'I have decided to . . . . Chloe, the priest said decisively, running his finger up and down her most sensitive erotic zone. 'Now, in order to do this, I am going to suggest that I tie you down.'

'Tie me down, Father?' she queried, her deep blue eyes wide.

'Yes. You see, I want you to experience the ultimate orgasm, and in order to do that I'll need to tie your hands and feet, to spread your limbs and open your body to receive the pleasures of the flesh. It is for your salvation, Chloë, that I offer you the sacrament of bondage.'

'But, Father . . . I thought that pleasures of the flesh were . . .'

'Sinful?'

'Yes, Father.'

'To derive pleasure from the flesh simply to satisfy one's lustful desires *is* a sin, my child. But to open your mind, your body, in order to cleanse your spirit, to drive out the evil dwelling within, is an act of contrition. The sacrament of bondage will procure you the grace of true humility.'

'Yes, Father. I understand.'

'Good. Now, wait there while I collect the necessary equipment . . .'

Depravicus

Ray Gordon

NEW ENGLISH LIBRARY
Hodder and Stoughton

British Library Cataloguing in Publication Data

Gordon, Ray
    Depravicus
    1. English fiction - 20th century
    2. Graphic novels
    I. Title
    741.5'941

ISBN 0 340 66054 6

Typeset by
Letterpart Limited, Reigate, Surrey
Printed and bound in Great Britain by
Mackays of Chatham plc, Chatham, Kent

Hodder and Stoughton
A division of Hodder Headline PLC
338 Euston Road
London NW1 3BH

CHAPTER ONE

The Rolling Stones blasted from the radio as The Reverend William Entercock sat in his office swigging lager from a can. Upturning the ashtray into the already overflowing waste-paper bin, he cleared the desk of screwed-up cigarette packets and crumpled beer cans and carefully flattened out the scathing letter he'd received from the bishop.

The bishop was unhappy, to say the least, and was demanding changes – 'mammoth changes' – in the parish of Cumsdale. Will Entercock had been parish priest for three years, during which time he'd managed to treble the congregation and accrue more than enough money for a new church roof – as well as 'defrocking' more than a handful of the local convent girls.

Witty, friendly, charming and extremely good-looking, he was particularly popular with his women parishioners. But his successes did nothing to appease his superiors when it came to his alleged unorthodox behaviour – sex, excessive drinking and smoking, controversial methods of taking confession at the convent, ads in contact magazines . . . They didn't know about the latter. At least, he hoped they didn't!

'Bloody hypocrite!' he swore, stubbing his cigarette out as he ran his fingers through his unruly black hair, wondering what to do about the problematic bishop. 'I'll bet *his* hands aren't virgin-clean,' he murmured, imagining the bishop defrocking a young nun. Taking another swig from the can, he sighed and read the letter again, the seriousness of his predicament beginning to sink in.

1

Dear Father Entercock,

As no doubt you are aware, rumours concerning your alleged outrageous behaviour are rife. The archbishop has asked me to get to the bottom of this and put a stop to the rumours before any damage is done to the reputation of the church. You leave me no choice, I am sorry to say. Either you drastically change your ways, or you will be excommunicated. To make matters worse, the archbishop has received more complaints from the Mother Superior of Hardmound Convent concerning your 'unhealthy interest' in the schoolgirls. He is well aware of the considerable amount of finance you generate, and of your popularity within the parish, but that doesn't outweigh your alleged dreadful conduct. I will be calling to see you tomorrow morning – Friday – to discuss the immediate and mammoth changes you will be required to make if you are to retain your post as Priest of Cumsdale Church.

Yours,
Bishop Simon Holesgood

'Fucking bastard!' Father Will breathed, tossing the letter on to the desk and opening another can of lager. 'Alleged dreadful conduct, my arse! He's jealous because I'm only thirty-two and he's an old git!' Taking a men's magazine from the desk drawer, he sat back in his swivel chair and gazed longingly at Miss August's ostentatiously bulging pussy lips, wondering what she'd have to say if he could get her into the confessional box. *Shit! Immediate and mammoth changes!*

'May I come in?' a soft female voice asked, breaking his reverie. Turning round, Father Will smiled to see a pretty young girl standing in the doorway. Wearing a very short pink gingham dress, he guessed she was a local farmer's daughter – or the devil's daughter, come to tempt him with her seductive young body. *Sexy little bitch*, he mused, wondering how sweet the soft cushions of flesh between her thighs, how savoury the taste of her vaginal juice. Creamy, warm, sticky, girlie. Long golden hair cascading over the swell of her excessive breasts, she was very well developed for her tender years – in fact, over developed!

'Of course you can come in!' he grinned, stuffing the magazine into a drawer as he stood up to introduce himself. 'Father Will Entercock,' he greeted her, holding out his hand.

'I'm Chloë,' replied the baby-doll-faced girl as he took her small hand in his and raised it to his mouth, planting a kiss on her warm, soft skin, imagining her hairless pussy lips against his mouth.

'Well, Chloë, what can I do for you?' he asked, begrudgingly releasing her hand, wondering where her slender fingers had probed. Had they explored her feminine curves, delved between her warm, soft pussy lips – wet, inviting and sticky with her come?

Wringing her hands, the girl glanced around the untidy office as if looking for something. 'Oh, I'm sorry,' Father Will smiled, moving a case of lager from a chair. 'Here, please sit down.' *Must clear up by tomorrow morning!*

Turning the radio down, he returned to his desk and smiled at the girl as she perched on the chair, nervously twisting her hair around her slender fingers. Lowering his eyes, he gazed hungrily at her slim thighs – firm, unblemished and shapely in their youth. His gaze transfixed between her legs as she fidgeted, he prayed for a glimpse of her panties – bulging, no doubt, with her full, fleshy girl-lips. Wet, pussy-stained panties – whiting-stained.

'Forgive me . . .' she began hesitantly, following his gaze and crossing her legs. 'Forgive me, Father, for . . . for I have sinned,' she finally stammered. Raising his head at the word *sin*, the priest looked into the girl's deep blue, dreamy eyes and smiled his understanding smile. *Forgive* me! he thought, imagining the wonderful sins he could commit with the young beauty's body as she returned his gaze, anticipation in her wide eyes.

'Then why not come to confession?' he suggested. *Or over my face!*

'I can't wait, Father.' *No, neither can I!* 'It's taken a lot of courage to come . . .'

'Yes, I understand. I do have a little time to spare, so what is it, my child?' His voice, soft and low, invited her to open up and reveal her innermost girl-secrets.

'I . . . I've sinned, Father!' she blubbered through her tears.

Christ! If I had a pound for every time I'd heard that! Sinned. He pondered the word, speculating if she'd been laid by a young farm hand, had her tight dress, her wet knickers, her virginity, crudely stripped during a romp in a haystack. *The horny little tart's probably pregnant*, he guessed, eyeing the gentle swell of her stomach as she shifted in her chair.

'And what was the nature of your sin, my child?' he enquired evenly, despite his ever-rampant and rising arousal, his imagination running wild now with images of young hairless cracks in their vestal virginity.

'Father, forgive me – I touched myself!'

Shifting uneasily in his chair in an effort to conceal the bulge beneath his cassock, the priest imagined the girl masturbating, her hands, her fingers, wandering over the contours of her naked body, seeking out the tight groove between her thighs, stroking her clitoris as she lay in her bed at night. His erection now menacing, tenting his cassock, he cleared his throat.

'How old are you, Chloë?' he asked gently as she wiped her eyes on the back of her clenched fist.

'Eighteen, Father,' she whispered.

Christ! Tight, hot and bloody wet or what? 'Ah, eighteen! You are going through the years of discovery, my child – difficult years. Now, before you can be forgiven your sins, I need to know a little more about the nature of the beautif— the terrible sins you have committed! Where, exactly, did you touch yourself?' *Your cunt, your clitoris?*

The girl's cheeks reddened as she dropped her head in shame. Uncrossing her legs, she inadvertently allowed her thighs to fall apart, answering the holy man's prayers. Gazing at the triangular patch of red material hugging her girlish bulge, he imagined her fingers there, massaging the warm, soft flesh, the stiffening bud-lette of her clitoris. Eighteen – her knickers would certainly be absorbing high-dosage creaming. *Oh, to breathe in the heady scent of the nymph's soiled panties!*

'I touched myself down there, Father – between my legs,' she confessed as she raised her head and looked at him with her innocently inviting bedroom eyes. He smiled again, wondering how to get *his* fingers inside her knickers, his penis inside her vagina – tight, hot, wet with teenage girl-come.

'And why did you touch yourself?' he asked concernedly, adjusting his cassock, remembering an advert he'd seen in one of his magazines offering soiled knickers for twenty pounds a pair.

'Because it's . . . it's nice, Father,' she replied with an air of surprise.

Nice? It's bloody wonderful! 'Tell me, child – what did you do? I mean, touching yourself isn't a sin. You have to touch yourself when you wash, for example, and that's far from sinful.'

'But I rubbed myself – and that's a sin!'

We all rub ourselves, baby! 'Rubbed yourself? But why?'

'It makes me feel good, Father.'

'Ah, so you've done this before, then?'

Chloë lowered her head again, her tears running down her cheeks as she admitted to rubbing herself frequently. 'Will I be punished for all my sins?' she sobbed fearfully. Father Will grinned, wondering if he could get away with putting her over his knee, pulling her knickers down and giving her taut, rounded buttocks a damn good spanking by way of punishment for her loveliness.

'You will go home and write in an exercise book, in explicit detail, about touching yourself,' he said firmly. 'You will write down all your wicked thoughts, exactly what you do to yourself, and how often you do it. You will write your confession by way of a penance – write about the sensations you have when rubbing yourself. I want you to continue to rub yourself every day and . . .'

'But, Father! I thought that it was . . .'

It is – gloriously sinful! 'You must rub yourself at every opportunity to drive out the demon in you – at *every* opportunity!' he instructed firmly. 'You will report to me at the presbytery next door, with your exercise book, every evening at seven o'clock, starting from today.' *Careful, Entercock – don't let her off the hook!*

The girl's face brightened as she brushed her blonde tresses from her tearful eyes. 'For how long will I have to go on rubbing myself and writing about it before I can be forgiven, Father?' she asked in her apparent naïvety.

Until you beg for my penis to penetrate your tight cunt hole! 'That depends, Chloë. A week, maybe two or three, I don't know.' *Or until I become bored with you and your bloody rubbing.* 'Go home now and start your book, my child. And be explicit! Write down every detail – where, when, what you did, what it felt like, what clothes you were wearing – if any. And there's one more thing, Chloë. You are to tell no one about this. We don't want the world to know what a dreadful sinner you are, do we?' *Or me, for that matter!*

'No, Father, we don't,' she smiled as she stood up. 'I'll see you this evening at seven o'clock – with my book.'

And your wet panties!

Gleefully, Father Will watched the girl breeze out of his office, her tight dress following the contours of her shapely young body, billowing over her ample buttocks. As he manipulated his solid member through his cassock, he hoped he'd brought her some relief – lifted the unbearable weight of anxiety from her young heart, creamed her young vagina with his suggestion of daily masturbation. She'd be pleased that she'd confessed her sins, he knew. He was pleased that he'd been able to help her in her plight, her quest for sexual fulfilment – but he'd sooner have helped himself to her fresh young body, to her tight, wet crack.

As he swigged at his lager, wondering about his still-rampant erection and the money to be made from peddling schoolgirl-soiled knickers, the telephone rang. 'Father Entercock,' he intoned lazily, pressing the receiver to his ear as he lit another cigarette.

'Will, you sad old pervy!'

'Christ, if it's not the bloody Vicar of Hallworth!' Will exclaimed, puffing on his cigarette. 'How's the C of E?'

'Not too bad. Much the same as you lot, I suppose – full of frustrated vicars. Anyway, how's it going, me old mate, me old buddy, me old pervy?'

'It's going all right, Bob. Hey, I've just had a young girl . . .'

'That doesn't surprise me!'

'No, I mean, she came to see me. She confessed that she wanks herself off, would you believe?'

'I presume you gave her a hand – or a knob?'

'I'd like to have done! Anyway, I told her to carry on rubbing herself, as she put it, and to write about it, in explicit detail, and bring me her notes every evening. I told her that she had to rub herself every day to drive out the demon in her.'

'Christ, that's a good one! I suppose you're going to toss yourself off while you're reading her notes?'

'No, I'll read her notes while she sucks me off! Seriously, though, she's a right little beauty! If I can take her under my wing, or better still, under my quilt . . .'

'Or under your body!'

'Ah, sheer bliss! If I can win her confidence, then I'm sure I'll also win her tight little pussy.'

'There's no stopping you, is there? You're a dirty old bastard, you really are! Anyway, I'm calling to tell you that I'm having some of the convent girls here for an evening of Bible-bashing and, this is the good bit, that old slag-bag, the Mother Inferior, won't be accompanying the little beauties! But better than that, guess who else is coming?'

'Me, I hope!'

'Yes, but there's someone else coming along to our perverted gathering – that little tart you shagged the arse off.'

'God, don't remind me, Bob!'

'Why, what's the problem? Repercussions?'

'The archbishop's pissed off.'

'Yeah? Where's he gone, Las fucking Vatican?'

'No, he's pissed off with *me*, you fool! I had a letter from the bishop this morning. He's coming to see me tomorrow about my supposed dreadful behaviour.'

'Fuckin' hell!'

'I hope they do, for our sakes! Anyway, I'll get it sorted. So, when's this schoolgirl orgy taking place? And why is it at *your* poxy church? They usually come here – I don't get it.'

'No, I don't suppose you do! It's tomorrow evening. The Mother Superior asked me if I'd mind the girls coming over me, I mean, coming to my church, as she can't trust you with her nubile, hot, wet, tight young virgins.'

'That doesn't surprise me!'

'Get here about six and we'll have a few beers before they arrive. I've bought four bottles of vodka and a case of tonic, just to loosen the beauties up a bit.'

'I'll loosen them up a bit! Listen, you shouldn't have bought the booze, I could have supplied . . . no, I'll tell you when I see you.'

'OK. Anyway, about sex o'clock, ha ha.'

'Great! Look, I have to go now, some nosy prat's wandering around the church, probably trying to nick the fucking silver – not that there's much of it left after my trip to the antique dealer! I'll see you tomorrow.'

'OK, Will – look forward to it.'

'And me! See you.'

Replacing the receiver, Father Will combed his hair back and stubbed his cigarette out before emerging from his office into the church. Eyeing a young couple, he quickly brushed the cigarette ash from his cassock, squirted a shot of Gold Spot into his mouth and walked over to greet them.

'Good morning,' he said warmly. 'Welcome to Cumsdale church. I'm the Reverend William Entercock.' The couple turned, smiling nervously as he approached them.

'Good morning, Father,' the young man replied. 'We . . . we wish to be married here, in your church.'

Poor misguided sod! 'This isn't *my* church, my son – it's God's church.' *More like the fucking money-making Catholic hierarchy's church!*

'Right. Whatever you say, Father. Anyway, we want to be married here – Josie and I. And we'd like some guidance.'

So would I – right up your bird's skirt!

Smiling benevolently at the young bride-to-be, Father Will imagined her screaming in orgasm on her wedding night as her new husband spread her legs and thrust his hard cock deep into her hot, wet body, desecrating her sanctuary. The delectable morsel was in her early twenties, with short brown hair cut in a bob framing her pretty, suntanned face. A child-like innocence shone from her big brown eyes as she gazed at her boyfriend, clutching his hand with love in her heart. And, no doubt, sex in her sodden knickers!

The ugly git didn't deserve a pretty little thing like her, the priest thought, surveying the girl's short skirt and tight top accentuating her young curves, her full, rounded breasts. A delightful sight, he mused, wondering how long her nipples were, how wet her vagina – and whether or not she masturbated.

'Right!' he beamed enthusiastically with a clap of his hands. 'Marriage – excellent!' *Bloody pathetic idea!* 'Now, normally, you'd have to make an appointment to see me but . . . well, I have a little time to spare so . . . I'll need to speak with you both – separately, of course.'

'Separately?' the young man queried.

Fuck off! 'Er . . . yes, separately. Now, Josie, isn't it? You follow me and . . . sorry, I didn't get your name.'

'Brian.'

That figures! 'Brian, right. You stay here, Brian. Or take a walk outside.' *And have a wank.* 'It's a lovely day for . . . we won't be too long.'

Leaving her boyfriend to wander outside, Josie followed her mentor into his office. 'Take a pew,' Will invited informally as he shuffled behind his desk and sat down. Resting his elbows on the desk, he clasped his hands and waited for her to make herself comfortable before beginning his lecture.

'Sex, Josie!' he began firmly, shocking the young girl into opening her mouth wide and staring at him in disbelief. 'Sex and love go together. You're in love with Brian, are you not?' *Wonder what colour her knickers are? White – stained white?*

'Yes, very much in love,' she replied softly.

'Good, good! Now, have you had sex with him yet?' *Has he fucked the arse off you?*

Josie blushed, lowering her head to conceal her guilt, he surmised. Her short skirt did little to cover her shapely thighs and Will found it pleasingly easy to imagine her naked, her pussy bared, opened, filled with her boyfriend's throbbing penis – *his* throbbing penis! Wondering if she'd taken Brian's pulsating knob into her pretty mouth and swallowed his gushing sperm, he continued.

'Sex to a man is like food, Josie – it's a need. A need that, sadly, is often neglected by women. That's why so many men turn to . . . anyway, I'm asking you whether or not you've had sex with Brian as it's important that a young couple be compatible in that area. So, have you had sex with him?'

'Well . . . yes, sort of,' she replied hesitantly, wringing her hands in her anxiety.

'Sort of?' Father Entercock persisted. *Sex is sex, for Christ's sake!*

'We haven't gone all the way, Father – not yet, anyway.'

'Ah, I see. So, how far, exactly, have you travelled along the beautiful path of sexual enlightenment?' *Sexual debauchery!*

'Petting – heavy petting, I suppose.'

'Good, good! And, tell me, Josie, do you enjoy heavy petting?'

'Oh, yes, very much, Father.'

One step at a time, Entercock. 'Excellent! Now, heavy petting, as you call it, can take many forms. What, exactly, do you get up to with Brian during your heavy petting sessions?'

'Well, we touch each other, I suppose. But what's all this got to do with our getting married, Father?'

What indeed? Fuck-all! But Will was enjoying their intimate chat, and his rising penis, and he wasn't going to let her spoil his fun. Looking up to the ceiling, wondering if he could buy soiled, girl-perfumed knickers in bulk, he took a deep breath before sitting back in his chair and folding his arms authoritatively.

'Sex, Josie, is important in a relationship, as I have said. Problems arise within marriages because the sexual side of relationships often falls short of one or the other's needs.' *The woman won't open her fucking legs!* 'I need to know about your sexual activities with your boyfriend, your future husband, so that I can advise you properly. Now, what do you get up to, sexually, with that young . . . with young Brian?'

'We play with each other, Father. He . . . he likes me to do it to him.'

'Do what?' *Wank him off?*

'Make him . . . you know, make him finish.'

'Ah, bring him to orgasm, you mean?'

'Yes, Father.'

'That's very good, Josie. It shows that you have an understanding of his male needs. Yes, that's very good indeed! Tell me, do you enjoy bringing him to orgasm by using your mouth?' *Shit! Cool it, Entercock!*

Watching the girl's reddening face, the priest was sure he'd gone too far. Still wringing her hands, she looked up to him and opened her mouth as if to speak, but only sighed. He glimpsed her tongue – soft, pink, wet. *The mouth – the orifice!* Problems in the oral sex department, he surmised, imagining her on her knees, her head beneath his cassock, his penis pumping sperm into her virginal mouth, bathing her pink tongue.

'I don't like doing that to him, Father,' she admitted flatly.

'Do you like him doing it to you?' *Cunt lips open, hot tongue darting, licking . . .*

'Yes, very much, but . . .'

'In a relationship, Josie, one has to be fair, unselfish. A marriage based on unfairness, on selfishness, is a marriage based on problems – a marriage doomed from the start. I don't want to worry you but you do have a serious problem. You enjoy Brian between your . . .' *Cunt flaps.* 'And yet you refuse to return the pleasure. Sexual pleasure should be mutual, shared. Now being unfair to your partner is no way to begin married life, is it?'

'No, I realise that, Father, but . . .'

But fucking what? 'Wives must obey their husbands as they would obey the Lord, remember that, my child. Look, I have an idea, Josie. I have to go out shortly, so why don't you come and see me this evening, at the presbytery next door, and we'll discuss your problem further?' *Look into your problem – into your wet panties!*

'Brian's busy tonight, Father, he has to . . .'

'Good! I mean, I'd like you to come alone. After all, it's not Brian who has this dreadful sexual problem, is it?' *It's me!* 'It's you, Josie.'

'But . . . but I've never looked upon it as a sexual problem.'

'I can assure you, my child, that you have, indeed, a sexual problem. But let's talk it over later – I really must be going now.

Oh, by the way, I wouldn't tell Brian about our meeting this evening if I were you – I mean, we don't want him to know that you have sexual problems, do we?'

'No, no – I suppose we don't.'

'Think on this, my child – thy wife shall be fruitful as the vine that grows on the walls of thy house. Now, the vine will wither and die, will it not, if not watered? So, you must drink the seed of your young man's loins to be fruitful!' *And my seed!*

'Yes, Father.'

'That's settled, then. About nine o'clock?'

'That's rather late, isn't it?'

'I'm afraid I'll be tied up with a young girl from seven till about half-eight.' *She'll be tied up.*

'Oh – nine o'clock, then.'

Sixty-nine o'clock? 'Good! Tell Brian that I'll see him some other time. You're the important one, Josie. After all, it's you who has the problem,' *the wet cunt,* 'isn't it?'

'Yes, Father, I suppose so.'

'But never fear, my child, for I am here to guide you, to advise you on such matters. I've met many young couples in my time and I have been able to help them, counsel them, before they embark on the often bumpy road of marriage. In fact, my bishop is calling on me tomorrow to congratulate me' *give me a bollocking* 'on my success with young women. Anyway, I don't want to blow my own trumpet.' *I'd rather you did.* 'Until this evening, then. Go now, my child. And mayest thou live to see thy children's children.' *And mayest I live to lick your pretty cunt!*

Watching Josie walk through the church, Father Will grinned. He'd soon have her begging for a man's penis throbbing in her mouth, filling her cheeks with gushing sperm – *his* penis, *his* sperm. Looking up to the beams supporting the church roof, he smiled and, cross-fingered, intoned his prayer. 'Thanks be to God!

13

How fair are the chaste, how glorious the young maidens! I pray that they may welcome the pleasures of my flesh and be nourished by the fruits of my loins – Alleluia!'

Back in his office, he popped another can of lager and reclined in his swivel chair, wondering, again, what to do about his ever-lurking erection. Should he spill his seed on the floor? Turning to a knock at the door, he grinned to see a young nun entering.

'Sister Teresa!' he beamed, rising to his feet. 'And what brings you to see me on this beautiful summer's morning with the sweet scent of God's flowers filling the air?' *The sweet scent of young girls' knickers!*

'Cut the fucking crap, Will!'

'Oh, right – sorry. PMT, is it? Wrong time of the month? Anyway, how are things at the convent?'

'Don't ask! The old bag had me in her office this morning.'

'How nice for you! I didn't realize that you were a lesbian.'

'Someone saw me in the pub last night and rang the convent to report my, and I quote, ungodly behaviour, unquote.'

'Shit! What were you doing?'

'I didn't think I'd be recognized wearing my blonde wig and miniskirt! Anyway, I got slightly pissed and was all over this bloke. I can't remember too much about it. I remember his hand up my skirt . . . Look, it doesn't matter what I was doing, the point is, some bastard obviously knew that I was from the convent and . . .'

'Mistaken identity – the old bat will believe that!' Father Will interrupted excitedly.

'What, for the third time running? No, this is it, I reckon – I'm done for!'

'I'm in the shit, too. The bishop's coming over tomorrow to have a go at me. Sod it! Bloody problems, all I get these days are bloody problems!'

'Tell me about it! I wonder who grassed me up?'

'Could be anyone, I suppose,' the priest ruminated, gazing into the young nun's green eyes.

'There was this sad old pervert in the pub. He kept trying to look up my bloody skirt! He was a funny old geezer, with a sort of mole on the end of his nose that reminded me of a nipple.'

'Are you sure?'

'I know what nipples look like!'

'Was he balding and plump?'

'Yes, do you know him?'

'That's your man – he's the one who rang the convent.'

'How do you know that?'

''Cause he's my fucking bishop!'

'No, he can't be! This bloke was with a young girl.'

'Who?'

'I don't know who she was, do I?'

'This could be my salvation!' the priest exclaimed. 'Don't you see? If that was my bishop, and I'm pretty sure it was, and he's screwing some young tart, he can't really do much about me having my fun, can he?'

'Blackmail! That's a thought! If I had something on the old cow, she couldn't threaten me, either. The problem is, she's squeaky bloody clean – the asexual old bag!'

'Is she? You don't know that for a fact, do you? Anyway, I reckon that you've just saved me my job. Now, how can I thank you?' *Fuck you?*

Taking the fledgling sister of God in his arms, Father Will kissed her full mouth, pressing his erection against her soft belly. Lifting her habit, he groped between her legs, running his hand up her silky-smooth stockings to discover her knickerless pussy – warm, soft and wet. Ripping her head-dress off, she gasped as the holy man slipped a finger between her moist swelling cunt lips, opening her tight sex-duct.

With cropped black hair and half-a-dozen gold studs adorning each ear, Sister Teresa hadn't surrendered her punk-rocker image gracefully. Forced by her father, Judge Widdlesby, into taking the veil after being arrested for committing an act of gross indecency with another girl in a park, she was far from settled – a square peg in a round hole. But she was trying to make the most of it, helped by the ever-helpful Will Entercock – and his ever-wandering hands and ever-erect penis.

'You look horny this morning, Sister T,' Father Will whispered as he gently bit on her lip, tasting her warm saliva.

'I *feel* bloody horny this morning!' she gasped as he continued to massage her wet inner flesh. Dragging her cream up her sex-groove, he lubricated the intimate folds, running the tip of his finger round the base of her stiffening clitoris as she panted and swayed on her weakening legs.

'Christ, you really do know how to turn a girl on, don't you, Father?' she breathed as he slipped his finger into her hot vaginal sheath again. 'No wonder young Sister Emily fell prey to your charm.'

Repercussions! Don't remind me! 'And *you* know how to turn a *man* on,' he replied as she lifted his cassock and grabbed his solid rod.

'You are naughty, wearing nothing under your frock!' she giggled, running her finger over the silky surface of his glans. 'Like wearing dresses, do you?'

'It's not a dress!'

'Are you a transvestite?' she giggled impishly as she moved the loose skin back and forth over his ballooning knob.

'I can be anything you like.'

'I'll tell you what I like – I like you coming all over my tits.'

'All right, if that's what you want, my horny little angel! Just let me lock the door.'

Slipping out of her habit, Sister Teresa stood before him, feet apart, wearing only her hold-up stockings and peep-hole bra. Father Will grinned as he confronted the familiar gold rings dangling from her pierced nipples, the colourful bird tattoos

darting up her curvaceous thighs and around her darkening areolae. As she jutted her hips forward to present her soft mound to
his hungry eyes, he dropped to his knees, peeling her inner petals
apart to lap up the small globules of opaque fluid hanging from the
glistening pink flesh.

Gasping, Sister Teresa grabbed his head, pulling his face firmly
against her trembling body, grinding her open pussy into his
mouth. 'God, that's good!' she cried, gyrating her hips as he
slipped his tongue into the wet heat of her tight vagina. 'Ah, that
makes me feel weak in the knees.'

'Blessed are the weak, for they shall inherit my cock!'

'Shut up, you're putting me off! Keep licking! I want to come
in your mouth!'

Clinging to the cleric's head, steadying her slender body as her
orgasm rose from the depths of her womb, Sister Teresa closed her
eyes and flung her head back. 'I'm there!' she cried as her clitoris
throbbed rhythmically in its coming. 'Ah, God! I love it! Suck
me! Suck . . . Alleluia!'

Thrusting his fingers deep into the young nun's contracting
sex-sheath, the pastor heightened her orgasm, prolonged her
shuddering pleasure until her knees sagged and she crumpled to
the floor. 'Ah, God!' she gasped as she lay with her legs open,
massaging the last ripples of sex from her budlette. 'God, that was
bloody marvellous!'

'You taste just like a woman should,' Father Will smiled,
licking his lips as he cast his eyes over her irrigating groove.
'Christ, look at you – the second coming!'

'Then drink it. Lick me clean or it will stain my habit and the
old bat will know what I've been up to.'

'Couldn't get me some dirty knickers from the convent, could
you?'

'What for?'

'A business venture . . . I'll tell you later.' *Schoolgirls' knickers
for sale – stained, aromatic – twenty quid a pair.*

Settling on the floor between the nun's thighs, Father Will lapped up her girl-come, savouring the warm, slippery cream as he cleansed her. 'It's no good,' he moaned, moving over her body. 'I've got to come!' Lifting his cassock, he pulled her bra from her firm breasts and rested his heavy balls in her cleavage. 'So, you want me to come over your tits, do you?' he grinned, moving the bulging head of his penis nearer to her pretty mouth. 'In that case, you'd better suck me off!'

Lifting her head, she pulled his solid organ to her mouth and engulfed the purple knob. 'Ah, that's nice,' he breathed as she ran her tongue round his glans. 'I'd love to get the Mother Inferior on the floor and fuck *her* mouth!' Sister Teresa could say nothing – her mouth full with him, she could only suck and lick and await her gift.

Panting in the beginnings of his climax, the priest yanked his knob from the nun's hot mouth and moved back. 'Now!' he groaned. Grabbing his shaft, she ran her hand up and down it as fast as she could, her eyes transfixed on the small slit at its tip as it appeared and disappeared in time with her wanking motions.

'Sperm over my tits!' she cried. 'I want your come all over me!'

Suddenly the priest grimaced as his shaft bulged in her small hand. 'Coming!' he grunted. Sister Teresa moved her hand faster as the sperm spurted from his knob, splattering her heavy breasts, her long, brown, beringed nipples. Moving her head closer, she pushed her tongue out, catching the white liquid as it flew through the air. Unable to help herself, she lifted her head further and took the pulsating knob into her mouth, her eyes rolling as she swallowed his sacred offering.

Licking her lips as she pulled away, she ran her hands over her breasts, her erect nipples, collecting the sperm and licking her fingers clean. Her other hand between her thighs, she began to massage her clitoris, slowly, rhythmically. The priest rose, adjusting his cassock as he gazed down at the insatiable young nun, lost now in her masturbation.

'Fuck!' he gasped as someone knocked on the door. Oblivious, the young nun continued her massaging – her body shaking, her back arching as she neared her goal . 'Sister, there's someone at the fucking door!' he breathed, wondering what the hell to do.

'Ah, coming!' Sister Teresa cried out, her words reverberating through the church. 'God, I'm coming! Ah, my cunt! How I love my beautiful, wet cunt!'

Pressing his ear to the door in an attempt to listen above the nun's orgasmic whimperings, Father Will prayed that the visitor would go away. But again came a loud knock. 'Get dressed, for fuck's sake!' he whispered urgently as she bathed in the afterglow of her multiple orgasm. 'Quickly, Sister, get dressed!'

Rising to her feet, her senses returning, Sister Teresa pulled her bra down, easing her long nipples and gold rings through the holes in the red silk bra before slipping into her habit.

'I know you're in there, Father!' a grumpy female voice called.

'Yes, yes. I . . . I was on the phone, I'm just coming!' Will stammered as he unlocked the door. 'Ah, Mother Infer— I mean, Superior,' he greeted, easing past her into the church. 'How nice to see you.' *Fucking old bag!*

'Likewise, I'm sure. I wouldn't normally come here to see you, as you know, but I have something of the utmost importance to discuss with you,' she said stiffly, brushing him aside as she propelled herself into the office. Father Will gulped, his heart racing as he watched the matronly penguin disappear through the doorway. *Christ! The end is nigh!*

Seating herself, Reverend Mother Mary looked around the untidy office and shrugged her shoulders. 'This place could do with cleaning up!' she snapped as Father Will lounged at his desk, wondering where Sister Teresa was hiding. Suddenly, he jumped.

'What's the matter?' Mother Mary asked starchily.

'Nothing, nothing,' the priest murmured as Sister Teresa moved beneath the desk, her hands sliding up his inner thigh.

'Now, I've come to talk to you about the comparatively vast

sums of money you are supposedly collecting from your congregation. It has come to my notice that you have other forms of income. Before I speak to the bishop about this, I want to hear *your* explanation.'

The priest rolled his eyes and sighed as Sister Teresa took the head of his penis into her hot mouth and began her licking. Trying to push her away, he smiled at the Mother Superior. 'I . . . Ah! I . . . I don't know what you're talking about!' he gasped as Sister Teresa kneaded his balls and took half the length of his solid shaft into her mouth.

'So you deny that you are earning money from the sale of alcohol and tobacco, do you?'

'Alcohol?' he breathed as the nun ran her tongue over his knob.

'Yes, alcohol! It has been put to me that you are bringing in wines, beers, spirits and tobacco from France and selling them to your parishioners. Is this true?'

Of course it's true! 'No, of course it's not . . . Ah, no! I'm sorry, I'm feeling rather . . . Oh, my God!'

'Do not take the Lord's name in . . .'

'Ah, please . . . I'm so sorry! Your accusations hold no truth whatsoever, I can assure you that . . .'

'Can you explain what this case of beer is doing here?'

Yes, I intend to get pissed-up on it later! 'Yes, I can. A friend gave it . . . Ah, no . . . Is giving . . .'

'What is it? What's the matter with you, Father?'

'Nothing, I'm . . .' *I'm coming!*

His knob exploding in Sister Teresa's hot mouth, Father Will rolled his eyes and trembled violently.

'What's wrong?' Mother Mary demanded as his sperm gushed over the young nun's tongue.

'God!' he cried as he shuddered his last shudder and collapsed over his desk, knocking the ashtray over the Reverend Mother's habit. 'Oh, God – I'm there!'

'Are you drunk, Father?' she challenged, standing up and

brushing ash from her habit. 'I have never seen such disgraceful behaviour in all my life! And who was in here with you earlier? I want to know why the door was locked! I'm convinced I heard a woman's voice. What were you up to?'

'Sorry, I . . . Ah, that's better! No, where were you? Oh, yes, disgraceful behaviour. Firstly, I was on the phone, secondly, I locked the door because it was a private call and I didn't want the cleaning woman wandering in here as she usually does about this time of day, thirdly, the voice you heard was on the radio, and fourthly . . . what was fourthly?'

'There was no fourthly! I shall be contacting the bishop immediately to report you . . . your peculiar behaviour to him! I shall tell him that I firmly believe that you are on drugs. There is no other explanation for your behaviour!'

'Drugs? But I . . .'

'Don't allow another lie to pass your lips, Father! You are a disgrace, not only to yourself, but to your faith – if you have one!'

'Just because I've been able to pay for a new roof, and trebled the congregation, you accuse me . . .'

'You may have put some money into the church from your illicit earnings, but the rest, no doubt, lines your pocket!'

No doubt at all! 'There is no evidence, no proof, to substantiate your wild allegations, Mother. All I have done is . . .'

Slamming the door behind her, the Mother Superior stormed from the church. 'Fuck, now I'm in the shit!' Father Will groaned as Sister Teresa emerged from beneath the desk, licking spunk from her full lips.

'Old bag!' she complained as she stood up. 'How the hell does she know about the booze runs to France?'

'Christ knows! Some bloody Judas must have told her!'

'She'll fall from her pedestal one of these days!'

'Just be their fall, who wrong me scornfully,' the priest breathed. 'Just be *her* fall!'

'I'd better be going,' Sister Teresa sighed, adjusting her habit.

'OK. It was nice, we'll do it again sometime, shall we?'

'Definitely! But next time, I'll make sure the old bag's well out of the way. I suppose I'd better get back before she does. See you, Will – 'bye.'

Quite an eventful morning, Father Will mused. Checking his personal diary to ensure that he was free that evening, he realized that he was due for a lager delivery. 'Shit!' he swore, dashing from his office to collide with a young man.

'Ah, John, I've only just realized that you were coming today,' he admitted, shaking the young man's hand.

'Head like a sieve, that's your trouble! Anyway, the van's out the back. Open the basement doors and I'll meet you there.'

Unlocking a huge oak door concealed behind heavy velvet curtains, Father Will slipped through the doorway and descended the stairs. Walking across the basement, he climbed half a dozen steps and flung back the outside doors, shielding his eyes from the bright sunshine.

'Fifty cases!' John called. Flinging open the van doors, he began unloading the cases of lager, piling them high on the grass. Emerging from the basement, Father Will looked around the graveyard, praying that no one was about – in particular, the Mother Superior.

'Need any fags?' John asked as he dumped another three cases on the pile.

'I'll have to check. It's good of you to do this run for me. There was no way I could go to France this week, not with the problems I've been having recently!'

'What, the rumours, you mean?'

'What do you know about rumours?'

'I keep my ear to the ground, Father. You have to in my business!'

'Yes, I suppose you do. How's that court case going?'

'Which one, the dirty videos or the gross indecency?'

'Videos? What's that all about?'

'I'd rather not say, Father.'

'You'd better come to confession, John!'

'Hadn't we all!'

'Anyway, the bishop's coming over to have a go at me tomorrow. But worse than that, the Mother Superior has been here this morning, and she knows about the booze runs – God knows how!'

'Christ, you'll be in for it if they discover this little lot!' John laughed as he unloaded the last case.

'In for it? I'll be cast into the eternal fires of hell!'

'At least the beer's free there!'

Taking the last case of lager down the basement steps, Father Will turned to John, passing him a wad of notes. 'I think you'll find that's right,' he said as John counted the money.

'Spot on – thanks, Father. It looks like a bloody pub cellar down here. I hope for your sake that no one sees this lot!'

'So do I!' the priest replied as they climbed the steps.

'I'll be doing another run next week if you need any more.'

'I'll let you know. I'm hoping to go myself, but we'll see. I'm OK for cigarettes, by the way,' Father Will replied, closing the outer doors to the basement.

'So I noticed! It looked as if you've got more fags stashed down there than John Player!'

'I like to keep about fifty thousand in stock.'

'Bloody hell! I hope you don't get robbed!'

'God's house!' Father Will winked. 'High security!' Lighting a cigarette, he looked around the graveyard and smiled. 'See anything unusual?' he asked. John turned on his heels, scanning the headstones, the shrubbery.

'No. What am I supposed to be looking for?'

'Follow me, and I'll show you,' the priest grinned, walking off towards a high hedgerow.

Making their way through a small gap in the hedge, they emerged into a grassy clearing. 'There it is!' Father Will declared with a proud flourish, walking the few paces to a new greenhouse.

Opening the door, he waved his hand at forty or so plants, potted in neat rows. 'Well, what do you think?'

'If you knew anything about gardening, you wouldn't have sited the greenhouse here, it's far too shady. Anyway, what's all this about?' John asked.

'You're right, I know nothing about gardening – but I do know about these plants. They need sun, yes, but they also need to be hidden from prying eyes.'

'They're not . . .'

'They are! They'll be ready in a few days, if you're interested.'

'Christ, is there anything you're not into?'

Yes, Josie's knickers – and Chloë's! 'If there's something I'm not into, then I want to know about it! Anyway, I'd better get back to the church. I'll ring you with an order, if I need to. And thanks again.'

'Any time, Father,' John replied as they made their way back to the van. 'You down the pub tonight?'

'No, I shouldn't think so. I'll be entertaining this evening.'

'Anyone I know?'

'No, just a couple of young women who need my intimate attention.'

'Lucky bugger! Talking of young women, I'm off to Hardmound Convent now. Hopefully, I'll get to see some of those lovely sixth formers playing netball!'

'Why are you going to the convent?'

'Can't tell you, Father. But put it this way, they don't know that I come here to see you – and you don't know that I go there to see . . .'

'Not the Mother Superior?' Father Will gasped.

'God, no! Sister Felicity, if you must know.'

'The rest of the stuff in your van, is that for . . .'

'Can't tell you, Father, I'm afraid. Sworn to secrecy and all that.'

'Hypothetically speaking,' Father Will began. 'What would

nuns be into? Wines? Spirits? Not lager, I'm sure.'

'Hypothetically speaking, I'd say they'd be into candles, fucking great candles with . . . Seriously, I'd say wines and spirits – and tobacco, I reckon.'

'Thanks, John. You may have saved a young nun her life.'

'Always pleased to help. I must get going – see you around sometime.'

Back in his office, Father Will opened a can of lager and retrieved his men's magazine from the desk drawer, planning the downfall of the Mother Superior. 'Wines, spirits and tobacco,' he chuckled. 'That won't look too good in the Sunday tabloids!' Imagining the headline, he laughed aloud. 'Mother Superior Gets In The Spirit!'

CHAPTER TWO

Drinks on the table, the lounge uncustomarily tidy, Father Will checked his watch. 'Five minutes,' he breathed against the soft background music, pulling the net curtain aside. 'Come on, Chloë, let's be having you, my little sex-pot!'

Wearing his blue jeans and white open-neck shirt, the priest combed his hair back, wondering just how gullible, how easily led young Chloë was. Sensing a swelling in his jeans, he grinned. 'As my champion, you shall rise to greatness and penetrate our young virgin!' he pledged.

Pouring himself a large whisky, he pulled the curtain aside again to see the girl walking up the front path, clutching a red exercise book. 'This is it,' he murmured as he walked through the hall and opened the front door. 'Chloë, it's good to see you. Come in, my child!' *Come off, my child!*

Her dangerously short red skirt barely covering her rounded buttocks, her skimpy white blouse revealing her deep cleavage, Chloë was, indeed, a young beauty. Her full lips curled into a sweet smile as she greeted her confidant, extending her hand to receive his kiss. Her long blonde hair arousingly dishevelled, flowing behind her as she followed the priest into the lounge, she radiated an air of innocent sexuality. Her perfume filled the air, stiffening Father Will's penis as he led her to the sofa.

Step into my parlour, said the spider . . . 'Have a seat, Chloë,' Father Will invited. Crossing her long, unstockinged legs she made herself comfortable, unwittingly causing his balls to roll in expectation.

'Drink?' Father Will smiled, pouring a large vodka and lime, wondering how wet the girl's tight vaginal sheath was and how to get hold of her stained knickers. *Twenty quid a pair*.

'Oh, thank you,' she replied surprisedly, placing her exercise book on the sofa as he passed her the glass. Watching him refill his glass to the brim with neat whisky, her deep blue eyes frowned. 'I didn't realize that priests drank,' she observed disarmingly.

'Priests are normal men, Chloë. Normal in every sense, I can assure you!' *Normally perverted!* 'Now, let's have a look at your notes, shall we? Or, better still, why don't you read them aloud?'

'I . . . I'd rather not, Father.'

'You must, Chloë. This is all part of your penance, my child.'

Vantaged opposite the young girl, in his favourite armchair, Father Will gazed at her slender legs, her youthful thighs. The epitome of femininity, he mused, raising his eyes to her cleavage as she opened the exercise book and brushed her golden tresses from her pretty face.

'Three p.m.,' she began, uncrossing her legs and tossing her hair back. 'My mother went out shopping, leaving me alone in the house. I went up to my room to change. Slipping my skirt off, I was about to put my jeans on when I remembered the exercise book – my penance. I remembered Father Will's words – "rub yourself at every opportunity" – which gave me a funny feeling in my stomach – the same feeling I always get when I think of rubbing myself. I slipped my knickers off and locked the door. Climbing onto my bed, I lay back and began touching myself with . . .'

'Not explicit enough, Chloë!' the priest admonished. *What colour were your knickers? Were they wet?*

'No, Father – sorry. I'll make it more explicit next time.'

'And one other thing, Chloë. Rather than say "rubbed yourself" I think it would be better to say "masturbated". Do you know what it is that you rub? Do you know what it's called, my child?' *Your cunt.*

'I call it my thing, Father.'

'It's called a cun— . . .clitoris, Chloë. That hard little spot that you rub is your clitoris.'

'Yes, Father. Shall I continue, now?'

'Yes, read on, my child.'

Relaxing a little, Chloë leaned back on the sofa, allowing her thighs to fall apart, unwittingly displaying her tight red panties to the priest's bulging eyes. His penis aching, he imagined the young girl lying on her bed, her legs spread wide, her fingers between her swollen pussy lips as she brought her clitoris to fruition. A sight to behold! he thought, wondering if reading her notes aloud excited her – wet her.

Having a young girl willing to expose her masturbation sessions was, indeed, a rare occurrence. The scope was endless, he knew, and he was determined to nurture the relationship, to coax her gently, win her confidence – and slip her panties off. *Perhaps I could masturbate her, show her how it's done,* he mused as she held the book up to conceal her face as she continued her confession.

'My thing . . . my clitoris was hard and felt nice when I touched it. Rubbing . . . masturbating makes me tremble, my whole body shake uncontrollably. I moan as the wonderful fluttering sensations grow. It feels as if my entire body is alive and vibrant and I rub . . . masturbate, faster and harder as the sensations build up and wash over me, engulf me in a welcoming warmth. Faster I rubbed my clitoris as I lay on my bed until, my body twitching, I squeezed my eyes shut. Then the feeling came. Rising from somewhere deep inside me, it gripped me, took me to that beautiful place where I feel as if I'm swimming, floating, drifting above my body. I call that place my secret heaven, and I visit it often. When the ripples subside, like the sea rushing out, leaving me exhausted on the sandy beach, I reach down and push my fingers between my lips and into my hole, which is always very hot and wet by that time.'

And tasty.

Her thighs parting more as she touched her secret world, Father Will noticed a small wet patch on the girl's panties. Wondering how to make a move, how to peel them from her girlish mound, he realized that he'd never seen her in the village before. He knew most of the local families, had interfered with most of the teen-aged daughters, but never had he set eyes on this particular young beauty. He swore to be more observant, to take more interest in his young female parishioners in the future.

'That's very good, Chloë,' he encouraged, trying to conceal his bold erection. 'Tell me, how long have you been masturbating?'

'Ever since I can remember, Father,' she confessed, her thighs now wide open in her innocence, the dark wet patch of material growing as her juices flowed, oozed from her tight vagina. The priest could barely contain himself as his penis twitched within the confines of his tight jeans. But how to coax the girl? How to get her to slip her panties off and allow him to feel her, touch her, finger her – taste her slippery girl-juice?

'Is there anything else, Father?' she asked, closing the exercise book as she reclined on the sofa.

Yes, my cock, for a start! 'You've done very well, Chloë. But . . . but I feel that you need a little tuition. You're not going to drive out the demon in you unless you know how to masturbate properly.'

'Properly, Father?' she echoed, sipping her drink.

'Yes, properly. You're doing very well, by the sound of it, but there's so much more, my child.'

'More, Father? I don't understand – what else is there?'

What else? God, give me strength! Shifting awkwardly in his chair, the priest wondered how near he was to taking the young girl's panties off and masturbating her, rubbing her budlette until she cried out in her coming. Instinctively, he decided to take a different line, a line that he was sure would reap him his reward.

'It's no good,' he said firmly. 'You're far too young, Chloë. I was going to suggest that we . . .'

'Too young?' she queried disappointedly. 'Too young for what, Father?'

'You need some sexual experience, my child. You're at the age when you should be discovering sex with boys. You should be learning with boys of your own age, rather than having a mature, experienced man such as myself teaching you.'

'But I *want* you to teach me, Father! You've already told me that it's called masturbation, and not rubbing – and that my thing is my clitoris.'

'I know, Chloë, and I regret having told you. You should be learning these things for yourself. It would be wrong of me to reveal the secrets of sex to one so young and naïve.' *And so delectable!*

'But, Father – you have to help me drive out this demon! Is there nothing you can do for me? I mean, I can't fumble around masturbating, knowing that I'm not doing it properly! If you know about masturbation, then you must tell me!'

'That is the difficulty, Chloë. It's not just a question of telling you – you need to be shown.' *Fucked!*

The crunch had come, Will knew, as he gazed into the girl's big blue eyes. Would she fall for it? he wondered. Was she really that stupid? Would she now beg him to show her – to fuck her?

'What would your parents say if they knew that I'd shown you, at first hand, the delights of masturbation, my child?' he ventured, gazing at her huge rounded breasts straining beneath her blouse. *They'd go berserk!*

'I live with my mother – my father left some years ago.'

'What would your mother say, then?'

'She won't know – no one will.'

'I'm not sure, Chloë. You're so young – are you really ready to learn the fine art of masturbation?' he asked, refilling her glass with neat vodka.

'Yes, more than ready, Father.'

'And what about male masturbation? I mean, there's so much you need to learn that I . . .'

'Male masturbation? Why do I need to learn about . . .'

So you can wank me off! 'Chloë, my child – you need to learn how to pleasure a man if you're going to make a good wife one day.' *A good tart!*

'The world is full of mysteries and secrets, Father, and I must learn of these secrets if I am to . . .'

'It's true that if you are to go out into the world you'll need to be prepared, but I don't know if I should . . .'

'Then I'll have to find someone who *will* teach me! I need to be rid of the demon in me – and I need to learn.'

The girl seemed overly keen to learn, Father Will decided. Was she delighting in what she perceived as an awkward and embarrassing situation for him? Or was she genuinely concerned about a lurking demon? He was the only demon, he knew, as he gazed hungrily at her inner thighs, her tight panties hugging her young sex. Whatever, it was now or never, he decided.

It was a risky business, he knew. He visualized his picture in the Sunday tabloids, exposed as a pervert along with the dozens of other vicars and priests who thronged the pages of the enlightened gutter press. That was the last thing he needed. But taking young Chloë, spreading her legs and penetrating her tight vagina was fast becoming a priority. And, as the girl had herself said, no one would know.

'All right, Chloë,' he began, his penis straining for freedom, aching for relief. 'I'll teach you how to masturbate properly but you must tell no one of our meetings. I am prepared to do all I can to help you in your plight. I am prepared to go over and above my duty as a priest, but I will deny all knowledge of you should it come to light that I have helped you in this way.'

'Of course, Father. It will be our secret, I promise!'

Christ, I've bloody well done it! the priest thought excitedly. But he knew that he'd have to lead the girl along the path of sexual discovery slowly, gently. One step at a time, he mused, wondering where to start. Knickers off? Yes, definitely, but worded carefully, of course.

'All right, Chloë, let's get to grips with female masturbation. If you'd lie on the sofa and slip your panties down and show me how you masturbate, I'll tell you where you're going wrong.' *What happened to the careful wording?* No matter, he thought. Who needs words if she takes her knickers off?

Trembling, his heart racing, Father Will watched as Chloë peeled her panties from her dark mound, pulling them down her slender legs and dropping them onto the floor as she lay full length on the sofa. A dream? he wondered. A dream come true. Placing one foot on the floor, her thighs apart, she spread her young, swelling pussy lips and began to massage her clitoris – her thing. Her eyes closed, she breathed deeply, moaning slightly as she stiffened her budlette as the priest gazed on in wonderment.

'How am I doing, Father?' she asked, breaking the silence, opening her legs further to display her intimate pink flesh, glistening delightfully with her milky juices.

'Yes, you're . . . God, you're doing . . . I mean, you're doing very well! But you'll need to lubricate your fingers, Chloë. Slip your fingers into your . . . into your vagina, to wet them.'

'Like this?' she panted, opening her outer lips further and easing two fingers into her creamy hole.

'My God! Yes, yes, like that, my child.'

Stage one complete, thought Father Will, his penis now frighteningly near to orgasm as he rose from his chair and walked over to Chloë. Kneeling on the floor beside her, he gazed longingly at her wet, pink, inner petals – her fingers, massaging her ripening flower. God, give me the weakness to succumb to temptation, he prayed as he reached out and tentatively ran a finger up the smooth, warm skin of her inner thigh.

His hand trembling as he neared the glistening entrance to her inner sanctum, he tentatively eased her pussy lips apart, exploring the lobby of her vaginal sheath with his finger as she brought herself ever closer to her climax.

'This will make it better for you,' he breathed shakily as he gently eased his finger into her young love tube. She gasped, massaging her clitoris faster as her breathing became heavier. 'And this will make it better still,' he panted, slipping a second finger into the heat of her trembling body.

'Oh, yes – that's nice, Father. Ah! Yes, much better!'

The girl shuddered as the priest thrust his fingers in and out of her spasming young pussy. Her fingertips vibrating over her solid clitoris, she tossed her head from side to side, arching her back as her orgasm rose from the hot depths of her virginal womb. Throwing her leg over the back of the sofa, her thighs stretched, her crack asunder, she opened her girlish intimacy to the man of God's sex-hungry gaze.

He dared not take the liberty of tasting the cream flowing from her young body as she gasped and grimaced in her coming. All he dared do was continue his fingering, massaging her inner flesh as she cried out, writhing in the incredible new-found pleasure between her legs.

'Ah, the feeling . . . The feeling is coming!' she cried. Her blouse falling open as she squirmed, the priest glimpsed her breasts – unblemished, firm, rounded. God, give me her nipples so that I may suck upon them! he prayed as he slipped his other hand inside her blouse and kneaded the beautiful, solid spheres of warm flesh.

His fingers still now, absorbing the heat of her contracting young sex, he allowed her to rest as her climax gently subsided.

Her hand fell limp by her side as she opened her deep blue eyes and looked up at him, smiling sweetly. Her hair matted with perspiration, her angelic face flushed, she gasped as he began to move his fingers, to excavate her sex-duct.

'That's nice, Father,' she whispered as he twisted his fingers, moving them slowly back and forth to induce a copious flow of lubricant. Smiling longingly at her pretty face, her full mouth, he leaned forward and kissed her cheek.

'Lesson one,' he whispered, slipping his fingers from her vagina.

'What's lesson two, Father?' she asked eagerly, innocently licking her lips provocatively as she stretched her arms behind her head, her breasts heaving, straining for their freedom. What indeed? he mused, his penis urgently craving relief. What indeed?

'You'd better dress now,' he murmured solicitously, praying that she'd beg for lesson two. 'That's enough for today, Chloë.'

'But, Father! I want to learn everything!'

Christ! 'You must take this in stages, my child. Little and often, that's the way to . . .'

'You mentioned male masturbation, Father. I need to know about male masturbation if I'm to . . .'

Bring me off! The very thought of the young girl's head gripping his solid penis sent a shiver up Father Will's spine, a delightful quiver through his heavily laden balls. He imagined his seed spurting, bathing her slender fingers, splattering her exquisite hand as she massaged his hard shaft. Yes, she was ripe for initiation into male masturbation – and his penis was over-ripe!

'Have you ever seen a man naked?' he probed.

'No, Father,' she replied, her fingers working between the soft swell of her pussy lips.

'Have you ever seen, or touched, a penis?'

'Never, Father – never.'

Never sucked sperm from a throbbing knob? 'Then I will show you, Chloë. I just pray that you're ready for this,' he breathed, tugging on his belt and slipping his jeans down to his knees. 'This, Chloë, is a penis.' *And I want to shove it up your tight, wet cunt!*

Kneeling beside her, he presented her with his massive organ, grinning at her awed expression as she confronted the huge rod, the purple, ballooning head. Moving his erect shaft nearer to her wide eyes, he took her hand and tentatively pulled it nearer to his rod. Gasping as she took the member in her small hand, she turned onto her side to examine the organ intimately.

'It's very hard, Father!' she exclaimed.

'It is, Chloë. Now, I will tell you how to pleasure a man. Move your hand up and down, like this,' he instructed, taking her hand and showing her the movements of male masturbation.

'Like this?' she asked as she pushed him away and moved her hand up and down the hard shaft, her eyes glowing with an inner desire as she watched the loose skin moving over the solid purple knob.

'God, yes!' he gasped. 'A little faster, my child! That's it!'

Her free hand exploring his full balls, Chloë continued her exercise of male masturbation to the accompaniment of the priest's gasped thanksgiving. Nearing his climax all too quickly, he knew he should warn her about his sperm, enlighten her as to the gushing, the pumping of his male fruits.

'You may kiss it, Chloë!' he breathed, deviating from his planned gentle initiation. 'Now, Chloë! Take it into your mouth!'

'But, Father . . .'

'Suck it, girl! If you are to learn how to pleasure a man, you must do as you are told!' *Disobedient bitch!*

Her hand still moving up and down his solid shaft, her eyes looking up to his, seeking praise for her efforts, Chloë parted her pouting lips to engulf the head of his penis in the wet warmth of her virginal mouth. Will gasped, instructing her to run her tongue over the silky glans, to keep her hand moving while she licked and sucked. Praising God for allowing him to teach the young girl the art of oral sex, he sensed his seed rising to the throbbing head of his penis.

'I'm . . . I'm going to come in your mouth!' he gasped as his sperm exploded from his glans, bathing her tongue, filling her cheeks as he gripped her head and moved his hips back and forth. Spluttering, breathing heavily through her nose as he rammed the back of her throat, his young pupil swallowed hard, savouring her first-ever taste of male cream.

Trembling as he pumped the last of his seed into her sullied mouth, the priest groaned, his eyes closing as he shuddered his last shudder and pulled away, collapsing to the floor, his balls drained. 'That was very good, Chloë!' he panted, his penis shrinking before the girl's wide eyes.

'It tasted funny, Father,' she appraised, licking her full lips.

'It'll do you good, my child. You must drink the male fruits from my fountainhead daily, Chloë. Every evening at seven o'clock, you will drink from my fountainhead to drive out the demon in you.'

'Oh, yes, Father, I will! Shall I dress now, or is there another lesson?'

Another lesson? Christ, were they not infinite? Aware that she might not return, might choose instead to enjoy the new-found delights of her body with younger men, the priest knew he should exploit his sacrificial lamb while he could. Her breasts heaving as she rolled onto her back, Chloë's young body demanded exploration, caresses. She was ready for her sexual awakening, he decided. As God's servant, he would bring the girl life.

'There are many beautiful lessons to be learned, Chloë. You are a virgin, are you not?'

'I am, Father.'

'Then I suggest that you surrender your virginity to me, as your priest – surrender your virginity by way of a penance, my child.' *Let me fuck you.*

'Yes, Father – I will.'

'Then allow me to disrobe you in preparation for the surrender, Chloë,' he said softly, climbing to his feet and taking her hand.

The girl stood meekly before him, her arms by her sides as he unbuttoned her blouse, opening it to reveal her tight cleavage. Slipping the garment off her shoulders, he admired the fullness of her heavy breasts, straining in the confines of her red lace bra. Reaching behind her back he unclipped it, deftly, unhurriedly, allowing her breasts to balloon as the bra cups fell away.

Her nipples grew, standing to attention as he encircled each one in turn with his fingertip, her areolae darkening in her arousal as he cupped her heavy spheres, weighing them, kneading them. 'You have a fine body,' he breathed as he unzipped her short skirt and let it fall around her ankles. 'A fine young body, indeed!'

'Thank you, Father,' she whispered, her cheeks blushing with her embarrassment as he leaned forward to examine her elongated nipples, squeezing them between his finger and thumb.

Falling to his knees, he kissed her smooth stomach, the sun-tanned skin around her navel – warm, taut, unblemished in its youth. Moving down, he parted her soft pussy lips, gazing at her inner folds as he moved his head, his hungry mouth, nearer.

'This is called foreplay,' he enlightened the girl, kissing the wet flesh between her swelling lips. Her knees weak, she held on to his head as he pushed his tongue out and licked the length of her reddening sex-groove. 'This is how a man gives a girl oral sex,' he murmured in his teaching, breathing in the heady scent of her intimate folds, savouring the sweetness of her girl-juice as he ran his tongue around the entrance to her sacred cavern.

'Pull your cunt lips open,' Will ordered his pupil as his tongue ran up her valley, ever nearer to her budding clitoris. Reaching down, she breathed the word *cunt* as if it were the first time she'd heard it. 'Yes, this is your cunt, my child,' he intoned with the solemnity of celebrating holy communion. 'Your beautiful, wet cunt.' *Take ye and eat, for this is my body.*

Opening the curtains of flesh veiling her intimacy, gasping as he located her clitoris and gently sucked it into his mouth, again, she breathed the sacred word. 'Cunt. My beautiful, wet cunt.'

Guiding her towards the sofa, he pulled her down gently,

positioning her on the edge of the soft cushion, her young thighs spread, her chaste cunt open to his every whim. Reclining, she pushed her hips forward, offering her virginity to her mentor – her priest. Ordering her to peel her cunt lips apart, he licked the entire length of her rubicund sex-valley, bringing her unknown pleasure, new sensations, as she lay back, lost in her desire.

'Now, I will return the pleasure you gave me and allow you to come in my mouth,' he murmured, engulfing her pulsating clitoris and running his tongue over the sensitive tip. Arching her back, her breasts heaving with her gasps, her fingers stretching her pads of intimate flesh wide apart, she exposed the full length of her clitoris to the priest's hot mouth, his caressing tongue.

'That's nice, Father,' she whimpered. 'I've never . . .'

'Never had your sweet cunt licked before?'

'Never. Oh, that's nice! Don't stop, Father! Please, don't stop!'

The girl came quickly, writhing, crying as her clitoris bloomed, flowered in the hot, male mouth. Never had she experienced such intense pleasure between her legs, a multiple orgasm, the waves of sex rolling over her body, heightening her passion, her desire for more. Lapping up her come, Father Will teased her inner folds, stroking her clitoris with every sweep of his tongue until she closed her legs and rolled on to her side, fulfilled.

His penis stiff, ready for penetration, the priest sat his rag doll upright and parted her legs, pulling her hips forward. 'And now for your deflowering, my angel,' he breathed as he knelt between her thighs and presented his purple knob to her open hole. 'Lie back and relax – and surrender your virginity.'

Gently easing his knob past her sweet pink folds, he watched his shaft sink into her young body. Slowly opening her virginal sex-tube, awakening her inner being, he completely impaled the young beauty, his balls resting against her warm buttocks, his knob caressing her silky-smooth cervix. Her eyes closed, her expression a mixture of desire and anxiety, she reached down between her legs to explore the base of the invading male organ.

Feeling her taut cunt lips encompassing the root of the man's penis, she ran her fingers beneath his rod and stroked his balls.

'That feels good,' she murmured, opening her eyes and looking down at her stretched pussy lips, the huge organ impaling her very being.

'And now I will fuck you,' the priest said, slowly sliding his piston in and out of her tight vagina.

'Yes, fuck me now!' she gasped, locating her clitoris with her fingertip and massaging the glowing tip.

'Can you feel me inside your hot cunt?'

'Yes, inside my hot cunt!'

'Can you feel my hard cock fucking you?'

'Oh, yes! Your hard cock fucking my hot cunt!'

'Do you want my sperm inside you, Chloë?'

'Yes – please, Father – fill my hot cunt with your sperm!'

How sweet the innocence of virgins! Lost in his sexual frenzy, the priest took his cherub with a vengeance, rocking her trembling body, pummelling her cervix as she cried out in her delight. 'Fucking me, my cunt!' Harder, faster he took her, stripped her of her virginity, tore down her protective curtains of youth, opened, for the first time, her tight cunt with his male organ.

'It's coming!' she cried, gazing at the glistening shaft as it drove into her torn body. 'The feeling's coming!'

'Coming!' Father Will echoed as his seed coursed its way up his shaft and erupted from his throbbing knob, baptizing her inner walls, her cervix.

Her cunt spasming, her breasts heaving, Chloë opened her legs to capacity to take the holy man deeper into her tight sheath, shuddering as her climax gripped her very soul. Making his last thrusts, the priest groaned, collapsing over the girl's breasts, gasping his satisfaction, praising the Lord for the beautiful gift of sex – of young girls.

'You're now a woman!' he gasped, slipping his penis from her drenched chasm. 'A real, fully-fledged woman, Chloë.'

'I've been fucked!' she cried disbelievingly. 'My cunt has been fucked by a real cock!'

Stupid child! 'Indeed it has, my child – indeed it has! Would you like me to fuck you every evening?'

'Oh, yes, Father! Every evening, I want you to fuck my cunt! God, it was so beautiful! I thought I was dying!'

Just you wait until I slip it up your bottom-hole! 'No, Chloë – you were living! And now you must go. Go home to your mother, no longer a girl – but a woman!'

Asking if the demon had gone as she dressed, Chloë smiled at her mentor, her eyes afire with desire. 'Yes, my child,' he replied reassuringly. 'I have sent the demon from you. But you must continue to masturbate and bring me your notes to ensure that the monster doesn't return. And I will fuck you every evening, continue with the lessons of love.'

The girl's full lips curled into a grin at the word *love*. My God! thought Father Will – wrong bloody word!

'Is this love, Father?' she asked coyly as she slipped into her skirt. 'What is love? Is it sex?'

'Love is the crest of a wave upon which you surf – before you crash alone onto a lonely beach.'

'What?'

'Love is . . . Sex is love, yes, Chloë. What we had was . . .'

'We had sex, Father – we are in love, then?'

Naïve or just plain stupid? Both! 'In a way, yes. But you still have much to learn about sex, so be sure to return tomorrow.'

'I will, Father!' Chloë enthused as she finished dressing. 'I will come every evening at seven!'

And so will I! 'And tell no one, my child!'

'I promise, Father – I promise.'

'Where do you live, Chloë? I could give you a lift if . . .'

'No, I'll walk home. I like walking, especially in the summer. I always walk to school and back.'

'School?'

41

'The convent, Father – Hardmound Convent.'

Shit! Gulping, Father Will gazed into the girl's innocent eyes. Christ! The bloody convent! Should she tell her friends, it was bound to get back to the Mother Inferior. 'Are there spies there, at the convent?' he asked.

'Spies, Father?'

'You know, girls who go running to the Mother Superior telling tales on the other girls.'

'There are one or two, yes – why?'

'You must tell no one about our meetings, Chloë – do you understand?'

'It's all right, Father, believe me – I know who the spies are. I'll only tell Samantha, my best friend.'

'No! Tell no one, Chloë!' *Stupid bitch!*

Showing the girl to the door, Father Will asked casually if he knew anything about the Mother Superior's private life. Chloë smiled as she turned. 'There are rumours,' she volunteered.

'Rumours? What sort of rumours?'

'Word has it that a few girls, the chosen few, as they're known, go to see Reverend Mother late in the evenings.'

'Chloë, you will find out all you can about these girls, and what they go to Reverend Mother for.' *A spanking session, with any luck!*

'Yes, I'll do that – I'll make notes about their activities in my exercise book and show you every evening. But why do you want to know, Father?'

'It's important that I know what's going on at the convent, Chloë, but I can't tell you why – not yet, anyway.'

Closing the door, Father Will sighed. He was sure that the stupid girl would go running to her friends with stories of wild sex with a priest. There again, perhaps the girls would all come running to nim for lessons in love. 'A gaggle of schoolgirls all eager to be fucked!' he laughed as he sat in his armchair and glanced at his watch. 'Shit, Josie! It's five to nine! There's no peace for the wicked, thank God!'

Lighting a cigarette, he planned his tactics. Josie wouldn't strip, bare her naked body to him, he knew. Neither would she suck the sperm from his orgasming penis! He decided that he'd have to frighten her into sex, but how? The fear of demons had worked admirably with young Chloë, but he doubted very much that Josie would fall for such a weak line. He was surprised that Chloë had been so easily taken in, that she was so incredibly gullible. Putting it down to her age, her stupidity, her sheltered upbringing, he checked his watch again – nine o'clock.

Leaping from his chair at the sound of the doorbell, he knew that he'd have to play it by ear, see what developed and ad lib as best he could. Opening the door, he donned his charming smile to welcome the girl into his house – his lair.

She appeared prettier than he'd remembered her, her eyes sparkling, her face bright, glowing with life as she walked to the lounge. Perhaps, away from Brian, she was free to be herself? he wondered, waving his hand towards the sofa, indicating for her to sit down.

She'd changed her clothes, he noticed as she dumped her handbag on the coffee table and sat down. She appeared to be different somehow, but he couldn't quite put his finger on it. Her skirt was short, her legs long and slender, her top open at the front, revealing virtually all she had. Had Brian sucked on her firm breasts, her nipples? he wondered. Sod Brian! he thought, pouring a large vodka and lime. But the change wasn't simply her clothes. She had a strange air about her – an air of cunning.

'Here, have a drink, Josie,' he invited, offering her the glass.

'Oh, thank you, Father,' she replied cheerily, her smile bright and summery, her big brown eyes mirroring an indefinable desire.

'I hope you don't mind me mentioning it, Josie, but you seem different somehow. You appear to be happy, full of the joys of spring, and all that.'

'I *am* happy, Father. I suppose I see too much of Brian, that's the trouble. You see, he keeps his eye on me all the time, never lets me out of his sight. He doesn't know I'm here, by the way – he'd go mad if he did!'

Father Will was beginning to see his way in – into her knickers. So, the young Brian was the jealous type, was he? Liked to keep her under wraps, away from other men, no doubt. A sign of insecurity, he mused. But what *was* his insecurity? A few tentative questions could reveal the truth.

'Do you find that Brian tends to suppress you, Josie?' he probed, eyeing her thighs.

'Suppress me, Father? How do you mean?' she asked, a strange glint in her eye as she followed his gaze.

'Well, does he tend to live your life for you, tell you what to do, what not to do, that sort of thing?'

'Yes, I suppose he is rather like that. I used to be happy-go-lucky, carefree, but now . . .'

'This sexual problem, Josie – I'm beginning to understand why you have a problem in that area. Forgive me, but I must tell you that Brian is suppressing your sexuality.'

'You mean that Brian is the cause of my problem, Father?'

'I wouldn't say the *cause*, exactly, but he certainly isn't helping you. You see, sex, as I told you earlier, should be mutual, a shared pleasure – and Brian, with his dominating attitude, is being highly selfish. Although I said that it was you who was being unfair, selfish, by not returning the pleasure he gives you, I can now see that you don't want to return the pleasure because . . . Brian's domineering attitude isn't helping you, Josie.'

'Then what do you suggest I do, Father?'

God, don't ask! 'That's not an easy question to answer.' *Take your knickers off and sit on my face*, he thought as his penis stirred in anticipation of her wet pussy hole. But why was the girl so very different? Earlier, she had come across as shy, nervous, timid, but now . . . He was suspicious – there was something about Josie, something strange, as if her words were scripted, as if she were play-acting.

'I suggest you go home and think about Brian and your future together. Before embarking on marriage, give yourself time.'

'But what about my sexual problem? You said you could help me.'

'Yes, I can, but you're not ready, my child.'

'I am ready! Listen, Father, I'll be honest with you. Brian isn't the one for me, I realize that now. There's someone else I'm interested in and I need to be free of sexual problems if I'm going to make any headway with this man. I love sex and . . . I need to know all about it, to be rid of my inhibitions if I am to enjoy my body.'

You need to be rid of your clothes! Noticing Josie's eyes darting to her handbag every now and then, the priest's suspicions grew. Unlike Chloë, she wasn't stupid, he knew. So what was her game? 'I can only teach you, guide you towards the Lord,' he proffered in his ministerial voice. 'I can only help you by talking, listening. I don't know what you thought I was going to do, my child, but I feel that you came here with the wrong idea in mind.'

The girl seemed agitated, her eyes turning cold, her expression one of anger now as if she'd failed in her mission. Again, she glanced at her handbag. Why? he wondered. Reclining on the sofa, she parted her thighs, deliberately exposing her panties. Moving her buttocks forward, her skirt rode further up her legs, her bulging panties unashamedly displayed to the priest's appreciative gaze.

'I was hoping that you were going to teach me about sex, Father,' she began. 'Brian is so . . . I don't know, he's strange when we're in bed. I don't take him in my mouth because I feel that he's using me. There seems to be no love on his part, only sex. Won't you help a young girl in her plight, Father? Won't you show me at first hand? Teach me about sex?'

In other words – won't you fuck me? Her panties disappearing up her young crack, her outer lips bulging invitingly as she opened her legs further, Father Will had a sudden flash of divine inspiration. 'Come out into the garden,' he suggested, rising to his feet. 'It's a lovely warm night, let's talk there.'

Grabbing her handbag, Josie moved towards the door. 'Leave your bag here,' Father Will said firmly, yanking it from her hand and placing it on the table. 'It will be quite safe.' She protested as he took her arm and propelled her through the hall. 'The garden's lovely,' he continued, ignoring her pleas for her bag. 'The night-scented stock is beautiful at this time of the evening.' *As is your pansy, no doubt.*

'I really do need my bag, Father!' the girl complained as he led her through the back door and out on to the patio. Almost pushing her on to the bed-chair, he smiled as he sat beside her, placing his hand on her knee as she reclined.

'Why do you need your bag?' *A Femidom, perhaps?*

'My . . . I need my make-up and . . .'

'All right, my child – if it's so important, I'll get it for you.'

Taking the bag from the coffee table, Father Will opened it and grinned. Switching the small tape recorder off, he placed it back in the bag, wondering which newspaper Josie worked for. I'll teach the bitch a lesson, he thought as he returned to the patio and placed the bag by the bed-chair. I'll have her knickers off and give her a bloody good fucking – the nosy little bitch!

'Tell me, Father,' Josie smiled. 'Do you have many young girls round here to see you?'

'Dozens!' laughed Father Will, sitting beside her and running his hand up her inner thigh. 'Why do you ask?'

'And do you always behave like this? I mean, putting your hand up my skirt isn't the way I'd expect a man of the cloth to behave!'

'I thought you wanted me to teach you about sex, Josie?' he replied as his finger slipped beneath the elastic of her panties.

'I do. I wanted to know about sex so that when I marry I'll . . . Father Entercock! Your finger's inside my knickers!'

'You have a nice cunt, Josie – it's all hot and wet! God you're a sexy little beauty!'

'Is this what you do to all the girls who come here for help?'

'Much more than this, my child! Now, you want me to teach you about oral sex, don't you? If you slip your knickers off, I'll get my hard knob out and we'll start with you sucking me off.'

Standing up, Father Will pulled out his erect penis and waved it threateningly before the girl's wide eyes. Poor thing, he thought as she gave her running commentary. She thinks she's got the story of the year! Moving his penis closer, offering her his male organ, he grinned.

'Do you want to suck it?' he asked, standing over her.

'Father!' she cried. 'Please, I'm a virgin!'

Not for long, baby! 'Then let me fuck you, my child! Let me strip you of your clothes, and your virginity! Let me eat your pussy, drink your hot come! Let me come in your mouth – fuck your pretty little face! Allow me to fuck your cleavage and give you a pretty pearl necklace!'

Grabbing her bag, Josie ran through the house and out into the lane – to meet her colleague, Father Will speculated as he zipped up his jeans. Would she return and try again in the realization that her tape recorder hadn't been working? She'd return, he knew – there was no way this wild little pussy would let a story like this slip through her claws! And when she returned, he decided, he'd reward her with the fucking of her life!

CHAPTER THREE

Bishop Simon Holesgood arrived at Cumsdale church at nine a.m. to find Father Will in the vestry donning his cassock in preparation to take confession.

'Greetings!' the priest beamed as he turned to face his bishop. 'You're earlier than I expected.'

'I thought I might catch you out,' the bishop returned agitatedly.

'Catch me out? I don't understand.'

'You're sailing close to the wind, and you know it! Now, I don't have a great deal of time so if we could retire to your office, we'll get this over with as quickly as possible.'

Pompous, pimple-nosed git! 'Yes, of course, Bishop – this way.'

Entering the office, His Grace appeared confused. Gazing around the room at the freshly-cut flowers, the open Bible on the highly polished desk, the neat pile of sermons, he frowned as he sat down, scratching his bald head.

'The Mother Superior of Hardmound Convent rang me yesterday,' he began. 'She . . . she seemed to think that you're selling alcohol and tobacco to the parishioners and . . .'

Shit-stirring slag-bag! 'Alcohol and tobacco, Bishop? Where on earth did she get that idea from? There must be some mistake.' *How the hell did she find out?*

'She told me that your office was a cesspit, with overflowing ashtrays and cases of lager strewn all over the place. She also informed me that you were either drunk or on drugs.'

'These are serious allegations, Bishop! Drunk? Drugs? I don't understand! You can see for yourself that my office is pristine.' *For a change*.

'She has informed me that you've been up to the convent and . . . As she put it, you interfered with a young nun – Sister Emily.'

Interfered with? More like fucked the arse off her! 'I'm always up at the convent taking confession, Bishop. Sister Emily came to me for help, advice, as do many of the nuns, and that is what I gave her. I really can't think why the Mother Superior is making these allegations. I mean, there must be a reason for what I can only describe as her blatant lies.'

The office door opening, both men turned to see a young woman wearing a scruffy raincoat, headscarf and dark glasses. 'Sorry, Father,' she began. 'I didn't realize that you were busy.'

'Come in,' the bishop invited. 'Tell me, what is it you want?'

'I only came to thank Father Entercock for all the good work he's been doing to help my grandparents.'

'Good work, my child? Of what nature?'

'He's been calling to see them three times a day. He takes Mass for them, holy communion and confession – they can't get out, you see.'

'Is that so?' the bishop replied, surprised. 'Then, you have no complaints about . . .'

'Complaints? Oh, no! Far from it! Without Father Entercock, I don't know what I'd have done. He's a pillar of godliness, such a good, kind man. Anyway, sorry to have disturbed you, I'll call back later, Father.'

'All right, my child. It was good of you to come,' Father Will smiled.

Turning to the priest as the girl left the office, the bishop's expression was one of undisguised anger. 'I know your game!' he snarled, his eyes piercing, bulging from his bald head. 'I'll catch you out, Entercock – if it's the last thing I do, I'll catch you out!'

50

And I'll catch you with a young tart in the pub! 'I hear you enjoyed a drink in the pub with a young girl the other night, Bishop,' Father Will smiled. 'Did you give her what she wanted? I mean, did you help her in her plight, whatever it was?'

'Listen to me, Entercock! You're trouble, and you'll get us all into trouble unless you stop . . .'

'I've written to the archbishop informing him of your good work. It's so nice to be able to help young girls during their years of discovery, their pubescent years, is it not? He'll be so pleased to learn that you took her to a pub for a drink. I hope she was of age, by the way – eighteen, I mean.' *Sixteen?*

Rising to his feet, the bishop's face reddened with anger. 'I have not taken anyone to a pub for a drink!' he stormed. 'I shall see the archbishop and advise him to have you defrocked without further ado!'

'You seem to enjoy defrocking people. Tell me, Bishop, how, exactly, did you help the young girl in the pub?' *Defrock and deflower her?*

'I have not been to a pub, and I have not taken any young girls out! I'll see you pay for this, mark my words!'

'And you mark mine, Bishop! I know more than you think about your private life, your exploits, and I won't hesitate to expose you unless you get off my back! Now, if you'll excuse me, I have to prepare for confession.'

As Bishop Holesgood stormed from the church, Father Will snatched a packet of cigarettes from his desk drawer. Pillaging the lower drawer, he grabbed a can of lager. 'Shit!' he cursed, his hands shaking with rage as he lit a cigarette and popped the can. He hadn't meant to threaten the bishop. Mentioning the young girl in the pub hadn't been a good move, he knew as he swigged down the lager. Trouble was brewing, he decided – serious trouble. Dangerous games – dangerous consequences.

A few people were gathered in the church waiting for confession to begin. They disturbed Father Will, dragging his thoughts, his contempt, away from the bishop. Finishing his lager, he stubbed his cigarette out and walked across the church to install himself in the confessional box. As he made himself comfortable, someone shuffled behind the metal grille, kneeling to confess their sins.

'Forgive me, Father, for I have sinned,' a soft female voice drifted through the grille. 'For I have been greedy and selfish.' Haven't we all? Father Will reflected idly as the woman continued her whispered confession. 'And I have committed adultery . . .' This is more like it! the priest thought, craning closer to the grille in an effort to discover the woman's identity. 'I have committed adultery with . . .' Her words tailed off.

Cough up, woman! 'Speak, my child,' Father Will gently coaxed.

'I have committed adultery with another woman.'

Father Will shifted on his seat, imagining the young lesbian naked with her lover – their bodies entwined, writhing in orgasm as they licked and sucked between each other's legs. He didn't usually ask questions, but on this occasion, he had little choice!

'How long has this been going on, my child?'

'For two months, Father,' came the tearful admission.

'And where does this sin take place?' *Between your wet cunt lips!*

'In . . . in the woods, Father – behind Cumsdale village hall.'

'And how often do you commit this dreadful sin?' *This beautiful sin.*

'Most afternoons, Father.'

'You will say three Our Fathers and six Hail Marys as your penance. Go now, my child, and make a good act of contrition.'

As the woman left the box, Father Will looked out through a chink in the grille and smiled. 'Young Mrs Harris!' he breathed disbelievingly, eyeing her slim legs as she walked across the church to join another young woman. Her lover, he mused, not recognizing the pretty girl dressed in a miniskirt and skimpy top revealing a band of naked flesh around her middle. *Really must pay more attention to my young female parishioners!*

The woods behind the village hall were no more than a large clump of trees surrounding a couple of grassy clearings, and Father Will resolved to take a trip there that afternoon to witness the wonderful sin – the lesbian sex show. Another sinner moved behind the metal grille as he imagined joining the naked women on the soft grass in their debased games of lesbian lust.

'Forgive me, Father, for I have sinned,' came the familiar dirge as the priest stifled a yawn, wishing he'd brought a can of lager with him into the confessional. 'I have wicked thoughts, Father,' the woman continued. 'I think about killing my husband. He behaves like an animal in bed, and I hate him for it.'

Think yourself lucky! God, give me strength, it's Mrs Harper again! Father Will thought as the woman droned on. He knew her husband well and smiled as he imagined the man taking his wife from behind, using her, fucking her bottom like an animal. Lucky sod, he thought, wondering if Chloë would allow him to slip his hard penis into her tight bottom-hole. *Must get some K-Y jelly.*

'He forces me to commit vile acts of indecency, Father,' the woman whined. She loved every minute of it, he knew, and got a great kick out of coming to confession twice a week to tell her sordid secrets. 'He ties me down and does it to me from behind. He uses my body to satisfy his perversions, Father. He makes me take him in my mouth and . . . I can't stand it any longer, Father. The trouble is, it's Friday, and on Friday nights he brings a friend home and they both use me at once – one in front and one behind.'

That's a new one, thought Father Will, imagining the woman being fucked by two men. Her fantasies are improving nicely!

Shame to leave her mouth vacant – void of a bulging, purple glans, throbbing in orgasm.

'You must learn to endure your husband's demands, my child. You are his wife, and a wife should obey her husband as she would obey the Lord. Go now, and remember my words,' he advised. 'Give your body to your husband, and share it with his friend. Be not selfish with your female form.'

The phone was ringing as he returned to his office after confession. 'Father Entercock,' he volunteered, pressing the receiver to his ear.

'Father, it's me, Chloë.'

I can almost smell the perfume of your panties! 'Ah, Chloë, my child, how are you?'

'Fine, Father. I'm ringing from the Mother Superior's office, so I'll have to be quick. I've discovered that she's having some girls visit her this evening, and I'm trying to get myself invited, so I might not be able to see you as planned.'

'As it happens, I've got to go over to Hallworth church this evening, so it doesn't matter, Chloë.'

'I was wondering if I could come and see you later, after I've been to her rooms, to tell you what happened?'

'I won't be back until . . . well, until at least ten o'clock.'

'That's all right. My mother's away for a couple of days, so I can stay out all night if I want to.'

God permit! 'Really? Well, in that case, I'll see you around ten. There's a key under the flowerpot by the front door. If you get there before I do, let yourself in.'

'All right, Father, I'll see you tonight.'

The priest could barely believe his luck as he replaced the receiver. 'Alleluia!' he cried, ransacking the drawer for another can of lager. 'Praise be to the Lord!' Hearing a knock on the door, he swung round in his swivel chair. 'Annie, come in! You did so well in front of the bishop!'

The young woman sat down and smiled, taking the can of lager offered by the priest. 'It was brilliant! I loved the raincoat and headscarf!' he enthused, passing her a cigarette.

'The bishop's a client of mine,' she enlightened him.

'What? Are you sure?'

'Course I'm sure, I've been entertaining him for six months!'

'Were you in the pub with him the other evening?'

'Yes, but it was only this morning that I realized he was a bloody bishop!'

'Annie, you're an angel! I needed something like this to . . . I won't worry you with it now. Christ, it's just as well you wore a disguise! If he'd recognized you . . . Are you seeing him again?'

'Yes, regular as clockwork. The thing is, I've got problems,' she confided, blowing smoke high into the air. 'It's been difficult recently, Father. My neighbours are becoming suspicious so I may not be able to work from home any more. If my old man finds out . . . I need somewhere else to work from, somewhere well away from the house – and my husband!'

Father Will rubbed his chin, deep in thought as he gazed into her brown eyes. He'd been sending her the odd male client, usually businessmen, and taking a twenty per cent cut, for some time. Her business could never be classed as booming, but she was able to charge well above the going rate, not only because she was stunningly attractive but because she'd do literally anything. With her long, crimped blonde hair and full sensuous mouth, her menu ranged from whipping to stuffing her knickers into her hot, wet cunt and allowing her clients to pull them out with their teeth.

'I might be able to help you out, Annie,' the priest smiled. 'As you know, I live alone at the presbytery next door. There are no neighbours, it's secluded, and there's a huge spare bedroom so . . .'

'Really, Father? That would be ideal!' she squealed excitedly. 'But I couldn't take the bishop there, could I?'

'I'll sort something out, somewhere else you can take him. Now, we'd have to work out the details, the times you'd be there, things like that. Financially, I reckon it's worth you giving me fifty per cent of your earnings. What do you think?'

'Fifty-fifty? Well, I'd have to take on more clients and without advertising, which I'd never do, I don't know how I'd get them.'

'I can take care of the clients, Annie, don't worry about that! There's twenty pounds for this morning's little stunt, by the way. I did wonder if you'd turn up dressed as you are now, in your red, thigh-length leather boots and microskirt, which would have blown the whole thing!'

'Was the bishop taken in by my story?'

'I think so, I'm not sure.'

'I hope it helped you, Father. Anyway, when can I start working from your place?'

The priest lowered his eyes to the girl's long legs, images of her young pussy, her wet, bloated cunt lips filling his mind. Not wanting to mix business with pleasure, he'd never had his wicked way with her incredibly sexy body before. But now, he was beginning to think that he should sample the wares on offer to the clients – *gratis*, of course.

'You can start straight away,' he decided. 'But there's just one thing, Annie. I'd like you to do me the odd favour now and then, if you get my meaning.' Lifting her skirt to reveal her knickerless pussy, she smiled. Her blonde pubic curls neatly trimmed, exposing her full, pouting cunt lips, a globule of milky fluid clung to her pink inner petals – inviting a tongue, Father Will thought as his penis twitched delightfully.

'This is yours for the taking whenever you want it, Father,' she smiled, lowering her skirt.

A gift from heaven! 'That's settled, then,' he grinned, his penis stiffening.

'I'll move my things in now, if that's all right with you.'

'Yes, that's fine. I'm having a visitor this evening so, if you could make yourself scarce by about ten, I'd appreciate it.'

'No problem. Anyone I know?'

'Er . . . No, no – I don't think so.'

Passing the girl a front door key, Father Will wondered what she'd meant by her *things*. Imagining whips, handcuffs, bondage gear, leather and rubber garments, his penis stiffened even more. But the minute she'd gone, his thoughts returned to the bishop. What was his particular fetish? What kinks turned him on? he wondered. Spanking? He'd ask Annie later, he decided – once she'd moved her tools of sex into the spare room. And her pussy.

Things were looking good, he reflected. The plants were coming on nicely in the greenhouse and the basement was positively overflowing with bootleg goodies. Annie's earnings would certainly give his income a boost – and she deserved a good fuck the minute the opportunity arose. Chloë was eager to learn more about sex. But there were still problems – Josie, the bloody newspaper reporter; the bishop's threats; and, not least, the archbishop and the Mother Fucker Superior!

Deciding to take a walk to Hardmound Covent, Father Will locked his office and left the church. The morning sun was hot, bright in the clear blue sky, and he imagined, again, the two lesbians writhing naked on the grass behind the village hall, their knickers and bras scattered around them in their wanton abandonment. Making a mental note to take his Pentax with him, he realized he could earn a small fortune by blowing the pictures up and selling them. Good thinking, Entercock! he congratulated himself as he passed the presbytery – the brothel.

'May I speak with you, Father?' Josie panted, running up the lane, her skirt shorter than ever, her naked legs shapely, ready for parting – her handbag swinging by her side.

'Good morning, Josie,' he replied pleasantly.

'I'm sorry I ran off last night only . . . Well, I was rather shocked by your behaviour.'

That was the general idea. She wanted him to speak words of sex, to incriminate himself, he knew as he glanced at her bag. But he was pleased that she'd returned to try to get her scoop. What to say? With the tape recorder running, he had to choose his words very carefully.

'I'm going for a walk,' he smiled pleasantly. 'It's such a beautiful day, don't you agree?'

'It is, Father. But about last night – the way you . . .'

'Forget about last night, my child. I did rather go on about teaching you the Lord's way, and I apologize. So, what are you up to this morning? And how's your husband-to-be?' *Ugly git!*

'He's all right. Last night, Father, you said . . .'

'Not another word, my child – it's forgotten, as far as I'm concerned. Now, will you walk with me to the convent?'

'Could we speak in the presbytery, Father? It won't take long.'

A determined young filly if ever there was one, he mused. He longed to get her into the house, but how to switch her wretched machine off? Leading her to the front door he had an idea and grinned as he let her in. Placing her bag on the coffee table, she was about to sit down when he asked her if she'd mind leaving the room while he made a private call.

'I'll wait in the kitchen,' she said, grabbing her bag.

'Thank you, Josie, only this is a most private call, a call of an intimate nature to a fellow priest – top secret stuff.'

Predictably replacing her bag on the table, she left the room and closed the door. Carefully removing the small cassette from the machine, Father Will pulled the tape out and snapped it. Slipping it back, he knew that she'd check that the recorder was running before beginning her questioning – blissfully unaware that the tape was broken.

'All right, Josie, you can come in now!' he called after some minutes. Returning to the lounge, she snatched her bag, discreetly checking the machine before sitting on the sofa. 'So, what did you want to talk to me about?' he asked, reclining in his armchair. She grinned, believing that, this time, she'd got him by the balls.

'Last night, Father Entercock, you rather frightened me. I mean, pulling your penis out and asking me if I'd like to suck it took me by surprise. Is that really what you to do to all the young girls you lure here?'

'Oh, I don't lure them, Josie. They come here because . . . To put it frankly, they want the pleasure of my hard penis throbbing in their young mouths, their tight, hot cunts. I mean, it is rather a fine specimen, isn't it?'

'Er . . . yes, from what I saw of it, it is! Now, you said that you'd help me with my sexual problems – what do you want me to do?'

Strip off and open your legs! God, she's changed her tune now that she thinks the recorder's running! he thought, delighting in the game. 'Slip your panties off, my child, and I'll begin by teaching you how to masturbate properly,' he said briskly, concealing his wicked grin.

'But Father Entercock, you're supposed to be a man of God! Don't you think that what you're suggesting goes against the teachings of the church, against your religion?'

'Oh, yes, of course it does! Anyway, I only got caught up in this God thing because I was working for MI5.'

'I don't believe you!'

'Good, because I'm not supposed to tell anyone.'

'You're mad, aren't you?'

'We're all mad, my child. Listen, Josie, I like sex as much as the next man – more, in fact – and I'm not going to give it up just because I'm priest of Cumsdale Parish. The things I could tell you about the church would make your hair stand on end, believe me!'

'Tell me, Father – tell me everything!'

'Not until you've slipped your knickers off, my child. Take them off for me and allow me to help you in your plight, and I'll tell you some juicy secrets about me, the convent, and the church!'

Standing up, Josie was about to oblige when she had a change of mind. She desperately wanted all the gory details, but to prostitute herself? Sitting on the sofa again, she frowned as Father Will joined her, thrusting his hand up her skirt and tugging on her knickers.

'What are you doing?' she cried as he manhandled her, wrenching the silky garment down to her ankles.

'I'm going to show you how to masturbate,' he boomed, much to her delight as she glanced at her handbag.

Parting her soft thighs, he groped between her swollen cunt lips, trying to push a finger into the heat of her vagina. Putting up a perfunctory fight, she knew that if she wanted her story, she'd have to go so far, allow him some pleasure.

'Oh, what are you doing, Father?' she exclaimed as he parted her young pussy lips and pushed a finger deep into her wet vagina.

'Fingering your cunt, Josie. I need to do this to teach you about masturbation,' he enlightened her. 'Now, I'll massage your clitoris and thrust my fingers in and out of your beautiful cunt and make you come as you've never come before!' he muttered crudely, his penis quivering in anticipation of slipping into another tight, wet sheath.

Josie was obviously enjoying herself as she began to squirm and writhe a little. 'Tell me, Father,' she gasped as he worked expertly on her stiffening clitoris. 'Tell me, do you do this sort of thing to your parishioners' wives?'

'Many of them, Josie. You see, they look upon me as their mentor when it comes to sex. I've taken most of the women around here to bed – some regularly.'

'What if it came out? I mean, what if the world discovered . . . Ah, that's lovely, you certainly know what you're doing!'

'If the world knew, then I'd be finished! God, can you imagine it? Father William Entercock corrupts convent girls, screws his parishioners' wives, sells . . . God, you're becoming extremely wet, my little angel!' *My little whore!*

Slipping his erect penis out from beneath his cassock, Will took

Josie's hand and forced her to grip the solid shaft.

'Father, please!' she exclaimed for the benefit of the tape recorder. 'You're forcing me to hold your penis and I don't want . . .'

'I want you to move your hand up and down, Josie. I want you to make me come all over your hand,' he gasped as she obligingly followed his instructions, continuing her protests.

'Oh, Father Entercock! You're making me do things to you that I don't want to do! You're forcing me to . . .'

'I always force the young girls to wank me off!' he breathed as she quickened her movements, bringing him nearer to his climax with every stroke of her warm hand. 'You see, they trust me, and I betray their trust by forcing them to wank me off.'

'But don't they tell . . .'

'No, no. Once they've enjoyed an hour or so of enforced perverted sex with me, they come back for more!'

Reclining on the sofa, his cassock pulled up around his stomach, his penis ballooning, Father Will grimaced. 'Coming!' he cried as Josie worked her hand up and down. 'God, I'm coming! Suck it, and I'll tell you about the spanking sessions at the convent!'

Pulling Will's foreskin right back, Josie leaned over, engulfing the purple head of his penis in her hot mouth as the first spurt of sperm jetted from his knob. Sucking, licking the throbbing glans, she swallowed hard, drinking the priest's fruits as he gasped, his body contorting in his coming.

Gripping her head, he moved her up and down, fucking her mouth, filling her cheeks with his gushing sperm until the pleasure became almost painful. Pushing her away, he lay back, his body trembling, every nerve ending ultra-sensitive.

'God, that was good!' he praised as she licked the sperm from her glossy lips.

'Father, I didn't want to do that!' she complained.

'Tough!' he laughed. 'It's too late now, isn't it? So, how about me giving you a bloody good fucking?'

'I want to know about the convent first,' she said. 'About the spanking sessions.'

So do I! he thought, pulling his cassock down. She was obviously prepared to do virtually anything to get her story, Father Will surmised, deciding to give her a little false information in exchange for her sucking his knob. Then, he'd offer her a little more for taking her wet pussy, and finally, a little more – for slipping his penis deep into her tight bottom-hole.

'They have regular lesbian spanking sessions at Hardmound Convent,' he began. She glanced nervously at her bag. 'It's mainly the nuns, but some of the schoolgirls, the sixth-formers, join in.'

'How do you know this?' she asked, wide-eyed.

'Contacts, I have contacts. The nuns, one or two of them, anyway, keep me supplied with ripe young girls. Mostly, they're right little tarts willing to do anything and everything!'

'The girls always come here, do they?'

'Not always. Sometimes I go there, to their dormitory.'

'You're allowed into the dormitory?' she asked, amazed.

'Not allowed, exactly! I sneak in through a back door. Sometimes, *I* wield the whip – they like that.'

'I don't suppose you have any photographs of the goings-on?'

'No, I'm afraid not. But there's more – the nunnery, for example.'

'The nunnery? What goes on there?'

'The nunnery is in the grounds of the convent and . . . No, I've said enough already. God, imagine the Sunday tabloids getting hold of this story!' *You dozy cow!*

More than imagine, Josie was already mentally writing up her story. Asking for a drink, she knew she'd have to offer more in the way of sex to get the priest to open his mouth, spill the beans.

'Fancy a little more fun?' she asked as he filled a glass with vodka. 'I want to know about the nunnery, so how about swapping some sexy fun for the info?'

'Info?' he echoed, frowning.

'Er . . . yes, about the goings on. I . . . you see, it excites me, listening to dirty stories.'

This was too easy! She was actually offering him her body, her tight cunt! Father Will suggested that she lie back and open her legs as he placed his drink on the coffee table and knelt at her feet. Lifting her buttocks, she moved forward, opening her legs as she reclined on the sofa. Bared, open to his every whim, her young crack seemed to smile at him invitingly as he moved closer to admire the naked centre of her body. Breathing in her girl-scent, he sucked each puffy outer lip into his mouth in turn, swelling the warm cushions of flesh, stiffening her clitoris as her sex-valley opened in response.

Stretching her slit wide open, he moved down and tasted the milky juice now oozing from her tight love-sheath. Squirming, she closed her eyes, opening her legs further to allow the priest better access to her femininity. 'That's nice,' she breathed softly as he located her clitoris and gently flicked the tip with his tongue. 'Keep doing that, and I'll come for you.'

Placing her feet on the sofa, flanking her buttocks, she allowed her knees to fall apart, exposing the entire length of her girl-slit to the cleric. Bulging, hot, wet, her fleshy *labia majora* glowed a fire-red in her arousal as he worked on her budding clitoris, stiffening the small protrusion until she began to gasp her delight.

'It's coming, don't stop!' she cried as she opened her legs further. 'God, you're good at this!' Good? Bloody brilliant! he thought as she squirmed and writhed as her clitoris exploded in his hot mouth. Her body shuddering uncontrollably, she reached down and peeled her bulging girl-lips wide open to expose her rubicund inner flesh. 'My cunt!' she cried. 'Lick inside my cunt!'

Moving down her glistening flesh to the hot, wet opening of her vagina, Will poked his tongue inside the humid cavern. She shuddered, gasped in her climax, grinding her open cunt into his face, his mouth, until she finally fell limp, quivering in the wake of her orgasm. 'God, that was lovely!' she breathed as he lapped up her sex milk, cleansing her open hole in readiness for his rock-hard penis.

Wiping his mouth with his hand, he sat back on his heels, admiring the girl's open sex, her inflamed inner flesh. His penis stiff and ready to delve deep into her body, he smiled. 'Information,' he began. 'The nuns hold orgies at the nunnery. Priests come from miles around to join in the fun. There's whipping, bondage, lesbian shows, body piercing, water sports, shaving – you name it, they do it.' *Would that they did!*

Josie's eyes lit up before turning into a frown. She was becoming suspicious – he was rather too keen to reveal his secrets for her liking. But he wants sex, she told herself. That was the deal – sex for information. She'd have to allow him to have his wicked way with her, she knew, as she followed his gaze to her creamy slit.

'These nuns' orgies,' she began. 'Is there any way you can get me an invite?'

'Probably,' he replied, imagining her dressed in a habit. 'But it won't be easy. Do you live nearby?'

'No, no, I don't. I'm, er . . . I'm on holiday. I live in London and . . . Brian and I were thinking of moving down here. I could leave you my home phone number.'

'All right. I'll make some enquiries and let you know about the orgies. Now, I suppose you'd like to know about confessions – what goes on between the young married ladies and myself through the hole in the grille of the confessional?'

'Oh, yes!' she replied eagerly, visualizing her editor promoting her. 'Tell me everything!'

'After you've enjoyed this,' he smiled, slipping his erect penis out from beneath his cassock.

Josie lay back, her legs open again, her body bared for sex in exchange for the priest's lies. His penis in his hand, he homed in, rubbing the purple head over her glistening folds of girl-flesh. 'Come on!' she coaxed in her rising desperation for satisfaction. 'Fuck me!'

Aligning his knob with her open entrance, the priest thrust his hips forward, driving deep into her hot body, his shaft disappearing between her splayed cunt lips until his heavy balls came to rest against the warmth of her buttocks. This was his penultimate goal – her hot, juicy cunt. Next, he'd slip his rod into her bottom-hole and really make her squeal!

Slowly, at first, he slid his piston in and out of Josie's tightening sheath, causing her stomach to rise and fall. She lay back with her eyes transfixed between her thighs, her swollen lips tightly encompassing the priest's huge organ. Lifting her feet from the floor, she placed her legs over his shoulders, allowing him deeper penetration. Her cunt lips bulging around his thick shaft, he looked down, drinking in the wondrous sight as he increased his rhythm, ramming her young cervix – fucking the cocky newspaper reporter's tight little cunt.

Grabbing her hips, he took the girl with a vengeance, rocking her young body, pummelling the very centre of her being. 'Coming!' she gasped as he drove deeper and deeper into her hot cunt. 'Fuck me hard!' Suddenly realizing that she might not allow him to fuck her bottom-hole, he decided to slip his knob out and thrust it into her smaller hole before she could stop him. Nearing his climax as she shuddered and tossed her head, Will knew that the time was nigh to commit his debauched sin.

Moving quickly, he withdrew his knob from her spasming vagina and guided it between her splayed buttocks. She opened her eyes and gazed at him in horror as he forced his knob into her tight bottom-hole, opening her muscles to invade the sanctuary of her bowels. *Take that, baby!*

'Christ, what are you doing?' she cried as he pressed his knob deeper into her tight anal tube. 'Take it out, you bloody pervert!'

Ignoring her ranting and raving, he pushed his shaft deeper into her tight orifice, filling her bowels with his male girth. 'I'll get you for this!' she screamed as he began his gentle fucking.

'This is what the Mother Inferior likes!' he gasped. 'She likes it up her bum!'

Stunned by his words, Josie seemed to forget that her bottom-hole was being crudely violated by the priest's stiff penis. Was there no end to the church's debauchery? she wondered as she gazed at him, a man of the cloth, forcing his male organ into her bottom.

'Is this what you do to her, then?' she asked as he thrust harder between her splayed buttocks.

'Oh, no, not me. I mean, I have fucked her bum, but it's the convent schoolgirls she likes.'

'But how can girls . . .'

'Strap-on dildos, Josie. They give her one up the bum by wearing strap-on dildos.' *That's a good one.*

Incredible as the idea was, Josie had to believe what she was hearing. After all, the priest was taking her bottom-hole, so why not the Mother Superior's? And from the apparent corruption abounding within the church, why should the convent girls be spared from the debauchery?

Thrusting his shaft in and out of her private duct, bringing his seed ever nearer to his glans as he rolled his eyes, soaking up the fiery heat of her inner being, Will imagined that he was indeed screwing the Mother Superior's arse.

'Don't, please don't!' Josie begged as he grimaced and gasped while his sperm gushed, baptizing her virginal hole to lubricate their lewd joining. 'I don't want spunk dripping out of my bum all day long!' But she knew now that, to get her scoop, there were no holes barred!

On and on the priest thrust, delighting in her perfunctory protests as he emptied his balls, pumping his sperm deep into her body until, his muscles rigid, he finally stopped. Resting, absorbing the dank heat of her bottom-hole, he gazed into her wide eyes and grinned. She hadn't expected this, he knew, as she wiggled to free herself, to pull away from the massive shaft buried deep inside her tight anal sheath.

Would she come back for more when she realized that the tape was broken? he wondered. Without an incriminating word, she could do nothing to substantiate her wild claims. But would she return to offer more sex in an effort to nail him? Sliding his spent penis from her slippery tube, he knew she'd be back for the story of the year – the scoop of the decade. And she'd have to give her entire body to get it!

'God, you've a beautiful bum-hole!' he gasped as he fell back onto the floor, his shrinking penis glistening with sperm.

'You bastard!' she returned. 'I'll see that you're . . .'

'That I'm what?' he smiled, looking up to her reddening face.

'You'll find out, you sad pervert!' She knew that she had to protest, but not too much.

'Didn't you like it, Josie?'

'No, yes . . . I don't know. I just wish you'd told me what you were going to do! I was shocked!'

'But you loved it, didn't you? You loved having your bottom-hole fucked, didn't you?'

'Yes,' she replied softly as she retrieved her knickers from the floor and dragged them up her legs, realizing that the more she encouraged him to speak, the more incriminating words she'd have to nail him.

'We'll do it again, if you like,' he suggested as she stood up and retrieved her bag.

'I . . . I don't know if . . .'

'If you want more information, and an invite to the nunnery, then you'll have to let me do it again, Josie.'

'Tell me more about the Mother Superior,' she said as he climbed to his feet.

'I've told you, she likes having her bum fucked.'

'I don't believe it! I mean . . .'

'You'd better believe it! The things that go on at Hardmound Convent, and the nunnery, would astound you. For example, when I go up to the convent to take confession, I sit in the box, the girls kneel behind the screen and . . . No, no, I'd better not say too much.'

'Oh, please tell me!'

'Well, there's this tiny hole in the screen. I slip my penis through it and the girls have their fun.'

'What, you mean . . .'

'They suck it – or slip their knickers down, bend over and back on to it. We have some bloody good confessionals, believe me!'

Josie glanced at her bag for the umpteenth time, images of her promotion swirling in her mind. Realizing that the tape might have run out, she decided to call it a day. 'I'll come back tomorrow, and you can tell me more,' she said as she rose to her feet. 'I'm really interested. I'd love to hear everything – it turns me on no end!'

'So you *did* like it up your bum?'

'You tell me all you know tomorrow, and you can have my bum again.'

'It's a deal – I'll even write it down for you, in the form of a story, so you can read it in bed and get all excited.'

'Great! Write it all down – names, the lot.'

'What do you want names for, Josie?'

'Well, to make it more like a real story.'

'Oh, right. By the way, the nunnery is the headquarters of the FRO.'

'What's the FRO?'

'The Free Rutland Organization. The county of Rutland was squeezed out by the larger counties surrounding it. The people were oppressed, and depressed, so they formed the FRO to regain their county.'

'You really are mad!'

'Don't tell a soul that I revealed this sensitive information to you, Josie. You've never heard of the FRO, OK?'

'Whatever you say. Until tomorrow, then.'

'Yes, until tomorrow.'

Father Will smiled as the girl left the house. 'Quite an accomplishment!' he chuckled, grabbing his cigarettes. In a way, he felt sorry for her. Having to sell her body to get her story, only to discover that she had no story at all, was quite sad. Still, he consoled himself, she's had her bum fucked by a priest – and not many can say that! Or can they? *Wonder if the people of Rutland were really oppressed?*

'Enjoy yourself?' a soft female voice enquired from the doorway. The priest jumped round to face Annie.

'Annie! How . . . how long have . . .'

'I saw the whole thing! I was bringing my stuff in, heard noises, and saw you both through the crack in the door!' she laughed.

'Christ, you gave me the fright of my life!'

'And you gave *her* the fuck of her life – up her bum!'

'Fancy watching me, Annie! You are naughty!'

'*Me*! God, you can talk! Anyway, I've got my things in the car, I'll bring them in – unless you have another client, that is?'

'No, no.'

'What was all that crap about the nunnery and the convent and Rutland, anyway?'

'It's a long story – or it would have been if . . . Never mind. Go and get your things.'

Father Will smiled. Having Annie work from the presbytery was going to be most rewarding, not only financially but sexually. His penis stirred as he recalled her words as she'd lifted her skirt and shown him her pouting pussy lips. 'This is yours for the taking'. A sweet young thing, he mused as she lugged a cardboard box up the hall. A sweet young thing – with a sweet young bottom-hole, no doubt.

'Which room?' she asked, her arms cradling the box.

'In there – it should be more than big enough for . . .'

'For what, Father?' she grinned as he tried to peer into the box.

'Well, for whatever it is you get up to, I suppose. There's a double bed and . . .'

'I'll need a table, something big and strong like those old-fashioned dining room tables.'

'What the hell for?'

'My clients are a weird lot. Some of them like me to bend over a table so that they can tie me down and whip me, others like me to lie on a table with my legs . . .'

'Annie, sorry to interrupt you, but I've just had a thought. Talking of tables, how about using the altar?'

'What, bring the altar in here?'

'No, no. I'll bet some of your clients are real pervs. Now, how about offering yourself as a sacrifice?'

'What, and end up dead?'

'No, of course not! What I mean is a sort of cult thing – you know, satanic stuff. They could fuck you . . . I mean, do it to you over the altar. They'd pay well for that.'

'That's good! Yes, that's very good, Father! They *would* pay well for something like that.'

'It would have to be at night, of course. Look, I've got to go up to the convent so we'll talk about it later. By the way, if that girl, Josie, comes back, or if you ever see her, say nothing to her. She's . . . she's a newspaper reporter.'

'What?'

'It's OK, I've got her where I want her – just say nothing.'

'OK, you're the boss.'

'The pimp, you mean! Anyway, I must be going. I'm off to take confession – or should I say, to give the girls something to confess! I'll sort a table out for you – nick one from the nunnery or something. See you later.'

Wandering down the front path to the gate, Father Will caught a glimpse of Brian dashing into the bushes across the lane. Christ!

he admonished himself. Of course, Brian's the bloody photographer! Had he taken pictures through the lounge window? Pictures of his penis slipping into Josie's bum-hole? Or of Annie entering the house with her gear?

Things were hotting up, and he didn't like it. He'd have to deal with Josie, and Brian, once and for all. What had been a game was now becoming a serious business. He should never have spoken to Josie, he chided himself – let alone fucked her bottom-hole!

CHAPTER FOUR

Arriving at the convent, Father Will was shocked to see Josie hovering outside the main entrance. 'What the hell's that little bitch doing here?' he breathed as he slipped around the back of the building. Trouble was brewing, he knew, as he entered the convent by the rear door.

'Father, what are you doing sneaking in the back way?' Sister Teresa whispered as she wandered down the corridor towards him.

'I can't explain now. Where's the Mother Fucker?'

'In her office, why?'

'There's a girl at the main entrance . . .'

'I know, she's gone in to see the old bag.'

'Shit! I've gone and done something that I think I'm going to regret. I wish I knew what they're saying.'

'We can listen, under the window outside her office – follow me.'

Slipping outside, Sister Teresa led Father Will along the side of the building to an open window. Crouching behind the bushes below the window they listened to Josie's questioning, her digging – her investigative journalism.

'You see, Reverend Mother, my sister has always wanted to join a convent school,' Josie lied. 'She's a devout Catholic, as I am, and it's her greatest wish to become a nun. But, from what I've heard about Father Entercock and the goings on in his church, I'm beginning to wonder whether it's a good idea for her to come here to Hardmound Convent.'

'What have you heard?'

'Only rumours. Everyone speaks very highly of *you*, of course. But when it comes to Father Entercock, it seems that he's not as godly as he makes out. I wouldn't want my sister to involve herself with anything like . . .'

'You said that you're a journalist with a Sunday tabloid.'

'Yes, I am.'

'Want a good story?'

'Well, I came to see you about my sister, but . . .'

'Father Entercock's behaviour is despicable, and not only do I want him defrocked and thrown out of the church, but publicly disgraced as well! Now, I'll get your sister a place here at Hardmound Convent if you can expose him for what he is – a low-down . . . I'd better not say it. So, what do you say?'

'I'll help you if I can, but . . . How much are the convent fees?'

'Don't worry about that! You get that priest defrocked, and your sister can attend the convent for nothing.'

'Really? That's good of you. The priest must be terrible if . . .'

'He brings alcohol and tobacco over from France. He interferes with the young nuns, not to mention the sixth-form girls. He drinks, smokes, and takes drugs. Is that enough to get you started?'

'Well, yes, but I'll need proof.'

'Surely, you newspaper types can get all the proof you need?'

'Yes, but I'll need leads, clues.'

'I've told you what he's up to, all you have to do is get the evidence. I'll help you as much as I can, of course, but . . .'

'Could you set him up?'

'Set him up? What do you mean?'

'I don't know, lure him into a trap or something.'

'I don't want to get involved, you must understand that. I don't want the convent or the nunnery connected with Father Enter-cock. But I'll tell you this – I believe that he's going to Hallworth Church this evening to . . . A group of my sixth-form girls are going there for Bible studies. As I'm unable to accompany the girls, I'm rather concerned for their welfare as, rumour has it, that Father Entercock might well be going along to . . . I dread to think what he has in mind, but I have a pretty good idea.'

'Can't you trust your girls?'

'They are young, impressionable, vulnerable. It's not a ques-tion of trusting the girls – I don't trust Father Entercock.'

'I'll go there this evening and see what I can unearth. I have a photographer covering this assignment with me . . . I mean, another assignment we're on, so I'm sure that between us we'll sort out Father Entercock. I'll be in touch about my sister, by the way.'

Creeping along the side of the building, Father Will turned to Sister Teresa. 'Now I've got more bloody problems!' he moaned.

'Who is this woman, anyway?' the nun asked.

'She works for a newspaper and . . . Well, basically, she's trying to expose me. I told her a string of lies so I could have my wicked way with her and it seems that I've whetted her appetite as well as her . . . I should have known better!'

'But it's only her word against yours.'

'Yes, it is at the moment. She had a tape recorder in her bag, but I snapped the tape so she's got nothing on me. But she *will* have if she keeps digging around, poking her nose in like this.'

'How did she get on to you in the first place?'

'Fuck knows! Someone obviously tipped her off. Who, one wonders.'

Sitting on the grass with his back against the wall, the priest lit a cigarette. Imagining Josie discovering that Annie was working as a prostitute from the presbytery and, worse still, that he was acting as her pimp, he sighed. 'I'll have to put everything on hold,' he decided as Sister Teresa sat beside him, pulling her habit up to sun her long legs.

'But the church basement, the greenhouse – you can't hide everything.'

'I was just about to start a new business venture, but that's fucked now – everything's fucked!'

'What venture?'

'Soiled knickers – they fetch twenty quid a pair in the men's mags.'

'So that's why you asked me to collect the girls' dirty knickers!'

'Yes, the convent's a bloody good source, don't you agree?'

'God, yes! We've got four hundred girls here! All I'd have to do is raid the laundry room once a week and . . .'

'Do it anyway. Collect the knickers – only the sixth-form girls' knickers, though!'

'OK. Look, I'd better be going. I'll let you know if I hear anything.'

'OK, and thanks. You'll get a cut for the knickers, of course.'

'Fifty per cent?'

'Twenty.'

'You're a hard bastard, Will!'

'You should know, my naughty little angel! By the way, I may have something on the Mother Inferior before long.'

'Really?'

'Yes, one of your girls . . . no names, but I may be getting some inside information. I'll let you know the minute I hear anything.'

'Great! Look, I'd better bugger off. See you later.'

'You don't know anything about the sixth-formers going to the Mother Fucker's room at night, do you?'

'No, I don't – but it sounds interesting. As you know, I've only been here for a few weeks so I don't know the ropes yet. Look, I really must go or she'll start creating.'

'OK, I'll be in touch.'

★ ★ ★

Wandering around to the front of the building, Father Will entered by the main door and made his way to the school chapel where half a dozen or so young girls were kneeling in the pews, waiting to confess their sins. Fidgeting and giggling, they brought a smile to the priest's face. He eyed their coltish legs, their skirts, hoisted – against the Mother Superior's wishes – well above their knees to display their shapely thighs. Their virgin white school blouses swelling with their petite young breasts, he imagined them naked, queuing up to squat over his face – their young cracks open, oozing with fresh cream. Trembling, he adjusted his cassock and made for the confessional box, his penis, yet again, hard and ready for sex.

Appeasing the beast through his cassock, he listened to the shuffling going on behind the screen, imagining the girl's pussy lips bulging in her stained knickers as she knelt to repent.

'Forgive me, Father, for I have sinned,' she began softly to the accompaniment of giggles from the waiting girls. 'Father, in my leisure time, I watched an immoral film.'

'What was this immoral film called, my child?'

'It was called . . . *Two girls, two tongues*, Father.'

Two tongues, two cunts! 'Where is this immoral film now?'

'Here, in my bag, Father.'

'Then pass it to me for confiscation. For your penance you will say three Hail Marys and ten Our Fathers . . . Go now and make a good act of contrition.'

'Yes, Father, thank you.'

Taking the video tape as the girl thrust her hand through the grille, Father Will grinned. Naughty little lesbian, he thought as he peered through the grille to see the young Janice Watts walking back to her friends. More giggles emanated from the girls as she reported the tape's confiscation.

He'd been set up again, he knew, but he was more than pleased to play along with their games. Inspecting the video box, he realized that the amateurish cover photo of a young woman's naked buttocks had been taken by the girls. Remembering that the convent had recently had video equipment installed in their media studies department, he guessed that they'd made the tape themselves – used the equipment late one night to film raunchy lesbian scenes to try to shock him.

How delightful! he thought, imagining their young pussies open, dripping with girl-come. But they wouldn't show their faces in the film, surely? Slipping the tape beneath his cassock, he awaited the next girl's confession.

'Forgive me, Father, for I have sinned,' she whispered. 'I have had an immoral conversation with another girl.'

'And what was this conversation about, my child?' he enquired, his penis tenting his cassock yet again.

'Sex, Father. We talked about sex.'

Wonderful! 'What did you say, exactly?'

'We talked about boys, Father – about their penises, how big they are, how hard and stiff and long and thick and . . .'

'Did you talk about girls' privates?'

'Yes, Father, we talked about this girl who shaved her . . . she shaved the hair off her private parts, Father.'

'What is this girl's name?'

'I can't tell you that.'

'But you must, my child.'

'Forgive me, Father, for I have lied to you. I am the girl – I shaved my pubic hair off.'

Smooth as a billiard ball! 'Why did you commit this vile act, my child?' *God, she must look wonderful!*

'It was for a dare, Father.'

'You will come to the presbytery later this afternoon to receive your punishment!'

'But, Father—'

'Later this afternoon! At five o'clock, after your classes.'

'I have to go to Hallworth Church this evening, Father. I'll have to get ready and—'

'Then I'll meet you at the church. I'll be attending the Bible-bash . . . the Bible studies, so I'll meet you there.'

'Yes, Father. What punishment will I receive for my sins?'

'I will think about the vile sin that you have committed against your young body and' *have a wank* 'inform you of your punishment this evening.'

'Isn't that rather unorthodox, Father? I mean, asking me to go to the presbytery, and then asking me to meet you at the—'

'Your sin is unorthodox to say the least, and I would consider having you dismissed from the convent. Think yourself lucky that confession is strictly confidential! I am appalled by your wanton act of depravity! Never in all my years as a priest . . . I will inform you of your punishment this evening!'

'Yes, Father.'

Before he'd had a chance to peek through the grille and see who the girl was, she'd rejoined her friends. 'Shit!' he breathed, praying that she'd approach him that evening so he could administer his punishment like a real man. As another girl entered the confessional, he thought of the video tape, wondering how much he could sell copies for.

'Forgive me, Father, for I have sinned.'

Yeah, yeah – what is it this time? Fucked yourself with a church candle? Bent over and had your arse buggered with a carrot?

'Father, it's me, Chloë.'

'Chloë! How are things going?'

'I've been invited to the Mother Superior's room this evening.'

'Good girl! Listen, who was that girl who came in here before you?'

'Samantha Lovejoy.'

'What do you know about her?'

'Her father's an MP and her mother's a doctor. They've got lots of money and she really upsets her parents. She's a right one! Always in trouble, she is.'

'What sort of trouble?'

'I'm not sure what she gets up to but I've heard Reverend Mother having a go at her hundreds of times about hanging around the perimeter fence, down by the pond. I don't know what she does down there, but Reverend Mother is far from pleased.'

'Right, I'll have to look into it and discover what young Samantha Lovejoy's into. Look, tell the other girls that confession is over, will you? I've got one or two things to do. I'll see you tonight.'

'All right, Father. I'll see you later.'

Poor Chloë, he thought as he listened to the girls disperse. She has every faith in me. Faith the size of a grain of masturbated seed can move the earth! Waiting until the coast was clear, he slipped from the confessional box, praying that the Mother Inferior was busy in her office as he stole down the corridor.

'Father Entercock!' came the old bag's voice as he was about to leave the building.

So much for prayer! 'Yes, Mother?' he asked, turning to confront her angry face.

'In my office, if you don't mind.'

I do fucking mind! 'Certainly! There's nothing I'd like more than—'

'I don't think you're going to like this one little bit!'

No, I don't suppose I will.

Sitting before her desk, Father Will raised his eyes as she began what he thought was going to be a lecture. 'This evening, I'd like you to visit Hallworth Church and help with the Bible classes,' she said, much to his astonishment.

'Certainly!' he replied enthusiastically.

'There will be a dozen or so sixth-form girls attending and, sadly, I shall be unable to accompany them. I wouldn't have asked you, under the circumstances, but I have no choice. I can't let the Reverend Cummings cope alone.'

'I'd be delighted to help,' he enthused, realizing that she was setting him up.

'I know that you'd rather be drinking and debauching in a public house. Anyway, get there at seven and give the Reverend a hand, will you?'

'Right you are. By the way, Reverend Mother, I overheard a young woman speaking to a man down the lane earlier. It rather intrigued me as they were talking about you. They were saying that they wanted photographs and that they needed to question you about something.'

'Question me? What about?'

That's got you worried! 'She was asking about the convent and—' *Think, Entercock!* 'She was saying something about wishing she'd been to a convent instead of a state school, and she mentioned a fictitious sister—'

'Fictitious sister, are you sure? What was her name?'

'Josie, I think. I was hiding behind a tree . . . I had to make radio contact with MI5, you see.'

'MI5?'

'Yes, but tell no one! Anyway, she was going on about infiltrating the sixth-form ranks to get information. I really don't know what she was talking about. She also mentioned a group of girls known as the chosen few, whoever they are.'

'I . . . I really don't know anything about this. Are you sure that they were talking about *my* convent?'

'Oh, yes. The young man said something about cases of wine being delivered to Hardmound Convent. Perish the thought!'

'There must be some mistake. Anyway, I have things to do so—'

'Right. I'll be going, then.' *Chew on that, you old hag!*

Walking back to his church, Father Will reckoned that by now Josie would have discovered the broken tape and be fuming. He desperately wanted to penetrate her bottom-hole again, but he knew that the next time she came to him for information she'd make doubly sure that the tape was running. He couldn't pull the phone call stunt again, he knew. But he knew also that he couldn't allow a horny little tart like Josie to go without another good fucking.

As he approached the presbytery, clutching the confiscated video tape, he thought of the woods behind the village hall, imagining the lesbians writhing on the grass, gasping as they licked between each other's pussy lips. Too late for the show now, he thought sadly, glancing at his watch. But there was always tomorrow, and the next day, and the next . . .

Wonder if they're into spanking?

'That's a thought!' he cried as he opened the front door. 'Tie her down and give her a damn good thrashing!'

'Give who a damn good thrashing?' Annie asked as she emerged from her room – her brothel.

'That young Josie. Sorry, I was just thinking aloud. So, how's it going?'

'Not bad. I've just about set the room up for . . . By the way, some bloke came round here looking for you.'

'Fuck! What did he look like?'

'Youngish, ugly . . . Said something about him marrying in your church. I said that I was the cleaning woman. Anyway, he pushed past me and insisted on waiting for you in the lounge. The odd thing is, he'd only been in there for a couple of minutes, then he left.'

Ushering Annie into the spare room, Father Will closed the door behind them, his dark eyes frowning. 'He's bugged the lounge,' he whispered.

'What?'

'An electronic bug – a listening device.'

'How do you know that?'

'I don't, it's just a shrewd guess. Anyway, MI5 use them, so why not the *Sunday Grovel*? Perhaps Josie's working for MI5?'

'Working for MI5?'

'On second thoughts, no, I don't think she is. The stuff these newspaper people have nowadays, they'd have no problem in bugging the place. Her partner's probably sitting in a car somewhere down the lane listening to my grandfather clock ticking.'

'What will you do?'

'No doubt Josie will be round to prise some info out of me, thinking that this time she's nailed me. Her accomplice, that ugly git, Brian, will be in his car taping the conversation.'

'Take her into the garden, or use my room—'

'No, no, I can't do that. I'll just have to find the bug and disarm it. The trouble is, I don't know when she's coming round.'

'He asked if you'd be in around four-thirty so I said you probably would as—'

'Half an hour! Christ, that doesn't give me much time! Look, stay in here while I find the bug, OK?'

'OK – good luck.'

Noisily entering the lounge, Father Will flopped into his armchair. 'The cleaning woman's done a good job,' he said loudly, scanning the room for the bug. 'Well, better get on with Sunday's sermon, I suppose,' he added, looking under the coffee table. 'I'll watch this fascinating video tape later. I'll bet Josie would like to watch it, too.'

Realizing that the chances of finding the small device were minimal, he took a quick look behind the picture of the Pope hanging over the fireplace. Moving to the bookcase, and then to the standard lamp, he shook his head despondently. No sign of a bug.

Where the fuck is it?

Suddenly remembering a film he'd seen, he walked through the hall to the kitchen and switched his radio on, tuning the dial up and down the FM band. 'Got it!' he breathed as he turned the knob right to the end of the dial and heard his grandfather clock ticking loudly.

Find the thing, and bug the Mother Fucker's office!

Back in the lounge, he knew that time was running out. He had to act quickly. Looking round, he couldn't see that anything had been disturbed. If it came to it, he decided, he'd not allow Josie in. He'd pretend that he was out until he'd found the bug – then welcome her into his lair and—

That's it!

Bending down, he unplugged the two-way adaptor from the wall socket. His adaptor was black – this one was white. Clever bastards, he thought – but not clever enough! Back in the kitchen he switched his radio on, only to hear a loud hissing on the spot where the signal had been. Knowing that Brian and Josie would realize that the bug had been unplugged, he dashed back to the lounge to reinstate the adaptor.

Within minutes, the front doorbell rang. Instructing Annie to stay in her room, the priest shot into the lounge and ripped the adaptor from the wall socket, positioning the magazine rack to conceal the empty socket before dashing to the door.

'Josie! What a pleasant surprise!' he beamed as he showed the girl into the lounge. *No handbag.*

'Don't mind me coming back so soon, do you?' she smiled, her pink skirt so short it was hardly worth wearing.

Come as often as you want – you horny little bitch! 'Not at all! I'm very pleased to see you.'

'I thought we could carry on with our chat, if you've got the time, that is,' she said.

'I've always got time for you, my sexy little beauty. So, how's that pretty little pussy of yours? Nice and wet for me, I hope?' *Dripping, no doubt!*

'Would you class yourself as a pervert?' she asked bluntly. 'I know it's rather an odd question, but I've never met a priest who . . . well, who's so sexually orientated.'

'A pervert would sum me up perfectly! Yes, The Reverend Will Entercock of Cumsdale Parish – a first-rate sexual pervert!' *Nice one, Entercock!*

'Are you into dirty videos?'

I'm into dirty knickers! 'Damn right, I am!' he chuckled, taking the tape from the sideboard. 'Those naughty lesbian convent girls made this one especially for me – I'll put it on.'

Ramming the tape into the machine, he switched the TV on and joined Josie on the sofa. The screen flashed, and then a picture of a young girl's shaven crack appeared.

Amateurish or what?

A girl's hand came into view, clutching a huge candle. Opening the naked girl's pouting pussy lips, she did her best to stuff the candle between the swelling cushions of flesh and push it deep inside the ravenous cavern, but the greasy phallus slipped from her hand. There was no sound-track – but who needed sound with pictures like this?

'That's disgusting!' Josie exclaimed. 'Look, someone's fingering the girl now! Good God, is this really what goes on at Hardmound Convent?'

'This is nothing! Christ, they earn themselves a small fortune from making dirty tapes! Look – she's managed to get the candle up the girl's cunt now! God, just look how stretched her poor pussy lips are! Shit, if it goes in much further she'll split open!'

Another shot showing a sixth-former's thick black bush came on to the screen. Someone squirted white foam from a can over the 'vegetation' and massaged it into the girl's young mound. Clutching a razor, the unseen girl began to drag the blade through the foam leaving soft, smooth, white flesh in its wake.

'I like my girls shaved,' Father Will enthused. 'We used to shave the typist at MI5.'

'Shave the typist?' Josie echoed.

'Yes. She hated it, but we told her that we'd send her to Moscow on an assignment if she didn't let us shave and fuck her.'

'I can't believe that!'

'Good, because I haven't told you, OK?'

'I've never seen anything so disgusting!' Josie cried, turning back to the television.

'I have! How about letting me shave *your* crack?' *How far will she go to get her sordid story – the little tart?*

'Father Entercock! You're a priest! I simply cannot believe the debauchery, the perversions, the—'

You'd better believe it, baby! 'Well, there it is in full living colour! You can't deny that they have some bloody good fun at the convent! Can I shave you?'

'No! Good God! You're a complete pervert!'

'Yes, I am, aren't I? Do you know, it took me fucking years to become practised in the fine art of perversity. I'll tell you what, Josie – you let me shave your cunt, and I'll tell you all about the Mother Superior's little business venture.' *Come on, come on – go for it!*

'Really? I don't know . . . I don't like the idea of—'

'The choice is yours. By the way, I overheard the old hag speaking to some newspaper reporter on the phone earlier. She was saying that she'd accept twenty grand for the exclusive story . . .'

'Which newspaper?'

'No idea.'

'What is her story?'

'Ah, you let me shave your fanny, and I'll tell you.'

Becoming increasingly aroused by the shaving scene on the television, Josie looked to Father Will and smiled. Her pubic hair would soon grow, and the itching would be well worth suffering for what could easily be the story of the decade. Deciding to pull out all the stops, she stood up and slipped her panties down her long legs, kicking them from her ankles and lifting her skirt up over her stomach.

'I might look quite nice without my pubes,' she muttered pensively, eyeing the now completely naked crack filling the TV screen. 'Okay, go and get a razor and you can remove my ugly bush for me.'

'Right, lie on the floor and I'll be back in a minute.' *Wonder if there's a market for pubic hair?*

Returning with a can of shaving foam and a razor, the priest pulled the girl's skirt well clear of her mound and settled on the floor by her side. 'You'll like this,' he murmured as he covered her bush with lavish quantities of foam.

'Tell me about the Mother Superior's story. It must be bloody good if they've offered her twenty thousand!'

'Hang on, I'm trying to concentrate.'

Dragging the razor down either side of her swelling pussy lips, Father Will grinned to see the veil falling away, exposing more and more of her young intimacy. Her firm stomach rose and fell, her legs twitching as he worked between them, exciting her, arousing her, wetting her vaginal sheath. Pulling her lips up and apart, he removed the last remaining hairs, revealing her full naked beauty to his wide eyes.

Her pink inner lips unfurling as she opened her legs wider, the entrance to her sex-duct lay open, glistening with her lubricant in readiness for penetration. Stroking the soft hillocks of flesh on either side of her fresh, youthful groove, the priest's penis swelled and twitched. Wondering what equipment Annie had set out in her room, he imagined thrashing Josie, whipping her taut young buttocks by way of punishment for her prying, her questioning, her persistent digging.

'Take a look,' he said, wiping the last of the foam from her smooth crack with his handkerchief. Lifting her head, she gazed at the nakedness between her shapely thighs.

'God, I look like a bloody schoolgirl!'

'Indeed you do!' he laughed, leaning over and licking the length of her soft, hairless valley.

'Tell me what the story's about, then,' she persisted as he sucked her swollen outer labia into his mouth.

'I'm just going to get something, I'll be back in a minute – and I'll reveal all!' he grinned, climbing to his feet and leaving the room.

Creeping into Annie's room, Father Will smiled, grabbing two pairs of handcuffs as Annie gazed at him in bewilderment.

'What are you going to do?' she asked anxiously.

'I'll cuff the bitch, and then you can come in and play with her.'

'I'm not a bloody lesbian!' she whispered loudly.

'Come on, you must have done lesbian scenes in your time!'

'Well . . . I suppose so, but—'

'Give me five minutes, and then join us.'

'What if she doesn't like the idea of me—'

'She wants her story, right? And I want to see just how far she's prepared to go to get it. Besides, she won't have any choice.'

The handcuffs concealed behind his back, Father Will returned to the lounge and switched the TV off before joining Josie on the floor – her legs spread wide, her fingers between her naked lips, stiffening her clitoris.

'What are you doing?' she asked fearfully as he deftly fastened a handcuff around her ankle, pulling her foot up and cuffing it to her wrist. 'For Christ's sake!' she exclaimed, struggling as he attempted to cuff her other foot to her free wrist.

'You want to know all the gory details of the old hag's story, don't you?' he laughed.

'Yes, but—'

'Come on, then – you know what a sad pervy I am, so allow me my fun in return for the story.'

Sitting up, her knees against her chest, Josie allowed him to finish his job of handcuffing. 'That's the idea, Josie. Now lie down, arms out straight and place your feet either side of your bum and you'll feel much more comfortable.'

Lying helpless on her back, Josie's pretty, hairless crack bulged invitingly between her firm thighs. Parting her knees, Father Will gazed longingly at her open sex-groove, her pinken inner lips, unfurling, gaping, glistening with girl-milk. 'You can come in now, Annie!' he called. Cursing the priest, Josie rolled on to her side, desperate to cover the very epitome of her femininity as the door opened.

'This is Annie,' Father Will chuckled as he rolled Josie on to her back and parted her knees to blatantly display her wares.

'You're a bastard!' Josie screamed hysterically. 'I'll expose you for what you really are!'

'Come now, Josie. We're only having a little fun! Besides, no one will believe that I'm working for MI5, so there's little point in trying to expose me.'

'You call this fun?' she cried as Annie knelt on the floor and massaged the cuffed girl's sex-valley, slipping a finger into her tight, creamy vaginal sheath. 'Bugger off, you dirty lesbian!' Josie cried in her rising anger.

'Unless you shut up, Josie, I'll have to gag you!' the priest threatened.

'Brian will be here in a minute!' she warned.

'What makes you think that Brian's coming here?'

'He . . . I just know that he'll be here in a minute to rescue me, so you'd better let me go!'

'When Brian gets here, I'll free you,' Father Will assured the girl as Annie lay on the floor and tucked her head beneath Josie's legs, kissing the swelling lips of her crudely bared pussy.

'You've got about thirty seconds before he bangs on the door, and he won't be at all pleased to find me like this!' Josie stormed.

'I'm sure he'll be only too happy to find you like this!'

Opening his victim's blouse, the priest lifted her bra clear of her firm breasts and took her long, erect nipple into his mouth, darkening her areola as he sucked hard on the young milk bud. Her clitoris now receiving attention from Annie's hot tongue, her nipple stiffening in Father Will's mouth, Josie began to tremble, breathing heavily as two fingers slipped deep into the wet heat of her tightening love-tube.

'The Mother Inferior's into lesbianism in a big way,' Father Will enlightened Josie, circling his tongue around her long, brown nipple. 'As I told you, she's into spanking, bondage, water sports, rubber and leather gear – you name it, she fucking well does it! The sixth-form girls are wonderfully vulnerable. Talk about taking candy from a baby! Christ, they offer sex—'

'Ah, God, that's good!' Josie cried as her clitoris swelled in Annie's hot mouth. 'Suck it! Lick my cunt! I'm coming!'

Pushing the girl's knees up to her chest, Annie licked her wet slit, inducing a torrent of girl-come to flow from her trembling body as her orgasm exploded from her pulsating clitoris. Moving the priest aside, Annie squatted over Josie's face, her knickerless pussy only inches from the other girl's mouth as she buried her face in the warmth of Josie's shaven cunny lips.

'Go on, Josie, lick her cunt out!' Father Will coaxed, pushing Annie down to force her open sex against Josie's tightly closed mouth.

'No!' Josie cried. 'I don't—' Annie's engorged pussy lips settled over the girl's mouth, quietening her, halting her protests.

'Come on, Josie, give her a good licking!' the priest insisted as Annie sucked and licked between their prisoner's swollen pussy folds. Averting her head, Josie couldn't bring herself to suck another girl's fanny – story or no story.

Grabbing her ears, Father Will gently turned her head, aligning her mouth with Annie's gaping vagina. 'I'll tell you about the archbishop if you give Annie a good licking and make her come in your mouth,' he bargained. Peering up at the priest, Josie smiled. Opening her mouth, she tentatively tasted Annie's hot quim lips before lapping up the juices as they flowed from the young prostitute's cavern.

Sitting back on his heels, Father Will watched the two girls mouthing and licking between each other's legs, both obviously delighting in the lesbian coupling as they moaned and writhed in their new-found sexual heaven. Their bodies locked in lust, they drank each other's slippery come, sucked on each other's rubbery cunt lips, stiffened their clitorises – shuddered in their lechery.

'There's nothing I like more than to watch two pretty mouths sucking on two pretty cunts!' he declared gleefully, his ever-rampant cock in his hand. 'Christ! Why can't the Pope get it into his head that men are men – and we love to fuck the arses off young birds? Just because he's not hungry, why should we starve?'

'You're vile!' Josie blubbered through a mouthful of dripping flesh.

'That's me, baby!' he laughed. 'Vile in my vileness! Unto the vile, all things are vile!'

Slipping into Annie's room, the priest examined her tools of sex. Whips, chains, leather straps, vibrators of all shapes and sizes were strewn everywhere. Grabbing a massive metal dildo, he grinned as he returned to the lounge. Josie was trembling as her orgasm threatened to erupt from the hot depths of her young body. Annie, too, was shuddering, her girl-cream decanting from her gaping cunt, flowing over Josie's face, filling her thirsty mouth.

Taking the phallus, Father Will presented the cold metal tip to Annie's bottom-hole, gently easing the rounded end past her tightening muscles. She didn't protest as he pushed the entire length of the metal rod deep into her bowels, leaving only the stub nestling between her splayed buttocks.

Licking, drinking Annie's come juice, Josie eyed the metal phallus protruding from the girl's stretched bottom-hole and gasped. Would Josie like it up her bum? the priest wondered as the girls continued their frenzied writhing. Better still, he mused, pulling his penis out, let's give Josie a bird's eye view of my cock up Annie's little nest!

Desperately mouthing at his heavy balls as he knelt behind Annie and pushed his knob between her open pussy lips, Josie watched as the huge male organ slipped deep into the young whore's body, stretching her rubicund flesh, opening the very centre of her tight sex. Licking and nibbling on his bollocks as they swung back and forth over her mouth, she lost herself in her debauchery.

'Coming!' the girls cried in unison as they sucked each other's clitorises into their hungry mouths. Father Will, too, was ready for his communion – all too soon, he thought sadly as his knob throbbed within the wet heat of the whore's spasming sheath.

Collapsing over Josie's perspiring body, Annie gasped as the priest filled her, and the girl drained her climax from her swollen clitoris. Grabbing the metal dildo, Father Will rammed her tight bottom-hole, taking her to hitherto unscaled sexual heights as she lay panting, trembling with the sheer bliss exploding between her splayed thighs.

Ramming his last thrusts, the priest slipped his penis from her hot sheath, positioning his jettisoning knob over Josie's open mouth. She gasped, taking the fountainhead into her facial orifice, sucking, gulping the male come as it gushed. It was a new, cosmic experience. Her story blown from her mind, she slurped, mouthed, drank the last of the priest's sperm as her clitoris exploded yet again in Annie's mouth to send terrifyingly powerful waves of lust through her tethered body.

'More, more!' she gasped ravenously as Annie fingered her dripping sex-tube, manoeuvred a thumb into her tight bottom-hole, bringing her more pleasure than she'd ever dreamed possible.

Pulling away from Josie's hot mouth, the priest lay on the floor, his penis glistening with saliva, sperm and girl juice, his balls drained. Annie climbed from Josie's spent body, collapsing on the floor beside him, her cunt open, gaping, her bottom stretched to capacity with the huge metal phallus. Easing the shaft from her tight anal tube she tossed it to the floor, grinning wickedly as she caught the priest's eye.

'Christ, I enjoyed that!' she gasped, tugging her skirt down to cover her inflamed holes.

'Me, too!' he endorsed. 'How about you, Josie?'

'I've never . . . Bloody hell, I thought I'd never stop coming!'

'Well, now you know what priests really get up to! I thought you said that young Brian was coming round?'

'He . . .'

'You were lying, weren't you?'

'No, no.'

'She was!' Annie interrupted gleefully. 'I don't like little girls who lie! They need to be severely punished! I'd better go and get my whip!'

'No!' Josie protested, rolling onto her side as Annie dashed from the room. 'Father, let me go, please!'

'I can't do that, I'm afraid – you see, Annie's in charge now.'

'For God's sake – you can't let her whip me!'

'It's in His hands, Josie – I'm sorry.'

Returning with her whip, Annie stood over Josie, a wicked glint in her eye as she dangled the leather tails over the girl's body. 'Let's have her on her hands and knees so that her bum's up in the air,' she suggested, turning to the priest. In silent acquiescence he rolled Josie over, pulling her hips up and positioning her with her knees against her chest, her head resting on the carpet, her buttocks high in the air.

'Now, you *were* lying, weren't you?' Annie taunted, running the leather tails up the dark crease between the girl's splayed buttocks.

'Please! Father, help me!' Josie screamed hysterically as Annie landed the first stinging lash across her taut, pale orbs. Rolling onto her side, she tried desperately to evade further punishment but, merciless, the priest rolled her back into position, pinning her down as Annie resumed her beating. Swishing the tails through the air, the mistress giggled gleefully as she watched the thin weals appear across her victim's buttocks.

'I love this!' she cried. 'Look at her cunt lips bulging out! Why not fuck her from behind when I've finished?'

'Good idea, Annie!' Father Will enthused, his penis rock-hard yet again.

'Please!' Josie cried as the whip cracked again and again. 'I'll do anything!'

Finally dropping her weapon, Annie knelt behind Josie and examined the girl's crimson buttocks. Burning, inflamed, her flesh glowed a fire-red. But her pussy lips bulging in their arousal beneath her small brown hole, her juices flowing in torrents, she had evidently enjoyed her punishment.

'Shall I lick her clean now?' Annie asked the priest. 'Or shall I wait until you've fucked her?'

'Wait until I've filled her with sperm!' leered Father Will, moving behind the girl, his massive weapon in his hand.

'I'll get you both for this!' Josie warned as Annie took the priest's penis and guided the head between the girl's swollen labia.

Projecting his hips, Father Will drove his shaft deep into her used body, filling her vaginal sheath to capacity with his huge organ.

'God, she's got a lovely body!' Annie gasped admiringly, watching the whipped girl's pussy lips rolling in time with the priest's thrusting. 'I think I'd better attend her bottom with this!' she giggled, grabbing the metal phallus. 'You'd like this up your bottom, wouldn't you, Josie?' she grinned, waving the shaft in the girl's face.

'You dare!' Josie screamed. 'You bloody dare!'

Parting the girl's buttocks, Annie forced the metal phallus past her defending muscles, deep into her bowels. 'I can't take it!' Josie cried as Annie thrust the phallus in and out of the girl's bottom in time with Father Will's penis.

'Yes, you can!' Annie laughed.

'Coming!' Father Will grunted as his sperm coursed its way up his shaft and erupted from his throbbing glans. 'Ah, yes! Coming in your wet cunt! Feel it, Josie – feel my sperm spurting!'

Shaking, her face flushed, her breathing heavy, Josie cried out as her clitoris pulsated, sending wonderful ripples of orgasm throughout her tethered body. 'Harder!' she ordered, delighting in the obscenity. 'Both holes . . . Harder!'

Thrusting for all he was worth, Father Will pumped the last of his seed deep into the girl's spasming vagina as Annie rammed her bowels with the metal shaft. Finally falling backwards, his penis slipping from the tight sheath, he lay on the floor, gazing at Josie's exposed, exploited pussy. Her outer lips swollen, her inner petals distended, dripping with a cocktail of sperm and girl-come, she was the epitome of female debauchery.

Slipping the hard shaft from Josie's sore bottom, Annie took her pew on the floor beside the priest, smiling at their prisoner's used body. 'The whip again?' she smirked, turning to Father Will.

'No!' Josie screamed, rolling onto her side.

'I think she's had enough for now,' deemed Father Will, crawling towards her.

Josie frowned as the priest released her handcuffs, wondering if Brian had the whole sordid episode on tape or not. Glancing to the wall socket, she lifted her head, trying to see if the adaptor was still intact.

'Brian didn't turn up, so you were lying, weren't you?' Father Will accused.

'I wasn't lying! Perhaps he had a change of mind,' Josie retorted, craning her neck now to see the adaptor. Not wanting her to see the empty wall socket, the priest moved across the carpet, positioning himself with his back to the magazine rack. Discreetly slipping the adaptor into the socket as Josie pulled her panties up her thighs, he stood up.

Leaving the room, he opened the understairs cupboard, switching the mains off before returning to the lounge. 'There's a power cut,' he complained. 'I went to put the kettle on for coffee, but the power's off.'

'I wonder how long it's been off for?' Josie mused, her face falling as she realized that all she'd endured had been for nothing – apart from some bloody good orgasms!

'Don't know,' Father Will replied as Annie slipped out of the room. 'It's probably sabotage, a last ditch attempt by the FRO to regain the county of Rutland. Still, not to worry – we can go without coffee, can't we?'

'Yes, I suppose so,' Josie smiled, moving towards the magazine rack to see the adaptor securely in the socket. 'I'm going,' she added. 'I need a shower. What you did to me was vile!'

'You loved it! Why not come again!' Father Will enthused as he followed her to the front door.

'Yes, maybe,' she smiled as she stepped out into the summer sun.

'Maybe? You're not leaving, are you?'

'How long do you reckon the power was off for?' she asked again as she reached the gate, rubbing her sore buttocks.

'Ages, I expect – why?'

'It doesn't matter. I might be back tomorrow if—'

'I'll look forward to it, Josie. Take care. And be careful when you sit down!'

Joining Annie in her room, the priest grinned. 'That was perfect!' he whooped, sitting on the bed.

'Yes, I loved every minute of it,' she smiled as she organized her equipment. 'We must do it again.'

'Definitely! But better still, I now have an electronic listening device! Imagine planting it in the Mother Inferior's office! God, I'll have her over a barrel!'

'That'll be nice for her! Anyway, my old man will be in soon for his meal, so I'd better get going. I've got a randy old judge to deal with tomorrow, so I'll start work around mid-morning, if that's OK?'

'Fine! Let's hope that our arrangement is successful – for both of us. Christ, I've got to be at Hallworth Church this evening, I'd better wash and eat in readiness for—'

'What are you going to get up to there?'

'Ah, that would be telling!'
'You get worse, Father – or better! Anyway, see you tomorrow.'

Retrieving the adaptor from the power point, Father Will switched the mains on and returned to the lounge. Sitting in his armchair, he examined the device. 'Clever!' he breathed. 'Very clever – but not clever enough! Poor Josie – failed three times! How many more times will she try to screw me, I wonder?'

CHAPTER FIVE

Picturesque Hallworth Church, nestling in its extensive wooded grounds, was the ideal setting for convent girl romps, Father Will mused as he opened the church gate. Turning his thoughts to the young Samantha Lovejoy and her shaven pussy, he reflected that the woods would provide ample seclusion from prying eyes. Imagining her lying naked on the soft grass, her legs open, her young slit yawning, oozing with slippery girl-cream, he prayed that she'd allow him to drink from her young hole, lick her clitoris to a shuddering orgasm.

To finger a young girl's tight vulva in the woods or, better still, slip his penis deep into her hot bottom-hole would be heaven, he decided. Would she approach him and ask what her punishment was to be? Would she beg to be spanked? He doubted it very much – but he'd approach her and beg her! *Should have brought my bloody camera!*

'Will! How are you, mate?' the Reverend Bob Cummings greeted him as he entered the church.

'As well as can be expected, what with a Sunday tabloid reporter hounding me, the Mother Inferior trying to string me up by my balls, the bishop having some private vendetta to see me excommunicated, the archbishop . . . I won't bore you with all that. How are you doing?'

'Brilliant, compared to you! Christ, you're in the shit, aren't you? Still, try and put it out of your mind because, tonight, we are going to have the time of our lives!'

'Don't count on it! The Mother Fucker has set me up.'

'How d'you mean?'

'She asked me to come here this evening to help you out, and she also told the reporter to come along to make notes, watch my every move, try to catch me out, trip me up. I'm thinking of joining the FBI.'

'The FBI?'

'Yes, but it's hush-hush at the moment. Anyway, this bloody reporter is a right pain up the—'

'We'll soon sort that out! Don't let it worry you, mate! What's this reporter bloke look like?'

'*She* is young, stunning, horny—'

'Sounds nice! Look, this is what we'll do. When she turns up, I'll tell her that the venue has been changed – send her off to Castlegate Church or something.'

'There's no such place as—'

'Exactly! Good idea, isn't it? Come on, let's go to my office and have a beer. And don't worry about the hierarchy, either – they'll never get anything on you.'

'I'll get something on them, if I'm lucky. Bastards, trying to blast the people with God music!'

'What?'

'Nothing.'

The Reverend Bob Cummings was left in comparative peace by *his* superiors. Having no nuns or Reverend Mother to cause him problems, no convent schoolgirls to tempt him, he had only his bishop to answer to and, with the old man living some miles away, he hardly ever saw him.

Swigging beer with Bob, Father Will felt a pang of envy. The vicar's office was far larger and more comfortable than his. With a television, hi-fi, a huge Chesterfield sofa and a drinks cabinet concealed in the wall behind a picture of the queen, it was luxury by comparison – home-from-home.

But, Will consoled himself, Bob Cummings wasn't into any

money-making rackets, and his only regular sexual encounters were with a couple of young women from the village who, by the standards of Chloë and Josie, weren't worth having. There again, he mused, a cunt's a cunt – or is it?

This was going to be the first time the Reverend Cummings had ever been blessed with a bunch of convent schoolgirls, and he was eagerly looking forward to it. Passing Will a can of lager, he swept his light brown hair back and grinned, his brown eyes mirroring his growing excitement.

'There's one girl in particular I'll introduce you to,' Father Will promised as he swigged his lager. 'Her name's Samantha Love-joy, an MP's daughter. She came to confession and, whether it's a wind-up or not, I don't know – but she told me that she'd shaved her fanny. Whether I'll get to see it or not, I don't know, but I'll have a bloody good try!'

'God, you have all the bloody luck, don't you? I've a good mind to defect to your lot, it sounds much more exciting.'

'Don't you believe it! The convent's an asset in many ways but, as I said, I've got the slag-bag Reverend Mother up my arse half the time. She came to the church going on about . . . oh, never mind. As you said, let's have some bloody fun this evening!'

'Shit, someone's just come into the church!' Bob observed, rising to his feet and moving towards the door.

'How do you know?'

'My security system. See that control panel – the red flashing light – that means the main door's been opened. It comes in handy when I'm having a good wank! Anyway, I'll get rid of whoever it is – you wait here.'

Wandering through the church, the vicar smiled at Josie, guessing straight away who she was. 'Can I help you?' he volunteered, eyeing her long legs, her cleavage, ridiculously accentuated by her tight bra.

'The Reverend Mother of Hardmound Convent sent me over to observe the Bible class,' Josie smiled. 'I'm a friend of hers and—'

'The venue's changed, I'm afraid. It's now at Castlegate Church. Follow the lane until you hit the main road, turn left and—'

'Changed? But—'

'Yes, it was a last-minute decision.'

'But I don't understand—'

'Sorry, but there's not much *to* understand, really – the venue's changed, and that's that.'

'OK, I'll leave it, then. Although I only left the Reverend Mother fifteen minutes ago and she said—'

'Er . . . yes, I've only just this minute had the phone call informing me of the change – it's rather messed up my evening.'

'Oh, well. I suppose you couldn't tell me anything about Father William Entercock, the priest of Cumsdale Parish, could you?' Josie asked, her handbag swinging ominously by her side.

'Depends what you want to know.'

Making herself comfortable on a pew, the reporter reclined with her legs parted just enough for the vicar to spy her bulging panties – a trick she'd increasingly accustomed herself to using when wanting information from men. Her trip to Cumsdale had taught her a lot – not least, the power ensconced between her thighs! Pulling a chair up, the vicar sat before her, gazing at her red panties and wondering what fantastic stories he could dream up about his friend. As he was about to speak, Father Will banged loudly on the office door to attract his attention.

'Who's that?' Josie asked as the vicar stood to attention.

'Er . . . the cleaning woman. I'd better see what she's up to. The clumsy so-and-so's always breaking things! Excuse me for a moment.'

Peering round the office door, he frowned at Father Will. 'What is it?' he asked.

'There's a bloody tape recorder in her handbag, so be very careful what you say!'

'Christ! I'd better not say anything, then!'

'No, no, it's all right. Tell her a load of lies about how good I am, how well-respected by the bishop, the parishioners, that sort of crap.'

'Got it. Help yourself to the beers – I'll soon send her packing. She's a sweet little thing, isn't she?'

'She's the devil's daughter!'

Wandering back to Josie, the vicar smiled and sat down. 'It's OK,' he reported. 'Nothing broken. Anyway, Father Entercock has been priest of Cumsdale Church for only a short while, and he's worked miracles. A new church roof—'

'But what about *him*, as a man, I mean?'

'Oh, I see. Er, he's well-respected by his bishop. His parishioners love him. He's done so much for the community. He works all hours, visits the sick and the elderly—'

'But what about his private life? Which way does he lean, politically, I mean?' Josie asked irritably, moving her handbag closer to the vicar.

'I've no idea about his private life, or his politics. I suppose, what with working all hours, he doesn't get the chance to have much of a private life. Why all these questions, anyway?'

'Oh, nothing. I'll be off then. Thanks.'

'Sorry about the change of venue!' the vicar called, eyeing her rounded bum, the backs of her knees, as she left the church, anger eating away inside her, suspicion filling her journalistic mind.

Closing the main doors, the Reverend Cummings joined Father Will, frowning and shaking his head as he sat down. 'I've a hunch that she's going to be trouble,' he declared, taking a can of lager.

'A hunch? I *know* she's going to be bloody trouble! She *is* bloody trouble!'

'She didn't believe a word I said to her, I know that! I reckon she'll be back later. Just let me make a phone call and I'll get her sorted out – for tonight, at least!'

Strangely, Father Will was developing a soft spot for Josie, although he couldn't for the life of him think why – apart from her tight, shaven pussy, that is! If only she'd stop her infuriating digging! He knew only too well that, the way things were going, his days as a priest were numbered. He wondered about settling down – with Josie, perhaps – and retiring on his illicit earnings. But he doubted very much if she'd be willing to settle down with *him* – a perverted priest! Besides, he knew nothing about her, her private life – apart from the fact that she worked for a newspaper. Or the KGB!

She might even be married, he thought, trying to imagine what sort of man her husband would be. Brian, the ugly git, was nothing more than a photographer – there was no way she'd want the likes of him! She seemed only too keen to open her legs, so perhaps she wasn't getting fucked on a regular basis. His mind in a whirl, he realized that his thinking was completely off course. No way would he ever consider settling down – not while there was a crop of young virgins ripening at the convent, anyway!

'Right!' Bob Cummings said. 'I've just phoned the convent. That Josie has just been on her mobile phone to the Mother Superior and told her what I said. I denied it, of course – told her that the girl hadn't even been here, that she must have gone to the wrong church. I don't give a toss whether she believes me or not as she's nothing to do with me. Anyway, the upshot of it is that Josie's on her way back here, so Christ knows what we do!'

'Fuck it!' Father Will cursed.

'That's a good idea! I'll hold her down while you—'

'This is serious, Bob! The evening's ruined! The girls will be here soon and . . . If I don't get to sow my seed up some bird's tight cunt, I'll end up wanking – again!'

'That's it!'

'What, have a wank?'

'No, you hide somewhere, I'll let her watch the Bible-bashing and when she realizes that you're not going to turn up, she'll bugger off.'

'Hide where?'

'That door leads outside into the church grounds. Take a wander around or something until I give you the all-clear.'

'Got any dynamite?'

'What the hell for?'

'To blow up the nunnery.'

'Are you mad?'

'Probably!'

'Good evening, Father Cummings,' a gaggle of sixth-form girls, led by Sister Teresa, sang in unison outside the office door.

'Ah, good evening, girls!' the vicar replied, wishing he'd noticed the red warning light flashing. 'And good evening to you, Sister.'

Closing the door behind him, he left Father Will hiding behind the desk in the office and showed the girls to a group of chairs he'd set in a circle. 'Sit down, girls, and I'll pass the Bibles round,' he smiled as they made themselves comfortable.

'Isn't Father Entercock coming?' a petite redhead asked.

Probably! 'No, he won't be along until later,' the vicar replied, gazing in disbelief at the girl's incredibly short skirt and her firm breasts, straining for their freedom beneath her tight blouse. Wondering which of the little beauties had shaved her pussy, he began distributing the Bibles – visions of tightly closed cuntcracks with soft shaven hillocks of flesh rising either side filling his mind.

'So the venue *hasn't* changed?' Josie asked accusingly as she wandered through the doors towards the vicar.

'I'm so sorry,' he smiled appeasingly. 'I had another phone call just after you'd left – there was some kind of mix-up. It's all very confusing but . . . Well, you're here now so, please, take a seat. Now, would anyone like a drink?' he asked, moving to a table with glasses neatly set out. 'I only have lemonade' *laced with vodka* 'I'm afraid.'

Father Will slipped through the door into the church grounds,

wondering when his chance to ravish the young girls would come
– *if* it came at all! He'd heard Josie's voice in the church and was
becoming despondent, disappointed that the evening was going to
be a total flop. Although he'd known that the girl would turn up,
he'd thought that Bob would have come up with a good solution,
as he usually did in awkward situations. 'She's becoming a pain in
the butt!' he murmured as he lit another cigarette.

Negotiating a small path through the woods, he stopped as he
heard young female voices. Gingerly peering through some
bushes, he spied two sixth-form girls lying on the grass in a small
clearing, sunning themselves. 'Samantha Lovejoy!' he breathed,
gazing at the young filly lying with her slender legs outstretched,
her firm, rounded breasts ballooning her blouse, pointing sky-
wards as if begging to be sucked. Licking her full lips, her long
golden hair spread out over the grass, she was a voluptuous beauty
– ripe for the taking.

'I wonder what punishment Father Will has thought of,'
Samantha remarked to her friend, a dark-skinned girl with huge
black eyes and long brown hair framing her angelic face.

'You don't think he believed that you shaved your fanny, do
you?' the girl asked, turning over to lie on her stomach, her
rounded buttocks beautifully outlined by her tight gymslip.

'I don't know – maybe, maybe not.'

'You could always show him!' she suggested, chewing on a
blade of grass.

'I'd like to do more than show him!'

'Really? You don't fancy him, do you?'

'Why not? Anyway, rumour has it that he's a randy old sod!
He's supposed to have screwed half the nuns, and several girls
reckon they've been bedded by him!'

'Yes, but they're only rumours. I can't imagine a priest—'

'Why not?' Samantha asked. 'You read about vicars and priests
in the papers every day – they're a randy lot, to say the least!'

Father Will moved uneasily behind the bush. *A bunch of perverts!*

'Did you really shave your fanny?' the dark girl asked.

God, I hope so!

'Yes, 'course I did. A dare's a dare, isn't it? I'd lose face if I—'

'Yes, but I've only got your word for it. I mean—'

'God, no one ever believes anything round here! I had to show Mary Harwood-Smith, Becky Collins, Judy Rooks, Shirley Gray – and now you want to see my baby cunt! Didn't you see the video we made of Julia Jackson shaving me?'

'No, no one will lend me a copy.'

'That's because you're a new girl. The priest's got a copy. I wonder what he thought when he saw my fanny being shaved!'

'Christ, he hasn't really got a copy of the tape, has he?'

'Yes – for a laugh, Janice Watts gave it to him during confession! Anyway, I'll show you what a shaved fanny looks like – seeing as you don't believe me!'

Standing up, Samantha lifted her gymslip up over her stomach and pulled her panties down, exposing her hairless crack to her friend's bulging eyes – and to Father Will's. Crouched behind the bushes, the priest couldn't believe what he was seeing as the dark girl knelt before Samantha, examining, at close quarters, the soft cushions of unblemished flesh either side of the girl's long crack.

His penis hard as rock, he longed to lay the girl down, open her young legs and bury his face in her beautiful virginal slit. Praying that his chance would come as he manipulated his rampant erection through his cassock, he ogled the wonderful scenario. *You show me yours and I'll show you mine!*

'Your piss flaps are much bigger than mine!' the dark girl exclaimed crudely as she inspected the pink protrusions emerging from her friend's young sex-valley.

'What do you mean?' Samantha asked, opening her outer lips and pulling them up to examine the pinken, glistening flesh within.

'Well, yours stick out – mine don't.'

'Show me,' Samantha said, sitting on the grass and pulling her panties over her ankles in readiness for the comparing of cunts.

The evening may not be a total failure after all, Father Will thought optimistically as he watched the dark girl stand up and tug her panties down her long, coffee-coloured legs. Lifting her gymslip, she showed Samantha her black bush, opening her young pussy lips to reveal her inner petals. 'See!' she exclaimed, pulling her swelling lips further apart. 'They're minute, compared to yours!'

'Christ!' Samantha squealed. 'Your clitoris is *much* bigger than mine! Just look at it! D'you wank a lot or something, Rosa?'

'Not a lot, no. Let's see yours, then.'

Hardly daring to breathe, the priest gazed in wonderment at Samantha as she peeled her vermilion lips further apart to display her cerise budling. 'See,' she said. 'Mine's much smaller, isn't it?'

'Yes, but it must get bigger when you—'

'Is that why yours is so big, 'cause you're feeling randy?'

'S'pose so. Lie down and let me rub it, and we'll see how big it gets,' Rosa suggested, to the priest's great glee.

Spreading herself full-length on the grass, Samantha opened her slim legs as wide as she could as Rosa settled by her side. The priest's view was perfect as the girl began to caress Samantha's hairless hillocks, running her slender finger up and down the opening valley. Poor Bob, he thought – always seems to be in the wrong bloody place at the wrong bloody time!

Samantha closed her eyes and let out a gasp as her friend spread her cunt lips and gently massaged her clitoris, swelling the budlette to twice its size. As Samantha began to writhe, Rosa slipped a finger into her sex-duct, massaging the creamy inner flesh. Inserting another finger, she began to thrust in and out of the girl's hole, rubbing her clitoris faster with her other hand as Samantha's cries of ecstasy reverberated through the wood. *Wish I'd brought my bloody camera!*

'God, I'm going to come!' Samantha wailed, pulling her gymslip high up over her stomach and virtually doing the splits as her sex-sheath gripped her friend's fingers like a vice. 'Don't stop!' Her cries growing louder, Father Will settled on the grass behind the bush, his penis beginning to throb, dangerously near to orgasm as he watched the young lesbians at play.

To his great delight, Rosa leaned over her friend and kissed the smooth flesh of her flat stomach, poking her tongue into her navel. Moving down, she licked Samantha's naked mound, causing the girl to gasp and cry out as her imminent orgasm swirled deep within her young womb. Moving her fingers away from Samantha's clitoris, Rosa pulled her pussy lips wide apart and tentatively licked her swelling cumbud.

'God, that's . . . that's incredible!' Samantha cried as Rosa fervently massaged the rubicund flesh with her hot tongue. 'Come . . . Coming!' Writhing, gasping, grabbing Rosa's head and grinding her young cunt into her mouth, Samantha reached her sexual heaven, her perspiring skin glistening, glowing with sex. Fingering and licking for all she was worth, Rosa didn't stop until Samantha brought her knees up to her chest and rolled on to her side, her body quivering as her orgasm gently subsided.

Unable to restrain himself any longer, Father Will almost fell through the bush into the clearing, his massive weapon in his hand as he staggered towards the girls. 'Father Entercock!' Samantha cried, trying to cover her intimacy. 'Have . . . have you been watching us?'

'Yes, my child – and it's the most vile sin I have ever witnessed!' *The most beautiful!*

'Father!' Samantha screamed as he waved his erect penis threateningly above her cowering body, his cassock high, his heavy balls swinging. 'Father, what are you doing?'

'I'm going to administer your punishment, my child. You have committed a dreadful sin, both of you, and you must both be severely punished. I shall drive out the demon in you with this!' As he knelt on the grass, Rosa gazed at his weapon with a mixture of terror and awe in her huge dark eyes.

'But, Father . . .' Samantha began as he gently pushed her back on to the grass and spread her legs, opening her inflamed slit in readiness for his rod – for her deflowering.

'You are both possessed by demons!' he cried, moving his rigid cock ever nearer to the girl's oozing slit. 'You must receive my penis, *both* take my penis deep into your vaginas to drive the demons from your bodies!'

Stabbing the purple head of his solid tool between the girl's drenched pussy lips, the priest slowly moved his hips forward, sinking his glans into her tight sheath. Kneeling beside her friend, Rosa gazed at her pussy lips, opening, stretching, as the massive weapon drove into her quivering young body, knowing that her turn would come. Further the priest burrowed his shaft until his balls came to rest against her buttocks and she was completely impaled.

Her mouth open, her blue eyes wide, Samantha lifted her head to behold her naked pussy lips, forced open by the sheer girth of the priest's huge organ. 'God, it's big!' she whimpered as he began to withdraw his glistening member. 'Christ, it's *big*!' she cried out as he drove deep into her young sex again, desecrating her curtain of youth, stripping her of her virginity.

'The bigger, the better, my child!' The priest gasped like a hungry wolf as her vaginal muscles spasmed and gripped his piston.

Rosa could only stare in amazement, emitting little gasps as the priest quickened his pace, driving his rod harder and deeper into her friend's bare honeypot. Samantha lay back, gazing up to the trees as she was taken by the priest, her girlhood disappearing – womanhood arriving. A smile curling her pretty lips, she closed her eyes, her body tensing as she neared her first-ever cock-induced climax. Her cunt tightening, she began to shake violently as the priest rammed her young cervix with a vengeance. 'By virtue of this sacramental rite, may you be delivered from the wiles of demons!' he cried.

Pulling Samantha's gymslip off her shoulders, Rosa unbuttoned the girl's blouse and lifted her bra clear of her firm breasts. Taking a nipple into her mouth, she sucked on the budlette, causing her friend to arch her back and gasp with the sheer bliss her body was bringing her. Tossing her head from side to side, her golden hair veiling her face, Samantha dug her fingernails into the soft grass and filled the wood with her cries of orgasm as her young sheath crushed the priest's penis. 'Coming! Fuck my cunt harder! Coming! Ah . . . God . . . Coming!'

As she reached the crest of her climax, Father Will shuddered and pumped her tight vagina full of sperm, lubricating his pistoning shaft, splattering her cervix until the male come oozed from her crudely stretched love sheath and ran down between her firm, rounded buttocks to bathe her smaller hole. Finally, spurting his last spurt, he collapsed over the girl's heaving body, pushing Rosa aside to suck Samantha's nipple into his mouth.

Small, hard, hot, the erectile tissue stiffened as he ran his tongue around her areola. Lost now in her debauchery, her lust, the girl uttered incoherent words of sex as his penis withdrew from her hot cunt, leaving her stretched flesh bathed in a cocktail of sperm and girl-come.

'More!' she managed to beg in her delirium as he moved by her side and sucked harder on her nipple. Reaching down, he located her erect clitoris nestling between her swollen, hairless pussy lips and began to massage the small protrusion, using her sticky come to enhance the masturbation.

'What about me?' Rosa asked petulantly, jealous of her friend's euphoric expression as her budlette stiffened and nectar seeped from her open hole. Releasing Samantha's nipple from his mouth, the priest turned to the girl. Standing behind him, her dark body naked, silhouetted against the evening sun, her pointed breasts topped with incredibly long milk buds, her dark bush sparse, barely covering her young virginal slit, she was the finest young specimen he'd ever set eyes upon. Still massaging Samantha's clitoris, he beckoned Rosa, his eyes wild with lust as she moved towards him and stood with her feet wide apart, her hips jutted forward, her smiling crack only inches from his mouth – his tongue.

Licking the crease between her thigh and her pouting pussy lip, Father Will breathed in her heady girl-scent, lost now in his lust as she reached down and spread her swollen cushions, inviting his tongue to explore her very femininity. 'Lick inside my slit!' she breathed as his tongue moved ever nearer to her pinken cunt folds. 'My spot! Lick my spot!' she ordered excitedly, swivelling her hips to align her solid clitoris with his caressing tongue. 'Ah, yes! Make me come with your tongue!'

Ignoring Samantha's writhing body, the priest centred his attention on Rosa's budding clitoris, sucking it into his mouth, flicking the sensitive tip with his tongue as she towered over him, swaying with the overwhelming sensations. Her legs sagging, she gripped his head, gyrating her hips, grinding her young cunt into his face as her body trembled in her new-found ecstasy.

Lying on his back, the priest pulled the girl down, her knees either side of his head, her open cunt lips settling over his hungry mouth. Reaching up, he pinched her hard nipples, causing her to gasp and beg for more as her orgasm welled up from her womb to explode in his hot mouth. Wailing, Rosa threw her head back and pushed the open centre of her young sex hard against the priest's face, filling his mouth with her nectarous milk as she rode the crest of her climax.

Mouthing, sucking, drinking, the priest looked up over the sensual swell of her stomach to her firm, pointed breasts. Her dark skin shone, glistening in the evening sun with her sweat, glowing with sex as she ground her clitoris harder into his mouth to sustain her shuddering climax. Finally falling back, resting on her hands, her open sex dripping with her hot come, she relaxed as the priest cleansed her, lapping up the milky product of her orgasm until she rolled to one side and spread herself out on the grass – taken, spent.

'And now it's my turn!' Samantha enthused, kneeling either side of Father Will's head, her naked body fresh, tight in youth. Her rounded breasts were as hard as rock, her nipples small but beautifully formed, her shaven cunt open, oozing with slippery opaque fluid. 'Come on, lick me out!' she instructed shakily as he pulled her down, pushing his mouth between her wet, rubbery girl-lips. 'That's it, lick me out and then fuck me again!'

Praise be to girls in their youth!

Grabbing a fallen branch, Rosa swiped Samantha's taut buttocks, giggling as thin weals appeared across the pale orbs. Screeching, Samantha leaned forward, resting on her hands to expose her rounded buttocks, her open cunt pressed hard against the priest's mouth as the thrashing continued. Her come decanting from her spasming sheath, her buttocks twitching with every stinging lash of the branch, she trembled violently, grinding her clitoris harder into the priest's mouth as she reached the pinnacle of her massive orgasm, the depths of her corruption.

Her young naked body rolling on to the soft grass, she lay on her stomach, quivering as Rosa continued to lash her buttocks in a wild frenzy. 'Stop!' Samantha cried as the branch landed again, tightening her glowing buttocks. 'Christ, Rosa – that's enough!'

Dropping the branch, Rosa climbed on top of the priest, pulling his cassock up over his stomach, sitting upright and settling her yawning chasm over his pillar. Teasing, swivelling her hips, she massaged the length of his glistening shaft, running her creamy slit, her clitoris, back and forth over the solid penis.

Grabbing the priest's cock, Samantha guided the huge head between her friend's splayed cunt lips. Rosa squeezed her eyes shut as she lowered her body, the massive organ slipping deep into her vaginal sheath, filling her pelvic cavity to the brim. 'Now rock!' Samantha squealed as, facing her friend, she knelt astride the priest's head. Settling her inflamed pussy lips over his face, decanting her copious juice into his thirsty mouth, she smiled at Rosa. Rocking their hips back and forth, they leaned forward, kissing each other's mouths, gasping their delight as they feasted in unison from the holy grail.

Samantha's tongue drove into Rosa's hot mouth, exploring, tasting, savouring the hot female saliva as the priest's tongue explored her open femininity. His penis locked, crushed within Rosa's gripping vaginal sheath as she found her sexual heaven, he released his sperm, gushing, spurting into the young girl's body as Samantha's clitoris exploded in his mouth.

The threesome gasping and writhing in unbridled lust, they didn't hear the camera shutter clicking, the motor whirring, with shot after shot of their lewd coupling. As one, they trembled, spasmed, came, the girls falling over the priest to collapse in a quivering heap of limbs.

'I want to know how a virgin can get pregnant!' a tedious sixth-former asked the vicar as she swigged down her potent lemonade.

'So do I!' the vicar replied, unaware that his colleague was being crushed beneath two young girls' naked bodies.

'It's just not possible!' the girl persisted, determined to bring the subject round to sex.

'Anything's possible,' Father Bob replied as orgasmic screams of lust filled the church, reverberating through the roof.

'It's a sign!' the girl called. 'It's the virgin—'

'It's not a bloody sign!' the vicar returned. 'Sister Teresa, are there any of your girls missing?' he asked.

'Er . . . yes, Samantha Lovejoy and Rosa . . . They'll be all right. They were tagging behind us down the lane. They're probably picking flowers in the wood. I'll go and see.'

Outside the church, Sister Teresa followed the wails of ecstasy, the whimperings of lust, until she emerged into the clearing to find her girls and Father Will naked, his penis between their mouths as they lay either side of him, licking and sucking on his orgasming glans.

'Christ!' she cried. 'What the fuck's going on here?'

'It's all right, Sister,' Samantha smiled sweetly as she licked the last of the sperm from the priest's purple knob. 'We're taking our punishment for—'

'I think you both need punishing – by me! Your behaviour is despicable! You're behaving no better than common sluts! And as for you, Father Entercock! I can't imagine what you think you're doing lying naked on the grass with two of my sixth-formers!'

'It's all right, Sister. We were just—'

'I don't want to hear another word! Good heavens, I have never witnessed such—'

'Beautiful young girls, Sister?'

Taking a branch, Sister Teresa ordered the girls to lie on their stomachs and receive their punishment. 'Just you wait until the Mother Superior hears about this!' she shrilled as she slipped out of her habit and stood over the pupils in her stockings and bra, her naked pussy inflamed with arousal, her pouting labia swelling, glistening in the orange evening sunlight.

The camera clicked and whirred as the young nun began her thrashing, landing blow after blow on the girls' fresh young bottoms. Her nipple rings protruding through the holes in her red lace bra, her pussy lips bloating, opening as she continued to lash the girls' taut buttocks, Sister Teresa's shrieks rocked the wood. 'I'll see you both expelled for this! Your only hope is to make your vows to me – vow to be my personal slaves!'

'Please, Sister – we'll do anything!' Samantha pleaded as the branch swished through the air to land squarely on her crimson buttocks.

'You'll attend me as and when I tell you to! You'll become my personal slaves!' the sister ordered.

'Yes, yes – anything!' Rosa promised as her dark buttocks tightened in anticipation of the next blow.

Finally discarding her weapon, the nun turned her attention to Father Will. Doing his Stan Laurel look-alike, he scratched the top of his head, grinning stupidly. 'Sorry, Sister. They made me do it! I didn't want to—'

'Shut up, Will! And bend over!'

'Yes, bend over!' the girls squealed in unison, grabbing the priest and pinning him to the ground, his buttocks exposed, bared for the beating.

With Samantha straddling his back and Rosa pinning his legs down, Sister Teresa retrieved the branch and began her thrashing. On and on she lashed the priest's buttocks until they glowed a fire-red, and his penis stiffened against the grass. Her arm aching, she finally collapsed to the ground, her cunette dripping, her clitoris throbbing.

'Roll him over!' she instructed her new recruits. 'I haven't finished with him yet!'

Hoisting Father Will over, the girls gazed at his penis, pointing skyward – a proud monument to the male species. Climbing aboard his naked body, Sister Teresa knelt astride him and lowered her dripping slit over his mast, commanding her galley slaves to guide him into her hot cunt.

Grabbing the solid organ by its base, the girls watched in awe as it disappeared deep into their mistress's gully. Releasing the shaft, they moved behind her, gazing now at her bloated lips encompassing the root of the priest's cock.

Bobbing up and down, Sister Teresa gave the girls a magical display of the priest's knob appearing and disappearing inside her ravenous hole. Her honey pouring from her nectaries as she rested on her elbows placed either side of his head, she afforded her new slaves a wonderful view of her splayed buttocks, her bottom-hole – her cunt, stretched wide, filled, dripping as the invading penis exploded in orgasm to shower her inner flesh with sperm.

Each grabbing one of his balls, Rosa and Samantha kneaded them, jiggled them as they drained, satiating the nun's cunt. Leaning forward, they nibbled her buttocks before moving their darting tongues down to lap up the holy come as it spewed from the church coupling. 'Lick harder!' Sister Teresa ordered her sex-slaves. 'Lick his balls, and my fanny!'

Finally falling limp, her thighs wide, the priest's massive shaft impaling her open body, Sister Teresa gasped her appreciation. The girls had done well, and she wouldn't report them to Reverend Mother as long as they attended her intimately, as and when she required them to. Rolling from the priest's body, she lay on the grass, gazing up to the trees as the girls homed in, both kneeling astride her face and lowering their young slits over her mouth.

Their stomachs touching, their firm breasts kissing, they began to move back and forth, allowing the nun's tongue to taste first one and then the other wet opening. Lapping the fresh juice as it decanted from its sources, she sensed Father Will at her feet and opened her legs. Suddenly, her tight vaginal sheath was full, swollen again by his massive piston.

Lost in their licking and fucking, still the foursome didn't hear the camera clicking and whirring. 'I'll fuck the girls' bottom-holes next!' Father Will spluttered as his sperm rose quickly to the head of his penis to shoot deep into the nun's spasming love-hole.

'No!' Samantha protested as, resting on one hand, he located her small hole and pushed his finger into her velveteen tube.

'You'll do as Father asks or else!' Sister Teresa warned as Rosa shuddered and poured her hot come into her mouth, halting her threats. Spasming, all four came together, their perspiring bodies locked in their debauched, lustful union, their juices flowing, bathing, lubricating, until they collapsed to the ground, writhing in the wake of their heavens.

'What was that?' Father Will panted, looking nervously towards a bush. The rustling grew louder, twigs breaking underfoot as the voyeur fled. 'Christ! Someone's been watching us!'

'Fuck!' Sister Teresa exclaimed as she scrambled into her habit, scooping the come from her oozing slit and wiping her hand on the grass. 'Who do you think it was?'

'I don't know, but I've got a bloody good idea!'

'Who?' the young nun asked agitatedly.

'If it's who I think it is, then we're all fucked – and I mean fucked rotten!'

'Who was it, for fuck's sake?'

'An enemy agent – Brian, Josie's photographer friend.'

The girls dressed, oblivious to what was going on, who the priest was talking about. 'It's all right, isn't it?' Samantha asked as she slipped her grey convent knickers over her drenched crack. 'I mean, we're not in trouble, are we?'

'Trouble? Oh, no – we're only going to be plastered all over the Sunday tabloids, naked, writhing – fucking!'

'You don't *know* that!' Sister Teresa reasoned. 'And if it's who you think it is, then you'll just have to go after him.'

'You're right, I'll have to get the bastard's camera!'

Following the only path Brian could have taken, Father Will made his way through the woods. Emerging into the lane, he spotted the photographer running some fifty yards ahead.

'Bastard!' the priest yelled as he gave chase. 'Fucking cunt of a bastard!' As the photographer disappeared around the corner, the priest tripped, tearing his cassock as he fell into the ditch skirting the lane. 'I'll have your fucking balls for breakfast, you cunt-mouthed prick-headed little—'

'Father Entercock! I have seen and heard more than enough of your most vile and disgusting behaviour!'

Peering up from the ditch, the priest followed the Mother Superior's disgusted gaze to his penis, revealed in all its sticky glory through the gaping hole in his cassock. Trying to cover himself, he smiled his most charming smile and climbed into the lane.

'A lovely evening for a walk, don't you agree?' he beamed.

'I have never heard such language in all my days!' Mother Mary cried as he stood before her, brushing mud from his cassock.

You want to get around a bit more then, you cuntless old hag!
'Sorry, Reverend Mother, but I fell and—'

'Where are my girls? What have you done to them? And who was that man you were chasing?'

Your girls are in the wood, and I've fucked them rotten, and that man's the biggest bollocked-face bastard . . . 'The girls are fine, Reverend Mother. I do believe that they've enjoyed a nice evening with the Reverend Cummings. That man I was chasing was a Peeping Tom. I've only just arrived, you see, and I noticed him lurking in the church grounds. Well, I can't tell you what he was doing to himself as he peeped through the church window, it's too disgusting for . . . I reckon he's with the KGB.'

'That's enough of your incessant drivel! Ah, Sister Teresa, has the Father been troubling you?' she asked as the young nun ran towards them.

'Sister Teresa, I was just telling Reverend Mother about the Peeping Tom I was chasing – a spy, more than likely. Wouldn't surprise me if he's an anti-Rutlander.'

'Did you catch him, Father? The girls were so frightened. If it hadn't been for you—'

'Come, Sister – we have to take the girls back,' Mother Mary interrupted sharply. 'You'll be hearing from the bishop about your behaviour, mark my words!' she added, turning to glare at the priest as she took Sister Teresa's arm to lead her towards the church.

I'll screw your tight bum-hole if it's the last thing I do! 'I'll look forward to hearing from him, Reverend Mother!' he called as she walked off. 'Mind how you go!'

Back in his office, Father Will sank into his armchair and picked up the telephone. 'Bob, it's me,' he said despondently.

'Will! Where the fuck did you get to? The Reverend Mother was here and she—'

'It's a long story, mate. Anyway, how did the Bible-bash go?'

'Fucking boring! That Josie girl was here all the time, the Mother Superior turned up just as the vodka was taking effect on the crumpet . . . the whole evening was a total failure! Where did you get to, anyway?'

'You'd never believe it! Christ, it's ten o'clock! Look, I'll call you tomorrow and tell you all about it.'

'OK. By the way, the Mother Superior was talking to that Josie. She said something about a photographer. Then Josie rang someone on her mobile and told the hag that everything had gone far better than they'd ever dreamed possible – does that make any sense to you?'

'Sense? Fucking right it does! I'm finished, done for! Anyway, we'll talk in the morning – see you.'

No sooner had the priest replaced the receiver than the phone rang. 'Father Entercock,' he acknowledged, pressing the receiver to his ear as he lit a cigarette and rifled for a can of lager in the desk drawer.

'It's me, Josie. I've been trying to contact you—'

'Hello, Josie! Sorry, only I've been talking to a young couple about marriage. I heard the phone go several times, but . . .'

'But I thought you were going to Hallworth Church?' she asked surprisedly.

'I was, but another priest went along instead. I couldn't get away, you see.'

'Another priest? But—'

'Yes. Anyway, I have to go now. See you tomorrow, perhaps?'

'Who was the other priest?'

'Oh, Father Jones, or something – I don't know him personally.'

'But Brian said—'

'Brian?'

'Yes, he said that he saw you near the church – Hallworth Church.'

'He must have been mistaken, Josie. By the way, where are you both staying?'

'The pub – The Woodman's Arms, why?'

'Oh, right. I know the landlord, Jack. He's a nice chap. Anyway, until tomorrow.'

'Are you *sure* you weren't at the church?' she persisted.

'Josie, I'd know if I was, wouldn't I? Brian must have seen Father Jones and mistaken him for me. Either that or he spotted a KGB agent.'

'What?'

'Sorry, I can't talk about my undercover work as a spy. Now, I really must go – 'bye.'

Locking the church, Father Will ran his fingers through his dark hair and sighed. Things were becoming complicated – dangerous! He had to get his hands on the roll of film. 'The Woodman's Arms!' he breathed as he left the church. 'The Woodman's Arms . . . Must pay Jack a visit! He still owes me for that case of Scotch!'

CHAPTER SIX

Finding Chloë in Annie's room examining a buzzing vibrator, Father Will realized he had some explaining to do as he cast his eyes around the room at the collection of whips, chains and dildos. Chloë's eyes met his as she switched the phallus off, asking what the strange device was for.

'Before we go into that, what happened at the convent this evening?' he asked.

'Nothing! I went along to Reverend Mother's room and all that happened was . . . well, there were half a dozen of us, and we all sat there drinking tea and talking.'

'Is that all?'

'Yes, I don't know what you were expecting, but . . . What's happened to your cassock?'

'I fell into a ditch. As with most stories, it's a long one.'

'Oh. Anyway, what's this thing for?'

'It's . . . well, it's to help women achieve orgasm,' the priest smiled, imagining the girl with her thighs spread and the vibrator plunged deep inside her wet vaginal sheath.

'Help them?' she queried, switching the thing on again and, in her innocence, holding it provocatively against her soft cheek.

'Yes, it's to . . . Instead of using fingers to masturbate, most women use a . . . it's called a vibrator. You just hold the tip against your clitoris and—'

'I'd like to try it!' she interrupted excitedly, her blue eyes sparkling at the prospect of sex.

The priest lowered his gaze to the girl's short skirt and smiled. Chloë had been sent, he was sure – a gift from above, or below! Her long legs disappearing up her pink skirt, he recalled her pussy – warm, cosy, damp, perfumed. She wants to use a vibrator! Unbelievable, incredible – beautiful!

Wonder if she'd like it up her bum?

'As you're staying the night, Chloë, why don't we go into the lounge and talk about this? I don't know if you're ready for such things, really, but we'll talk about it,' he said, taking the buzzing phallus from her small hand and switching it off.

'What is there to talk about?' she asked, following him into the lounge.

'I'm becoming rather concerned, Chloë. I mean, I'm teaching you things that, to be honest, many women a lot older than you are only just discovering. You're learning fast – too fast, I fear. Next, you'll be asking me about shaving your pubic hair off, and that's something that girls of your age should know nothing about!'

'Shaving it off? But why . . .'

Because I'm a sad pervy!

'No, don't even think about it, Chloë! When you're older—'

'You're always saying that I'm too young for this and too young for that! What's age got to do with it?'

'You're right, Chloë. I'm being unfair, I can see that. It's just that I don't want you to learn too much, too soon, my child. There are certain things that may come as a shock to you.'

'What things?'

My throbbing penis filling your tight bottom-hole with sperm, for a start!

'To be told that most women shave their pubic hair off, for example.'

'But why do they do that? I don't understand.'

'Because they like to be feminine, and pubic hair is . . . Anyway, you want to try the vibrator, don't you?'

'Yes, I do! Shall I lie on the sofa again?'

'Yes, but first allow me to remove your clothes.'
And lick your cunt!
Unbuttoning Chloë's blouse, Father Will recalled his evening in the woods with the naked sixth-form girls, and then remembered Brian, the photographer. The photographs were more than enough evidence to . . . *Problems, problems.*

Slipping the girl's blouse off her shoulders, he decided to deal with Brian the next day – for now, Chloë needed his intimate attention. Unclipping her bra, he peeled the cups from her heavy breasts and gazed in wonderment at her nipples as they grew long, firm – erectile. Looking down at her fine young breasts, Chloë smiled as her areolae grew darker with her arousal. She was learning, discovering her young body, the secret pleasures it held.

Kneeling, Father Will admired her smooth stomach, her small navel, as he tugged her skirt down her legs. Now only her tight red panties lay between him and his goal and he kissed the warm material, inhaling her scent. Licking the dividing groove perfectly outlined by the bulging material, he sensed her tremble slightly as she gasped. She was more than ready for a night of lust! Peeling her panties from her mound, her pubic curls sprang to life, unfurling – ready for the razor.

'Father,' Chloë began pensively as she stepped out of her panties. 'Do you have other girls here? I mean—'

'No, Chloë, I don't. I am only doing this for you because you need to learn, as I have said. I am going way above and beyond my strict duty as a priest to help you in your plight. When you came to me and confessed your sins, I knew then that I had to help you. We were brought together, my child. By the powers that be, you were sent to me for help, and I am being guided in order to help you.' *Satan moves in mysterious ways!* 'You said the other day that you were in my hands – so, come over to the sofa and *put* yourself in my hands. Open your mind, your body,' *your cunt!* 'to me, your mentor. In my wisdom, I know that I have to teach you the delights of your young body. I will teach you to use the vibrator, Chloë.'

Positioning the naked girl on the sofa, the priest spread her legs, watching as her young slit opened, exposing the complex folds of pink flesh within her sex-groove. Chloë *was* in his hands now, and he knew that he could get away with anything, do whatever he liked to her young body. His mind reeling with perverted thoughts, he remembered the handcuffs and pictured the girl's body tethered, her limbs spread, her young sex vulnerable, defenceless.

'I have decided to teach you all there is to know, Chloë,' he said decisively, running his finger up and down her open sex-valley. 'When women use vibrators, they open their legs as wide as possible to increase their pleasure. Now, in order to do this, I am going to suggest that I tie you down.'

'Tie me down, Father?' she queried, her deep blue eyes wide.

'Yes. You see, I want you to experience the ultimate orgasm, and in order to do that I'll need to tie your hands and feet, to spread your limbs and open your body to receive the pleasures of the flesh. It is for your salvation, Chloë, that I offer you the sacrament of bondage.'

'But, Father . . . I thought that pleasures of the flesh were . . .'

'Sinful?'

'Yes, Father.'

'To derive pleasure from the flesh simply to satisfy one's lustful desires *is* a sin, my child. But to open your mind, your body, in order to cleanse your spirit, to drive out the evil dwelling within your womb, is an act of contrition. The sacrament of bondage will procure you the grace of true humility.'

'Yes, Father, I understand.'

'Good. Now, wait there while I collect the necessary equipment.'

Returning from Annie's room with handcuffs and rope, the priest glanced around the room. To tie her over the back of the sofa, or lie her on the floor and spread-eagle her limbs? Or in the armchair, her legs over the arms, her hips pushed forward, her cunt wide open?

'Sit on the coffee table, Chloë,' he instructed the girl, moving the table to the centre of the room and placing the armchair at one end of the table. 'That's it – now lie back on the table and rest your head on the chair.' Following his orders, Chloë reclined, her head on the chair, her arms limp by the sides of the table, her feet on the floor.

'Now, what I intend to do is tie your feet to the table legs, like this, to keep your thighs as wide apart as they'll go. And then tie your hands together, under the table, like this. There, now, are you comfortable?'

'Sort of, Father,' she replied nervously, closing her thighs a little.

'I'm just going to tie ropes around your legs, just below your knees, like this, and then pull them back and secure the ends to the table to make sure that your thighs remain wide open.' *Your cunt remains wide open!*

'It's rather uncomfortable, Father. My groin aches!' the girl complained as he tightened the ropes, gazing at her crack as her outer lips parted further to reveal the entrance to her vaginal sheath.

'The pain will soon ease off, Chloë,' he smiled, settling on the floor between her legs, gazing appreciatively at her buttocks resting over the edge of the table, the small brown entrance to her most private sanctum bared, open in readiness to receive his penis. Licking the length of her glistening slit, he reached for the vibrator and switched it on. 'Now, my child, you are going to experience the ultimate, heavenly, multiple orgasm.'

Pulling her pinken prepuce right back, he exposed her already erect clitoris. Presenting the tip of the buzzing vibrator to the sensitive protrusion, he grinned to see the budling pulsate and grow in size. Gasping, rolling her head from side to side, Chloë responded quickly to the beautiful vibrations coursing their way through her throbbing clitoris and deep into her womb.

'Father, I've never . . . God, that's . . .!' she breathed as her first climax stirred within the hot depths of her pelvis. Slipping three fingers into the fiery heat of her drenched cunt, Will massaged the creamy inner flesh, heightening her pleasure as she suddenly screamed in her coming. 'Ah! God! Father, I can't . . . Ah, yes, come, come!'

Her fresh girl-juices flowed, running over her stretched and inflamed pinken petals to lubricate the thrusting fingers. Pressing on the rubicund flesh surrounding her clitoris, the priest popped out the full length of the pulsating budling, pumping in orgasm against the tip of the vibrator. Unable to close her legs to halt the beautiful torture, unable to move her hands to push the vibrator away from her now aching clitoris, Chloë could only endure the incessant waves of orgasm tearing through her fettered body. Her cream pumping, bathing the priest's fingers, running down his hand, she reached another mind-blowing climax, crying out in her ecstatic pleasure, her body quivering uncontrollably.

'Please, Father, that's enough!' she begged as another shuddering peak of sensation exploded from her clitoris. The protrusion pulsating, bright red, her inner folds scarlet, drenched in her come, the priest allowed her some quarter, removing the vibrator and sucking her solid clitoris into his hot mouth. Running his tongue round the base of her cumbud, she shook violently, gasping as another orgasm stirred deep within her pelvis.

Slipping his fingers from her hot hole, he moved down, pushing his tongue out and lapping up her creamy offering, driving his tongue deep into her swollen cunt. 'Enjoying it?' he murmured seductively, persuasively, presenting the tip of his sticky finger to her smaller hole.

'No! Not there!' she cried as the well-oiled digit slipped into her tight bottom-hole. 'Please, Father, that's . . . Argh! No!'

'Oh yes, my child!' he disagreed gleefully as he invaded the privacy of her hot bowels, pushing his finger deeper into her tight anal tube.

Slipping his thumb into her vagina, he switched the vibrator on again and gently pressed the tip against her clitoris. Immediately, the small bud grew, becoming erect as she gasped and moaned in her ecstasy. Fingering her bottom-hole, her cunt, he licked her swollen outer lips, nibbled on her inner thigh as, once more, she flew to her sexual heaven.

'You must stop!' she pleaded as her sex juice gushed, drenching the priest's hand. 'Stop, *please*!' But he only pressed the vibrator harder against her clitoris, gazing in awe as the bud visibly throbbed with orgasm. 'I'll never come back here again!' she threatened as she trembled violently again, her body perspiring, glistening under the light.

'All right, Chloë. That's enough for the time being,' he smiled, slipping his finger from her bottom-hole, his thumb from her hot cunt.

Switching the vibrator off, he sat back on his heels and surveyed the girl's crudely opened slit – inflamed, dripping with come-juice, swollen in the wake of several enforced multiple orgasms. His penis stiff, throbbing in expectation, he lifted his cassock. On his knees now, he moved the purple head of his massive weapon towards Chloë's open hole, grinning as he gazed at her face, her eyes closed, her mouth open, her breathing heavy.

'God!' she cried as he slipped the entire length of his mighty shaft deep into her hot sheath. 'Oh, God, that's nice!' The ballooning head of his rock-hard penis bathed in her moist inner heat, he moved back and forth, pistoning deep into her trembling body, ramming her young cervix to the accompaniment of her whimpers of pleasure.

His balls swinging, slapping the girl's buttocks as he fucked her, he waited for his moment, the moment when he would slip his knob from her gaping cunt and ram it deep into her bottom-hole.

'The virtue of humility must be earned, Chloë!' he gasped as his moment neared. 'You will suffer the ultimate humiliation in order to find virtue!'

'Yes, Father – the ultimate humiliation!' she gasped.

'And degradation, my child.'

'Degradation, Father?'

'Yes, you must suffer the ultimate degradation to enable your spirit to find freedom.'

'But how, Father?'

'Like this, my child – hold tight and pray for your very soul!'

Slipping his penis from her hot sheath, his hands grasping her inner thighs, his thumbs parting her taut buttocks, he opened the private entrance to her inner being. Swivelling his hips, he aligned the bulbous head of his organ with her small, tight hole and thrust forward, impaling the girl, sinking his eight inches deep into her quivering bottom-hole.

'Father! Father!' she screamed as he began fucking her there, taking her bowels with a vengeance.

'The ultimate humiliation, Chloë!' he cried as he rocked her tethered body with his ramming shaft. 'The ultimate degradation!'

'No, no! It's not right to . . . Ah, God, what's *that*?' she breathed as he thrust the buzzing vibrator deep into her spasming cunt.

'The ultimate, Chloë! Pray for your soul, my child! Pray for the demons, the evil spirits to leave you!'

Shuddering, the priest sensed his sperm rising and rammed the girl harder. 'Coming!' he wailed as his glans throbbed and his seed gushed, bathing her inner flesh. 'Fucking your bottom . . . Coming, my child! Pray that you may beg to receive my penis in your bottom-hole daily!'

'Praying, Father!' she shrieked as her clitoris pumped in its climax, her cunt gripping the vibrator, her bottom stretched open by the ungodly male shaft of lust.

Finally collapsing over the girl's fettered body, sucking on her erect nipples, the priest slipped his spent weapon from her anal sheath and rested. Her mound pressing against his belly, he sensed her pubic hairs, wet with her come, tickling him as he trembled.

'And now, Chloë,' he began, licking her hard nipples. 'And now for the sacramental rite that will cleanse you of your own transgressions, and absolve you from all sin!'

'What are you going to do to me, Father?' she whimpered.

'I am going to wash away the sins that stain your soul, Chloë.' *Shave your pubes off!*

'How, Father?'

'Depilation – the removal of your pubic hair to restore you to your former innocence, to turn your body away from the sins of womanhood and take you back to child-like innocence!'

Slipping the vibrator from her sodden sheath, he left the girl to ponder her return to pubescence as he dashed to the bathroom, washing his penis under the cold tap in preparation for the penetration of her shaven pussy. Grabbing his razor and can of shaving foam, his torn cassock flowing behind him, he returned to the lounge.

Lathering the girl's mound, he looked into her deep blue eyes and smiled his reassuring smile. 'You will keep your puss— . . .you will keep yourself smooth and clean-shaven, Chloë. Every day you will remove the stubble of womanhood to retain your innocence.'

'Yes, Father, I will,' she promised as he dragged the razor from her smooth belly down over her swollen labia. Carefully removing every last hair, he wiped the residue of foam from her smooth pads of flesh and smiled.

'Now you are as innocent as the day you were born!' he enthused, gazing at her pubescent mound, her gaping sex-valley, her pink inner folds protruding delightfully, inviting his mouth. 'I must enter you once again, my child. Push my male organ deep into your vagina and baptize your very womb with my seed.'

'Oh, yes, Father!' she squealed as she lifted her head to admire her naked innocence.

Parting her swollen cushions of flesh, he stabbed his knob into her open hole, driving his shaft deep into her hot body to the accompaniment of her gasps of delight. Rocking his hips back and forth, he watched her inner petals clinging to his sticky rod, her swelling outer lips rolling in and out with his every thrust. 'And now I come!' he cried triumphantly as his sperm gushed into her tight canal.

'God, I'm coming up your tight girl-cunt!'

'Ah, yes! My girl-cunt! Coming in me!'

'Feel my sperm, Chloë – feel my sperm gush!'

'God, yes! Filling my girl-cunt!'

His stamina waning, he lay over the slight swell of her belly, licking her areolae, breathing in her perspiration, her female perfume, as he rested, his knob glued to her cervix, his drained balls stuck to her buttocks.

'Can't you do it again, Father?' she wheedled softly as he slipped his penis from her sex-duct. 'Can you not find the energy, the love, to do it again?'

Love? 'Later, my angel – later. Rest now and I will cleanse your cunt, lick you clean, suck you dry.'

'Finger me, Father – please!' she begged as he moved between her splayed thighs and licked the length of her yawning valley. 'Do everything to me – anything you want!'

Anything? Bloody hell's bells!

Dashing to Annie's room, Father Will rummaged through her incredible assortment of sex equipment. Discovering a box labelled 'Vaginal Developer' he returned to the lounge and grinned. 'Anything, Chloë?' he asked.

'Yes, I want to come again, Father,' she whimpered.

Settling between her thighs, he opened the box and took out the thick cylindrical device. Parting her now hairless lips, he eased the shaft into her creamy pussy hole, leaving only the rubber tube and bulb hanging from her used body. Pumping the bulb in his hand, he watched her lower abdomen rise as the device swelled within her tight cunt.

'God, what's that?' she shrieked as he pumped the rubber bulb, opening her vaginal sheath to its limits. 'No more, Father! I . . . God, no!' she screamed as he crushed the bulb rhythmically in his fist, still gazing entranced at her lower belly rising, ballooning. 'Stop!'

Her cunt bloated to capacity, her rosy outer lips full, swollen in lust, Chloë lay tethered to the coffee table, gasping as the priest massaged her clitoris with the buzzing vibrator. His penis hardening again, he looked to her huge breasts, heaving as she breathed heavily through her nose. To splatter her elongated nipples with sperm would be wonderful, he decided as she cried out that she was coming. And to come in her hot, gasping mouth would be even better!

'Ah, my cunt's on fire!' she screamed as her clitoris throbbed against the vibrator. 'God, my cunt's burning!' Affording the girl no mercy this time, Father Will worked the tip of the vibrator over her pulsating nodule to her pleas for him to stop. Again and again she shuddered, her orgasms tearing through her body, tightening every muscle, touching every nerve-ending until, her eyes rolling, her body rigid, she appeared to faint with the unbearable pleasure emanating from her gaping sex.

Switching the vibrator off, the priest climbed on to the armchair, kneeling astride her face and lowering his solid shaft towards her open mouth. Semi-conscious, her eyes closed, her golden hair matted with perspiration, she sucked on the purple head like a babe at the breast, moaning her pleasure through her nose until, unable to control his rampant lust any longer, the priest drove his shaft deep into her hot mouth and released a stream of sperm. Choking, she swallowed hard, spluttering as she drank the fruits of his loins, drained his balls. Clinging to the chair to steady his quivering body, he pulled his penis from her mouth, his sperm dripping over her pretty face, her long hair, as he collapsed on to the floor.

'Please, take that thing out!' Chloë begged as she licked the sperm from her chin with her long tongue. 'My cunt . . . take it out of my cunt!'

'All right, hang on,' he gasped as he crawled between her thighs and tugged on the rubber pipe. 'It won't—'

'Argh! Don't pull it! Argh! No!'

Pulling the rubber bulb from the pipe, he let the air rush out, watching the swell of her abdomen slowly fall as he slipped the wet rubber cylinder from her bloated love sheath. Licking her inflamed crack, he cleansed her, lapped up her juices – thick, sticky, slippery, hot. Moving back, he contemplated her crudely exposed femininity – swollen, sore, used. Had the demon gone?

'I think that's enough, Chloë,' he smiled as he untied the ropes. 'More tomorrow, my child, if that's what you want.'

'God, yes! I want more, Father! Every day, I want to come here and . . . Why don't I come and live with you, permanently, I mean?'

'But . . . Chloë! Your mother . . . you . . .'

'She won't mind. I'll tell her that I've moved in with a girl-friend or something.'

'We'll talk about this tomorrow, Chloë. I mean, it's a big step, moving in with . . .' *A perverted priest!*

'All right, tomorrow, then. I must sleep now, I'm tired,' she grinned coyly, lifting her aching body from the coffee table.

'So am I! Come on, this way,' he smiled, taking her hand and leading her to his bedroom.

Lying beside Chloë, his relentlessly stiffening penis pushed between her closed thighs, absorbing the wet warmth of her pussy lips bulging sweetly below her bottom, Father Will thought about Brian and the incriminating photographs, planning his next move as sleep engulfed him.

'For fuck's sake!' Jack yelled as Father Will rang the pub doorbell for the fifth time. 'I'm fucking coming! It's seven o'fucking clock in the fuck— Oh, Will, what on earth are you doin' up at this ungodly hour?' he exclaimed as he opened the door.

'Sorry to drag you from your pit, Jack, only I need a massive favour.'

'Oh, right. You'd better come in. Scotch?'

'Christ, no!'

'OK. I think I'll 'ave a nifter. So, what's this all about?' he asked, brushing his thick hair back with his fingers as he led the way to the bar.

'Christ, it stinks like a Dutch prostitute's arse-hole in here!' the priest observed.

'Yeah, it's the beer and fags. It always reeks in 'ere in the mornin'. So, what's the problem?'

'You've a couple staying here – Brian and Josie.'

'Oh yeah, the sales reps – what about 'em?'

'Brian has a camera and . . . Look, it's a long story, but I want his camera and any rolls of film he might have with him.'

'What, you want me to nick 'em, you mean?'

'Something like that. Christ, your gut's getting bigger and bigger!'

'Yeah, it's the fucking booze! So, what's in this for me?'

'I'll let you off that case of Scotch you owe me for.'

'Oh, fuck, I'd forgotten about that! You should 'ave been 'ere last night, Will. There was a bloke in the bar tellin' jokes. A right laugh 'e was, too. You 'eard the one about this brunette bird what goes to a fancy dress party wearing nothin' but black socks and black gloves?'

'No, I can't say that I have.'

'Some geezer asks 'er what she's come as, so she stands with 'er feet apart and 'er 'ands in the air and she goes – the five of spades!'

'Very droll. Anyway, *I* told you that one last week. Look, it's a bit early for jokes. Can you get your hands on this camera and film or not?'

'Yeah, no prob! You in tonight?'

'That depends. I'm being hounded by those two . . . those sales reps, so I'm having to keep a low profile, as far as boozing in pubs is concerned, anyway.'

'Oh, right. Look, they bugger off out about nine so I'll raid their room and see what I can lay me 'ands on, OK? Shit knows 'ow I'm going to explain the missing camera, but—'

'Tell them that MI5 raided the place.'

'What the fuck are you talkin' about?'

'Nothing. Just take the film – leave the camera.'

'Right, got it.'

'I'll pop in lunchtime to see how you got on.'

'OK, squire, see you later.'

Parking his car a short distance from the convent, Father Will crept through the woods and dashed across the lawn, clutching the two-way plug adaptor. Crouching under the Mother Superior's window, he looked up to see that it was ajar. *Alleluia!*

Climbing in, he looked around the neat office, noticing a socket virtually concealed behind the filing cabinet. 'Wonder how far this thing transmits?' he breathed as he slipped the adaptor into the socket. Leaping through the window at the sound of voices in the corridor, he fell into the bushes and dashed across the lawn to the cover of the trees. *Wish I had some dynamite!*

'Christ, the things I do!' he panted as he climbed into his car and switched the radio on. Tuning to the top end of the FM band, he grinned as he heard the Reverend Mother's voice blasting from the speakers.

'Sit down, Sister Felicity,' she instructed as a chair scraped across the wooden floor. 'Now, I want to talk to you about the accounts. I can't keep taking money from the funds for wine and batteries. I know that you've only been here for a short while but . . . You can't keep spending and spending. We're going to have to cut back, I'm afraid.'

'But, Reverend Mother, I've planned another session for this

136

evening. The girls have arranged for that Chloë to be there and—'

'Yes, I know. Look, we've more than enough wine for tonight's little bash, and there's still some gin and vodka left. As for batteries, we'll just have to share the big vibrator, the one you plug in. And don't worry, you'll have the new girl!'

'I hope so! Apparently, it went well last night.'

'Why, what happened?'

'Oh, nothing happened. I wasn't there but the girls did as you said, talked and drank tea, just to check her out. I think she's OK. I'm sure she'll like you dressed in your governess outfit!'

'I hope so. She's quite delectable, don't you agree? She's a nice little bum on her, too! By the way, did you manage to get hold of a new whip?'

'Yes, I did. And some more nipple clamps.'

'Good. Anyway, I've a job for you.'

Lighting a cigarette, Father Will could barely believe his ears. 'Whip? Nipple clamps? Christ, and I thought—' he muttered to himself.

'Father Entercock is causing me problems, and I want you to sort it out, Sister,' Mother Mary continued. 'I know what he gets up to, and I want him exposed.'

'But why? I mean, he's not doing us any harm, is he?'

'He's getting on my nerves. He's been trying to get something on the bishop, and if he does . . . Look, he'll be on to *us* next, and I want him out of the way. Permanently. Besides, I want to take over his booze business, and whatever other money spinners he's into. The money he makes is incredible! Someone I know at the bank checked out his account for me – he's earning a small fortune, but not all from the booze. I want to know how he's making so much money. What I want you to do is this – befriend him, get to know him well. Use your body, if you have to, but get as much information as you can out of him.'

'Use my body! You *are* desperate, aren't you?'

'You'll never know how desperate I am to be rid of him!

137

Anyway, go and see him this morning.'

'Oh, by the way, there's a problem with the laundry. It seems that a hundred or so pairs of knickers have gone missing.'

'Knickers?'

'Yes, apparently.'

'I wonder if . . . Look, just get as much on Entercock as you can. I'll look into the knickers.'

'Right, I'll go there this morning – and I'll use my body!'

Chloë had gone to school by the time Father Will returned home. Wondering if she really wanted to move in with him, he filled the kettle for coffee and switched the radio on. He didn't expect to pick up the bug as the convent was some four hundred yards down the lane and so he was delighted when he tuned in to hear the Mother Superior, loud and clear, on the telephone.

'All right, Simon, I'll see you later,' she trilled. 'Yes, and me! I'll look forward to it. No! I'm not telling you what colour they are! No! Because I'm not wearing any, that's why! Oh, you are naughty! Yes, until later, 'bye.'

Frowning, Father Will repeated her words. 'Simon. Because I'm not wearing any . . .' Simon Holesgood? The bishop? Surely not! Not wearing any knickers? 'Christ, this is a turn-up for the bloody books!'

The Reverend Mother evidently leaving her office, closing the door behind her, he switched the radio off and checked his watch. Nine o'clock. *Whips, nipple clamps and Simon Holesgood!*

Pouring his coffee, wondering what Sister Felicity would offer in exchange for information, he decided to place an advert offering soiled knickers in his favourite men's magazine. Taking his coffee into the lounge, he lifted the receiver and dialled.

'Good morning – Ballcock, Allcock and Moore-Cock Solicitors. How can I help you?' a young woman asked.

'Oh, I'm sorry, I seem to have the wrong number,' he replied, replacing the receiver and dialling again.

'Good morning, Cuntry Interiors,' a woman's voice trilled. Put through to classified ads, he gave his credit card number to the girl and read out his advert.

'Genuine convent schoolgirl soiled knickers,' he enunciated, wondering when Sister Teresa would deliver the hundred or so pairs she'd lifted from the laundry room. 'Yes, a box number, please. The Presbytery, Church Lane, Cumsdale. Yes, I *did* say The Presbytery. That's good, thanks very much.' Replacing the receiver, he sipped his coffee. The next issue, he thought glee-fully, making a mental note to buy some plastic bags to keep the goods fresh – girl-cunt fresh! *Schoolgirl pubic hair, five quid a bag?*

Finishing his coffee, he lit a cigarette and walked to the church. It was going to be a good day, he could feel it. The sun already hot in the clear blue sky, Jack taking care of the rolls of film, the bug in the old hag's office, Sister Felicity's fresh young cunt – a good day, indeed!

'Good morning, Father!' Josie called as she ran up the lane towards him.

Ah, the handbag! 'Good morning, Josie! How are you?'

'Fine, thanks. Although I feel rather itchy after you . . .'

Tape recorder, Entercock! 'How's young Brian?' he quickly interrupted.

'He's gone back to London. As I was saying, I feel—'

The films! 'I've a lot to do this morning, Josie, so if you don't mind . . .'

'Oh, right. Anyway, shall I come round this evening? I thought we could have another mind-blowing—'

'How did you get on at Hallworth Church last night?' he asked. 'Brian was sure that he saw you there.'

'As I told you on the phone last night, I couldn't get away.'

'That's funny because he swore blind that you were . . . any-way, how about some fun this evening? I really enjoyed the—'

'I must go, Josie. I'll see you later, perhaps. Oh, by the way, the

139

Reverend Mother rang me this morning. She's getting her twenty thousand soon and—'

'I asked her about her newspaper story and she said that she knows nothing about it.'

'You've seen her?'

'Er . . . yes, I . . .'

'She would say that, wouldn't she? I mean, she doesn't want the world to know that she's earning herself twenty grand, does she?'

'No, I suppose not. Thanks for the whipping, by the way, it was—' Josie began, determined to get the priest on tape.

'I'm only too pleased to have been able to help, Josie.'

'It was really . . .'

'I used to enjoy horse riding, but I don't have the time now, so you're more than welcome to the whip.'

'Horse riding?' Josie frowned.

'Must go – see you later!'

Slipping into the church, Father Will closed the door behind him and breathed a sigh of relief. 'That girl and her bloody tape recorder!' he fumed as he made his way to his office. 'I'll have to deal with her once and for bloody all!'

Dialling the Woodman's Arms, he lit another cigarette. 'Jack, it's me, Will,' he said as the man grunted something unintelligible down the phone.

'Ah, Will. That bloke's gone off to London.'

'Yes, I know, but did you manage . . .'

'No probs, squire – three rolls of film.'

'Good man! Hang on to them, guard them with your life!'

'Will do. Listen, when you come over lunchtime, can you bring me a case of vodka and a dozen cases of lager?'

'Sure. Cash, of course.'

'Right you are. Oh, and have you got any cheap plonk?'

'Yes, red or white?'

'A case of each. The real cheap stuff, I mean. The punters can't tell the bloody difference, especially as I rebottle it! They think it's some bloody expensive German stuff!'

'The brewery will have you one of these days! Not to mention Customs and Excise!'

'Ah, there's been a slight problem on that front. Some git from weights and measures caught me fiddling the optics – bastard! Anyway, must shove off – see you later.'

'I'll park round the back with the stuff.'

'OK. Cheers, Will.'

Downing an early morning can of lager before checking on his cannabis plants, the priest was about to leave his office when Sister Teresa appeared in the doorway.

'Knickers!' she said, dropping a black plastic sack on the floor.

'Bras!' he laughed.

'You said knickers, not bras!'

'It was a joke. Anyway, let's have a look,' he smiled, opening the bag and pulling out a handful of grey convent knickers. 'Talk about creaming!' he laughed. 'Look at the stains in these!'

'You really are a sad pervy, Will! I suppose you're going to put them over your head and sniff them while you have a wank?'

'Certainly not! I'll put them over my head and sniff them while you suck me off!'

'God, you get worse – or better! It was funny you falling in the ditch last night. Shame you didn't catch the photographer.'

'It's been dealt with – there'll be no pictures.'

'Thank God for that! The Reverend Slagger went mental! Said that she'd never heard such foul language!'

'She ain't heard nothing yet, baby! I'm about to nail her! I've got the bitch by the bra straps, so your job's safe.'

'Yeah? What have you got on her?'

'I'll reveal all later. If she has a go at you about anything, just say that you hope that she's pleased with the new whip and nipple clamps – that'll shut her up!'

'Whip? Nipple clamps?'

'Just say it, and wait for her reaction. I really must get some work done now. I've got to get an order ready for the pub . . .'

'By the way, I saw a young woman going into your house with some old geezer.'

'Ah, good – more money!'

'Who are they?'

'Just . . . it doesn't matter.'

'Right, I'd better get going or she'll be screaming the place down for me. What was it? Oh, yes, "I hope you like the new whip and nipple clamps." I'll let you know how she reacts.'

'She'll have a heart attack!'

'That would be good, except she hasn't got a heart! Catch you later, Will.'

Leaving the church by the rear door, the priest slipped through the hedge into the presbytery garden and crept up to Annie's window. 'Christ!' he gasped, gazing at an old man wearing stockings and a bra. Lying on the bed naked with a lighted candle emerging from her beautiful pussy, Annie was masturbating with a vibrator, the old man looking on as he climbed on to the bed and offered his huge penis to the girl's mouth. Turning her head, she gobbled the purple crown, her lips stretched around the thick shaft as it drove down her throat until only the root remained visible.

'Talk about deep throat!' the priest whispered as the old man began his thrusting, his heavy balls swinging, battering Annie's face. Suddenly pulling his penis from her mouth, he splattered her face with his sperm. Licking the throbbing knob, Annie appeared to reach her own climax as she arched her back, the candle shooting from her pussy galore and landing on the floor. *Better check my fire insurance*, thought Father Will as the girl sucked the old man's knob into her mouth again and swallowed the last of his cream.

His penis tenting his cassock, the priest gazed in amazement as Annie rolled onto all fours, lifting her buttocks high in the air as the old man crawled beneath her and began licking her gaping vagina. His penis vertical, he began masturbating as he sucked and licked on the girl's swollen pussy lips. Within minutes, he was on his knees, pushing his tool deep into her bottom-hole, fucking her there to the accompaniment of her exaggerated cries of bliss.

'Ah, there you are!' Turning, Father Will gulped to see the bishop walking across the lawn towards him. Annie's orgasmic cries drifted through the summer air as His Reverence drew closer, his expression angry, his lips twisted. Dashing towards him, Will led him hurriedly out of the garden.

'I was just going to the church, Bishop,' he smiled, unflustered.

'I've just come from there. There was a woman waiting for you.'

'A woman, Bishop?'

'Yes, I sent her off. I had no choice, seeing as you'd disappeared. Anyway, it has come to my notice that you have placed an advert in a disgusting magazine.'

'Advert, Bishop?' *How the fuck . . .*

'You know damn— you know very well what I'm talking about! There are over one hundred pairs of . . . of undergarments missing from the convent laundry room, which ties in very neatly with your vile advert and—'

'Undergarments, Bishop?'

'Look, Entercock, I've got you this time, so don't try and wriggle out of it! Twenty pounds per pair! You are the most vile, disgusting, perverted—'

'What colour are they? I can't tell you because I'm not wearing any! Ring any bells, Bishop?'

'What *are* you talking about, man?'

'Your phone call to the Reverend Mother this morning.'

'I . . . I don't know what—'

'No, and I don't know what *you're* talking about, either! Now, if you'll excuse me!'

Leaving the bishop standing dumbfounded in the lane, Father Will stormed through the church to his office and snatched another can of lager from his desk drawer. 'How the fucking hell does he know about the ad?' he cursed. 'How in God's name does he know?'

CHAPTER SEVEN

Checking the lines to his house, Father Will knew that the phone must have been tapped. There could be only one person prepared to go to such lengths to nail him – Josie! With the financial backing of a national newspaper, he wondered what other tricks she had up her sleeve – and up her skirt! *Bloody MI5!* But, he consoled himself, at least the pimple-nosed bishop would be lying low for a while. *I can't tell you because I'm not wearing any!*

Finding no signs of a phone tapping device, he hid in the bushes as Annie saw her client out. Wondering how much she'd charged the old man for letting him spurt his come into her pretty mouth, he imagined Josie conscripting Annie as a spy. Now he was beginning to trust no one. He imagined Annie taking money in exchange for spilling the beans as he emerged from the bushes and greeted the girl. The story was well worth having, and what was a few grand to a national newspaper?

'What were you doing hiding in the bushes?' Annie asked on his approach.

'Waiting for your client to leave. You've got sperm on your face, by the way.'

'Oh, God! I'd better have a shower, the next one's due in an hour. Oh, here's twenty-five pounds – half the take.'

'How are you fixed for money, Annie?' he asked, noticing her new and obviously expensive thigh-high leather boots.

'So – so, why?'

'Things looking up, then?'

'They could be worse, I suppose.'

'So you're all right for a few grand, then?'

'God, I wish! Why, are you short?'

'No, no, it's OK.'

'Some girl phoned for you earlier. Said that she desperately needed to see you. She left her number, it's by the phone.'

'Oh, thanks. I'd better give her a call. What's her name?'

'Don't know, she didn't say.'

In the lounge, Father Will gazed at the telephone, wondering whether that ugly git Brian had fitted some kind of bug inside the instrument. Following the lead to the wall socket, he smiled, noticing a thin wire running from the socket to a small black box. So, he mused as he ripped the wire out of the box. Brian's been telling the bishop all about me – but why?

The only way Holesgood could have known about the call to the men's mag was if Josie, or Brian, had told him. But why involve the bloody bishop? What was to be gained? Unless it was all part of the plot to have the priest defrocked. Had Brian really returned to London?

Dialling the number Annie had scribbled on the pad, he pressed the receiver to his ear, happy in the knowledge that the call would be private, but desperately trying to remember what other incriminating calls he'd made. *Wonder if the church phone's tapped?*

'Hello,' a woman answered softly.

'This is Father William Entercock, you called earlier.'

'Oh, yes! I was wondering if I could come and see you. I have a problem and . . . well, I'd like to see you.'

'Do you live locally? I mean, are you one of my parishioners?'

'Yes, I've recently moved to the village. I couldn't come and see you now, could I?'

'Er . . . yes, all right. You know where the presbytery is, do you?'

'Yes, I do. I'll be about ten minutes.'

Strange, the priest mused as he replaced the receiver, suspicion welling in his mind. Just some girl with a genuine problem? Or a set-up? *Soon find out*, he thought as Annie called out that she was going to have a shower.

He found the phone tap worrying. If Brian *was* back in London, Josie must be in sole charge of the operation, the bugging, the tapping – planting this girl, perhaps? Josie was becoming a formidable foe! Or had the newspaper sent someone else to take charge? There were so many entities baying for his blood. Apart from Josie, there was the pimple-nosed bishop, Reverend Mother Fucker, Sister Felicity – who else was fighting the cold war? And what would Brian do when he discovered that his rolls of film had mysteriously disappeared? Apart from tape recordings, the paper would want pictures. They'd sent Brian back, he was sure. Either that, or send another photographer.

Father Will felt alone now. He had to discover exactly who was on whose side and draw up his battle plans. Apart from Sister Teresa, it seemed, he had no allies, and that was no way to fight. A war cabinet was the answer, he decided. Conscript those he could trust and launch a full-scale war on the church hierarchy!

The mysterious girl arrived at the presbytery within five minutes, increasing his suspicion. Irresistibly attractive, with never-ending legs and a microskirt, the late-teenaged blonde smiled sweetly as he invited her into the house. Definitely a set-up, he surmised, although she didn't have a handbag and there was nowhere she could conceal a tape recorder – not under her tight T-shirt, anyway! *Up her hot, wet fanny, perhaps?* he mused as he showed her into the lounge and offered her a seat.

Her full, red lips smiling, her enormous green eyes sparkling, she appeared innocent enough. But there was something about her he couldn't quite put his finger on – apart from her clitoris! Her long fingernails perfectly painted, her make-up immaculate, she looked ready to stroll down the catwalk. What was a girl like her doing in a sleepy village like Cumsdale? the priest wondered warily.

'I'm new to the area,' the young blonde began. 'I want to make some friends and I thought the best way to do it would be to join in with some of the church activities.'

Church sex romps! 'But I thought you said that you had a problem?' he queried, eyeing her slim thighs, wondering how wet and tight her pussy was, and whether she masturbated or not. *All women masturbate, Entercock!*

'Yes, I do have a problem. I find it very difficult communicating with people, making friends. The reason being . . . well, I have these blackouts, you see. I'm usually out cold for about half an hour. It's not dangerous – it's just that it's embarrassing.'

'Oh, I see. Well . . . sorry, what was your name?'

'Amber.'

'Well, Amber, we don't have much in the way of church activities, I'm afraid. We have the odd fête, perhaps a coffee morning, but that's about all, really.'

'Oh, never mind, then,' she sighed despondently.

'If you want to meet people, I suppose you could call in to the church now and then. Give me a hand, perhaps, and get to know a few of the locals. We have confession, which is becoming increasingly popular, what with the way the world's going, and . . .'

'Give you a hand?'

That would be nice! 'Yes, help with the Bibles, the flowers, that sort of thing. In fact, the woman who used to do the flower arranging has left. After the incident in the vestry with the candle, she . . . well, it doesn't matter why she left, but you could take her job – if you want to, that is?'

'I'd love to! I've done some flower arranging before and, even though I say it myself, I'm not bad at it.'

I've done some deflowering! 'Good. Look, I've got things to do, sadly, but call in to the church this evening about seven and I'll show you the ropes.' *And my prick!*

'Right, I'll see you later, then.'

'Do you live with your parents, Amber?'

'No, on my own.'

Perfect! 'Bought a place, have you?'

'Yes, a cottage just down the lane.'

'Not Thornycroft Cottage, surely?'

'Yes, that's the one.'

'You must be doing well to be able to afford that place!'

'The money was left to me. I . . . I'm fairly well off so I don't need to work.'

'Ah, I see. Right, until this evening, then.'

Showing the young filly out, Father Will was convinced she'd been sent to spy on him. The newspaper could easily have rented the cottage as part of the plan to expose him. But would they really go that far? Yes, he decided, they would! But he'd play along with the game until he'd discovered just what was going on. Besides, there was a chance that he'd have his evil way with the young Amber, and he couldn't let her slip through his fingers!

Answering the phone, he grinned to hear Chloë's summery voice. 'Samantha Lovejoy has just gone down to the perimeter fence, by the pond!' she enlightened him excitedly.

'Really? Right, I'll do some nosing around and see exactly what it is that she gets up to down there. Thanks, Chloë.'

'May I stay with you again tonight?' she asked shyly.

'Yes, but don't come round until about ten. I'm having a visitor, you see.'

'A girl?'

'No, no! The bishop . . . he's coming to talk . . . Anyway, about ten o'clock.'

'All right, 'bye. Oh, and Father.'

'Yes, Chloë?'

'I love you!'

Oh Christ!

Wandering into the lounge naked, her body wet from the shower, Annie smiled at Father Will. 'I've got some free time if you feel like—'

'I haven't got any free time, I'm afraid – but I'll make time for you, Annie! Come here, you sexy little thing!'

'You are awful, Father!' she squealed as he cupped her pouting cunt lips in his palm and gently sucked on her elongated nipple.

'Yes, and I get worse!' he laughed. 'Tell me, Annie, what does your husband like in bed?'

'Nothing! That's one reason I'm on the game – it's the only way to make sure I get fucked regularly!'

'I'll fuck you regularly, my dirty little whore!'

'You'd better answer the phone first.'

'There's no fucking peace for . . . Hallo, Father Entercock speaking.'

'Father, it's me, Josie.'

'What is it this time?' he asked irritably as Annie knelt on the floor and lifted his cassock.

'I just wanted to make sure that your phone's working all right.'

'Of course it is – why shouldn't it be?'

'I . . . I tried to ring you earlier and . . . Can I come round?'

'No, I'm busy just now. What is it, Josie, what do you want?'

'Nothing – forget it.'

'I'm . . . Ah, God! Sorry, I'm very busy . . . Ah, ah! We'll talk later, Josie. Ah . . .'

Dropping the receiver, Father Will looked down at his hard penis, the solid head engulfed in Annie's hot mouth. 'Do that deep throat bit you did to the old man!' he gasped.

'You were watching, you sad pervy!' she spluttered, her big brown eyes gazing into his.

'Yes, 'fraid so. It was an incredible sight!'

'All right, here goes.'

Adjusting the angle of her neck, Annie went down on the priest's penis, taking the entire length of his solid knob deep down her throat like a sword swallower. 'God, that's good!' he cried as she began to move back and forth, massaging his glans with her hot tonsils. Quickly, his sperm rose and gushed from his pulsating knob, Annie savouring his male come as she murmured through her nose – delightfully, she had the *savoir faire* to swallow, suck and breathe simultaneously. His balls drained, he shuddered as he watched his long penis withdraw from her mouth, the thick shaft glistening with her saliva, the knob shining.

'Sorry I was so quick,' he apologized. 'It's just that I've never experienced anything like that before!'

'I thought you'd enjoy it,' she smiled as she stood up and licked her lips.

'What other tricks have you got up your knickers?' he asked as he pulled his cassock down to cover his limp penis.

'Oh, you'd be surprised!' she laughed. 'And I never wear knickers!'

'I once saw a film where this girl fucked a door . . .'

'A door?'

'Well, the door *knob*. She . . .'

'I can do that! Watch!' she giggled as she bounded across the room.

Opening the lounge door, Annie stood on her toes, her legs parted, and manipulated her pussy lips over the huge brass doorknob. Clinging to the door, she began her fucking motions, gyrating her hips, taking the whole knob into her tight, wet hole.

'See!' she panted triumphantly. 'It's easy!'

'Christ! Show me some more tricks!' he enthused as she slipped the knob from her hole.

'Here's one you'll love!' she giggled, laying her naked body on the floor. 'I'm a bit of a contortionist – watch this!'

Bringing her knees up either side of her head, she grabbed her buttocks, moving her head ever closer to her now gaping crack. The priest watched in sheer disbelief as her mouth neared her swollen pussy lips, sure that she'd never managed to lick them. Rocking on her curved back, she poked her tongue out and licked the entire length of her bulging slit, finally managing to poke her tongue into her open hole.

'God, I wish I could do that!' he gasped, watching her tongue disappear into her tight fanny.

'You can, come on!' she laughed, moving her head back.

'Stay just as you are!' he ordered her, kneeling down and plunging his stiff penis between her swollen lips. 'God, deep penetration or what!' he cried. 'I can almost get my balls in!'

'Ah, that tastes good!' she breathed, licking the cream off his glistening shaft as he slipped it in and out of her orifice.

'Bloody hell! I've never been fucked and licked at the same time by the same girl before!'

'There's a first time for everything. Now give me a bloody good shafting!'

As his sperm spurted from his throbbing knob, he withdrew from her squeezing vaginal sheath and drove his tool deep into her mouth, filling her cheeks with his seed until it dribbled down her chin and splattered on down over her vaginal lips. As he sat back on his heels, his knob dangling, spent, he watched the girl lick the spilled sperm, still unable to believe that she was actually licking her own fanny.

Straightening out, she lay on the floor, smiling as she caught the priest's incredulous gaze. 'Well, what do you think?' she asked as she opened her legs and gently massaged her clitoris.

'I think it's incredible! I'd love some pictures of you licking your cunt like that. Christ, I could make a fortune . . .'

'I never do pictures. Anyway, my next client will be here shortly, so I'd better get ready for him.'

'OK, I'd better be going. Have a good one!' he called as he left the room.

Slipping into his office to check his diary, he realized that he was getting behind with church work and decided to spend the following day catching up. 'There'll be no screwing tomorrow, Entercock!' he breathed. 'A wank maybe, but no fucking! Oh, shit – tomorrow's Sunday!' Hearing movement in the church, he investigated to discover a young nun walking down the aisle. *Must go down to the pond.*

'Good morning!' he called. 'Father Entercock – Will Entercock.'

'Good morning, Father – I'm Sister Felicity,' the nun replied softly.

Thought as much! 'And what can I do for you, Sister?'

'I just thought I'd come and make your acquaintance – I'm from the convent.'

'Come into my office, Sister. Would you like some coffee?'

'Have you anything stronger?'

Scotch, gin, vodka, lager, bitter . . . grass! 'Stronger, Sister?'

'I like a little tipple now and then.'

Don't we all? 'This *is* a church, Sister!'

'Sorry, I just thought I'd ask. It's a lovely church, isn't it? I noticed the new roof when I walked up the lane.'

'Yes, it was completed earlier this year.'

'How on earth did you manage to raise the money?'

'Fêtes, coffee mornings, the collections . . .' *Prostitution, alcohol, tobacco, wacky-back . . .*

'You must have a fête every day of the week! The roof must have cost a fortune!'

'It did! Anyway, how long have you been at Hardmound Convent?'

'Only a few months. To be honest, I'm leaving, getting out of this game altogether,' she smiled, lifting her habit to reveal her long stockinged legs. 'I'm going back to stripping, there's good money in that. I'll give you a demo, if you like.'

'Certainly not, Sister!' *She must have a tape recorder!*

'Come on, you look like a normal man – enjoy yourself! Besides, I need to get some practice in.'

'I have to ask you to leave my church, I'm afraid. And all I can say is that the convent will be far better off without the likes of you! I'm sorry, Sister, but I'm a man of the cloth. I've taken vows, as you have – and I'm celibate!'

That'll confuse the Mother Fucker! he thought jubilantly as the nun lowered her habit and fled the church. *Me*, turning down the offer of a young nun's wet cunt? That'll screw the old hag!

Walking down the lane, Father Will slipped through the bushes and made his way through the convent grounds to the pond by the perimeter fence. He'd left it rather late, but he hoped to discover exactly what the pretty Samantha Lovejoy got up to. Stealing past some bullrushes by the pond's edge, he spotted Samantha lying on the grass, sunning herself. Nothing untoward here, he thought as he crouched behind a bush.

As he was about to walk over to the girl, he noticed someone wandering around the far side of the pond. The middle-aged man, wearing a dark suit and carrying a briefcase, waved to Samantha as he approached her, a broad grin across his face. The priest recognized the man, but he couldn't for the life of him think where he'd seen him.

'Hi, Sam!' the man smiled as he sat next to the girl, dumping his briefcase on the grass.

'Hi, Tom. You're late,' she reprimanded.

'Yes, I'm sorry – I couldn't get out of the house. There's a Green Paper . . . anyway, you don't want to know about that.'

'How's my old man?'

'Stirring it up, as usual.'

Suddenly Father Will remembered where he'd seen the man before – on television. 'Christ, Tom Gower – the MP for Piddlington South!' he gasped, wondering what on earth he was doing meeting the young Samantha.

'I haven't got much time,' the man said, pulling at Samantha's gymslip. 'So let's get started, shall we?'

'Money first!' Samantha said firmly as he pulled her blouse open.

'Don't you trust me?' he asked, pulling on her bra to release her young breasts and tweaking her erect nipples.

'Trust you? Trust a *politician*? You must be joking!'

'Go on then, there's your money,' he laughed, pulling some notes from his pocket.

Standing up, Samantha instructed the Honourable Member to

remove her gymslip. In his desperation, he almost tore the garment from her young body. 'God, I've waited for this!' he cried, tossing her bra aside as he tugged her panties down to reveal her smooth mound. 'You've shaved your cunt!' he observed gleefully.

'Yes, I did it for the priest!' she laughed as he buried his face between her soft pussy lips, breathing in her sweet girl-scent.

'The priest?' he echoed, licking the length of her young crack.

'Yes – he fucked me in the woods.'

'What? A priest fucked you?'

'Why not? You're an MP, so why not a priest?'

'Yes, but I've never fucked you.'

'That's because you're weird.'

'Talking of weird, let's get started!' he enthused, hurriedly stripping off as Samantha lay her naked body on the grass.

Pulling a plastic bag from his briefcase, he passed it to Samantha and lay back on the grass, his long penis pointing to the blue sky. Taking several pineapple rings from the bag, the girl slipped them over his shaft, piling them high until only his purple head remained visible. Reaching for his case, she grabbed a can from inside it and squirted cream over his glans.

'That feels good,' the MP breathed appreciatively as the girl covered his heavy balls with thick cream. 'Get the banana now.' Taking the fruit from his case, the girl kneeled astride his head, her gaping crack hovering invitingly above his mouth as she leaned forward and began licking the cream from his knob. Peeling the banana, he slipped it between her swollen pussy lips, pressing the soft fruit deep into her tight hole before grabbing the can and squirting cream between her thighs.

Father Will looked on in amazement as the couple licked and sucked between each other's legs. His own penis stiffening as he watched the MP eat the banana from the girl's sex, he resolved to try the same trick with her at the earliest opportunity.

'My bum!' Samantha cried as she nibbled the pineapple rings from the hard, twitching penis. Grabbing another banana, the MP parted the girl's buttocks, massaging cream into her dark crease before presenting the tip of the banana to her small hole. As the fruit slipped into her tight anal sheath, Samantha gasped, her naked body visibly trembling as her hole was stretched and filled. Taking another banana, the Honourable Member for Piddlington South slipped it deep into her creamy sodden cunt, leaving only the tip emerging between her shaven lips. Both eating ravenously, their faces covered in cream, the unlikely couple writhed on the soft grass as their orgasms neared.

'Coming!' the politician warned as he slobbered on the banana emerging between Samantha's buttocks. Suddenly, his own delicacy shot from his knob, covering the girl's face as she licked her fruity prize. Engulfing his throbbing member in her hot mouth, she swallowed his spurting cream, her cunt expelling the remains of the banana as her muscles spasmed in orgasm.

Licking between her legs, the cream from her clitoris, as she shuddered, the MP ordered her to lick his balls. Both lost in their debauchery, they cleansed each other's genitalia, lapping up the remnants of the cream, their slippery come. Rolling from the man's body, Samantha lay on her back, the hot sun bathing her pert breasts and her inflamed pussy as she rested.

'That was bloody good!' the MP asserted as he sat up, wiping his mouth. 'How did you get those weals across your bum?'

'One of the nuns thrashed me,' she enlightened him.

'Bloody hell! It all happens in Cumsdale, doesn't it!'

'Sure does! Are you going to fuck me now?'

'I . . . no, I'd rather not.'

'Why not?'

'You know that I . . .'

'I don't understand why you only like fucking my mouth. What about my bum, then – fuck my bum.'

'Really? I didn't realize that you're into . . .'

'The priest fucked my bum – it was great!'

'I must meet this perverted priest!'

Rolling on to her stomach and raising her hips, Samantha offered her bottom to the Honourable Member. 'Slip it in, then!' she coaxed as he knelt behind her, his ample rod in his hand.

'Some lubrication, first,' he murmured, squirting a good helping of cream between her buttocks.

Father Will watched the MP's solid knob sink into the girl's bottom-hole, the cream smothering his shaft as he drove his weapon deeper into her quivering body. 'More!' Samantha begged, pushing her buttocks higher to receive her prize.

'God, you've got a tight little arse!' he cried as he pushed his rod further into her bowels until his balls came to rest against her swollen cunt lips.

'And you've got a big prick!' Samantha panted, reaching for her clitoris as he began his shafting.

Suddenly remembering that he had to make a delivery to the pub, and pick up the rolls of film, Father Will prayed for the couple to hurry up – to writhe in their climaxes before he had to leave. Answering his prayer, Samantha frigged her clitoris and cried out, wailing her appreciation of the MP's penis as he pumped her full of his come. Both gasping, they collapsed onto the grass, rolling to one side, giving the priest a beautiful view of Samantha's gaping cunt – and of her brown ring stretched tightly around the base of the honorable member.

'Will you allow me to thrash you?' he asked as he slipped his penis from Samantha's tight bottom-hole.

'I didn't know you were into that!' she returned.

'And I didn't know that you were! So, how about it?'

'You haven't got a whip.'

'No, but my leather belt will suffice.'

'Go on, then – but not too hard,' she grinned, rolling over to present her taut buttocks.

'No, not like that. Stand up, feet apart, and touch your toes,' he instructed briskly.

Eyeing the girl's pouting cunt lips bulging beneath her splayed buttocks, Father Will knew he should be leaving. But he had to stay to witness the thrashing. Pulling his belt from his trousers and positioning himself behind the girl, the MP tested his swing as if about to drive a golf ball down the fairway.

Raising the leather belt above his head, he brought it down, landing it squarely across the girl's buttocks. 'Argh! That hurt!' she complained as the belt swished through the air again and cracked across the reddening flesh. This time, she didn't screech, but parted her feet further and bent further over. Again, the belt lashed her burning flesh. Her muscles tightening, squeezing the sperm from her anal sheath, the priest watched the creamy liquid run down to bathe her inflamed labia.

'More!' Samantha begged as the MP lashed her crimson buttocks. 'Harder!' Both lost in their lust, the thrashing continued until they collapsed to the ground, exhausted, panting their expletives. 'More! I want you to thrash my arse again!' Samantha demanded.

'Only if you do something for me,' the MP grinned, his solid penis in his hand as he lay back on the grass.

'What?' she asked with curiosity, resting on her elbows to admire his organ.

'Truss me up. Take the belt, and bind it around my cock, my balls.'

'Are you sure?' she laughed, taking the belt and wondering exactly what to do with it.

'Do it, and then wank me.'

Looping the belt around the base of his penis, Samantha ran one end under his thigh and tied it to the loose end. Pulling the leather tight, she watched as his penis bulged, the shaft swelling around the belt. 'Tie my balls up!' he ordered.

'What with?' she asked, a puzzled expression on her pretty face.

'In my case – there's some sticky tape in there.'

Taking the tape, Samantha began binding his heavy balls,

running the tape around his penis, his thighs, until only three inches of his shaft emerged from the entanglement of leather and tape. 'Now pull your knickers over my head,' he instructed the girl. Taking her stained panties, she tugged them over his head, positioning the damp crotch over his face before leaning back to admire her handiwork.

'They smell good!' he breathed. 'Now wank me!'

'The things you're into!' Samantha giggled as she took his penis in her small hand and began her wanking movements. 'You're a typical MP!'

'This is nothing,' he murmured through a mouthful of panties. 'I'll show you what I really like the next time we meet!'

Leaning over his tethered penis, the girl took the swollen knob into her mouth and sucked. Running her tongue round and round, she reached down for her clitoris, massaging the hard nodule. Her eyes closed, her blonde hair falling over her face, she masturbated her bud, sucked on the MP's throbbing knob, until his come spurted. Pulling away, she ran her hand up and down his shaft, the sperm splattering her face as she licked and slurped at his fountainhead. Finally engulfing the exploding glans in her hot mouth, she reached her own shuddering climax, her fingers vibrating over the tip of her clitoris as she sucked the remnants of his sperm into her mouth.

As she shuddered, her fingers slowing, her orgasm subsiding, she moved up to his face. Opening her mouth to let the sperm run out and drench her panties, she buried her face in the wet material, wiping the sperm over her mouth, breathing in her own femininity. Kissing the MP through her wet knickers, she moaned, writhing as the sperm covered her face. Near to another climax, she sat astride his head and lowered her shaven labia over his face, rubbing her open crack over the material, decanting her girl-come, mixing her juices with his sperm until she threw her head back and cried out in her climax.

'Lick me through my knickers!' she begged. 'Push my knickers up my cunt with your tongue!' Doing his best to comply, the MP pressed his tongue against the sodden material, pushing her panties into her open hole. 'That's good!' she cried as she shook violently, swivelling her hips, manoeuvring her gaping sex-valley to massage her bursting clitoris over his hot tongue. 'That's it! Ah, God – yes!'

Close to orgasm, the voyeur slipped away, leaving the couple to their debauchery, saddened slightly by Samantha's infidelity. But the Honourable Member for Piddlington South had given him some good ideas that he'd experiment with later. Can't have the young tart all to myself, he rationalized as he emerged from the bushes into the lane to bump into Josie.

'Brian's gone and lost our holiday photos,' she confided despondently as they walked down the lane together.

'That's a shame,' Father Will commiserated.

'He's coming back to take some more pictures.'

'When?'

'Tonight. He'd taken some really good shots, but he's gone and lost the film – bloody fool that he is.'

'Why come all the way back from London to take a few snaps of Cumsdale village?'

'He . . . he likes the place very much. Where are you going, anyway?'

'Where's anyone going?'

'What?'

'I'm going home to pack. I'm going away for a week or so – church business, I'm afraid.'

'A week? Oh no!'

'What's the problem?'

'Nothing. It's just that I've grown to like you and . . . I'll be leaving soon so . . .'

'And I've grown rather fond of you, Josie,' he smiled. 'Haven't got any sticky tape on you, have you?'

'What?'

'Nothing – it's all right.'

'When are you leaving?'

'This afternoon, so I'll miss Brian.'

'Oh, no! I . . . I've just remembered that I have to make a phone call,' she stammered, running off down the lane.

'Nice to have met you, Josie!' he called after her. *Nice to have fucked you!*

Loading his car with the order for the pub, Father Will prayed that he wouldn't bump into Josie. The last thing he needed was for the girl to spot him making the delivery! But she'd be packing her bags to return to London now that she'd failed in her mission. Although, knowing Josie, she'd be back to get her story!

'I've got your order, Jack,' the priest called, entering the pub by the rear door.

'Thanks, Will. Here's the film you wanted.'

'Thank God for that! I'll bring the booze in.'

'What's all this about?'

'What?'

'The three rolls of film, what's on them?'

'Not a lot – just two naked schoolgirls and a nun fucking each other.'

'Fucking?'

'Yes, you know what . . .'

'Course I do! But—'

'You don't want to know, Jack – believe me!'

'Where are you going to get them developed?'

'I don't know if I'll bother. Anyway, I'll bring your stuff in. Haven't got any sticky tape, have you?'

'Er . . . yes, somewhere. I'll find it for you.'

Dragging the last case of lager from the boot of his car, the priest happened to look up to see Josie spying on him from her window. 'Damn that fucking girl!' he cursed as he closed the boot. 'Persistent little bitch!'

Taking the money and a reel of sticky tape from Jack, he leaped into his car and sped back to the church, knowing that Josie would be hot on his heels. What to tell her? How to explain the booze when she launched her barrage of questions? Sitting in his office swigging lager, he desperately tried to formulate his plan.

'Are you there, Father,' Josie called predictably as she entered the church. 'Father Will, are you . . .'

'Yes, Josie, I'm here,' he replied wearily, emerging from his office.

'What were you doing at the pub?'

'You saw what I was doing – unloading the boot of my car.'

'Where did you get all that drink from?'

'I picked it up from another pub for Jack, the landlord. It was a favour, Josie – all right?'

'Oh, I just wondered where you'd got it from.'

'Does it really matter? I mean, what I do is my own business, surely?'

'Yes, of course. I was just intrigued, that's all.'

'You've asked me a lot of questions since you've been here, Josie. Why? I wonder. It's as if you've been following me, spying on me . . . You seem to turn up wherever I go. Brian was always sneaking in and out of bushes with his camera. What's it all about?'

'Nothing! We're on holiday, as you know. He likes taking pictures of birds and things, that's all. And as I said, I've grown to like you – I like your company.'

'Well, this is goodbye, Josie. I'm catching the train this afternoon and, as I said, I'll be away for a week or so, probably two. No doubt you'll be gone by the time I get back.'

'I suppose I might as well go today. There's nothing to keep me here, is there?'

'I thought Brian was coming back?'

'Sod Brian!'

'Oh. Well, goodbye, Josie. It's been nice meeting you.'

'Yes, thanks for . . . well, thanks. I feel quite sad, really.'

'Goodbyes are never easy. I have things to do, the priest who's filling in for me will be here shortly.'

'The things you said about the Reverend Mother were lies, weren't they?' she pursued.

'No, no! It's all true, Josie. The things that go on at the convent are . . . Look, you might think badly of me, but what I get up to is nothing compared with . . .'

'Do you really screw your parishioners' wives?'

'Yes, why not? I mean, I like sex, as you do. We had some fun, didn't we? You enjoyed your romps with me, didn't you?'

'Yes, I did. I'll miss you.'

'And I'll miss you, Josie.'

'That girl, Annie . . . the one who did things to me when I was handcuffed. Is she your . . .'

'She's just someone I've known for a long time. We worked together when I was with MI5.'

'What's all this MI5 stuff?'

'Can't tell you, I'm afraid.'

'Does she live with you?'

'No. She comes to see me now and then – she's good at shampooing carpets. Why all these questions?'

'You never did get me an invite to the nuns' orgies, did you?'

'No, I wasn't able to. Why all these questions?'

'Oh, nothing. Well, goodbye, Father,' Josie whispered, a tear in her eye as she left the church.

With a pang of sorrow, Father Will returned to the presbytery, wondering when Josie would leave. He'd have to stay in hiding until he was sure that she'd gone back to London, but that wouldn't present a problem. Switching the radio on, wondering where Annie was, he sat at the kitchen table listening to the Reverend Mother working in her office.

Paperwork, he mused as she shuffled papers around on her

desk. How boring! Grabbing a can of lager from the fridge, he lit a cigarette and thought of Josie. He pictured her naked, her young pussy shaved, her cream flowing from her hot hole as he licked her clitoris. Nothing lasts, he reflected sadly – nothing lasts.

'Sorry to disturb you, Reverend Mother,' Josie's voice emanated from the radio. 'But I need to talk to you.'

'That's all right, Josie. Sit down.'

'Thanks. This business of exposing Father Entercock,' she began. 'I'm going back to London this afternoon. Brian's lost all the rolls of film he took of Father Will, and I've got nothing on him whatsoever. My tape recorder kept playing up, the bug we'd put in the presbytery didn't work, and the phone tap seems to have packed up, so . . .'

'You're going to give up?'

'Well, seeing as he's going away for a week or two, I don't see that I've any choice!'

'Going away?'

'Yes, church business, or something.'

'Did he tell you that?'

'Yes, why?'

'Just let me make a phone call – I've an idea that he's lying!'

Turning the radio up, Father Will knew that the Reverend Mother was going to ring the bishop. 'Shit!' he cursed. 'That'll blow it!' Dashing into the lounge, he quickly dialled the bishop's number, leaving the receiver on the table before returning to the kitchen.

'It's engaged,' Mother Mary said irritably as she replaced the receiver. 'I'll try again in a minute. Is there nothing you've been able to get on Father Entercock?' she pursued.

'Nothing at all. It seems that everything keeps going wrong. I can't think why, because the equipment has never let us down before.'

'Perhaps he got to it?'

'No, he couldn't have done. The tape broke, that was one

problem. The bug in his lounge . . . there was a power cut and then the thing packed up . . .'

'Have you got it back?'

'No, I've not been able to retrieve it. I'll have to leave it now.'

Redialling the bishop, the nun was infuriated to find that his number was still engaged. 'He's probably talking to the archbishop, I'll try later,' she fumed.

'I'd better be going,' Josie sighed. 'I know he's not lying, so there's not much point in my hanging around.'

'But you were so near to getting your story!'

'I've got the story – I know exactly what he gets up to. But without proof . . .'

'If you know, then keep trying! You can't just walk away from a story like this!'

'He told me all sorts of things about you.'

'Whatever he's told you, I wouldn't believe him, if I were you. He's a natural born liar.'

'I had thought of investigating *you*!' Josie laughed. 'When he told me what goes on here, I thought I'd expose you!'

'He's a liar, Josie. He'd have you believe that I was a man if he wanted to!'

'Yes, he's a liar, all right! They'll send someone else down to replace me, so don't worry – Father Entercock will have his comeuppance! And I'll probably be sacked for my incompetence! Anyway, goodbye, Reverend Mother.'

'Goodbye, Josie. Let me know who they send to replace you, won't you?'

'Yes, I'll make sure that they contact you. Here's my mobile phone number. Give me a call if anything develops.'

'I'll keep in touch. What about your sister?'

'Sister? Oh, right – I'll let you know. Goodbye.'

'Tell your replacement to keep away from the convent, won't you?'

'Why?'

'I don't want reporters nosing around here. I've nothing to hide, of course. It's just that I don't want people nosing around, it would upset the girls, among other things.'

'Brian saw Father Will with two of your girls and a nun in the grounds of Hallworth Church.'

'What were they doing?'

'They were all naked. Brian had taken pictures—'

'Why didn't you tell me this before?'

'Without proof, there was little point in telling you.'

'Sister Teresa! Right, I'll have her for this!'

Switching the radio off, Father Will puffed on his cigarette, wondering who'd replace Josie. Sister Teresa would be all right. All she'd have to say to the Reverend Mother was *nipple clamps* and she'd be in clover. But the old bat would soon discover who the two girls were – and expel them.

Whatever, he was free, for a while, at least, and he decided to throw a party – an orgy. Suddenly realizing that the Reverend Mother would ring Josie the minute she discovered he hadn't gone away, he frowned. He had Sunday mass in the morning – he could hardly hide.

Wandering into the lounge to replace the telephone receiver, he flopped into his armchair, desperately trying to plan his next move. Why had everything started to go wrong? he wondered. Perhaps it was time to get out. Get out before the going got too tough. If only he could expose the Mother Superior, catch her red-handed – red-knobbed – with the bishop. Nail the pair, and at least Sister Teresa and the girls would be safe for ever.

The time had come to go on the attack, he decided. 'No more pussy-footing, Entercock!' he breathed aloud. 'Only pussy-fucking! It's time to launch a full-scale attack!'

CHAPTER EIGHT

Amber arrived at the church at seven that evening complaining that she felt a blackout coming on. Placing the reel of sticky tape he'd been contemplating back into the desk drawer, Father Will sat the girl down, praying that she wouldn't pass out in his office.

'It starts with a slight feeling of dizziness,' she explained breathlessly. 'Don't be alarmed if I fade out – as I told you, it only lasts for half an hour and then I'll be as right as rain.'

Flopping back in her chair, Amber's head lolled and her eyes closed, her arms falling limp by her side. 'Oh, great!' Father Will exclaimed softly. 'That's all I need!' Eyeing the girl's short skirt, her slender thighs, he grinned – the devil lurking, coaxing. 'Could just take a peek at her panties,' he murmured, closing and locking the office door. 'Deliver me unto temptation!'

Dropping to his knees, he gingerly lifted the girl's skirt. Gazing at her tight red panties, bulging slightly to restrain her swelling pussy lips, he smiled. 'Just take a look inside,' he whispered, pulling the elasticated waistband away from her smooth skin.

Her dark bush had been neatly trimmed, her soft, warm mound rising high from her valley. Her tightly closed crack opened slightly as her thighs fell apart, affording the priest a good view of her pinken inner lips, protruding from her sex-valley – begging for his tongue.

Sticky-tape her lips open?

It was too good to be true – an attractive young girl, lying there, her young pussy defenceless, vulnerable! And he had at least half an hour to enjoy her young body. 'This is wrong of me, Amber, I know, but I simply can't help myself!' he whispered as he lifted her buttocks and tugged her panties down to her knees. Slipping the garment over her feet, he spread her thighs, gazing at her glistening pinken slit as it opened fully to reveal her intimate sex-folds.

Settling between her legs, he leaned forward, kissing her fleshy hillocks, licking the soft inner folds as they unfurled, breathing in her heady yin bouquet. 'God, you taste wonderful,' he murmured as he parted her inner lips with the tip of his tongue, seeking out the entrance to her vaginal sheath, savouring the milky globules within.

His beast solid beneath his cassock, he looked up to the girl's face – serene, innocent, a sleeping beauty. Her pretty mouth open slightly, he imagined his penis there, between her full red lips, resting against her wet tongue. But no – her nether orifice.

'I'm just going to slip my cock into your tight cunt, my child,' he breathed, his hands trembling with the excitement of dangerous sex as he lifted his cassock. 'You won't get anything out of this, I'm sorry to say – but I will!'

Pulling her forward in the chair, he ran the head of his penis up and down her slippery crack, lubricating his warhead with her cream. 'And now in!' he whispered as he watched his knob disappear between her swelling pussy lips. 'Ah, nice and warm and wet!' Pushing his hips forward, he inserted the full length of his solid rod into her vaginal sheath. His glans resting against her cervix, he absorbed the heat of her young body, pulling her engorged cunt lips up and apart to see the root of his shaft encompassed by her wet inner flesh.

His lust rising, he began his pistoning rhythm, ramming the girl's soft cervix, gazing at her inner lips clinging to his glistening shaft, her juices lubricating their coupling. Wondering whether to fill her spasming cunt with his sperm, or to pump his fruits deep into her bottom-hole, he lifted her T-shirt to admire her firm young breasts.

Her red lace bra straining, her heavy breasts ballooning, creating a deep cleavage, he lifted the garment up and away from her body, releasing his prize. Given their freedom, her nipples lengthened, her areolae darkening in response to the priest's attentions. Leaning forward, he took first one and then the other nipple into his mouth, hardening the protrusions until they stood proud from her brown discs.

Moving his attention back to the centre of her femininity, he massaged her erect clitoris, wondering whether she'd be able to achieve her orgasm while in her apparent coma. The budling grew, hardened as he caressed its sensitive tip. Her juices flowing, bathing his full swinging balls, he plunged in and out of her love tube. Her breathing becoming heavier, he wondered if she'd open her eyes and discover his lewd infringement, his defilement of her luscious young body, and scream her disgust – her delight.

Thrusting deeper and harder into her young body, he sensed his seed rising, his balls rolling. 'This is it, my child!' he cried as he spurted his first spurt into her spasming cunt. Gasping, she tossed her head, licking her dry lips as her body convulsed, shuddered as her climax rocked her very soul.

Filling her chasm with his copious sperm, he thrust even harder, battering her cervix, ramming her quivering body until he'd drained his balls. Falling depleted over her heaving breasts, mouthing her elongated nipples, he relaxed, breathing in the perfume of her breasts, luxuriating in her vaginal heat.

Finally withdrawing his penis from her flesh-depths, he adjusted his cassock, wondering when she'd return to waking consciousness. Slipping her panties over her feet, he tugged them up her legs, lifting her buttocks to cover her dripping sex, to conceal the evidence of his lechery. The red material soaking up the cocktail of sperm and girl-come oozing from her young pussy, he lifted her heavy breasts into the cups of her bra and pulled her

T-shirt down. Eyeing her wet panties, he prayed that she'd not realize what had happened – that her vagina had been invaded, pumped full of sperm.

Settling back in his chair, he opened a can of lager and lit a cigarette, blowing smoke high into the air, relaxing, waiting for the teenage beauty to join him. She hadn't been sent by the newspaper, he was sure – from heaven maybe, but not a newspaper! They'd hardly send someone prone to half-hour blackouts, he decided.

'Oh, hallo,' the girl murmured, within minutes, opening her eyes and adjusting her buttocks to make herself comfortable in her chair.

'Ah, you've returned to the land of the living,' Father Will smiled benevolently.

'Yes, I'm sorry about . . .'

'No, no – it's not your fault, my child. How do you feel?'

'Sort of . . .' Her words tailed off as she reached discreetly between her legs, feeling the discomfort, the wetness there. 'Did anything happen while I was out?' she asked anxiously.

'Happen?' he echoed. *Priest comes on to blackout girl.*

'I feel as if . . . My clothes are . . . Did I fall on the floor or something?'

'No, but you did slide down in the chair.'

'Perhaps that's it, then. How long was I out?'

'Not long. Anyway,' *now I've deflowered you* 'about the flower arranging . . .'

'Where do the flowers come from?'

'Gifts, mainly – but I do buy some in.'

'May I take a look around the church?' she asked, rising to her feet and making for the door. 'Oh, it's locked!' she exclaimed, turning to face him as she tried the handle.

'Yes . . . I . . . I locked it earlier. The cleaning woman tends to be somewhat nosy and . . . I was on the phone, you see, and . . .'

'Oh, right. I do feel strange,' she murmured, pulling her panties out from between her buttocks. 'Are you *sure* nothing happened?'

'I told you, you slipped down in the chair, that's all.' *And then I fucked you!*

She'd know exactly what had happened the minute she got home and slipped her drenched knickers off, the priest thought. Maybe it hadn't been such a good idea to fuck her after all. Perhaps she *was* a plant – but who could have resisted such temptation?

'Take a look around the church, Amber. I've just got to make a quick phone call, and I'll be with you,' he suggested. The minute she'd left the office, still pulling on her panties through her skirt, he grabbed the phone book and rang the village estate agent, hoping that he'd be working late, as usual.

'He's popped out, can I help?' a girl asked.

'Is Thornycroft Cottage still on the market?' he enquired.

'Yes, it is, sir. Would you care to view it?'

I wouldn't mind viewing yours! 'Er, I'll get back to you. Thanks.'

Lying little bitch! he cursed as he replaced the receiver. Josie, Brian, the newspaper – *they*'d sent the girl. Christ! Her so-called blackout! Faked? Obviously! But she had no handbag, no recorder, no bug, so . . .

Play it cool, Entercock!

'So, Amber, what do you think of the church?' he asked, joining her at the altar. *Must talk to Annie about the altar*.

'My only criticism is that there are no flowers, but that's what I'm here for, isn't it?'

'Indeed, it is. I'll order some from the local nursery tomorrow morning. Come round at, say, ten, and you can show me your arrangements.' *I've already seen them!*

'OK. What about Bibles and things?'

'We'll discuss that tomorrow, I expect you want to get home after your . . .'

'Oh, yes . . . I do feel a little strange. I have to wear this,' she said, showing off her doctor's name and phone number engraved on her gold identity bracelet. 'If anything serious happens to me during a blackout, my doctor can be contacted.'

'It's a serious condition, then?'

'Fairly. I forget the medical term for it. Anyway, I'll be going.'

'I'll walk down the lane with you. I'd like to see your cottage.'

Gotya, bitch!

'No, it's all right. I won't be going straight back to the cottage as I've one or two things to do first. I'll see you tomorrow morning.'

'Very good, I'll order the flowers.'

'About ten o'clock, then – 'bye.'

Slipping out of the church, Father Will followed the girl down the lane and watched her climb into a car. She was obviously the bait – but where was the trap? No one could prove that he'd used her delectable young body for his own pleasures, so why go to the trouble of feigning a blackout? Although, having seen her bracelet, he was now in two minds.

Walking towards Thornycroft Cottage, he wondered if she was staying at The Woodman's Arms. A phone call to Jack would soon establish that, but for now he decided to view the cottage – through the windows, at least.

The front gate fallen off, the garden overgrown, paint peeling from the woodwork, the place looked forsaken. Peering in through the dirty lounge window, the priest smiled. Bare boards, no furniture – nothing.

Lying little bitch!

Quite an eventful day, he mused as he made his way to the pub, not really giving a damn now whether he was seen drinking at the bar or not – or by whom.

If a man can't have a bloody drink, then what's the point in living?

'Evening, Will,' Jack beamed as the priest approached the bar and grinned.

'Evening, Jack. Lager, please – a pint. Haven't got a young girl staying here have you?'

'Christ! You still after young birds?'

'I'm always after young birds! But this one's different. Her name, or so she tells me, is Amber – she's about eighteen, blonde, painted nails, make-up . . .'

'Nope, no one like that staying 'ere, unfortunately,' he replied, sliding a pint across the counter.

'Did Josie check out?'

'Yep! First that ugly git and then 'er.'

Finding a corner table, Father Will sat down and lit a cigarette, thankful, but sad, in a way, that Josie had left. But where was the young Amber staying? And why lie about the cottage? It was pretty obvious that sooner or later it would come to light that the property was empty. Crazy! he reflected. In their desperation to nail him, they'd all gone bloody crazy!

Noticing a young woman enter the pub, the priest gazed at her long shapely legs as she walked up to the bar. In her early twenties, with short blonde hair and a damned good figure, she was an extremely delectable young filly. Taking her drink from the bar, she turned, wondering where to sit, he surmised. Smiling his charming smile as she neared his table, he stood up.

'Please, do join me,' he invited.

'Oh, thank you, Father,' she replied as she sat opposite him, her low-cut blouse revealing her heaving spheres, her deep cleavage.

'Father William Entercock,' he proffered, extending his hand. *Women trust men of the cloth – misguided fools!*

'My name's Cheryl,' she smiled, reciprocating.

'I haven't seen you in the village before – have you recently moved to Cumsdale, or are you just visiting?'

'I'm on holiday. Well, not a holiday exactly. You see, my husband and I have split up.'

'Oh, I'm sorry to hear that.' *You'll be needing some physical comfort, then?*

'It's a sort of trial separation. I've come here for a week or so just to think – to get away from it all.'

'Where are you staying?'

'There's a small boarding house on the other side of the village. It's rather quaint, as is the landlady.'

'Ah, that'll be Mrs Weston. A lovely old lady.'

'Yes, she's been so kind to me. Anyway, I thought I'd take a walk through the village and visit the local pub, as it's such a lovely evening.'

His gaze transfixed between her rounded breasts, the priest was sure that he knew the woman from somewhere. There was something familiar about her, but he couldn't think what it was. Can't suspect everyone! he thought, raising his eyes to meet hers. Rolling her glass between her palms, she returned his smile.

'I don't know where I went wrong in my marriage,' she confided dolefully. 'He . . . he had an affair, you see, and I couldn't forgive him for it. I tried, God knows . . . sorry, I mean, I really tried to put it out of my mind, but I kept picturing him in another woman's bed and . . .'

'I understand. You feel betrayed, cheated . . . But don't blame yourself, as so many people do in a situation like this. I'm sure that it wasn't your fault.'

'*He* blames me. He said that if I'd been more loving, more understanding, then . . .'

'Sex, was it? Incompatible on the sexual front?'

'Yes. You see . . . look, don't get me wrong, but there are things he likes that I simply couldn't bring myself to do.'

'Some men are very demanding, I know.'

'Yes, but I had my demands, too.'

Really? 'What, sexually, you mean?'

'Oh, yes. I don't know why I'm telling you all this. I suppose, as you're a priest, I feel that I can talk to you.'

'That's what I'm here for, my child. Sexual problems often arise within marriages, and they often destroy marriages.'

'I hope mine's not destroyed. I do love him, but . . .'

'But what, Cheryl?'

'There are certain things I like. To find sexual satisfaction, sexual fulfilment, I . . . I like to be used. I've shocked you, haven't I?'

'No, no! I've heard it all in my time as a priest! You see, I don't just preach the Lord's way, I offer counselling, help to those in need – whatever their need may be. What do you mean by *used*, exactly?' *Fucked up your tight little bottom-hole?*

'When I was at school, a very strict boarding school, I was always in trouble – and always getting the cane. My form mistress was . . . She'd take me into the stock room after lessons and bend me over and . . . she used to pull my knickers down and cane my bare flesh.'

Firm, rounded, taut . . . 'I see. But, what has this to do with your marriage?'

'I came to enjoy the cane. It made me feel . . . I don't know, I shouldn't be telling you all this, really.'

'It helps to talk, Cheryl. A problem shared, as they say.'

'Yes, I suppose it does help. I've never told anyone about this before. I've told my husband, of course, but he doesn't understand.'

'So, how do you like being used, as you put it?'

'Well, I grew to like being caned and . . . I suppose he's not into that sort of thing – some people aren't, are they?'

'We all have different tastes, likes and dislikes. So, what you're saying is that you enjoy being caned, and he won't do it, is that right?'

'Yes, but there's more.'

More? Deo Gratias!

'Apart from the cane, I enjoy being tied up. It all came from my experiences at school.'

'What, your form mistress tied you up?'

'Once or twice, yes.'

Better and better! 'And your husband wouldn't do that, either?'

'No, he wouldn't. He has no understanding whatsoever. He wouldn't even try to understand me – he just called me a pervert.'

Join the club!

Father Will was sure that he'd met Cheryl before as she sipped her drink, her eyes fluttering, catching his now and then. But, he concluded, he'd met, and fucked, so many women in his time, he couldn't remember them all! He found Cheryl captivating – not only because she was extremely attractive, or the fact that she was heavily into bondage. There was something else about her – something indefinable. He felt as if he'd known her for years, as if they were old friends recounting memories, chatting about the good old days. With her he could talk – open up and talk about anything and everything. An ideal conscript to fight the church hierarchy, he decided.

'We all have problems, Cheryl,' he smiled. 'I have more than most! In fact, I have so many problems just now that . . . I'm sorry, you're supposed to be unloading *your* problems, not taking mine on board. This may seem like an odd question, but do you masturbate?' *Me and my big mouth!*

'Yes, I do. I started when I was at school. In fact, that boarding school has a lot to answer for!'

'And a lot to be grateful for.'

'Grateful?' she queried.

'Yes – masturbation is perfectly normal. You discovered yourself at school, your sexual identity.'

'But I also discovered caning and bondage and . . .'

'What's so terribly wrong with that? If you enjoy it, as you obviously do, then what's the problem?'

'My husband, for one thing!'

'Then . . . look, I shouldn't be telling you this really, but why not find yourself a man who *does* understand your wants, your needs?'

'Have an affair?'

'Yes, it might help to . . . Affairs often take the pressure off marriages, Cheryl. They relieve the pressure, the demands partners make on each other.'

'I can see your point, but . . . I don't know any men. And besides, how do I know if a man's into . . . into the things I like?'

Aren't all men? Suspicion looming, Father Will observed the girl, trying to see behind the façade, if there was one. She appeared genuine enough, but didn't they all? There again, she hadn't asked him any searching questions. She hadn't pried into his private life. In fact, she hadn't asked him anything.

'Would you like to come back to the presbytery for a coffee?' he asked, finishing his pint.

'I'd love to!'

'Good! We'll sit out in the garden. The night-scented stock is wonderful at this time of the evening.' *And I'll bet your cunt is, too!*

'You're into gardening, are you?'

'No, I'm a plumber by trade – or I was.'

'A plumber? What made you turn to the priesthood?'

'It's a long story. I left university, rebelled against the government for a while, worked at a girls' school as PE master for a year or so, and then, having been thrown out, I became a plumber. Shortly after that, I was recruited by MI5.'

'MI5?'

'Yes. But I can't tell you about that.'

'You've had quite an interesting life.'

'No, not really.'

Jack winked and mouthed something obscene as Father Will left the pub with Cheryl. Grinning, the priest gave him the thumbs-up as he closed the door. Another challenge, another conquest, he reflected as they wandered down the lane, the evening sun warming their backs, the birds singing. Thank God

Josie's buggered off back to London! he thought as they entered the presbytery. Annie'd done a disappearing trick, too.

Annie's tricks!

Filling the kettle, Father Will talked about the weather, eyeing the girl's thighs as she sat at the table and crossed her long legs. Wonder if she'd enjoy a session in Annie's room? he mused. Bondage, caning, masturbation – what else was she into? *Soon find out!* he thought, pouring her coffee.

'Sugar?' he asked, heaping three teaspoonfuls into his cup.

'No, thanks,' she replied. 'Do you mind if I smoke?'

'Be my guest. Here, have one of my roll ups, they're, er, aromatic. So, what other things are you into that your husband doesn't understand?'

'Nothing much, really,' she replied, lighting her cigarette. 'It's just the caning and bondage. Mind you, I've never tried anything else, so I wouldn't know. What's it like being celibate?'

'Celibate? I'm far from celibate!'

'But I thought . . .'

'No, no. I'm a man, Cheryl – a normal man with a normal sex-drive. Just because I'm a priest, it doesn't mean to say that I'm not sexually aware – or active, for that matter!'

'Do you have a regular woman friend?'

'No, no.'

'Then do you sleep around?'

'I suppose you could put it that way.'

'God! I always thought that men of the cloth were . . .'

'You obviously don't read the Sunday tabloids!' he laughed as he joined her at the table.

'I do, but I didn't believe it! So, do you have kinks, fetishes, or whatever they're called, like I do?'

'Very much so! As it happens, one of my favourites is bondage.' *Well, it is now!*

Cheryl held her hand over her mouth to stifle a gasp. She was genuine, all right – not from a poxy newspaper, he knew. 'I'm going to change,' he announced. 'I don't like wearing my cassock all the time – it chafes my—'

'I like it – don't change,' she smiled. 'To be honest, it really turns me on.'

'Turns you on? What, a cassock?' he laughed.

'Yes, must be another one of my kinks, I suppose. What do you like your women to wear?'

'God, I don't know! Got any suggestions?'

'Well, apart from wearing nothing, I enjoy going around without my knickers. I'm a bit of an exhibitionist, you see! I really shouldn't be telling you these things!'

'I'm a priest, Cheryl, so you can tell me everything. I don't suppose you'd like to . . .'

'There's nothing I'd like more!'

Standing up, the girl reached up her short skirt and slipped her knickers down. Father Will didn't glimpse her pussy as she pulled the garment off, but he knew that was part of the exhibitionist's game. She would allow him a peep as and when it suited her, as and when her pussy was ready, wet with arousal – and not before. Sitting at the table again, she crossed her legs and smiled as she held her black panties up, dangling them from her slender fingers.

'What shall I do with these?' she asked, deliberately showing him the crotch.

'Er . . . May I keep them?' *Another twenty quid in the bag!*

'I was hoping you'd say that. I like the idea of men sniffing my knickers while they masturbate!' she giggled, parting her thighs slightly as the aromatic 'tobacco' took effect. 'You do masturbate, don't you?'

'Of course – who doesn't?'

'My husband, for a start. At least, he says he doesn't,' she sighed, dropping her panties on to the table.

'I don't understand why he's not turned on by you, by bondage and caning and—'

'The woman he's been seeing is fifty-five. He obviously gets his kicks in the form of older women.'

'We're all different, I suppose,' Father Will replied, feasting his eyes on the girl's gaping sex-slit as she pulled her skirt up and parted her slender thighs a little further. 'Anyway, you seem a lot happier now. I don't like to see people upset, hurt by their partners.'

'Yes, I do feel happier now. I never thought I'd meet anyone like you. It's as if you've been sent – as if we were destined to meet. I'm so pleased that we bumped into each other.'

'Was all that true about your husband?'

'Of course it was! I wouldn't make it up!'

'It's just that you've changed so much since we met in the pub. You were lost, lonely – desperate, almost.'

'You've cheered me up. I really enjoy talking to you. This cigarette tasted nice!'

'Yes, it's home-grown tobacco. Do you know, I've only known you for half an hour, and it's as if we've been friends for life. It's strange, isn't it?'

'I have that effect on people. My husband couldn't stand the way I made friends so easily. He always accused me of flirting but I was just being myself, friendly.'

'Will you go back to him?'

'No. Not now that I've met you and discovered that there are men out there who appreciate the things I like.'

'Sex is rather like music,' the priest ruminated. 'You either love a certain piece of music, or you hate it. I'm into Hendrix, the Stones, Pink Floyd . . . I can't get on with Abba, but that doesn't mean to say that they're not brilliant – they just don't do anything for me. You're into bondage and whipping, as I am, and your husband can't get on with that – it obviously doesn't do anything for him. But that doesn't mean to say that he's not into certain aspects of sex. I love the wailing, howling feedback of Hendrix's guitar, perhaps your husband prefers Tchaikovsky. To me, both are brilliant, but Tchaikovsky doesn't blow my head off.'

'He always said that he wanted love *and* sex, not just sex, as I seem to.'

'Whatever gets you through the night, that's what I say.'

'We're very much alike, aren't we?'

'We seem to be. How about taking this further?'

'How about you giving me what I really want?' she grinned, pulling her skirt higher up her thighs.

'And what do you *really* want?'

'Well, I've never been tied over an altar and whipped for my sins,' she laughed, blowing smoke into the air.

'An altar? Yes, I like the sound of that!'

'Got any rope?'

'You'd be surprised what I've got in the spare room – rope, handcuffs, whips – you name it, I've got it!'

'Then what are we waiting for?'

Grabbing the necessary equipment from Annie's room, Father Will led Cheryl across the garden and through the hedge to the church. Closing and locking the door behind them, he marched the excited girl down the aisle to the altar. Clearing the candles away, he turned to her and smiled.

'Well, Cheryl, would you like me to disrobe you?' he asked, almost tenderly.

'Yes, only . . .'

'Only what? You do want to go ahead with this, don't you?'

'Yes . . . it's just that there's another kink of mine that I haven't told you about.'

'Oh?'

'I . . . I like the idea of being forced – raped.'

'Ah, so you want me to tear the clothes from your body and forcibly tie you over the altar, is that right?'

'Yes, be really rough with me.'

The priest grinned wickedly as he reached out and tore the girl's blouse from her body. Struggling, she tried to pull away as he ripped her bra off, exposing her firm breasts, her huge, wedge-shaped nipples. 'And now for your skirt!' he cried as she slipped from his grip and dashed up the aisle. Chasing after her, he caught her skirt, tearing the garment from her, revealing her knickerless pussy as she streaked across the church. Ambushing her as she dashed around the altar, he grabbed her arm. 'And now over the altar with you for a good fucking!' he bellowed, his words of debauchery reverberating around the church.

Struggling with her naked body, he bent her over the altar, face down, grabbing the rope and tying her down in readiness for the thrashing. 'That's got you!' he cried like a demon as he tethered her ankles, running the ropes around the altar, pulling on them until her feet were wide apart. Her hands tied behind her back, her feet asunder, she lay over the altar with her rounded buttocks exposed, her swollen cunt lips gaping beneath her small brown hole.

'Talk dirty!' she demanded as he grabbed a huge candle and knelt behind her, presenting the waxen tip to her drenched vaginal entrance. 'Ah, that's good – shove it right up me! And talk dirty!'

'OK, bitch! I'm going to fuck you with this candle. It's going right up your cunt, filling your cunt hole.'

'No! It's too bloody big. No!'

'You asked me to be rough with you, so shut up! Half of it's slipped in – another shove and . . . there, only the thick end is sticking out of your cunt now! And now you deserve to be whipped for your sins – you whore!'

'God, I'm going to split open!'

'No, you won't. But you might do when I drive my knob deep into your tight arse!'

Grabbing the leather whip, the priest raised it above his head and brought the tails down with a crack across the girl's splayed buttocks. Yelping, squirming with every stinging lash, Cheryl begged for more and more.

'I've barely started yet!' Father Will laughed, thrashing her crimson buttocks even harder. Again and again the leather tails cracked across her taut buttocks, leaving angry red weals in their wake. 'This'll teach you to go around without your knickers on and show your cunt off to men!' he yelled, landing several stinging blows before dropping the whip.

'Don't stop!' she cried as he lifted his cassock and grabbed his solid penis by the base. 'Please, whip me more!'

'In a minute. First, I'm going to fuck you in the bum as you've never been fucked before!'

Forcing her buttocks open, he pushed his purple knob against her tight brown ring. Suddenly, her muscles yielded and his bulbous head slipped into her hot body. Gasping her appreciation, she said that her husband would never take her there, that he'd never dream of using her bottom to bring her pleasure.

'I'll bring you pleasure!' the priest cried, sinking his thick shaft into her quivering body. 'This will pleasure you, you dirty little whore!' Further into her hot bowels he drove his solid rod until his balls pressed against the candle emerging between her bloated pussy lips. 'And now to fuck you!' he cried triumphantly.

'God, I think I really am going to split open!' she wailed as he withdrew half his length before thrusting again into her tethered body.

They didn't hear the knocking on the door as the priest took the young beauty's body with a vengeance. Ramming her open hole, he smiled as she shuddered and asked him to thrust the candle in and out of her vagina. Grabbing the wax rod, he drove it in and out of her spasming cunt in time with his thrusting penis, bringing her to her exploding climax. Her entire body shaking violently, she wailed in her coming, her orgasmic cries filling the church, echoing around the building.

His sperm suddenly spurted, creaming her anal sheath, filling her tight bowels. 'I can feel you coming!' she screamed as her orgasm peaked again. 'Sperm . . . I can feel your sperm coming out!'

'God, you're hot and tight!' he gasped as he pumped the last of his spunk-fruit into her perspiring body. 'Ah, God – I'm done!'

As he withdrew his glistening penis from her tight bottom-hole, he staggered, grabbing the altar to steady his trembling body. 'God, that was bloody good!' he breathed as someone knocked loudly on the door again. 'Christ, who the hell's that?'

'How do I know?' Cheryl gasped as she squeezed her vaginal muscles and expelled the huge candle from her sore sex-duct.

'I'll go and see,' he whispered as the impatient knocking continued.

'Don't let them in, for God's sake!' she pleaded as the priest lurched up the aisle towards the door.

Opening it an inch or so, he smiled to see the Reverend Cummings. 'What are you doing here, Bob?' he asked, relieved.

'I thought I'd come and join in the fun!' the vicar quipped.

'How the hell did you know . . .'

'I've been watching you through the window!'

'Bloody hell! Is there no privacy?'

'No, none,' Bob laughed. 'So, can I come and play, too?'

'You can play and come!'

Leading the vicar down the aisle, Father Will told Cheryl that she was going to receive pleasure from two hard cocks. 'One at each end!' she enthused as the vicar slipped his fingers deep into her drenched vagina. 'One up my cunt and one in my mouth!' she begged. 'I want to be used as a common whore!'

'You heard the girl, Bob – which end do you want?'

'I'll take her mouth!' he laughed, moving round the altar as he unzipped his trousers. 'Here, suck on this! *Accipite, et manducáte ex hoc omnes: HOC EST ENIM CORPUS MEUM. Take, all of you, and eat of this: FOR THIS IS MY BODY.*'

Offering his huge knob to the girl's pretty mouth, he gasped as she parted her full lips and engulfed the ballooning head. Her eyes rolling, she moved her head back and forth, taking the full length of his penis into her hot mouth. 'That's good!' the vicar breathed as she ran her tongue over his silky glans. 'Keep doing that and I'll give you a mouth wash!'

'She's a right little tart, isn't she?' quipped Father Will as he drove his penis deep into her bottom again.

'Where the hell did you find her?' Cummings gasped.

'Picked the little wench up in the pub!'

'This has given me an idea for my sermon tomorrow. "Thou shalt not covet thy neighbour's wife" – grab a whore from the pub instead and stuff her three holes rotten!'

'A prayer!' Will laughed. 'Deliver us from the pain of abstinence, deliver us from the boredom of purity and let us fuck! Alleluia!'

'Blessed are women, for they shall be fucked!'

'Blessed are tits, for they shall be sucked!'

Her hands trussed behind her back, her young body tethered, Cheryl squirmed and moaned as both men found their rhythm and rammed her orifices, pushing her back and forth over the altar like a rag doll. The vicar's penis suddenly bulged, the head swelling and throbbing as she sucked out his orgasm. His sperm pumping, filling her cheeks, she swallowed his offering as the priest, too, invoked his salvation. Spreading her buttocks with his thumbs, ramming his shaft deep into her anal duct, he forced himself ever deeper into her hole, slapping her drenched pussy lips with his heavy balls until he gave one last shuddering thrust. Gripping her hips, he pushed his belly hard against her buttocks, impaling her with his solid weapon until she'd finished drinking from the vicar's pulsating fountainhead.

As the two men slipped their organs from her quivering body, she spluttered, licking the sperm from her lips. 'That was heavenly!' she gasped. 'God, it was incredible!'

'You ain't seen nothin' yet, baby!' Father Will cried, releasing her bonds and laying her naked body on the altar. Her arms hanging limp by the sides of the altar, her legs spread, the men of God tied her wrists and ankles.

'A sacrifice!' Father Will laughed, tweaking her erect nipples as the vicar buried his face in the warm nest of hair between her legs. 'Lucifer, I offer you this female's naked body in the name of lust!'

'Christ, be careful, Will!' the vicar warned, looking up from the girl's pinken slit. 'You'll have the forces of evil upon us!'

'The forces of evil? No, I won't – she's at the convent! So, Cheryl, what would you like us to do to you now?' he invited, kissing her full mouth.

'Both fuck me! Take it in turns to fuck me until your cocks wither and die!'

Climbing on to the altar, the Reverend Cummings positioned himself between the girl's legs. Taking his solid shaft in his hand, he thrust it between the swell of her cunt lips and drove the head deep into her body. Gasping, Cheryl closed her eyes, grimacing as the organ moved in and out of her tight tube, the huge knob battering her cervix. Sucking hard on her nipple, Father Will reached down and massaged her erect clitoris, bringing her climax nearer, wetting her vagina.

'God, I'm going to come!' she whimpered as her clitoris ballooned under the priest's massaging fingertips. 'Don't stop, I'm coming! Fuck me harder! Fill my cunt with sperm!'

Suddenly, the vicar gasped as his sperm jetted once again. Bathing her inner flesh, he pumped her tight cavity to the brim with his white liquid as the priest brought out the girl's orgasm with his gently caressing fingertips. On and on her climax rolled, tensing her naked body, making her nostrils flare. Sucking harder on her nipple, Father Will sank his teeth gently into her areola, causing the girl to arch her back and let out a wail of satisfaction.

Resting at last, her body depleted, she opened her eyes as the vicar climbed from the altar and staggered over to a pew, his penis limp, his balls drained. Cheryl looked into Father Will's eyes as he took his friend's place between her legs and parted her rubicund pussy lips. Tensing her body as he drove his penis into her dripping hole, she let out a long, low moan of pleasure.

'Ah, yes!' she sighed. 'God, I love being fucked!'

'And I love fucking you!' the priest returned as he began his thrusting, rocking her tethered body, battering her cervix as the vicar looked on. Quickly, the sacrificial victim reached her sexual heaven again, her cries of orgasm filling the church as her young body convulsed. Releasing his sperm, the priest hammered her young body with his battering ram of a cock, racking her young cunt, splattering his spermatic lifeblood deep into her womb.

Finally collapsing on her heaving breasts, Father Will fell limp, his balls resting against Cheryl's taut buttocks, his knob teasing her cervix. Both depleted, they kissed, their tongues meeting, exploring. 'More,' she breathed, tightening her vaginal muscles around his shrinking penis. 'Please – more!'

'I can't!' he panted. 'I'm not a machine!'

'You, then!' she called to the vicar. 'Give me more!'

'You'll have to wait. I'm in no fit state to take you again!'

'In that case, release me,' she ordered, turning her head back to look into the priest's faraway eyes.

Freeing her used body, Father Will helped Cheryl climb from the altar. Staggering up the aisle, she grabbed the remnants of her clothes and opened the church door. 'I'll see you both again, I hope!' she called as she slipped through the door and disappeared into the dark of the night. Looking at each other, and then at the communion of girl-come and sperm spilled over the altar, the clerics laughed.

'It's Sunday tomorrow!' Father Will exclaimed, replacing the candles on the altar and mopping up the sex juices with his handkerchief. 'God, what a bloody mess!'

'Don't panic! I'll give you a hand,' the vicar soothed, climbing to his feet. 'Who the hell was she, anyway? The devil's daughter?'

'God knows! But I'm bloody glad I bumped into her! Christ, I've never met such an insatiable little whore like her in my entire life!'

'I can't say that I've come across a tart like that before, either!'

the vicar laughed as he placed the candles upright. 'She wanted more and more!'

'God, it's late – Chloë . . .'

'Who?'

'No one, I was just thinking aloud. Look, Bob, I've got to push off. I've not even prepared tomorrow's sermon!'

'OK. I'll talk to you tomorrow after the service. Oh, one other thing. If that little tart comes back, give me a ring, will you?'

'Too right I will – I can't handle her on my own!'

'Great! Talk to you tomorrow.'

Locking the door as the vicar disappeared into the night, Father Will recalled the evening's events, still unable to believe what had happened. 'Over the altar!' he breathed as he made his way to the presbytery, his wet, sticky penis dangling beneath his cassock. 'For God's sake – over the fucking altar!'

CHAPTER NINE

Waking early on Sunday morning, Father Will was anxious about Chloë. She'd not arrived at the house the previous evening as planned, and he was beginning to think that she'd found someone else to teach her the joys of sex. Whatever the reason, he'd have to look into it later. Time was running on and he hadn't even dreamed up the Sunday sermon, let alone written it.

The early morning sun already hot, he wandered out into the garden, naked. Sitting on the lawn, the grass tickling his heavy balls, he wondered about his sermon. Apart from that tedium, he loved Sundays, he reflected. Lunchtime spent in the bar drinking with friends – wonderful! Praise be to the Lord for the Sabbath! And for young girls' tight cunts!

Sermons were a pain to write, and even worse to read to the congregation, he mused. His eyes darting between the female parishioners, trying to look up their skirts to glimpse their moist knickers, any semblance of sincerity was virtually impossible. The evil of drink? he pondered. Vile and most beautiful pleasures of the flesh? What the hell to wax hypocritical about this week? Deliver us into temptation! No one wanted to listen anyway, so why bother with the bloody things?

'Morning, Father!' Amber called in summery tones, skipping across the lawn towards him.

God, she's fucking beautiful! The angel of sensuality, sexuality – perversion. Satan's gift to men. The temptress.

'Amber, good morning! I'm, er . . . I'm just sunning myself. I

189

didn't expect anyone this early on a Sunday morning – I'm sorry I'm not decent.'

'Don't apologize – it's your garden so you've every right to loll around naked.'

'All the same, I'll just nip indoors and put some clothes on. Back in a moment,' he smiled breezily, wondering what she thought of his long, thick penis as he stood up. *She doesn't know that it's been up her tight fanny!*

'Oh, no! I . . . I feel another funny turn coming on!' the girl moaned as she flopped onto the soft grass. 'I'm so sorry, Father, but I . . .'

As she slowly crumpled, her long legs parting enticingly, her short skirt riding high up her shapely thighs to reveal her tight pink panties, Father Will smiled. A faked blackout? he wondered, deciding to play the gentleman rather than the pervert for a change and take her into the house. Lifting her up, he carried her to the lounge and set her down on the sofa, her skirt now up over her stomach, her bulging panties exhibited before his wide eyes. She'd be aware of everything he said and did if she were faking it, he knew. Deciding to call her bluff, he lifted the telephone and pretended to ring the doctor.

'Doctor Barnes,' he said with some urgency. 'It's Father Entercock. I have a young girl here and she's passed out. Yes, I have. No, her breathing's fine. Would you? That's very good of you, doctor. My problem? Oh, that's fine now, thanks. Yes, it was very sore, but I suppose it's only to be expected. No, sadly, it died from asphyxiation – I buried it in the garden. Yes, all right, I'll be waiting for you. Thank you. Goodbye.'

Replacing the receiver, he turned to Amber and smiled. 'The doctor's on his way,' he informed the comatose form, pulling her skirt down to cover her bulging femininity. 'It's not normal to have these turns so we'll get the doctor to check you over, just to be on the safe side.'

The girl didn't flinch an eyelid as he placed a cushion under her head to make her comfortable. Perhaps she'd miraculously come round when she thought the doctor would be arriving? he wondered, eyeing her identity bracelet. There had to be a way to establish whether or not she was really unconscious, he reflected as he slipped into his bedroom and donned his cassock. Give her a good whipping, perhaps? Creeping through the hall, he spied through the crack in the lounge door, wondering whether she'd open her eyes or move slightly, giving the game away.

For several minutes he watched the sleeping beauty, breathing quietly, hardly daring to move as he monitored her. But not once did she stir, and he began to wonder if he was right in his assumption that she was a spy. Entering the lounge, he rolled her over, lifting her skirt up and peeling her panties away from her taut, rounded buttocks. 'A quick internal should sort things out!' he chuckled, parting her pale orbs and running his finger down her dark crease to her small brown hole. Easing his finger past her relaxed muscles, he pressed it deep into her bowels, wondering what it would take to make her jump up and scream. 'Would you like me to fuck you there, Amber?' he laughed. 'You'd like my hard cock pumping sperm up your bum, wouldn't you?'

Unmoved by the priest's threats, Amber lay still, completely relaxed as he massaged her hot inner flesh. Pushing a second finger deep into her tight anal sheath, his penis stiffened, tenting his cassock as he wondered if he had the time to carry out his threat before she woke. 'Damn!' he cursed, slipping his digits from her bottom-hole and covering her buttocks with her panties as she stirred. Turning her over, he adjusted her clothing and slipped out of the room as she opened her eyes.

Filling the kettle, Father Will smiled as Amber joined him in the kitchen. 'Ah, we're back in the land of the living!' he greeted her cheerily. 'Coffee?'

'Mmm, please. I'm so sorry about . . .' she began. 'It's really embarrassing, passing out like that all the time.'

'Don't apologize, Amber – it's not your fault. It's rather worrying though. I mean, what if you were standing on the platform and passed out and fell under a train?'

'I have to be careful about things like that. Usually, I sit or stand well back from the platform edge. The doctors can't do anything for me. But I suppose I've got used to it. It's become a way of life.'

'It can't be easy for you. Anyway, what brings you here so early?'

'I couldn't sleep. Sitting alone in my cottage bored me so I thought I'd pop round for an early morning coffee with you, if you don't mind, that is.'

Cottage, my arse! 'No, not at all. In fact, you can help me. I'm stuck for ideas for this morning's service – the sermon, I mean.'

'Tell people how lucky they are to be healthy. Tell them of my plight. By the way, there's something I haven't told you about my blackouts. Falling in front of trains isn't the worst hazard. I was walking across a common once when I passed out and . . . When I came round, I was completely naked! I saw a young man running off and . . . he'd taken advantage of me.'

'Amber, I'm so sorry! You poor child!'

'That's another reason I find it difficult to make friends. It's hard to trust anyone.'

'Yes, I understand. You're completely defenceless while you're out cold – it must be frightening not knowing what you're going to find when you come to.'

'It is. When I woke up on your sofa just now, I realized that you must have carried me into the house and . . .'

'And what, Amber?'

'Well, I wondered if . . . I felt as though—'

'You didn't think that I'd done anything to you, did you?'

'It crossed my mind, yes.'

It more than crossed mine! 'Amber, I'm a priest!'

'You're a man, Father.'

Point taken.

Pouring the coffee, Father Will wondered whether the girl felt any discomfort between her buttocks, whether she'd realised that the privacy of her beautiful bottom-hole had been invaded by his probing fingers. She would certainly have known if he'd driven his solid penis deep into her tight sheath and pumped his male come into her bowels! Lies, lies, lies – she'd believe almost anything he said, he was sure. After all, he was a priest – belief was a perk of the job! Passing her a cup of coffee, he sat at the table and smiled.

Better change the subject. 'What's your idea for my sermon, then? Apart from telling people that they should be grateful for their health, that is,' he asked.

'When I fainted in your office the other day, you . . . I was very wet, Father. The door was locked and . . .'

'Wet?'

'Yes, you know – down there.'

'I really can't believe that you're saying this, Amber! I am a priest, a man of God!'

'Then why was I so wet?'

Because I fucked you! 'I really have no idea! Look, if you suspect me of taking advantage of you, of raping you, then why on earth come and visit me here, knowing that I live alone?'

'I suppose I wanted to discover the truth.'

'And have you?' he asked, again wondering whether she'd faked the blackout to catch him out.

'No, I haven't,' she replied dolefully. 'I'm sorry, Father, I suppose I tend to get paranoid about it. I should never have suspected you.'

'No, don't apologize. I understand your concern, my child, but you must believe that you can trust me. I am your friend, Amber, and I am a priest, so you can trust me, I assure you. So, about my sermon, what do you think?'

'Trust, loyalty, fidelity, reliability – talk to them about that.'

Scepticism, treachery, infidelity, unreliability! 'Yes, but I'll need a hook, something to hang it on.'

'Sex.'

'Sex?' *Yes, please!*

'Yes, all those words relate to sex. Well, some of them, anyway. Talk to them about relationships, about the need to be truthful and honest in a relationship.'

'Yes, I'll preach about the values of a good, sound, sexual relationship,' he decided, eyeing her nipples pressing through her tight T-shirt. 'I mean, sex is an extremely important part of a marriage, don't you agree?'

'Sex is important whether one is in a relationship or not, whether one is married or not.'

'How do you mean?' he asked.

'I'm single, and I need the comfort, the pleasure of sex, as much as anyone else.'

God, so do I! 'So, what do you do about it? I mean, how do you find sexual fulfilment?' *Play with yourself?*

Turning her head, Amber gazed wistfully out into the garden, commenting that the lawn needed cutting. Watching the girl closely, the priest wondered whether she'd masturbated in her bed that morning, whether she'd allowed her fingers to wander between the swell of her soft pussy lips and caress her erect clitoris. He was always wondering whether the women he met masturbated or not! Facing him again, she smiled sweetly, an exotic glint in her eye. She fancies me, he thought – as all women do! Was she asking him for sex? he wondered. Was she desperate to come?

What a wonderful trick, he reflected. Had she never thought of faking a blackout in order to have her young pussy attended? What better way to offer her young body to a man for sex than to feign oblivion? Thighs deliberately open, panties on show, pulled up between her cunt lips, perhaps? What normal man wouldn't take a peek, at least? Or touch her there, caress her open cunt, breathe in her girl-scent – fuck her, even? Bob Cummings would!

He almost laughed aloud. But he was sure that her blackouts were genuine.

'I know the lawn needs cutting,' Will groaned. 'I used to have a gardener, but she left under embarrassing circumstances. I haven't had the time to cut the grass, or the hedge,' he added, still wondering what the girl did for sex. 'I must have the carpets shampooed, too.'

'She? You had a female gardener?' she asked surprisedly.

'Yes, a young college girl. She needed the money and . . . well, it's a long story but . . . There was some trouble over the rubber gloves she used to prune the roses. She got caught up on the thorns and I . . . well, I put the gloves on and my hand slipped and . . .'

'Did you order the flowers?' she interrupted as the doorbell rang.

'No, I didn't get round to it. Excuse me for a moment.'

Opening the front door, the priest smiled to see Chloë standing on the step. 'Chloë, how are you?' he asked, not wanting to invite her in because of her jealous disposition.

'Sorry I couldn't make it last night, Father,' she beamed. 'I was up at the convent and . . . well, it's a long story, but I think you'll be very interested.'

'Good, you've done well, my child.'

'There's also some bad news, I'm afraid. My mother came home and . . . well, she's far from happy with me. A neighbour told her that I'd stayed out all night. I had to tell her that I was here, with you.'

'God! What did she say?'

'She's coming to see you later today.'

'Oh, great! I suppose it's not your fault. Look, I'm preparing my sermon so . . . why not come back this afternoon, Chloë? After your mother has been to see me, perhaps?'

'All right. I hope you can convince her that I stayed in the spare room, because that's what I told her.'

Christ, she might want to look at the room! 'Don't worry, I'll sort it out. How old is she, by the way?'

'Thirty-nine, why?'

Does she fuck? 'Just wondered.'

'I'll see you this afternoon, then, Father. I have so much to tell you about the convent.'

'All right, Chloë, I'll look forward to it. Have you been using your exercise book?'

'Oh, yes – everything's written down.'

'Good girl!'

'My mother's mad, by the way.'

'I expect she is!'

'No – mad as in mental.'

'Mental?'

'You'll see what I mean when you meet her.'

'Oh. Well, I'll see you later, then – bye.'

Returning to the kitchen, Father Will politely asked Amber to leave. 'I have so much to do,' he explained agitatedly. 'It's Sunday, my busiest day. As there are no flowers to arrange . . . you do understand, don't you?'

'Of course, Father. Thanks for the coffee – I'll speak with you later,' she smiled as he saw her out.

No sooner had he closed the door than the bell rang. 'What is it?' he asked irritably as he opened the door, expecting to see Amber standing on the step.

'Good morning, Father,' a man in a dark suit greeted him. 'I'm from the water authority.'

'No, you're not! You're from a newspaper!'

'A newspaper?'

'I have nothing to say.'

'I've come about the water supply, Father.'

'On a Sunday morning? That's a good one!'

'It's urgent. I have to check the water supply.'

'I have no comment – good day!'

Slamming the door, the priest cursed aloud. 'Bastards! They won't nail me!'

Having completed his sermon, Father Will wandered over to the church to take the morning service. A few cans of lager inside him to calm his nerves, he stood by the doors, greeting his parishioners as they flocked into the church. Kissing the young women's hands as they passed him, he breathed in the scent of their perfume, wondering whether or not they'd been laid of late. Nothing like a Sunday morning fuck, he mused. Or perhaps they'd massaged their clitorises to massive orgasms while in their beds waiting for their husbands to bring in the morning tea?

'Good morning,' he greeted his congregation from the pulpit, the ritual of mass well under way. 'I really don't want to, but today, I am going to talk to you about values – the values of relationships, family life, loyalty, trust and dependability. But first, as usual, let's get the unpleasantries out of the way. Sadly, it has come to my notice that sales of contraceptives, and in particular, condoms, are soaring. Now, I have no wish whatsoever to destroy Mr Snort's village pharmacy business, or Mr Backenside's barber shop, but we must remember that the teachings, our religion, our faith, is totally against utilizing any method of birth control – apart from the rhythm method, that is.' *Or whipping it out and sperming all over the wife's belly!* 'As you all know, the use of contraceptives, of any kind, is forbidden. So, may I take this opportunity to remind you that, with all due respect to Mr Snort's and Mr Backenside's profits, we must abstain from using contraceptives.

'Miss Bareham-Puttocks, the chairperson of the residents' association, contacted me the other day and enlightened me with the distressing news that our village has, yet again, been plagued by dandelions. Now, this may seem trivial to some but, in fact, it poses a serious problem for the keen gardeners in the village. Apparently, many gardens are overrun with dandelions, and this is

Ray Gordon

far from acceptable, as you will all appreciate. So, I will ask all those with unsightly growths to burn them at the earliest opportunity. As Miss Bareham-Puttocks put it, there are too many fairies floating on the wind.

'Before I begin this Sunday's sermon, I would just like to say that I am hoping to instate a choir at Cumsdale Church. Now, in keeping with modern thinking and attitudes, I propose to have an all-girl choir. So, may I ask any parents who think that their daughter, or daughters, between the ages of sixteen and eighteen, might be eligible to join the choir, to contact me. I will be auditioning shortly, and will welcome any girl between the aforesaid ages to come forward and show me her oral capabilities.

'And so to this Sunday's sermon. We are all sinners. We all lie at times.' *Well, I do!* 'We lie to our loved ones, we cheat, we are selfish, we are inconsiderate, we are immoral. We are licentious, we are promiscuous. I am lust-crazed . . . I mean, *we* are crazed with lust. Not satisfied with our partners, our loved ones, we commit adultery. Husbands and wives must be able to trust each other. They must be able to live without the fear of lies, without clouds of falsehoods and adultery hanging over them. Should a husband be working late, then his wife should have no doubt in her mind that he really *is* working late and not out drinking and fornicating and enjoy— I mean, sullying his soul. Equally, a husband should be able to trust his wife, and know in his heart that, if she has said that she is visiting a friend, then she *is* visiting a friend and not committing vile acts of adultery with another woman – I mean, another man. It's in this context that I am going to talk to you today about relationships.'

The service over, Father Will bade his parishioners goodbye at the door before re-entering the church and locking up. 'Right!' he enthused, walking over to a group of twenty or so men and rubbing his hands together. 'Let's get the bar open, shall we?' Pulling the velvet curtain back, he opened the heavy oak door and led the way down the steps to the basement. Drawing a huge sliding door back, he switched on the music and lighting and stood behind the small bar. Like a tidal wave, the men surged forward, all holding their money out and ordering their drinks. 'One at a time, gentlemen, please! Now, Mike, lager for you, isn't it?' he asked, wishing he could employ a girl to help out behind the bar – a knickerless, miniskirted, young blonde with enough breast for everyone.

'Cigarettes, gentlemen!' he called above the laughter and music. 'I have some pre-rolled cigarettes which will waft away your blues and bring about a state of euphoria. At only fifty pence each, I'm sure you'll find it's money well spent.' His punters all happily drinking, smoking and chatting, the priest eventually poured himself a drink and began to mingle.

'A bloody hypocritical sermon if I may say so, Father!' a young man laughed.

'Indeed it was, Dave!' he replied, sucking in the aromatic smoke from his cigarette. 'How's the wife?'

'Much the same – won't let me near the pub and won't open her legs!'

'You don't need the pub, do you? Not when you can come here to drink.'

'But you don't open in the evenings, do you, Father?'

'When I get someone to run the bar, some horny little tart, I'll be open every evening. Anyway, you were saying that your wife won't open her legs?'

'That's right. She tells me not to look at other women, not to have vile thoughts, not to wank, not to do this or that . . . What's the point in having a nice, tight, wet fanny if she's not going to let me use it?'

'Beats me!' the priest laughed. 'Get yourself a bird.'

'No, too risky. I'm doomed, I suppose. Doomed to a life of wanking over my mags!'

'Have faith, Dave!'

'In what?'

'I don't know. Your cock, perhaps?'

'What is faith, Father?'

'Faith is the ability the dense have to believe in something unbelievable. Anyway, I'd better mix with the punters, I suppose.'

Moving on, Father Will slapped a man on the back as he walked up behind him. 'Simon! How goes it?' he asked as the man turned round.

'Not bad, Father – and you?'

'So-so. You still screwing that little blonde *au pair* of yours?'

'Bloody right I am! God, she's a little mover!'

'Good man! I was just telling Dave that I'm hoping to open the bar in the evenings before long, so you'll be able to bring her here rather than having to sneak off to The Nun's Dells.'

'Great! The Nun's Dell is a bloody long way to go for a beer but, being a QC, I can't be too careful, as you'll appreciate. I only wish I had somewhere to screw her other than in the back of my car! By the way, your condom machine's on the blink again.'

'Fucking thing! I've only just had it fixed! Anyway, how's the job going?'

'OK. I banged some poor sod up for three years this week for gross indecency.'

'What had he done, exactly?'

'He couldn't stop wanking in public.'

'Three years is a long time for . . .'

'Yes, but he shot his load over a group of schoolgirls on Victoria station.'

'That's not worth three years, is it?'

'Well, a porter gave chase, slipped up on the stuff and broke his leg. One of the girls fainted . . . I suppose we can't really have people like that on the loose, can we?'

'Sounds like a decent sort to me! Shame he doesn't live in the village, we could do with a few more lively people around who know how to enjoy themselves. Anyway, see you later – take care.

And don't get caught with your trousers down – or the *au pair*'s knickers!'

'Excuse me, Father,' a young man interrupted.

'Hi, Mick! Things OK with you?' Father Will smiled.

'Not too bad. I was just wondering if you still have any MOT certificates. My old Cortina is somewhat the worse for wear and . . .'

'No problem, Mick. See me later and I'll fix you up.'

'Still fifty quid, are they?'

'Yes, expensive at half the price!'

Back behind the bar, Father Will spent three hours lining his pockets, as he recalled the Mother Inferior describing it. Contemplating setting up private rooms for his male customers to use for their adulterous ways, he realized that he could do more than line his pockets – he could positively stuff them! As a priest, he reflected, his earning potential was infinite.

As, one by one, his drunken customers staggered out through the rear basement doors, he thought of Cheryl, wondering where he knew her from. He wondered, too, what sort of man her husband was. Running from his attractive young wife, who enjoyed bondage and whipping, into the arms of a much older woman, was something he simply couldn't understand. *The man must be deranged!*

Counting out his takings, he decided to spend a peaceful afternoon in the woods behind Cumsdale Village Hall – watching the lesbian show, if there was one. Locking the church, he wandered back to the presbytery to stash the money to find a package lying on the doorstep. Interesting, he thought, opening the front door. Ripping the brown paper from the box, he discovered an unmarked video tape and frowned. Odd, he mused, pushing the tape into the video recorder and switching the TV on.

His heart missed several beats as the screen lit up. Cheryl was lying over the altar, her wrists and ankles tethered, her naked body being crudely attended by the clergy. '*Sacre bleu!*' he breathed, realizing that the video camera must have been above the altar. 'Who the hell . . .'

Dashing back to the church, he looked up to the roof above the altar, but there was no sign of a camera. During the night, he thought. They must have had a key. Bloody hell, the basement, the booze! Dashing back to the presbytery, his mind reeling, his head aching with worry, he flopped into his armchair and grabbed the phone.

'Come on, come on!' he mumbled impatiently. 'Bob, it's me!'

'Hi, how are you doing?'

'We've been rumbled. Our fun in the church last night – the whole bloody thing's on video tape! I've got a copy here!'

'What? But how . . .'

'God only knows! It's obviously got something to do with the newspaper reporter, and the Reverend Fucker, but I don't know when or how the hell they got into the church to set the camera up.'

'That Cheryl tart, d'you reckon that she was in on it, too?'

'Christ, I'm a bloody fool! Of course she was – it was her idea to go to the church, and she wanted to play her game of pretending to be raped! God, I'm a fool!'

'We must get the master tape back. Grab the girl and beat it out of her!'

'I don't know where she lives. Well, she told me where she was staying, but she was obviously lying, as do most people around here. Listen, I'll contact the place and check it out. I'll talk to you later.'

'OK, Will – and good luck!'

Ringing Mrs Weston's boarding house, Father Will was shocked to discover that Cheryl was indeed staying there. And even more shocked when the landlady put the girl on the phone.

'Hello, Father,' she said innocently.

'I know your game, Cheryl, and I want the tapes, all of them!' he blasted.

'Tapes?' she echoed.

'Don't give me that crap! I know exactly—'

'What tapes? I don't know what you're talking about.'

'Can we meet?'

'Well, yes, I suppose so. Shall I come over now?'

'Yes, and make it snappy!'

Banging the phone down, he was in two minds as to whether she was guilty or not. She hadn't lied about the boarding house. And why would she agree to meet him if she was guilty? It didn't add up, but he still suspected her. After all, the rape game, bondage, sex over the altar – it was all down to her.

His thoughts turned to Josie. She'd gone back to London, so who the hell had installed the camera? Brian could be back, he mused, but he wouldn't have had the time to set up the equipment. Unless the whole thing was a con and he'd never returned to London at all. His mind in a turmoil now, Will poured himself a large whisky and lit a cigarette.

Cheryl arrived to be dragged into the lounge and thrown over the sofa. 'Who put you up to it?' growled Father Will, almost ripping her T-shirt from her trembling body as she cowered before him.

'Put me up to what?' she spluttered, her eyes wide with terror.

'Setting me up in the church, whose idea was it? Are you working for the newspaper?'

'Newspaper? I don't understand, Father.'

'I'll beat the truth out of you, girl!'

'What truth? Look, we had some fun together, that's all! What's all this about setting you up and newspapers?'

'I'm becoming rather fed up with people setting me up, spying on me, recording me, taking pictures of me! I know your game, Cheryl – if that's your real name. Do you really think that I'm completely stupid?'

'Yes, I do! You're talking utter nonsense! If you explain what it is that I'm supposed to have done, I might be able to help you.'

Realizing that she'd hardly send him the video tape and then call round to see him, Father Will sat in his armchair, gazing at her. An accomplished liar? he wondered. He was still sure that he knew her from somewhere, but where? She stood up, adjusting her T-shirt and straightening her skirt.

'I'm going now,' she sighed wearily, moving towards the door. 'I really have no idea what you're going on about, so I'm leaving.'

'I'll walk down the lane with you and explain what's been going on,' he volunteered, wondering what to do. 'I need to get out of the house and think. I need some fresh air.'

Eyeing the girl's enticing legs as he walked behind her, he decided to ravish her in the woods. Whether she was lying or not, it didn't matter – she deserved a damned good fucking. Should be able to find a branch to thrash her with, he mused, gazing at her rounded buttocks beneath her miniskirt. Her long legs and shapely thighs disappearing beneath her short pink skirt were a picture of sensuality. She was, indeed, a fine specimen, but he found himself missing young Josie as he quickened his pace and walked by her side.

There was something about Josie, something that he admired, apart from her shaven pussy! God, I hope I'm not in love! he thought. Apart from her looks, her beautiful body, there was a darker side to the girl. She was determined, stubborn, relentless in her quest to nail him, so why hadn't she checked out his story about going away for a couple of weeks? And where was her replacement? Cheryl? Word would have got back to Josie by now, and she'd know that he hadn't gone away at all. Putting her aside, he turned his attention to Cheryl. Admiring her long nipples pressing through her tight T-shirt, he decided to ask the girl a few searching questions.

'Heard from your husband, yet?' he asked as they walked down the leafy lane.

'No, we decided not to make contact with each other until . . .'

'Did Josie give you the copy?' he interrupted, watching closely for her reaction.

She stopped, turning to face him. 'Sorry?'

'Josie – did she give you the copy?'

'Copy? Who's Josie?'

Word association, he mused. That'll trap her – if she's guilty.

'Ever played word association?' he asked as they walked on. 'Let's see how good you are at it. I'll start. Radio.'

'Television.'

'Tape recorder.'

'Music.'

'Video camera.'

'Holidays.'

'Bollocks.'

'What?'

'Sorry, I mean, electronic bugging device.'

'Er . . . spy films, I suppose.'

'Newspaper editor.'

'Newspaper editor? You're supposed to say one word! Anyway, I don't associate a newspaper editor with anything.'

'All right, how about – tabloid.'

'This is getting stupid!' she laughed as they neared the village hall. 'You're weird!'

Thinking of the Mother Superior as they passed the convent, Father Will smiled. Could always tie her down and force myself upon her! he mused. The old hag, as Sister Teresa calls her, might really like it up her bum. And besides, whoever was in possession of the video tape would soon have the sordid affair plastered across the front pages of the papers, so he might as well screw the Mother Fucker anyway.

'Come on, let's take a walk through the trees,' he suggested, sure now that the girl was innocent. Nearing the clearing, he took her arm, pointing to a bird in a tree. 'There's a lot of wildlife round here,' he whispered. 'Let's make our way through the trees quietly.'

'Wildlife? I didn't think you were interested in stuff like that!'
she giggled.

'Oh, yes, I often come here to watch the birds.' *Naked, writhing
in lesbian lust, coming . . .*

Entering the clearing, Father Will was disappointed to find that
the young lesbians, if they had been there, had finished their
lovemaking and gone. Just my luck! he thought, sitting on the
grass. Cheryl joined him, her short skirt revealing her knickerless
pussy as she made herself comfortable. Gazing at her outer lips
bulging between her thighs as she rested her chin on her knees, the
priest smiled.

'I'll explain everything to you,' he began, his eyes meeting
hers. 'You see, there's a newspaper reporter after me. She seems
to think that it would be a good idea to expose me as a pervert or
something.'

'You are, aren't you?'

'Well, yes, but that's beside the point! Anyway, she's determined to nail me, and so are several other people. Why, I don't
know. I mean, I've done nothing to upset anyone, I've never gone
out of my way to harm anyone. They all want to see me fall, and I
just don't know why.'

'Well, the reporter is obviously out to make money. As for the
others, whoever they are, I don't know. You must have a lot of
enemies, that's all I can say.'

Lying back on the grass, Cheryl opened her legs, displaying her
swollen pussy lips to the priest's popping eyes. Where the hell do I
know her from? he asked himself as she reached down and ran her
hands up her inner thighs. Opening her legs wider and peeling her
outer lips apart, she massaged her erect clitoris, moaning as she
closed her eyes and breathed heavily. His penis solid, the priest
watched her masturbate, wondering what it must be like to be an
exhibitionist.

Lifting her T-shirt, the girl pulled her bra up, revealing her firm
breasts, pinching and twisting her nipple as she vibrated her

fingers faster over her clitoris. 'I love masturbating in the woods,' she breathed as the priest joined her. 'Finger me, will you?' Reaching between her splayed thighs, he gently pushed three fingers into her creamy hole, massaging her silky inner flesh as she writhed in her ecstasy. 'And suck my nipples, too!' she begged, offering him her firm breast.

Taking her elongated nipple into his hot mouth, Father Will sucked hard, stretching the brown milk bud, darkening her areola as he fingered her hot hole. Her fingers working between her swelling pussy lips, her body contorting, shuddering with lust, she arched her back and let out a long moan of sexual fulfilment. 'Oh, my God, I'm coming!' she cried, bringing her knees up to her chest. 'Finger my bottom!'

With one finger ramming her vaginal sheath and another invading her velveteen anal tube, the priest sucked and bit on her nipple as she tossed her head from side to side, wailing her appreciation for her clitoris, her spasming vagina, her tightening bottom-hole. 'Come in my mouth!' she pleaded as her orgasm subsided. 'I want you to lick my cunt and come in my mouth.'

Lifting his cassock and climbing on top of her perspiring body, Father Will buried his face in her wet nest as she took his rigid penis into her mouth and sucked. Rolling her tongue over his glans, she breathed heavily through her nose as her clitoris swelled. 'Wish I'd brought some sticky tape,' the priest mumbled through a mouthful of wet cunt flesh as his penis ballooned. His face grimacing, his body rigid, he pushed his tongue deep into her hot vagina as his sperm erupted from his throbbing glans, bathing the young whore's tongue, filling her cheeks as she, too, reached her paradise. Their mouths locked to each other's genitalia, they sucked out each other's orgasms, finally falling limp, spent – done in their coming.

'You really do know how to eat pussy!' Cheryl praised the priest as he rolled from her dripping body.

'And *you* really know how to suck a man's cock!' he laughed, pulling his cassock down.

'I'd like to fuck you in the woods all day,' she breathed as her fingers found their way between her wet pussy lips again.

'God, you're insatiable, aren't you?'

'I know, I just can't control myself when it comes to sex. We must do this again, now that you trust me. You do trust me now, don't you?' she asked, her eyes meeting his.

'Yes, I do. But I have a major problem, so I can't enjoy myself as much as I'd like to. Worrying is no good, I know, but I can't really appreciate your beautiful body to the full with things on my mind.'

'Well, hurry up and sort it out so that we can get down to some serious fucking! Masturbating with my vibrator is OK, but it's not as good as having a stiff cock up me.'

'How often *do* you masturbate?'

'Several times a day. When I wake up in the morning, I grab my vibro. Then, usually around mid-morning, I have another session. I don't know, what with the afternoon session and then having a good vibrate in front of the telly in the evening, I reckon four or five times every day.'

'Bloody hell! Your poor clit must get sore!'

'No, not really. My cunt does, though: it's the bottle I use, it's too big really, but I love it! Well, I'd better be going, I suppose. I have things to do so I'll see you later, perhaps?' she babbled, covering her breasts with her bra as she stood up.

'Yes, later, perhaps,' he smiled, imagining the girl with a bottle stuffed up her fanny. 'I'll stay here for a while – I need to think.'

'All right – and thanks, it was great!'

Lying back on the grass, Father Will toyed with the idea of visiting the convent and having the whole thing out with the Mother Superior. If he told her that he knew about the deliveries of wine to the convent, and that she hadn't been wearing any knickers when she'd spoken to the bishop on the phone, and that he'd bugged her office and built up a dossier on her . . . But no, the time wasn't right – not yet, anyway. He had a week until the

Sunday tabloids ran the story, a week in which to expose the Mother Superior, the bishop, and, possibly, the archbishop.

Don't panic, Entercock!

Wandering out into the lane, he was stunned to glimpse young Josie as she disappeared round the corner – with the bishop! Bloody hell! he thought as he followed, keeping his distance as they entered the woods. 'What are they up to?'

Moving cautiously through the undergrowth, he crouched behind a bush as they sat on the grass under a tree. Josie had her handbag with her, as usual. Had she lured the bishop into the woods for sex to record the sordid act on tape? Perhaps she'd given up trying to nail him, and moved on to richer pickings?

'It was good of you to meet me, Bishop,' Josie began. 'I'm sorry to have to drag you into the woods, but I can't be too careful since Father Entercock believes that I'm in London. Anyway, I have nothing at all on the priest. I have tried, as I told you on the phone, but I have no proof whatsoever. Now, if you were to help me out by telling me all about the Reverend Mother's escapades with the nuns and the schoolgirls so that I could run a damn good story about it, I'll return the favour – if you get my meaning?'

'Return the favour?' he queried.

'Yes, I'm sure you'd appreciate a sexual favour from me in return, wouldn't you?'

Fall for it, you pimple-nosed git!

'Well, I . . . I really don't know.'

Lying back on the grass, Josie lifted her skirt, displaying her shaved pussy to the bishop's disbelieving eyes. Gasping, he reached out and stroked the smooth skin of her bulging outer lips, running a finger up her glistening sex-groove. His cassock revealing his arousal, Josie reached out and grabbed his solid penis, gripping it tightly through the black cloth.

'You'd like me to give you a little pleasure, wouldn't you?' she murmured, lifting his cassock and pulling his shaft out. 'You enjoy a girl's hand stroking your knob, don't you, Bishop?'

'I . . . well . . .'

'You'd enjoy my mouth, wouldn't you? And my hot wet cunt, I'm sure. So, what does the Reverend Mother get up to? Is she a lesbian? Or is she bisexual? Come on, Bishop, my mouth and my cunt are waiting for your cock, so tell me all you know!'

Leaning forward, Josie took the bishop's staff into her hot mouth and ran her tongue over the silky glans. Gasping, the Right Reverend reclined, lying on the grass as the girl kneaded his heavy balls and took the entire length of his hard shaft into her mouth. Suddenly pulling away, Josie laughed. 'Well,' she said, releasing his penis. 'That's all for now.'

'But . . . but you can't leave me like this! Please . . .'

'Tell me what I want to know, and I'll finish the job. And if the information's good enough, I might even let you lick my cunt.'

'But I don't know anything!'

'Come on, I've been doing my homework and I . . .'

'All right, but keep me out of it, won't you? I'll expose the Mother Superior on the condition that you keep me out of it.'

'It's a deal, Bishop – it's a deal!'

Poor sucker! Father Will thought. Still, it would serve him right to be exposed. With the recorder running, Josie would have every incriminating word on tape. This could be my lucky day! he ruminated. With the bishop soon to be defrocked, and the Reverend Fucker thrown out of the convent – this *could* be my lucky day!

'The Mother Superior . . .' the bishop began as Josie placed her handbag nearer to him. 'She enjoys lesbian relationships with some of the convent schoolgirls.'

'How do you know this, Bishop?' Josie asked, her eyes sparkling with the prospect of promotion.

'We talk and . . . we often meet for a drink and . . .'

'And what, Bishop?'

'I have had a sexual relationship with the Reverend Mother, but I want that kept out of it. Anyway, she pays the girls to spank her in her room at night. They have parties . . . orgies would be a better word to use, I suppose. I don't think I should say too much more.'

Leaning forward again, Josie sucked the bishop's ballooning knob into her mouth. 'Are you sure you won't tell me anything else?' she asked, sitting upright.

'I . . . The Mother Superior plies the girls with alcohol. She also bribes them by threatening to expel them unless they pleasure her. Most of the girls' parents are rich society types, and the last thing the girls want is to be expelled, so they carry out the Mother's wishes – they have no choice, you see.'

'Interesting. And now, in return for the little information you've given me so far, I'll show you some pleasure,' she smiled, taking his knob into her mouth again.

Moving her head up and down, swallowing the entire length of the bishop's ample penis, Josie kneaded his balls. The cleric lay back on the grass, his eyes closed, his mouth open, gasping as the girl brought his seed ever nearer to his throbbing glans. Father Will watched on in amazement as his superior breathed his lewd demands. 'Suck it harder, girl! Use your tongue! Make me spurt down your throat, and then I'll fill your tight little cunt with my love-staff!'

Suddenly grimacing, his body rigid, the bishop cried out. 'Coming!' Slipping his knob from her mouth, Josie used her lips and tongue to sustain his orgasm. Lapping up the sperm as it jetted, mouthing his ballooning glans, moving her hand quickly up and down his veined shaft, she brought him his pleasure, paid for his information.

Finally falling limp, he relaxed as Josie sucked up the sperm from his shaft. Licking his come from her pretty lips, she sat up and smiled. 'Now, tell me more!' she demanded. 'And then you can lick my cunt.'

'No, not now! Later, my child. I can't do any more just yet.'

'All right, I'll meet you here again this evening, at seven, OK?'

'Yes, at seven. I'll fuck your tight, hot cunt at seven, and I'll tell you more about the Reverend Mother!'

Creeping out into the lane, Father Will walked back to the presbytery. 'Seven o'clock. I'll need my camera,' he breathed. 'Josie might let him off the hook and only drop the Mother Fucker in it, but I'll get the fucking bishop if it kills me!'

Who planted the video camera?

CHAPTER TEN

Watering his cannabis plants, Father Will contemplated the video tape of Cheryl lying naked over the altar and wondered again whether or not to confront the Mother Superior. He *had* to get the original copy of the tape, or face being defrocked and publicly exposed as the happy pervert he really was. Josie had told the bishop that she had nothing on him – so who the hell was the culprit? Hoping that the pimple-nosed git would reveal more than Josie when they met in the woods that evening, he closed the greenhouse door and returned to the presbytery to prepare for the unholy exposition.

Checking his camera, he planned the bishop's downfall. A Sunday tabloid would pay handsomely for a few rolls of film of His Lordship's knob being intimately attended by a young girl – especially a young newspaper reporter! One of Josie's rival papers would have a field day exposing not only the bishop, but the sleazy way the story had been acquired. The money would come in handy should Father Will find himself defrocked – and out of business! But God willing, his own sordid exploits would never come to light.

No sooner had he settled in his armchair to load a new roll of film than the doorbell rang. Christ! Chloë's mother! he suddenly remembered, jumping up to open the door. The young woman standing on the step smiled as she caught his eye. Almost as attractive as her daughter, she was slim and well-dressed in a short turquoise skirt and matching blouse.

'I'm Chloë's mother,' she announced, tossing her long dark hair over her shoulder as she entered the house. 'I won't take up too much of your time Father, it's just that I wanted to make sure that Chloë really did stay here with you the other night. She tends to lie sometimes, you see.'

Mad? 'Come into the lounge, Mrs . . . I'm sorry, but I don't know your surname.'

'Mary Baxter – but please, call me Sarah.'

'Right, come in, Mary – I mean, Sarah.' *Sarah?*

Showing the woman into the lounge, Father Will offered to make tea, but she declined. 'I can't drink tea, it upsets my system, my alimentary canal,' she explained dolefully.

'I'm sorry to hear that. Have you had it looked at?'

'Certainly not!'

'Oh. Anyway, Chloë did stay here – in the spare room.'

'I didn't come here to talk about my daughter, it was a ploy.'

'A ploy?'

'Yes, I want to be a nun.'

'A nun?'

'Did Chloë tell you that I'm divorced?'

'She did mention it, yes.'

'Will you kiss me?'

'Kiss you?'

'I need to enjoy the experience of a passionate embrace, Father. Before I don a habit and close the entrance to my womb forever, I need to be sexually embraced by a man – filled and fulfilled!'

'Well, I . . .'

'I hate men, I hate women, I hate everyone and everything – I even hate myself!'

'But, why?'

'I don't know. I even hate my daughter – lucky little bitch! I'm jealous, you see. She's young, pretty, sexy, and the men look at her with a burning desire in their eyes and a bulge in their trousers. They never look at me. Kiss me, Father! Release the male desires locked in your heart and take me in your arms and kiss me before I die from lack of passion!'

'But, if you want to become a nun, then why . . .'

'Nuns don't have sex, do they? No one will have sex with me, so I might as well be a nun. I might as well seal off the entrance to my womb forever – allow my barren slit to heal up.'

'I think you need help, Sarah. Why do you call yourself Sarah when your name's Mary?'

'It sounds sexier, and I want to be sexy – like Chloë. I used to call myself Fanny, but people got the wrong idea.'

'Have you seen your doctor about this?'

'I last saw him ten years ago. I had a passionate affair with him, a wild, wanton fling – and then he left me.'

'Oh, how awful for you.'

'It was worse for him, he almost died from shame. Am I attractive, Father? Do you find me sexually attractive?'

'You are a very attractive woman, yes.'

'Do I excite you – sexually, I mean?'

'Well . . . I am a priest, Sarah, and . . .'

'Do I arouse your most vile and depraved male instincts?'

'Well . . . you *are* very attractive for a woman of thirty-nine.'

'I'm twenty-five, Father.'

You bore your daughter at primary school? 'Chloë said that you were thirty-nine.'

'She's lying. Do you find my daughter more sexually arousing than me?'

'I find you extremely sexually arousing, but I feel that you should get some help.'

'Then help me, Father! I desperately need to feel my heart pounding, lust coursing through my veins! I need to feel the butterflies of love, of wild and wanton lust, swirling in my stomach as I'm taken in a man's arms and French kissed!'

Fruitcake! Father Will shifted in his armchair, frowning as the woman stood up. Tossing back her dark curtain of hair, she opened her blouse, lifting her bra up and baring her breasts.

'I am a woman, Father!' she announced triumphantly. 'See, I have breasts! I have nipples – a woman's body!'

'Please, Mrs Baxter! What are you doing?' he asked as she unzipped her skirt.

'You don't believe that I am a woman! Men ignore me, my femininity! Men look at my daughter, but not at me! I will prove to you that I am a woman – all woman!'

Kicking her skirt aside, she pulled her panties down her slender legs and walked across the room to the priest. Discarding her blouse, she unclipped her bra and dropped it into his lap.

'Touch me, Father! Prove to me that you find me sexually attractive!' she cried, sitting on his lap and running her hands over her breasts. 'Feel my body, it's electric! Touch me between my legs! Bring out the woman in me!'

'Please, Mary! I mean, Sarah. I think it best that you dress and leave. Find yourself a psychiatrist and . . .'

'You are a priest, a man of God – help me in my plight or I shall die from a broken womb!'

Taking Father Will's hand, the desperate woman thrust it between her legs. Cupping her breast, she offered her nipple to his mouth. 'Suckle as a babe!' she ordered as he ran his finger up and down her sex-groove. Pressing her nipple against his lips, she begged him to suck. 'You are my baby, drink the milk of love from my bosom!' Parting his lips, he took the erectile protrusion into his mouth, running his tongue round the brown bud as she squirmed and writhed in her ecstasy. Locating the entrance to her vaginal sheath, he pushed his finger deep inside, exploring the wet heat of her inner flesh.

'I want to come!' the euphoric woman cried. 'I haven't come for ten years, since my doctor lover gave me an internal examination in the back of his Jaguar!'

'My God, woman, you're completely mad!' the priest exclaimed as she opened her legs wide and lay across his lap. 'I'll make you come, but then you must go home and pray for forgiveness for your wicked sins! I'll make you come, but not for my pleasure, you understand. I'll do it to drive out the demon within you.'

'Yes, drive out the demon dwelling within my womb! Drive out the evil so that I may be cleansed and freed of lust! Free my soul so that I may become a nun and deny forever my base sexual yearnings!'

Massaging her stiffening clitoris with his wet fingertip, the priest sucked on her nipple. His penis bulging beneath her bottom, he wondered whether to take advantage of her and slip his organ deep into her bottom-hole. But no, she was totally insane. The best thing to do, he decided, was to pleasure her for a while and then send her packing.

'God, that's heavenly! Don't stop, I'm coming!' the neurotic woman gasped as her naked body contorted. Suddenly arching her back, her thighs spread wide, her head hanging over the arm of the chair, she quivered violently as she reached her illicit heaven. Her come oozing copiously from her gaping hole, she finally closed her legs, her juices liberally staining the priest's cassock.

'Did you enjoy that?' he asked as she rolled off his lap and fell to the floor.

'You forced me!' she screamed hysterically, grabbing her clothes as she fled the room. 'Rape! He raped me!'

'Christ, she's a fucking nutcase!' Father Will breathed as he moved to the window and watched her run naked down the lane, screaming her accusations.

'You in trouble again?' Annie asked, emerging from her room into the lounge. 'You and your women! They'll be the death of you one of these days!'

'She's a nutter, a complete nutter! Poor Chloë – that was her mother, by the way. Fancy having a mother like that!'

'She's not really mad, you know – she puts it on. I've known her for years.'

'Puts it on? She's bloody crazy!'

'She's unbalanced, but not completely mental. She was all right until her doctor refused to have an affair with her. She cried rape and he almost got struck off. Now, she pretends to be mad to block out the painful memory.'

'Well, I hope she stays away from me! Christ, all I need is a nutcase hounding me!'

'Anyway, I'm off now,' Annie smiled. 'There's three hundred on the kitchen table, by the way. I've been bloody busy recently – my poor cunt needs a rest so I'm going home to bed.'

'It's Sunday, isn't your husband at home?'

'No, he's away on business for a few days. I must go, I'm nearly falling asleep. I got you the plastic bags you asked for, and I brought that sack of dirty laundry over from the church. I put it by the back door. By the way, a man from the water authority called round to see you earlier.'

'Water authority, my arse – he's from a newspaper! What did you tell him?'

'Nothing, I just said that you were out and . . .'

'Did you let him in?'

'No. He showed me his identity card so he must be—'

'It's a fake.'

'Oh.'

'OK, Annie, I'll deal with him, should he come back. I'll see you later – take care.'

Opening a can of lager, Father Will grabbed the money from the kitchen table, wondering whether to install two prostitutes in the presbytery. Taking the black plastic sack, he emptied the convent knickers out onto the table and sorted through them, separating them into three piles. 'Filthy, slightly soiled – unsaleable!' he muttered as he sat down. Pulling the filthy pile towards him, he began folding them and placing them into the plastic bags. Suddenly he stopped. 'They're dry,' he observed aloud. 'Stained, smelly – but not damp.'

Sprinkling holy water over the dark grey knickers, he placed them in the bags, sealing them to keep the moisture in. 'Right, fifty pairs at twenty quid each – that's a grand! Excellent!' Disposing of the other piles as he checked his watch, the front doorbell rang. 'Six o'clock – wonder if that's Chloë?'

'Chloë, come in!' he invited as he opened the door.

'Has my mother been to see you yet?' she asked, her tight summer dress hugging her youthful body, following the contours of her heaving breasts.

'Yes, and you're right – she's completely mad!'

'It was after her imaginary affair with her doctor,' the girl said, clutching her exercise book as she followed him into the lounge.

'Yes, I know about that.'

'There was an official-looking man in a suit hanging around outside just now.'

'What was he doing?'

'Looking down the drain.'

'He's a spy.'

'What?'

'It doesn't matter. Anyway, what happened at the convent last night?'

'We all sat around, and the Mother Superior came in wearing some sort of leather suit. She had a whip and ordered the girls to strip off!'

'Did you join in?'

'No way! Once the girls were naked, they tried to rape me! The Mother Superior is a rampant lesbian! She told the girls to strip me so that she could have my bottom. I managed to struggle free and run off!'

'Good God! I can hardly believe that the Reverend Mother would—'

'Well, it's true! I'm not going back to the convent. I can't, not now.'

'What *will* you do?'

'Find a job, I suppose. Anyway, I've written it all down in my exercise book. And I've written about . . . well, you can read it for yourself, if you want to.'

'OK, leave it with me and I'll take a look later.'

'I need another sex lesson, Father – if you have the time, that is?' she smiled sweetly, reclining on the sofa.

'Er . . . I have an appointment at seven, so . . . all right, Chloë – I do feel rather . . . Remove your clothes, and we'll start straight away.'

Standing in the centre of the room, Chloë slipped her summer dress off. Unclipping her bra, she tossed it on to the floor and peeled her panties from her smooth mound. 'I've been shaving regularly,' she declared, looking to the priest for praise.

'Good girl!' he replied enthusiastically, gazing at her youthful body as she stripped.

'And I've been masturbating at every opportunity.'

'Well done, my child. Have you heard from your friend Haley yet?'

'Yes, she's coming down soon to stay for a couple of nights,' Chloë replied, laying her naked body on the sofa in readiness for her sex lesson. 'What are you going to teach me today, Father?' she asked, endearingly coyly, as he knelt on the floor beside her. *A good question!* Admiring her firm breasts, her elongated milk buds, he wondered what perversions he could put her through. She'd already had her bottom-hole invaded by his intrepid penis, and he'd spermed into her pussy, and her mouth. Where to next? he wondered, remembering how much Cheryl had enjoyed the whip.

'Today, Chloë, I'm going to teach you about domination and sexual slavery.'

'Sexual slavery, Father?' she queried as he ran his fingers up and down her naked sex-valley.

'Yes, it's important that young girls be initiated into the delights of domination and slavery because . . .' *Because what? Think*

Entercock! 'Because they have to learn to be obedient.'

'Obedient, Father?'

'Yes, my child. When you are married, as you will be one day, you will have to obey your husband. Now, in order to instil obedience in your mind, I will, gently, of course, whip you.'

'Whip me! But, Father . . .'

'Only gently, Chloë. Now, to introduce you to sexual slavery, go to the spare room and bring me the leather whip.'

'But . . .'

'Do it, Chloë!'

'Yes, Father.'

Returning to the lounge, the girl passed the priest the whip and stood before him, apprehension in her deep blue eyes. Ordering her to fetch some rope, he wondered where to tether her naked body. The coffee table again, he decided, placing it in the centre of the room.

'Right, Chloë,' he smiled as she passed him the rope. 'Lie face down on the coffee table with your knees on the floor, and I'll prepare you for your initiation into sexual domination.' Following his orders, the girl lay over the table, her knees on the floor, her buttocks raised and spread, ready to receive the whip. Tying her limbs to the table legs, he kissed her smooth, rounded buttocks before standing up and raising the whip above his head.

Bringing the leather tails down gently across her youthful buttocks, he smiled as her young body jolted. Again, he brought the tails down lightly, assuring her that she'd enjoy the experience when she'd become used to it. As he brought the tails down a little harder, she yelped slightly, her buttocks tightening as she turned her head for sight of her master. In his rising arousal, Father Will landed the first hard blow, causing the girl to cry out.

'Sorry,' he apologized. 'That was a mistake.'

'Please free me now!' she begged as he strengthened his grip on the whip and beat her harder. Dismissing her pleas, he began to thrash her buttocks for all he was worth, leaving thin weals across her pale orbs with every lash. 'Please!' she screamed, but he gave her no quarter, only beating her bottom harder until he finally fell to his knees to examine his handiwork.

Whimpering, the girl twitched as he kissed her crimson buttocks and ran his finger down the dark crease to the wet entrance of her tight vagina. 'The whipping has made you very wet, my child,' he murmured. 'You liked it, didn't you?'

'Yes, Father,' she whispered. Moving around the table, he lifted her head, smiling as he raised his cassock and waved his engorged penis before her tearful eyes.

'Now, as you are my sex-slave, you will suck this!' he instructed, pressing the bulbous knob against her pursed lips. 'Come on, Chloë – do as you're told or it'll be the whip again!' Parting her lips, she allowed him to push his purple knob into the wet warmth of her pretty mouth. 'There's a good girl!' he breathed as she closed her eyes and ran her tongue over his swollen glans.

Moving his hips back and forth, the priest watched the girl's lips cling to his wet shaft as she mouthed and sucked on his organ. She was a sweet little thing, and she deserved to have her mouth filled with sperm daily, he decided as his seed neared the throbbing head of his solid tool. 'I'm going to come now!' he enlightened her, grabbing her head and driving his shaft deeper into her mouth.

Moaning, she squeezed her eyes shut as his sperm gushed, bathing her tongue, filling her cheeks. 'Ah, yes!' he cried as he withdrew his shaft a little to massage his pulsating head between her pretty lips. His sperm oozing from her mouth, running down her chin, he drove his weapon in again, his glans pressing against the back of her throat as she was forced to swallow his ejaculate.

'You're doing very well, my child!' he praised as he slipped his penis from her mouth and sat on the floor. Licking her lips, she smiled, wondering what else she would have to do as the priest's sex-slave. Moving behind her again, he parted her taut buttocks and licked the length of her anal crease. 'Do you like that?' he asked, pushing his tongue into her small brown hole.

'Yes, very much!' she gasped as he reached beneath her trembling body and pushed three fingers deep into her spasming cunt. 'Ah, that's nice, Father! That's . . .'

'I'll make you come now, my child,' he murmured, slipping his fingers from her vaginal sheath and locating her stiffening clitoris.

Lifting his cassock, he massaged his penis, rubbing the swelling head between her buttocks as she neared her orgasm. 'Put it in me!' she begged as he probed around her tight bottom-hole. Driving his shaft deep into her quivering pussy, he slipped it out again. Wet, glistening with her cunt milk, he stabbed his glans between her buttocks. Her muscles yielding as he gently pressed his knob into her anal hole, she gasped. 'More, more!' she pleaded as he slowly drove the entire length of his organ deep into her bowels. 'Ah, yes! Do it to me hard!'

Her anal sheath stretched to its limit, Father Will began his fucking motions, slowly entering and withdrawing his shaft to the accompaniment of the girl's gasps. Still massaging her clitoris, he took her bottom-hole with a vengeance, ramming her fettered body for all he was worth until, his body rigid, he pumped out his sperm.

'I can feel it coming inside me!' she gasped as he spurted his come deep into her bowels. 'Now I'm coming too! Don't stop!' Massaging her pulsating clitoris, he brought out her orgasm, his shaft almost splitting her young body open as he fucked her tight bottom. Finally done, he collapsed over her back, breathing in the scent of her perspiration as his penis twitched within the heat of her bottom.

'I can feel it shrinking inside me,' Chloë breathed. 'It feels nice there, Father.'

'It does, my child. It feels very nice there, but that's enough for today.' Slipping his shaft from her hot tube, he lowered his cassock. 'I'll untie you in a minute,' he said as the phone rang. Lifting the receiver, he sighed to hear the Mother Superior.

'I thought you'd gone away,' she snapped.

'Whatever made you think that?'

'I heard that you were going away on church business.'

'Well, you heard wrong. Now, how can I help you?' he asked irritably.

'We must talk. There are things I wish to discuss with you.'

'Really? Such as?'

'I don't want to talk about it on the phone.'

'Has the water authority called at the convent?'

'Water authority? What *are* you talking about?'

'Ah, just as I suspected!'

'Are you completely mad, Father?'

'I suspect as much, yes.'

'Can you come over to the convent now?'

'Er . . . yes, give me ten minutes.'

'Ten minutes,' she echoed, hanging up.

Interesting, he mused as he gazed at Chloë's young naked body. Wonder what she wants to talk about? 'Please, Father, let me go now!' Chloë begged.

'All right. I've got to go out now anyway,' he replied, releasing the girl. 'Will your mother be a problem? I mean, she left here crying rape. Will she go to the authorities?'

'No, she won't, don't worry. You didn't do anything to her, did you?'

'No, no, of course not!' he laughed as she dressed.

'I'm pleased about that. I couldn't bear to think of you with another woman. Especially my mental mother!'

'Don't worry, my child. I am a priest, after all. Listen, I'll leave you to dress as the time's running on. I'll see you tomorrow, Chloë.'

'All right, Father. Will you give me another lesson tomorrow?'

'God, yes! I mean, if you feel that you're ready, then I will teach you more, my child.'

'I am ready, Father – I *am* ready!'

'Good. Until tomorrow, then,' he smiled, grabbing his camera before leaving the house.

Walking down the lane with his camera, Father Will bumped into the official looking man in a suit. 'I must check your water supply, Father!' the man demanded.

'You can't – there's a young naked girl in the presbytery.'

'A naked girl?'

'Yes, she's in the middle of dressing. It wouldn't be decent to allow you in there. Besides, you're from a newspaper, aren't you?'

'Father! I'm from the water authority! I'm checking the water supply in Cumsdale village for contamination. We've had complaints, you see, so . . .'

'There's no contamination in the presbytery – God sees to that!'

'I'm simply trying to do my job, Father – earn a wage . . .'

'The wages of sin is death!'

'I can't work for nothing, Father!'

'Charity shall cover the multitude of sins. Now, if you'll excuse me, I have an appointment at the convent. Good evening.'

Water authority, my arse! he thought as he wandered along the lane, leaving the man dumbfounded. Officials move in mysterious ways! Arriving at the convent, he entered by the main door, breathing in the arousing heady scent that wafts around girls' schools. Walking down the corridor, he thought about taking confession at the convent, and hiding a tape recorder in the confessional. Could always sell the tapes, he mused. Hearing giggles coming from a classroom, he stopped and spied through the crack in the door.

'No, I've got a better one!' a girl laughed, wielding the blackboard rubber.

'Go on, then!' another girl enthused.

"A young novice nun from Hardrod,
Delighted in tickling her pod,
As her pea in erosion,
Suffused its explosion,
She shouted "I think I've found God!" '

Grinning, Father Will walked down the corridor to Mother Mary's office. 'Come!' she called as he knocked on the door.

I just have! 'Good evening, Mother,' he greeted her as he closed the door behind him. 'And good evening to you, Sister Teresa,' he added, frowning at the young nun. *What the hell is this?*

'Now, it has been brought to my attention that you, Father Entercock, and Sister Teresa committed a vile act of gross indecency in the grounds of Hallworth Church. Is this true? And what's that camera for?'

'Certainly not! What on earth—'

'Why are you carrying a camera?'

'To take some pictures.'

'What sort of pictures?'

'Excuse me, Reverend Mother,' an elderly nun interrupted as she opened the door. 'There's a man at the main entrance. He says he's from the water authority.'

Bloody hell!

'Tell him to wait!'

'Yes, Mother.'

'What have you got to say, Sister?' the Mother Superior asked, turning to face Sister Teresa.

'I . . . Reverend Mother, I . . . How's the new whip, Mother? And the clamps?'

The older nun's face fell, her hands trembling as she shifted in her chair. *Got you now, you old hag-bag!* Father Will thought as he fixed a smile on her. Her eyes fluttering, she cleared her throat, not quite knowing what to say as she stood up and walked across the office to the window.

'What do you mean, girl?' she asked, turning on her heels to face the sister.

'The new whip, Mother – I just wondered if it was all right.'

'Is there something that I don't know about, Mother?' the priest asked, a huge grin across his face. 'What's this whip for? Are the schoolgirls going to have riding lessons? And what does Sister Teresa mean by clamps? Surely, they're stirrups, aren't they?'

'I have no idea what the girl is talking about! She's obviously been out in the sun for too long! Now, if you'd both leave – I have things to do.'

'But, Mother . . .' Sister Teresa began. 'You said that you'd summoned me to your office to banish me from the convent. To have me defrocked, denounced, de—'

'I've had a change of mind.'

Flashing a grin at Sister Teresa before turning to the Reverend Mother, Father Will smiled charmingly. 'If that's all, I'll be going. I have things to do, too. I like to keep abreast of my work.'

'Don't mention breasts in my office!' Mother Mary admonished. 'Please, both leave my office at once!'

'I am escaped with the skin of my teeth, Reverend Mother,' the priest teased.

'Please, go!'

'Go out into the highways and hedges . . .'

Walking down the cloister together, Father Will and Sister Teresa laughed. 'What's this whip and clamps stuff all about?' the nun asked as they left the building.

'It's a long story. I'm surprised that you don't know what goes on here.'

'I don't take a great deal of interest. No one tells me anything so . . .'

'How are your young sex-slaves?' he asked, picturing Samantha Lovejoy's young shaved pussy and the perverted MP.

'They've been doing very well. I shaved Rosa, she looks lovely now! The problem is, the Mother Superior has been sniffing around them. I think she's sussed me out, the old hag! I'd kick her up the cunt, but I'm frightened of losing my foot!'

'You and me both! So you shaved Rosa? I must see this! When can we all meet again for some fun?'

'I'll ring you. Where are you off to now?'

'To the woods. I'm going to . . . well, I'll tell you another time. Don't forget, I want those girls in the woods again – and you, you horny little devil!'

'I won't forget! I'll ring you. Bye for now.'

Apart from the bogus water authority official, things were looking good, Father Will decided as he walked to the woods. The Mother Fucker would shut up, for a while at least. The bishop was about to be deflowered, and defrocked . . . but there was still the video tape to worry about. Praying that Holesgood would open up and tell Josie something worth knowing, he crept into the woods and hid behind a bush, lying in wait.

Within a few minutes, Josie and the bishop arrived, creeping through the undergrowth to settle on the grass beneath the tree. Placing her handbag next to the bishop, Josie asked him to tell her all he knew about the Reverend Mother and her exploits at Hardmound Convent.

'You start taking your clothes off, and I'll tell you all I know,' the bishop instructed excitedly. Unbuttoning her blouse and unclipping her bra, Josie exposed her firm breasts to his oggling eyes. Her nipples growing, lengthening, hardening, Father Will felt a pang of jealousy as she cupped her breasts and suggested that His Lordship stroke her milk buds.

There was something special about the girl, he ruminated. But what? A crack's a crack, a nipple's a nipple. But of all the women he'd laid, all the sweet pussies he'd eaten, the breasts he'd sucked, there was something different about Josie. As she slipped her miniskirt off and peeled her alluring red panties from her naked mound, Father Will wondered again whether he was in love with her or not. But no – she was a newspaper reporter, a whore, who'd go to any penile length to achieve her sordid glory.

'I want promotion,' the bishop confessed, eyeing Josie's naked slit. 'I want the archbishop's job, so I will reveal one or two things about him before I tell you more about the Reverend Mother.'

'The archbishop!' Josie squealed in amazement.

Bloody hell!

'Yes, he has a woman friend who . . .'

'How do you know?' the girl interjected, her eyes darting between her bag and the lust-crazed cleric.

'I've seen them together. I phoned the archbishop's secretary a while ago, and she said that he was away on business somewhere down on the coast. I told her that it was imperative that I contact him and, against her better judgment, she told me the name of the hotel. I drove down to Brighton and saw the archbishop leaving the hotel with a blonde girl. They went for a walk down to the beach – hand in hand. She was young, about eighteen, I'd say. Anyway, as they walked, they stopped now and then to kiss each other. I was shocked, as you can imagine!'

'Do you know the girl's name?'

'No, but on enquiring at the hotel, I discovered that they'd registered as Mr and Mrs Dixon.'

'My God!' Josie breathed, imagining the balding archbishop in bed with a young girl.

Snapping away at the Right Reverend Holesgood fondling Josie's pinken slit, the priest grinned. The archbishop! Christ, was there no end to the debauchery, the filth permeating the very foundations of the church? The pictures would be perfect, he thought, taking several more shots of the bishop pushing his finger into Josie's open hole as she reclined on the grass and spread her legs. But pictures of the archbishop screwing some young blonde tart would be heaven.

'You said that you had nothing on Father Entercock,' the bishop continued. 'I have something that will destroy him, but it will cost you.'

'What have you got?' Josie asked excitedly, raising herself on her elbows.

'A tape. A video tape of him and the vicar, Bob Cummings, doing sinful things to a girl they'd tied over the altar. I also have proof that he's placed an advert in a men's magazine.'

My God! So it was the . . .

'Really?' Josie cried. 'Christ, that's just what I need! How do you know about the advert?'

'His phone, I had it tapped by a friend of mine.'

'I wish I'd known all this before! The trouble I've been to to nail the priest, and you've got all this on him! I even had to check out of The Woodman's Arms and move into a bed-and-breakfast place so that he'd think that I'd returned to London.'

'I've known that you've been sniffing about for some time now. I was going to tell you, but I needed to get as much as I could on him before I said anything. Anyway, as I said, it will cost you.'

'What do you mean, it'll cost me?'

'Money. It will cost you money.'

'But I'm paying you with my body, Bishop. Don't get greedy, or you'll find yourself in trouble alongside Father Entercock and The Reverend Mother.'

'Are you blackmailing me?'

'I'm just saying that you don't want your name involved when the shit hits the fan. I mean, you're hardly clean, are you? Imagine being sucked into the mire when all this comes out – you'll never get to be archbishop, will you? You'll never get to be anything, in fact.'

'Point taken. But, if you're paying me with your body, then you must allow me to do as I wish with you.'

'What do you wish to do, Bishop?'

'Lie down on the grass, and I'll show you.'

Standing up, the bishop slipped his cassock off. Josie gasped, and then, sitting up, laughed as she gazed at him in disbelief. Clad in fishnet stockings, a red suspender belt and silk panties fringed with lace, His Lordship stood over the girl, grinning. 'My little fetish,' he explained as he joined her on the grass. 'I hope you don't mind this sort of thing?'

'There's so much perversion around here that nothing surprises me any more!' she laughed as he leaned forward and sucked on her milk bud.

Transfixed by the bishop's bulging silk panties as he fingered Josie's tight cunt and licked her firm breasts, Father Will snapped away. Slipping her hand inside the clerical pervert's panties, the girl pulled out his long penis, running her fingers over his smooth glans as she opened her eyes to examine the organ.

'You're very big, aren't you?' she observed gleefully.

'Yes. The Reverend Mother likes it very much,' he replied proudly.

'Are you having an affair with her?'

'No, she's a lesbian, but she likes to wank me off in her office now and then. She loves watching my sperm shoot across the room and land on the carpet.'

'Do you interfere with the schoolgirls, the sixth-formers?'

'No, I'd like to, but she won't allow it. She wants them for herself, you see.'

'Why do you want Father Entercock nailed? I mean, you're as bad as he is, so . . .'

'Because he'll land us all in trouble if he's not careful. I mean, this advert he's placed advertising soiled convent schoolgirls' knickers, for example. It won't be long before he's tracked down by the porn squad or whoever, and then the whole thing will come out. I want to carry on as I am, having my fun now and then with a prostitute friend of mine and . . . If I can get the Reverend Mother out of the way, too, I'll be able to enjoy some of those schoolgirls' tight cunts. Also, I want to set up a little business venture – rent girls. That should pay well. And I want promotion. Father

Entercock will blow the lid off the entire church if he's allowed to carry on. Anyway, enough of that. Let's have some fun!'

The priest could hardly believe what he was hearing as he took several more photographs. Rent girls! Good God! he thought, wondering what else his revered boss was into as Josie pulled his panties to one side to reveal his heavy balls. Rolling the girl over, he spread her legs wide and parted her taut buttocks, examining the small entrance to her bowels.

'You've a nice bottom,' he proffered, leaning over and licking the full length of her crease.

'You can finger me there, if you want to,' she offered, opening her legs wider, affording Father Will a perfect view of her gaping, shaven cunt lips.

'Have you ever had a man's penis up your bottom?' he asked, pushing a finger into her small, tight hole.

'Yes, as it happens, I have. Why, is that what you'd like to do with me?'

'I'd like to finish off by doing that, yes. But first, I'm going to fill your hot cunt with my seed. Stick your bum in the air and I'll kneel behind you.'

Obediently, Josie got on all fours and rested her head on the soft grass, her buttocks splayed, open to the bishop's voracious eyes. Her chasming pussy lips already swollen and wet with her juices, she was ready to pay the man of God for his knowledge. 'Come on then!' she enthused. 'I've never been fucked by a bishop before!'

Kneeling behind the girl, Holesgood took his penis by its base and drove it between her pouting lips deep into her young body. 'God, you're hot and tight!' he exclaimed as he began his thrusting. 'When I'm rid of Entercock and the Reverend Mother and I'm the archbishop, how about coming to live with me?' he garbled, grabbing her hips and thrusting into her violently.

'That would be blasphemy!'

'In the eyes of the church, yes . . . But I could fix it so that no one would know.'

'I'll think about it,' Josie gasped, reaching between her legs and massaging her clitoris. 'I need a man who can give me a good seeing-to now and then – someone with some money so that I don't have to work.'

Another pang of jealousy stabbed Father Will as Josie's words echoed in his mind. Live with the bishop! Did she really fancy the pimple-nosed old fool? he wondered. No, she was just trying to extort as much information from him as possible before dropping him in it with everyone else.

'God, I'm coming!' the bishop groaned as he thrust into Josie so hard that she had to clutch at handfuls of grass to stop herself being impelled forward. 'Coming!' he cried again as he grimaced and filled her tightening cuntal sheath with his gushing come. Josie cried out too – but only to satisfy the bishop, Father Will hoped, in the realization that it was more than mere lust that he felt for her. For loath as he was to admit it to himself, the thought of her finding sexual happiness with another man churned his stomach.

Slipping his glistening shaft from the girl's body, the bishop fell to the ground leaving her vagina open, dripping with its cocktail of come. Josie continued to massage her clitoris until she too fell forward, her body shaking violently as her massive climax rendered her almost unconscious. Finally rolling onto her back, her rounded breasts bared, her shaven cunt open, she looked to the bishop and grinned.

'Where's the video tape?' she asked, caressing her drenched inner lips with her slender fingers.

'In my car, just down the lane,' he replied, moving towards her. 'I sent a copy to Father Entercock, just to worry him. With any luck, he'll run scared and be out of my way for good! The original copy's in my car: I'll give it to you when I've finished with your beautiful young body.'

Taking several more photographs, Father Will slipped from his hide and made his way to the bishop's car. Predictably, it was locked but, desperate to get his hands on the tape, he took a large stone and shattered the side window. 'The insurance company will pay,' he breathed as he opened the door and snatched the tape from the glove compartment. 'And Holesgood will pay for screwing my bird – with his job!'

Back in the woods, he was in time to watch Josie take the bishop's ballooning knob into her mouth as he began licking her creamy slit. Lying on the grass, their tongues licking, slurping, they were the perfect picture of obscenity. Quickly finishing his roll of film, Father Will wondered where to get it developed. Money, money, money, he mused as he watched the bishop roll on to his back, pulling Josie on top of him as she continued to lick and suck on the Right Reverend cock.

Her legs splayed, her swollen pussy lips spread wide open, she pumped out her girl-cream as His Lordship lapped at the entrance to her vaginal sheath. Poor girl, Father Will mused. She was selling her body for the story, for the video tape. But at the end of the sordid day, there would be no payment. The only evidence she had was on her tape recorder and her editor would be far from happy with a recording of a few incriminating words, punctuated by anonymous cries of lust. Words that were, after all, only hearsay. The bishop might well have had it in his mind to make up wild stories of lesbians and whipping sessions just to have his wicked way with her. Moreover, Josie wouldn't believe that the video tape had been stolen, but more likely she'd been set up, used for sex.

'Lick me just there, that's it!' Josie cried, breaking the priest's reverie. 'God, yes! I'm coming!' Licking and mouthing the girl's clitoris as she shuddered and squeezed out her hot come, the bishop trembled in harmony as his pulsating knob exploded in her mouth, filling her with sperm. Writhing, the odd couple rolled over and over as their orgasms took them to their illicit heaven. I'll whip her for this! Father Will decided, watching the bishop's knob slip from her mouth, his sperm covering her pretty face as her climax rolled on.

Finally coming to rest, the lewd pair lay back on the grass, their bodies glowing under the hot sun, their faces wet, their genitalia dripping – spent. Creeping away, Father Will hid a short distance from the bishop's car. There'd be a hell of a scene when Josie realized that she'd surrendered her body for nothing! She'd see the broken window, of course, but he was sure that she'd not believe that the tape had been stolen.

Arriving at the car, the bishop gasped, knocking pieces of glass from the window as he cursed the vandals. 'Just look at it!' he stormed. 'Bloody kids!'

'That's *your* problem,' Josie replied irreverently. 'Give me the tape and I'll get out of here before we're seen together.'

'It's gone!' the bishop cried as he opened the glove compartment. 'Christ! They've taken the fucking tape!'

'Lying bastard!' Josie returned. 'You lied about having a video tape so you could use me for sex! There *was* no tape, was there?'

'There was! It's been stolen! Don't worry, Entercock has a copy. I'll sneak into the presbytery and grab it.'

'You'd better, or I'll see that you're ruined!'

Suddenly realizing that Josie had left her bag in the woods, Father Will dashed back to the spot and grabbed the tape from the machine. 'Thank you, God!' he intoned, looking up to the heavens before sprinting through the woods to reach the presbytery before the bishop.

The car pulled up just as he reached the door. Smiling, he waved to the bishop as he climbed from his car and opened the front gate. 'Bishop, how nice to see you!' he beamed, hiding the tapes under his cassock.

'Ah, Father Entercock. I was wondering . . . may I come in for a moment?'

'Of course, Bishop,' Father Will replied, opening the door and leading the way into the lounge. 'Please, sit down,' he invited, discreetly placing the tape on the mantelpiece.

Eyeing the video tape, the bishop rose and walked nonchalantly across the room, admiring the picture of the Pope as he stood before the fireplace. 'I wanted to talk to you about . . . I don't suppose you're making coffee, are you?'

'I'm fresh out of coffee, sorry, Bishop.'

'Oh. Er . . . well, I just wanted to tell you that I'm sending a young curate to help you out. You'll have to put him up at the presbytery for the time being, just until he . . .'

'But I don't want a curate! I don't need one, Bishop!'

'Well, I believe that you do. Anyway, it was the archbishop's idea, not mine. Besides, it'll give you more time to yourself, having him to do the menial tasks, having him to lean on, so to speak.'

'A crutch, you mean?'

'You're incorrigible, Father! Couldn't get me a glass of water, could you?'

'Certainly, Bishop. After you,' the priest invited, waving his hand towards the door.

The bishop hesitated before leaving the room, anger mirrored in his piggy eyes as he realized that there was no way he could grab the tape. Taking the tape on his way out, Father Will slipped it under the armchair before following him to the kitchen. 'There's your water,' the priest said, offering the glass. 'I really don't need a curate. There's no room for him to stay here, for a start.'

'Of course there is! You have a spare room, haven't you?'

'Er . . . well, sort of.' *Oh my God!*

'That's settled, then.'

No, it's bloody not! 'I was just off out, so . . .'

'Thank you,' the bishop interrupted, placing the empty glass in the sink. 'I'll be going now, then. I'll speak to you soon about the curate. He should be arriving this week. He's well in with the archbishop, by the way, so best behaviour at all times, Father. Goodbye.'

'Goodbye, Bishop – *Dominus vobiscum!*' *And the bloody devil!*

Showing the bishop out, Father Will couldn't stop grinning. Another round to me, he thought as he watched him climb into his car and drive down the lane. A broken car window, retrieved cassettes and dozens of photographs of Josie and Bishop Holesgood screwing in the woods all added up to a successful day, he decided – a bloody good day! But a curate? That was all he needed!

Back in the lounge, he sat down. Monday tomorrow, he reflected, wondering what the day would bring. What to do about Annie's room? About the greenhouse, the basement – everything?

Shit – a curate!

Pouring himself a large Scotch, he flopped into his chair again. Hope Chloë pops round to see me, he thought, fondling his stiffening penis through his cassock. Could do with a bloody good fuck! Picturing Josie in the woods with the bishop, he wondered whether she'd want more sex. Another pang of jealousy attacked him. 'Fucking old git! I'll screw him!'

CHAPTER ELEVEN

The front doorbell was ringing incessantly. Climbing from his bed, still half-asleep, Father Will slipped his dressing gown on and opened the door to find Josie standing on the step. He looked her up and down, remembering her evening in the woods with the bishop. Her body was fresh, curvaceous, youthful, sensual, and he wished she'd not given herself to the pimple-nosed old pervert.

'I thought you were away on church business,' she snapped accusingly as he gazed into her big brown eyes.

No handbag. 'And I thought you were in London,' he replied, leading the way to the kitchen. Opening the back door and blessing the good weather, he filled the kettle, wondering what the girl had in mind – what she wanted so early on a Monday morning.

'I've been plagued with problems,' she began as she sat at the table. 'One thing after another has gone wrong for me, and I want to know why.'

'I'd want to know why, too, if I were you.'

'I thought that you might be able to tell me.'

'*Me*? Now, what makes you think that I'd know why things are going wrong for you? I am a man *of* God, Josie – not God himself.'

'Something was stolen from my handbag yesterday.'

'Oh? Where had you left it?'

'In the . . . I went for a walk in the woods and left it unattended for a while.'

'Ah, lovely weather for a romp in the woods, don't you agree?'

'A romp?'

'Just an expression. Write to the water authority, they might be able to throw some light on it.'

'What?'

'Never mind.'

Father Will was enjoying the game now that he was winning. Josie had nothing on him, not an ounce of proof, and he couldn't help feeling sorry for her. 'You've never told me what line of work you're in,' he said as he poured the coffee.

'I'm in sales – a sales rep,' she replied.

'Oh, what do you sell?' *Apart from your pussy.*

'This and that. Listen, Father, I didn't come here to talk about my job, I came here to ask you why everything keeps going wrong for me.'

Because I keep fucking things up for you! 'How would I know, Josie? I mean, we all have off days, times when everything goes wrong, but no one knows why. It's all part of life's threadbare tapestry, I suppose.'

'Yes, but I think you *do* know why. Brian didn't lose the rolls of film, by the way – they were stolen from his room. Now something's been stolen from my bag. It's not just a case of having a bad day or two, is it? Someone is out to get me.'

'Out to get you? Of course they're not! There's your coffee. What was stolen from your bag, anyway – Femidoms? Condoms? Tampons? Pantie liners?'

'You're crazy!'

'It's a crazy world!'

'Anyway, a tape was stolen. I have a tape recorder, for listening to music when I'm out walking. The other day the tape mysteriously snapped, and now another tape has been removed from the machine. Any ordinary thief would have taken the machine, not just the tape. They'd have taken my handbag and my money, wouldn't they? Where were you between seven and eight o'clock yesterday evening?'

Watching you screwing the bishop. 'What is this? Am I under arrest?'

'Just tell me.'

'Here, if you must know. Ask my bishop, he came round to see me just as I was going out. That would have been around eight, I suppose.'

'Can you prove that you were here up until the bishop arrived?'

'Of course I can't prove it! And why should I? Are you with the KGB?'

'Don't be bloody stupid!'

'Sorry, just wondered. I was with MI5, but that was a long time ago.'

'Yes, so you told me.'

'I still am, actually, but say nothing to anyone.'

'You're completely mad!'

'We're all mad, to a greater or lesser degree. So, why have you come back? Or didn't you return to London?'

The game was becoming ridiculous, but he knew he had no choice other than to play along with her. He was in two minds as to whether to tell her everything or not – that he knew she worked for a newspaper. But it was too early in the game to put his cards on the table. Eyeing the swell of her young breasts, her nipples pressing through her T-shirt, he smiled.

'I want to get out of the priesthood,' he confessed.

'Why? I thought you were happy . . .'

'No, no! Things have been going wrong for me, too. There's someone out there who doesn't like me, and they're trying to destroy me. God knows who, or why!' *A little pang of guilt, Josie?*

'Destroy you, how do you mean?' she asked, averting her gaze.

'I like to drink now and then, as most people do. I enjoy sex, as everyone does! But there's someone out there who is determined to expose me. They want to tell the world what an awful man I am, that I don't pay my water bills. They want to tell the world that I drink, smoke and enjoy sex. What I've done to whoever it is to deserve this, I've no idea – but they've really got it in for me!'

'But do you sell drink to your parishioners! I've heard that you're into all sorts of weird and illegal things!'

'Don't believe rumours, Josie! I wouldn't have the time or the inclination to sell drink to my parishioners!' he laughed. 'And as for paying my water bills . . .'

'Soiled knickers?'

'Have you? You know where the bathroom is, don't you?'

'No, I mean, do you sell soiled knickers?'

'What? Why would I sell dirty knickers? Who the hell would buy them? And where would I get them from, anyway?'

'The convent,' Josie said accusingly.

'What *are* you talking about? Soiled knickers? I'll have you know that I do my washing regularly! They haven't cut the water off – not yet, anyway!'

'God, it's like talking to a madman!'

Josie stood up and wandered out into the garden. Following her, Father Will gazed at her slim legs and grinned. Nothing like an early morning fuck, he thought, eyeing the swell of her buttocks. Sitting on the grass and crossing her legs, she looked up at him and smiled.

'It's your bishop,' she said. 'He's the one who's been hounding you.'

'What? My bishop? But . . .'

'You screwed some girl over the altar, didn't you?'

'Screwed a girl over the altar?'

'Don't deny it!'

'Good God! I have no idea what you're talking about!'

'Yes, you do – you have a copy of the video tape. Anyway, it was Sister Felicity. I'm surprised you didn't recognize her. There again, without her habit, I suppose you wouldn't.'

'My God! Sister Felicity? I thought that it was just some randy bird who . . .'

'So, you don't deny it, then?'

'Well . . . what *is* all this about? Why did Sister Felicity dress and act like a tart and tell me that her name was Cheryl? I don't understand any of this! And why is the bishop doing this to me?' *Thought I knew Cheryl from somewhere – bitch!*

'I believe he wanted to sell the story to a newspaper.'

'A newspaper? How do you know all this, anyway?'

'I . . . I overheard him talking to the Mother Superior of Hardmound Convent yesterday. He placed a video camera in the church to trap you.'

Astonished by the girl's revelation, Father Will joined her on the grass, covering his stiffening penis with his dressing gown as he glimpsed her bulging red panties. 'The bishop!' he breathed. 'I really didn't think he'd go that far! Why did you ask me why things are going wrong for you?' he queried, still gazing at the thin strip of bulging material between her shapely thighs.

'I thought that you . . . it doesn't matter now,' she smiled. 'Anyway, just keep your head low for a while and you'll be all right. I didn't return to London as I ran into an old friend. I stayed at her place and came back to Cumsdale last night. I'm now staying in bed-and-breakfast. Who do you think went through my handbag?'

'I've really no idea, Josie! This is a small village with virtually no crime, so I can't imagine who it could be. You don't happen to know a girl called Amber, do you?'

'Amber? No, I don't. Why?'

'Good. It doesn't matter why. Look, I'd better get dressed.'

'Oh, right. I'll go then, shall I?'

'Stay, if you want to.'

'Yes – I want to.'

Following the priest into the house, Josie tailed him to his bedroom. Turning, he gazed into her big brown eyes. What was she after? Not a fuck, surely? Insatiable or what? he thought as she sat on his bed and lay back, her skirt rising, revealing a damp patch on the crotch of her red panties. Slipping his dressing gown off, he joined her on the bed, wondering which orifice to deposit his sperm in this time. Her short brown hair framing her pretty face, her full lips smiling faintly, she was the epitome of innocence – and the devil's daughter! If only she really was a sales rep, he thought, instead of a conniving little bitch of a tabloid newspaper reporter!

'Where's Brian – still in London?' he asked as he slipped his hand beneath her T-shirt and lifted her bra from her breasts.

'Yes, he's working on another . . . he's gone back to work.'

'I thought he was going to come back to take some more pictures?'

'Someone else is going to cover . . . I mean, he was but . . . Oh, I don't know what he's doing. That's nice, I like you stroking my nipples,' she murmured, reaching down and grabbing his solid penis.

'And I like you stroking my knob,' he breathed in her ear. 'We should do this more often.'

'You've already got more than enough women to satisfy you!' she laughed, slipping her panties off.

'But I'd like one special woman.'

'Would you give the others up?'

'Would you? If you had just one special man?'

'I haven't got any others!'

Lying again! 'Are you sure?'

'Of course I'm sure! Anyway, are we going to have a chat or a damn good fuck?'

'I think a damn good fuck is in order!'

Lifting the girl's skirt, Father Will moved between her outstretched legs and kissed her smooth pussy lips. 'I've missed you,' he murmured as he ran his tongue up her opening slit. 'I've missed your pretty pussy.'

'That's all you want me for, isn't it?' she breathed as he located her clitoris with the tip of his tongue.

'No, of course it's not!' he laughed, peeling her swelling cunt lips apart to expose her erect nodule. 'Now, close your eyes and relax. I'm going to lick an orgasm from your beautiful little clitoris.'

Pressing on the pinken flesh surrounding her pleasure bud, he eased out its full length and sucked it into his mouth. Josie breathed heavily, opening her legs as wide as she could, pushing her naked sex hard against the priest's face. 'God, you're good at this!' she breathed as her clitoris began to throb. 'Lick up and down my crack, lick me all over!' she gasped, trying to force her legs open wider. 'Finger me, too. God, yes, that's good!'

Sucking her clitoris hard and flicking the sensitive tip with his tongue, the priest thrust three fingers in and out of her creamy sex-duct, reddening her swelling outer lips, bringing her more pleasure than she would have thought possible. Slipping his fingers from her hot cunt, he pushed his tongue into the flesh-cavern, lapping up her girl-come, licking her urethral opening to the accompaniment of her gasps. 'Oh, oh, that's nice! I want your tongue deep inside me!' Snaking his tongue out as far as he could, he licked the slippery walls of her tightening love-hole, breathing in the female scent, savouring her sex juices.

'Ah, I'm going to come!' she warned him as she threw her head back and arched her back. 'I'm nearly there! Don't stop! Lick . . . Ah, God! Coming . . . com . . .' Wrapping her legs around his head, she ground her young slit into his mouth, covering his face with her juices as she dug her fingernails into the quilt. Shuddering, gasping, her come flowing like a stream from her pulsating sheath, she suddenly became rigid, silent, her eyes rolling in her ecstasy. Her seemingly endless climax gripping her very soul, her face flushed, her nostrils flared, she remained locked in her lust. Father Will licked at her pulsating clitoris, sustaining her pleasure until she finally fell limp, pushing him away and rolling onto her side. Panting for life-giving breath, shuddering, clutching at the quilt, she cried.

'I've never . . . I've never known anything like it!' she sobbed.

'Don't cry,' he said softly. 'Why cry if it was so good?'

'Because . . . just because, that's all.'

'I've never known anyone cry before.'

'I don't suppose you've ever made anyone come who's in . . . Let's not talk about it now. Make love to me, Father! Please, I want you to come inside me.'

Climbing on to her young body as she rolled over and spread her legs, the priest slipped his shaft deep into her hot vagina, savouring her inner heat, her contracting muscles, as they rhythmically gripped and kneaded his penis. Pushing his tongue into her mouth, he kissed her full lips as he drove his shaft harder into her trembling body. 'Come inside me!' she breathed as he moved his head down and sucked on her elongated milk bud. 'I want your sperm inside my cunt!'

Lifting her legs, she placed them over his shoulders, opening her young sex to the priest, allowing him even deeper penetration as he gasped his approaching offertory. 'Coming! Can you feel it?' he panted as his seed jetted into her cavern, flooding into her womb.

'Yes, feel it . . . Fuck me harder!'

Ramming between her inflamed pussy lips, pummelling her cervix, driving her body up the bed, he pumped his sperm deep into her perspiring body. Crying again, she rolled her head from side to side, lost in her climax as his root invaded the very centre of her body. Her feet high in the air, she gave a last shudder as he made his final thrust. Lowering her legs, she lay still, absorbing his sperm, her vagina gripping his organ as he lay over her quivering body.

'I can feel you inside me,' she whispered, running her fingers through his hair.

'You like me inside you, don't you?' he breathed as he kissed her mouth.

'I want you inside me forever. Never take it out.'

'I won't, Josie – I won't.'

His limp penis finally slipping from her hot tube, he rolled over and lay by her side. There was something different about this one, he reflected again. Love, perhaps? God forbid! 'Work, Josie! Time for work!' he declared, brushing her hair from her face before leaping up from the bed.

'Don't go!' she begged. 'I want you again!'

'Later. I'm going to have a shower, and then I have to go to work. What are your plans for today?'

'I don't know. My plans seem to have gone out of the window now. I was going to . . .'

'What were you going to do?'

'Nothing. Go and have your shower.'

Returning to the bedroom after his shower, Father Will found that the girl had gone. Donning his cassock, he realized that he'd not taken confession at the convent for some time, but he couldn't face the Mother Superior now. Before going to the church, he packaged the rolls of film and addressed it to a seedy back-street company advertised in his dirty magazine. They'll probably make copies and sell them, he mused. But there was no other way to have the films developed.

Dropping the package off at the village post office, he made his way to the church and sat in his office, wondering what the day would bring. Thinking of the archbishop, he realized that he'd need proof of his debauchery if he were to expose him alongside the bishop. He'd need evidence of the Mother Superior's lechery, too. Perhaps Cheryl was the key? If he didn't let on that he knew that she was Sister Felicity, he might be able to use her to expose the Mother Superior – but how? At least now the war zones were clear – who was on whose side, who working with whom, and what they were up to.

So, he ruminated, it was the bishop who had the phone tapping device planted. And I should have known he'd hidden the video camera in the church as no one else has a key! Lighting a cigarette, he wandered outside and stood under the hot sun, his mind reeling with plans to expose the church hierarchy. Attack! he thought, remembering his original plan. But how? The bug in the Mother Superior's office might be of use. If he could record her talking openly of her debauchery . . . But photographs would be the real proof – photographs of her entwined in lust with the bishop. She liked to wank him off and watch his come shoot across her office floor, he thought, wondering how to capture the firecracker on film. Through the window, perhaps?

'Good morning, Father!' Cheryl called as she minced towards him in her microskirt.

'Good morning, Sis— Cheryl. And how are you on this fine morning?'

'Randy, as always!' she laughed.

Oh, no! Not another bloody handbag! 'I'm rather busy today, so . . .' he began, eyeing the bag.

'I've only come to say hallo, that's all,' she smiled.

'Oh, by the way, there was a phone call from your husband . . .'

'My . . . when?'

'He'd been trying to contact you, without any luck, so, Cumsdale being a small village, he tried the church. It was about ten minutes ago. I think you'd better call him back.'

'But . . . did he leave his name?'

'Surely you know your husband's name?' *Stupid bitch!*

'Yes . . . I mean . . . What did he say, exactly?'

'That you're on holiday here and . . .'

'You told him that you'd met me, then?'

'Oh, yes. I said that you were fine, and that you were enjoying the break and all that. Ring him back now. I think he's missing you, so ring him from my office.'

'No, no. I'll speak to him later.'

Frowning, Cheryl was obviously baffled. Father Will smiled. I'm getting good at this, he thought, deciding to confuse the poor girl even more. 'I was talking to my bishop last night,' he began. 'He was telling me about one of the nuns at Hardmound Convent

– her name's Sister Felicity. I shouldn't laugh, but it is rather funny. Apparently, she's into making porn videos and the police are . . .'

'Sister Felicity? Porn videos? But . . .'

'I know, it's terrible, isn't it? The things that go on at that convent! There's an undercover operation in progress so I'm keeping well away from the den of iniquity . . . The Mother Superior is under suspicion, too – according to the bishop, anyway.'

'I . . . I must be going . . .' the girl stammered before turning on her heels and running down the lane towards the convent.

Laughing, the priest returned to the presbytery and switched his radio on in readiness for the girl's predictable hysterical discussion with the Mother Superior. 'Set one against the other!' he laughed, taking a can of lager from the fridge. 'I'll confuse them all so much that they won't know who to believe, or who to trust!'

On cue, he soon heard Sister Felicity burst into the Reverend Mother's office, ranting and raving about the bishop.

'Father Entercock's a liar, and the father of lies!' the despairing Mother Superior countered.

'But he knows about the video tape, the porn, as he put it.'

'I don't know *how* he knows . . . unless the bishop told him. But why go to all the trouble of setting the camera up and organizing things with you only to tell Father Entercock what he'd done? There's more to Father Entercock than meets the eye, it seems.'

'A hell of a lot more! He told me that he used to be with MI5.'

'He's mad!'

'That's as maybe, but he's bloody clever!' the young nun cried.

'Perhaps he *was* with MI5. He's led a checkered life, I know that!'

'He once worked at a girls' school as PE master, but was thrown out. He said he's a plumber by trade. Anyway, apparently MI5 recruited him, and he ended up in the priesthood.'

'God, perhaps he's still with MI5?'

'Maybe. What shall we do?'

'I don't know. I need to think for a while.'

'We can't trust the bishop! If he's been telling Father Entercock that the thing in the church with me over the altar was a set-up . . . Why on earth tell him that I'm into porn videos? We can't trust the bishop at all!'

Laughing, Father Will wondered how to cause even more confusion. Confusion, the ideal weapon, he decided as he swigged more lager from the can. But why *had* the bishop sent him a copy of the video tape? To frighten him off, perhaps? he wondered. The enemy camp was becoming divided, at last, and he turned his thoughts to Amber. What was her part in all this? he wondered. Switching his radio off as Sister Felicity left the Mother Superior's office, he decided to check out Thornycroft Cottage again to discover the truth about Amber, once and for all.

Creeping around the back of the cottage, he was surprised to see washing hanging on the line. All part of the trick, he supposed as he peered in through the kitchen window to see a table littered with cups and plates. Easy enough to set up, he mused, moving to another window to see a double bed made up. 'Nice one!' he breathed, deciding to break into the place.

Forcing open the warped back door, he walked into the kitchen. There was no cooker, no food to speak of, so Amber could hardly be living there. In the bedroom, he pulled out a drawer and rummaged through some papers. There was nothing to say that she'd bought the cottage, nothing to show that she worked for a newspaper. The only thing of interest was a vibrator, and that didn't work. *Probably burnt the thing out!* Closing the drawer, he moved to the light switch. The power was off. The whole thing was a set-up, he was sure as he left the cottage. Placing Amber in the enemy camp, he returned to the church.

The rest of the morning didn't bring anything interesting, other than a huge order for drink and cigarettes from Jack. The afternoon passed without the merest whiff of a girl's tight crack. But the priest caught up with his work, drank too much, and left the church at six, wondering what the evening had in store for him. Sitting swigging still more lager in his back garden, he leaped to his feet as the front doorbell rang, hoping that Josie had returned for more sex.

'Oh! PC Bridlington! How nice to see you.'

'Good evening, Father. I'm sorry to trouble you, but I wish to speak with you about a somewhat delicate matter.'

'I see. Well, you'd better come in.'

'Thank you.'

Showing the constable into the lounge, the priest bade him sit down, wondering what the hell he wanted. 'Tea, or coffee perhaps?' he asked.

'No, I'm fine, thank you. Now, Father, I'll come straight to the point. There have been sightings of naked women . . . forgive me, Father, but those ungodly words were necessary.'

'Of course, Constable, please carry on.'

'These sightings have taken place in the woods behind Cumsdale Village Hall. Mrs Highmen, from the village knit-wear shop, alleges that the aforementioned women often indulge in . . . I'm sorry, Father, but I have to use an ungodly word again.'

'That's all right, Constable, I quite understand.'

'Thank you. These women were indulging in an unhealthy lesbian entanglement. Now, Mrs Highmen has never ventured close enough to identify the women but . . . well, Father, she alleges that she saw *you* in the woods last night. I just wondered . . .'

'Yes, Constable, I was there. I often take a walk in the evenings and, of late, I've been walking through the woods behind the village hall. I enjoy bird watching, you see. There are some fine specimens there – especially the tits.'

'Tits, Father? Oh, yes, I see.'

'Do you know anything about birds, Constable?'

'No, Father. I don't have the time for such things, I'm sorry to say.'

Thank God for that! 'Ah, that's a shame. I was lucky enough to come across a pale-breasted, long-teated, deep-throat warbler the other evening. Quite a rare sight these days.'

'Yes, Father, I'm sure it is.'

'And last night, that's when Mrs Highmen must have seen me, I spotted a pair of lesser-feathered bush tits. You can always tell the male, because he has virtually no plumage on his head and a sort of mole-like pimple just above his beak. And the female has a lovely furry mound beneath her lower belly. They really were a wonderful pair of tits! There are a few bustards roaming the woods, too.'

'I beg your pardon, Father?'

'Bustards, Constable – birds.'

'Oh. So, you haven't come across any . . . er . . . there were no naked women in the woods then, Father?'

'Good heavens, no! But I shall contact you immediately should I *come* across any naked women in the woods, Constable, I can assure you of that!'

'Well, thank you, Father. I'm sorry to have troubled you. Good night.'

'Good night, Constable.'

Seeing the police officer out, Father Will closed the door and breathed a sigh of relief. 'That bloody Mrs Highmen!' he cursed. 'Thank God she didn't see me with . . . What the hell's she doing skulking around the woods, anyway?' Grabbing the ringing phone, he smiled to hear Chloë's refreshing young voice.

'Chloë, how are you, my child?'

'Sore, Father – very sore!'

'Oh, yes, I . . .'

'Anyway, I'm just calling to tell you that my mother is going away for a few days again so I'll come round, if you'd like me to, that is?'

'Yes, of course, Chloë! Where does your mother go to on these excursions of hers?'

'I'm not sure. I believe it's some kind of rehabilitation centre for jilted, broken-hearted women.'

'She certainly needs . . . anyway, come round now, Chloë, and we'll enjoy a good . . . a nice drink together.'

'All right, Father. I'm in the call box just down the road so I'll be with you shortly. Bye!'

'Bye, Chloë!'

Answering the front door, the priest cursed his visitor before smiling his greeting. 'Oh, Cheryl, nice to see you! I'm afraid I'm rather busy this evening. What was it you wanted?' *Alleluia! No handbag!*

'I just thought I'd come and see you,' she smiled, walking past him into the hall.

'Actually, I'm expecting someone,' he faltered, following her into the lounge, scrutinizing her curvaceous buttocks rising beneath her microskirt.

'I'll go when they arrive. Aren't you pleased to see me?'

'Yes, of course I am, it's just that . . .'

'Just that you've gone off me, is that it?'

'No. Did you ring your husband?'

'Yes, I did – and I'm not going back to him. So, who are you expecting, anyone I know?'

'Er . . . no, I don't think so,' he replied, praying that the nun wouldn't recognize Chloë as one of her girls. In the light of Sister Felicity's transformation, there was no way Chloë would recognize her as one of her nuns! 'That will be her now,' he said as the doorbell rang.

Showing Chloë into the lounge, Father Will introduced his visitors to each other and offered them a drink, wondering how long Cheryl would stay. Obviously desperate for another lesson in sex, Chloë didn't seem too pleased to have company, particularly that of a sensual young blonde. But she'd learned a lot of late, and sat on the sofa with her young thighs parted just enough to display her bulging panties. Sure that Father Will would be driven to get rid of her rival, she opened her legs a little further. But, older and wiser, Cheryl, joined in the exhibitionism, parting her shapely legs to display not her panties to the priest's hungry gaze, but her pussy crack.

Talking and knocking back vodka, the competition between the girls hotted up. Cheryl now blatantly showing her gaping labia and Chloë sitting with her legs apart to the hilt, her panties buried between her pouting pussy lips, Father Will suggested that he sit between them.

'What are you after?' Cheryl asked, her eyes sparkling.

'After? I'm not after anything!' he laughed.

'Well, I am!' she returned with a glint in her eye.

'What do you mean?' Chloë asked in her innocence.

'A threesome!' Cheryl giggled, nudging the priest's arm.

'I still don't understand,' sighed Chloë.

'She means sex, Chloë,' Father Will smiled, turning to the girl. 'There are certain things that you know nothing about, as yet. Our lessons haven't yet taken you down the beautiful path of lesbian sex, my child.'

'Lesbian sex! But, Father, that's sinful!'

'No, it's only sinful if you indulge in lesbian sex simply to fulfil debased sexual desires. Lesbian sex can be an extension of a friendship, and you are among friends now.'

'What's all this about lessons?' Cheryl asked.

'I've been teaching young Chloë here the joys of sex.'

'I'll teach you the joys of lesbian sex, Chloë,' Cheryl suggested, smiling at the girl as she reached across Father Will to stroke her leg.

'Well, I don't know if . . .' Chloë began, looking to the priest for guidance.

'Come on, it's all right! You'll enjoy it!' Cheryl coaxed. 'You see, a girl knows what a girl needs, what she likes. I know what will please you, what you'll enjoy, because I'm a girl, too.'

'She's right,' Father Will smiled, stroking Chloë's thigh. 'Let her show you the delights of lesbian sex. You need to learn of all aspects of sex, Chloë.' *Especially from a nymphomaniac nun!*

Kneeling by the younger girl's feet, Cheryl parted her legs and kissed her inner thigh. The priest smiled reassuringly as, again, Chloë looked to him for reassurance. Moving nearer to the swell of her panties, Cheryl licked the young girl's smooth skin, breathing in her body scent as Father Will watched, his penis already hard beneath his cassock. Chloë lay back, closing her eyes and opening her legs further as Cheryl nibbled her panties, wetting the material with her saliva, blowing through the silk, warming the girl's shaven pussy lips with her hot breath.

'Lift your bum up,' Cheryl breathed, tugged on Chloë's panties and pulling them down to her knees. 'Oh, they're all wet!' she observed as she tugged them down her legs and pulled them off over her ankles. Eyeing the girl's baby-soft pussy lips, she gasped. 'My God, you've shaved!' she cried, moving forward and kissing the smooth cushions of flesh either side of the girl's pinken slit.

Chloë let out a rush of breath as Cheryl licked her sex-groove, swelling her pussy lips, opening them to expose the complex girl-folds within the moist valley. Peeling the girl's lips apart, the nun licked Chloë's swelling clitoris fervently, hardening the protrusion, reddening the glistening flesh. Chloë moved her hips forward, pressing her open groove hard against Cheryl's mouth as Father Will knelt on the sofa and lifted his cassock, offering his long, hard shaft, his distended knob, to her pretty mouth.

'Suck, my child,' he breathed, pressing the organ against her full lips. Opening her mouth, Chloë sucked his knob inside, running her tongue over the silky glans as Cheryl stiffened her clitoris even more. Chloë was learning of new things, new experiences, new sensations, and the priest was pleased that Sister Felicity had come round after all. He watched Chloë, monitored her expression as her cunt was licked by another girl's tongue, her mouth filled by a huge male organ. She was becoming lost in her arousal now, snorting through her nose as her clitoris swelled and throbbed and the priest's penis twitched in her mouth.

Cupping his heavy balls in one hand, she gripped the thick base of his solid rod with the other and moved her head back and forth. Father Will gasped as he gazed down at her full rosebud lips encircling his meaty shaft. She was quick to learn, he thought, as she withdrew his penis from her mouth and licked around his knob. The sight sent a quiver through his balls and he knew that he couldn't restrain himself for much longer.

'Nearly there?' he murmured through his quivering.

'Mmm!' she mumbled, nodding her head slightly.

'Then we will come together! My sperm feeding your mouth, and your juices Cheryl's!'

Stretching Chloë's cunt lips wide, exposing her erect nodule to her darting tongue, Cheryl worked feverishly on the girl. 'Make more cream!' she ordered as she licked around the entrance to her vagina. 'I want lots more juice!' Pushing three fingers into the girl's spasming cunt sheath, sucking her clitoris into her mouth again, her reward came in torrents as Chloë shuddered and writhed. Sucking for dear life on the priest's knob, Chloë's climax went into orbit as he released his spunk-flood in a cosmic explosion.

'Drink it, Chloë!' he cried, watching the girl mouth and suck as he filled her cheeks. Swallowing hard, she drank his magical fluid as Cheryl sustained her orgasm. Lost in the coupling, Chloë rolled her eyes, taking the full length of the male organ into her mouth as Cheryl licked the past ripples of pleasure from her throbbing cumbud. Eventually falling back on the sofa, leaving the spent penis glistening in the light, she rolled her head from side to side, murmuring her incoherent appreciation as Cheryl licked the last trickles of girl-come from her inflamed cunt.

'Well!' Cheryl grinned as she sat back on her heels and looked up to the girl. 'How did you enjoy your first lesbian-induced orgasm?' Chloë didn't answer. Her breathing still heavy, her head lolling, she reached between her legs and caressed her open girl-flesh, fingering her hot cunt, pulling and twisting her rubicund inner lips. 'She seems to have enjoyed it!' Cheryl chuckled, turning to Father Will.

'I know *I* did!' he smiled as he sat next to Chloë and kissed her full mouth.

'Me, too,' Chloë murmured, coming to her senses.

Wasting no time, Cheryl sat on the sofa, pulling her top off and unclipping her bra before slipping off her skirt. Turning to Chloë, she pulled the girl's T-shirt over her head and removed her bra. Tugging at her skirt, she pulled the garment down her slender legs and tossed it across the room before leaning forward to take the girl's nipple into her mouth, fondling her own budling as she sucked.

'Are you going to make me come with your tongue now?' she asked, breaking off briefly from her tonguing of the girl's areola, licking Chloë's full lips and pushing her tongue into her mouth. Glancing at Father Will, Chloë smiled.

'Yes, I will,' she conceded. 'But I want you both to lick me first.'

'You're learning fast, Chloë!' the priest praised, taking one of her nipples into his mouth and sucking hard.

The girl moaned her pleasure as Cheryl sucked at her other nipple. Looking down at the two mouths engulfing her milk buds, she shuddered. Now, two hands were between her thighs – fingers exploring, fondling, each stroking her outer labia. Locating her wet entrance, the fingers slipped into her creamy cavern, stretching the delicate flesh as they massaged her love tube. 'That's good!' she gasped as a finger located her clitoris and gently rubbed the hard protrusion. 'Both lick me now!'

Moving to the floor in unison, the priest and the nun pulled Chloë forward. Her buttocks over the edge of the sofa, they each opened her legs wide and nibbled her inner thighs. Moving closer to her gaping slit, their tongues licking her youthful skin, they sucked on her outer lips. Their faces pressed together, their tongues probing, licking the girl's open sex-valley, they reached up and squeezed her nipples.

'Oh, God!' Chloë cried as the tongues worked on her clitoris. 'God, I've never known such ... Ah, yes! Make me come!' Opening her legs wider, the servants of God stretched the girl's young cunt lips apart and licked at the reddening flesh. Both easing their fingers into her hot hole again, they began their thrusting, quickly bringing out her orgasm. 'Coming!' she wailed as her clitoris exploded beneath the darting tongues. 'Ah! Ah! Coming! Com—'

Her body shaking uncontrollably, she tossed her head from side to side as her orgasm rolled through her, touching every nerve-ending, tightening every muscle. Her cunt a fire-red, her areolae deep brown, her nipples hard, she cried out, filling the house with her wails of bliss. Finally falling limp, her head to one side, her eyes closed, her face flushed, she let out a long low moan of satisfaction. Cheryl licked the girl's slit, lapping her cunt milk up until she was clean. Lying on the sofa, her legs wide, her crack inflamed and gaping, she was the epitome of a woman satisfied. Her curvaceous body taut in youth, glowing in the aftermath of adult pleasure, she rested, allowing her climax to subside.

'She's a very pretty little thing, isn't she?' Cheryl observed.

'Yes, very. And so are you, Cheryl,' Father Will replied, admiring the swell of her rounded breasts, her long brown nipples. 'You haven't been attended to yet, have you?'

'No, and I think it's time I was, don't you?'

'Why don't you kneel in front of Chloë and bring her off with your tongue again while I take your sweet honeypot from behind?' he suggested.

'Which one?' she giggled, taking her position between Chloë's legs.

'Both, if you so wish!'

'My cunt first! Fuck my cunt first!'

Parting and lifting her buttocks, the priest gazed at the young nun's pouting labia, wet, glistening, swelling in readiness to encompass his massive shaft. As she leaned forward a little more to lick Chloë's open slit, he pushed the head of his penis between her quim lips and drove his shaft fully home, impaling the young beauty on his organ. Gently thrusting in and out of her tight cunt tube, he watched her inner lips clinging to his glistening shaft. 'Chloë can suck my come from your cunt when I've done!' he gasped as Chloë cried out in her rising arousal. 'It's all right, my child!' the priest laughed. 'I'll be fucking you next, so don't worry!'

Driving his rod deep into Cheryl's squeezing vaginal sheath as she reached her sexual heaven, he grunted and pumped out his sperm, filling her young hole to the brim. Trickling from her stretched entrance, running down her inner thighs, his come dripped onto the carpet. Slipping his penis out, he ran the jetting head up and down the dark crease between her buttocks. 'Chloë can lick you clean,' he murmured, pressing his knob into her bottom-hole. But, although it slipped past her yielding muscles, his spent shaft was powerless to dig deep into her bowels. 'You'll have to wait a while,' he sighed, pulling his knob out and moving to her side.

Her face dripping with perspiration and Chloë's girl-juice, Cheryl sucked the girl's orgasm from her pulsating clitoris. Barely able to utter her words of sex, Chloë twitched, her eyes rolling upwards as she fell to one side, her body consumed in its coming. Lapping up the girl's creamy offering, Cheryl finally fell back onto the floor and lay with her limbs outstretched, her eyes closed.

'You both look as if you've been fucked all day long!' Father Will laughed as he joined Chloë on the sofa.

'I feel as though I have,' the girl gasped, running her fingers up and down her gaping slit.

'God, so do I!' Cheryl gasped as she, too, massaged her swollen pussy lips.

Jumping up as the doorbell rang, the priest moved to the window and spied through the net curtain. 'Christ! It's the local bobby again!' he cried.

'Again?' Cheryl queried, climbing to her feet.

'Yes, he was here earlier. Both get dressed and slip out through the back door. Cut through the hedge and you can get to the lane through the church grounds.'

Making himself presentable, Father Will waited until the girls had slipped into their clothes and disappeared into the back garden before opening the door. 'Hello, again, Constable!' he smiled. 'Please, do come in.'

'Thank you, Father. I'm sorry to have to trouble you again, but there's been a development.'

'A development, Constable?'

'Yes, Father. Last night, while you were roaming through the woods behind the village hall, the bishop's car was broken into. The odd thing is that it was parked in the lane not far from the spot where the alleged incident concerning the lesbians took place. I find it odd that Mrs Highmen should be wandering through the woods, that you were bird-watching in the woods, that lesbians were seen at the very same spot, and that the bishop was also there. There seems to be a strange, if not downright unhealthy, interest in the woods behind the village hall.'

'Coincidence, Constable. The woods there are wonderful, a lovely place for walks, bird-watching, nature rambling and . . .'

'Yes, I take your point, Father. But there's more.'

'More, Constable?'

'Yes, more. Intrigued as to the unhealthy interest, I decided to take a look at the aforementioned wooded area myself. On investigating, I discovered this, Father – a large crucifix, such as the one you wear.'

'Well, I haven't lost mine. It must belong to the bishop.'

'Now, that's strange, because the bishop hasn't lost his, either. But stranger still is the fact that I discovered the crucifix only inches away from . . . from an item of clothing, a pair of . . . a woman's undergarment. The garment, now logged as exhibit X, was heavily stained, which leads me to believe that the owner of this crucifix was not only involved in some sort of sexual activity with a young woman in the woods that eventful night, but that he is also the man who broke into the bishop's car. On continuing my search, I found something else, Father.'

'What was that, Constable?' *A used condom?*

'Behind a bush, not too far from the spot where the alleged sexual activity occurred, I discovered that the vegetation had been flattened, suggesting that someone had been hiding in the bush, watching the proceedings. I also discovered a packet of ciga-rettes.'

'Suggesting that the person hiding behind the bush smokes, Constable?'

'Yes, Father. But more, the particular brand is of the duty-free variety. This was easily discernible as it states *duty-free* on the packet.'

'Very interesting, Constable. But what has all this to do with me?'

'Nothing, as yet. I just thought I'd tell you of my findings. Do you know of anyone who might have been to France, or away on holiday recently, Father?'

'No, but I'll ask around.'

'*I'll* do the asking around, thank you.'

'Yes, of course, Constable.'

'Well, that's all for now. Thank you for your time, Father.'

'Not at all, Constable. I'm only too pleased to help.'

Showing the policeman out, Father Will raised his eyes to heaven. But stopping by the front gate, the officer started ram-bling on again. 'There's one more thing, Father.'

'What's that?'

'Did you see the bishop's car parked in the lane, and if not, were you aware that he was taking a stroll through the woods?'

'No to both questions, Constable.'

'Right, then, I'll be going, Father. Good night.'

'Good night, Constable.'

'Oh, there is one other thing, Father,' the PC persisted, holding his hand to his head.

Who's he think he is, Columbo? 'What's that, Constable?'

'You mentioned that bustards roam the woods.'

'Yes, that's right.'

'On returning to the station, I did some homework and discovered that the bustard is a large game bird of Asia and Australia, with a wingspan of eight feet! Rather odd to find such a bird in Cumsdale woods, don't you think?'

'Little bustard.'

'Father!'

'The little bustard, Constable – sometimes called the turkey. They're often spotted in England.'

'Oh, I see. In that case, Father, I'll bid you good night.'

And goodbye! 'Good night again, Constable.'

Returning to the house, Father Will dashed to his bedroom to discover that his crucifix was missing. 'Shit!' he breathed. 'It might have my fingerprints on it, or a fibre from my cassock, or DNA from my sperm!'

Gazing out of the bedroom window, he desperately tried to think, to plan his next move – his alibi. With the crime rate in Cumsdale village almost non-existent, PC Bridlington would enjoy getting his teeth into a mystery such as this. The priest would have to plant some clues somewhere well away from the woods to put the officer off the scent – the scent of sin and sex. Because if he *were* to uncover the truth, the end would be more than nigh!

CHAPTER TWELVE

The heavens opening, Father Will decided to stay in his office, rather than brave going to the convent to take confession. It was Tuesday morning, and he still didn't relish meeting the Mother Superior. Planning his next move in the cold war, he thought of Cheryl – Sister Felicity – and wondered why she was still offering him rampant sex without so much as a tape recorder in sight. But she'd be into higher realms of artifice than tape recorders, he knew. God, not a video camera in the presbytery, surely? he speculated as he lit a cigarette. Or a bug up her fanny!

She could fuck away all day and all night, but she couldn't prove a damn thing without any evidence, he surmised, pulling the ring on a can of lager. He desperately wanted to know what her game was, but couldn't for the life of him work out her plan. She'd have heard that the video tape had gone missing and might try to gather more incriminating evidence. But she no longer trusted the bishop. What would she do? Go it alone, perhaps? Try to nail him single-handed? She had to be building up to something, he decided. Possibly trying to gain his confidence to lure him into a trap.

Emerging into the church, he walked over to the altar and looked up to the roof. No sign of a camera. But she wouldn't pull the same stunt twice, he was sure. So where was the trap to be set?

'Sorry to trouble you again, Father!' PC Bridlington's authoritative voice echoed around the church. 'But there's been a further development!'

Oh, Christ! 'Not at all, Constable. What is this further development?' the priest asked, walking up the aisle towards the officer.

'I . . . may I ask you why you're not wearing your crucifix, Father?'

Oh shit! 'You may, and I will tell you. I couldn't find my crucifix this morning. I didn't wear it yesterday, but I distinctly remember taking it off on Sunday afternoon and leaving it on my bedroom window sill. Now it seems to have disappeared.'

'That's odd. Was the window open?'

'Yes, during Sunday afternoon and evening I left it open as it was such a hot day. You don't suppose someone's stolen it, do you, Constable?'

'Mm, it looks that way, Father. I'd say that whoever stole your cross is the man who spent some time in the woods with a young woman and, possibly, the man who broke into the bishop's car.'

'Yes, I agree. What was the further development?'

'A young woman came to the station this morning to report a theft from her handbag. She told me that she'd left it unattended for a while and—'

'That was a silly thing to do!'

'Indeed, it was, Father. She'd left it unattended in the woods behind Cumsdale Village Hall. Now, what do you make of that?'

'Curiouser and curiouser! So, this young woman might well be the woman who had sexual relations with the man you're looking for?'

'That's what I thought, but she assures me that she was only picking flowers. Who was hiding in the bushes watching the aforesaid sexual activities? That's what I want to know.'

'I really can't imagine, Constable. Let's look at the facts. My crucifix was stolen and found lying next to the pair of . . . a certain item of women's stained underclothing. The bishop's car was broken into whilst parked in the lane. A young woman's handbag was raided while it was left unattended in the woods. And someone was watching the sexual activities from behind a bush – someone who smokes and might well have been abroad recently. Obviously the man who stole my crucifix was the very same man involved in the sexual activities. But who he is, I've no idea.'

'The young woman who reported the theft of a certain item from her handbag wasn't a party to the sexual activities, of that I'm sure. I believe her story about picking flowers because she looks like the flower-picking type. Anyway, I'll have to make further enquiries, Father. I'm pleased that we've sorted out the puzzle concerning your crucifix.'

'Yes, so am I. When will you be able to return it to me?'

'Not yet, Father – it's evidence, you see. I now have a cigarette packet, a pair of . . . an item of women's stained underclothing, and your crucifix. Anyway, I'll be off now. Thank you for your time, again. Goodbye, Father.'

'Goodbye, Constable – and good luck.'

Returning to his office, Father Will sat down and opened another can of lager. Christ, now the law's involved! he thought, wondering what the hell to do. Why on earth had Josie gone to the police? he wondered. She'd nothing to gain, and everything to lose by involving them. PC Bridlington wouldn't let it drop, he knew. He'd go on and on digging until the mystery had been solved. Not because he was conscientious, but because he had nothing better to do.

'Morning, Father!' Amber trilled as she skipped into the office.

'Morning, Amber, how are you?'

'Fine,' she smiled. 'I just thought I'd pop in and say hallo.'

'Well, I'm glad you did. How are your blackouts?'

'I'm having them more frequently, I'm afraid. Anyway, when will you be needing me to do the flower arranging?'

'Soon, Amber – soon. May I ask you something?'

'Of course!'

'The cottage, your cottage – are you actually living there?'

'Yes, of course – why?'

'I came to visit you and, as there was no answer, I took a peep through the window and . . .'

'It's a mess, I know. I'm waiting for my furniture to arrive and . . . well, it's chaos at the moment.'

'I see. I happened to be talking to the local estate agent yesterday and, apparently, the cottage is still up for sale. They have no knowledge of it being sold. Strange, that, don't you agree?'

'Very! I'd better go and see them! It's all gone through, the contracts and everything, so I don't understand it!'

'I suggest that you go and sort it out now before they try selling the place again.'

'Yes, you're right, I'll do that and then I'll come back.'

'All right, Amber, see you shortly.'

As the girl left the church, Father Will picked up the telephone and rang the bishop. 'Good morning, Bishop Simon Holesgood speaking,' the bishop replied.

'Ah, Bishop, it's Father Entercock. I've just been speaking to the village policeman and he told me that you were in the woods behind the village hall on Sunday evening.'

'Er . . . yes, that's right. I was out walking, you see . . .'

'The strange thing is that several people were in the woods that evening. Apparently, a couple were engaged in some sort of sexual activity, there was a voyeur in the bushes, Mrs Highmen was out walking there, you were out walking there, a girl had something stolen from her handbag – and your car was broken into.'

'Yes, I know the story. I *am* rather busy – what is it you want, exactly?'

'Well, I haven't told PC Bridlington this but . . . I know who the young man is. The one hiding in the bushes, I mean.'

'You . . . you know him? Have you spoken to him?'

'Yes, he rang me this morning. He said that he was out walking, as everyone seemed to be that evening, when he came across a couple indulging in some sort of lewd sexual activity. I remonstrated with him for watching, of course. Anyway, he had his

camera with him and . . . well, he assured me that I'd be astonished to see the photographs. He's bringing them over to me later
today.'

'Photographs? He took *photographs* of the couple in the
woods?'

'Yes, I can't think why.'

'Send him directly to me! I forbid you to look at such obscene
photographs! Contact him and tell him to come directly to me!'

'I can't send him to you because I don't have his phone number.
To be honest, I don't know him that well, Bishop. We worked at
MI5 together for a while, but we were in different sections.'

'MI5?'

'Yes, but that was some time ago.'

'You worked for MI5?'

'Yes, but don't say anything to anyone. It's the Official Secrets
Act, you see.'

'Official secrets . . . what time is this man coming to see you?'

'He didn't say. He just said that he'd bring the photographs over
later today. The point is, I was wondering whether he knows
anything about your car being broken into.'

'Listen, Father – whatever you do, don't look at the photographs!'

'I'll bring them straight over to you, Bishop. He told me that
he's still with MI5 and that he's on a special assignment that's
brought him to Cumsdale village. He didn't say what the assignment was, of course.'

'Are you sure he's with MI5?'

'Oh, yes. Things have changed a lot since I was with them, of
course, but—'

'This MI5 business, it's not on your record.'

'Well, no, it wouldn't be, would it? I mean, it's not the sort of
thing that—'

'I've got to go. Bring the photographs to me the minute you get
hold of them. And *don't* look at them!'

'Yes, of course, Bishop.'

Replacing the receiver, Father Will burst out laughing.

'Confusion, confusion!' he guffawed jubilantly.

'Confusion?' Annie frowned as she entered the office.

'Hi, Annie. How's it going?'

'Very well. Here's another fifty pounds. I've done two already this morning and I'm booked solid for today, so I can't stay.'

'Oh, right. About the table you wanted . . . I haven't got round to sorting it out, yet.'

'That's OK. By the way, I've a punter interested in the altar idea. He's willing to pay a fortune to have me over the altar so . . . is tonight all right?'

'Yes, what time?'

'Nine o'clock.'

'Right. I'll leave the rear door unlocked so you can both slip in that way. I'll also leave some lights on.'

'Thank you, Father. You won't be around, will you?'

'What, spying on you, you mean? Good gracious, no!' *You can bet your life I will!*

'Good, I'll be seeing you, then.'

'Have you had the bishop recently?'

'No, he's been lying low, for some reason.'

'I'll bet he has! Anyway, thanks for the cash – and good luck for tonight.'

'Thanks, Father – 'bye.'

A productive morning, the priest mused as the phone rang. 'Father William Entercock,' he intoned lazily.

'Ah, Father, it's me – Sister Teresa.'

'Hello, Sister T, how are you?'

'I'm all right. Listen, the Mother Superior has changed the laundry room arrangements. I'm having great difficulty in swiping the soiled knickers.'

'Oh, no! The advert will be out tomorrow! What's she done, exactly?'

'The girls now place their dirty knickers straight into a big tub of soapy water so—'

'Great! But, won't they get mixed up?'

'No, they've all got name tags sewn on.'

'What? I didn't notice any . . . Are you any good at sewing? I mean, can you take the name tags off?'

'Well, I could, but it would take hours.'

'Oh, God! I suppose the names won't mean anything to the punters. If anything, it adds a nice touch of authenticity. But you'll have to do something about this tub of soapy water.'

'I don't know what I can do, but I'll try and think of something.'

'Thanks, Sister T. You're an angel.'

'Hardly!'

'Well, a little demon, then!'

'I'll speak to you later. I can hear the old hag's voice bellowing down the corridor, so I'd better go.'

'OK, bye for now.'

A group of people murmuring in the church caught the priest's attention and he went through to see what they wanted. 'Good morning, I'm Father Will Entercock!' he greeted a middle-aged woman as she approached him.

'Good morning, Father,' she smiled. 'We were just passing through the village when we spotted your wonderful church. Would you mind if we looked around?'

'Not at all!' he replied, eyeing six young schoolgirls milling around behind the woman.

'Oh, good. We're from a Sixth Form College,' the woman smiled. 'We're on a touring holiday and we're trying to take in as many villages as possible. I must say that Cumsdale is one of the prettiest we've come across so far. When was the church built, do you know?'

'Well, there's a headstone in the graveyard that dates back to the fourteenth century, and I believe that's when the church was built.'

'We'll take a look round the graveyard first, then,' she smiled. 'Come on, girls, into the cemetery!'

The girls groaned as they followed the woman outside. Rather nice, Father Will thought, gazing at their slender legs and short skirts. An attractive young brunette turned and smiled at him as she passed through the doorway and, returning her smile, he wondered if she was wearing panties, and whether she shaved.

I'd love to show her my brass rubbings!

'Who are they?' Amber asked, rushing over to him.

'A bunch of schoolgirls on a touring holiday or something. Anyway, what did the estate agent say?'

'There was a mix-up with their filing system. They had a temp working for them for a while and she didn't know that I'd bought the cottage. By the way, the furniture should arrive today.'

So she wasn't lying! 'That's good. You'll be able to get yourself properly settled in.'

'Yes, I'm really looking forward to it. Have you ordered the flowers, yet?'

'Oh, God! I forgot. Look, why don't you go to the florist and pick some up? There's fifty quid, see what you can do with that.'

'All right, Father. I'll see you later.'

Hope she has one of her blackouts soon – I could do with a good fuck!

Sitting in his office, Father Will took stock of the situation. The bishop's confused – and terrified! The Mother Superior doesn't know what the hell's going on. Sister Felicity's posing as Cheryl. Josie's resolve to get her story might be weakening. Annie's doing very well. Chloë's learning fast! Sister Teresa's dealing with the soiled knickers problem. PC Bridlington is poking his nose in where it's not wanted. Amber is . . .

'Excuse me, Father,' a blonde schoolgirl interrupted as she leaned in the doorway.

'Oh, come in, my child!' he exclaimed over-invitingly, his gaze transfixed on her pert breasts, her long nipples pressing through her blouse.

'I wandered off on my own in the graveyard and came across a greenhouse.'

Oh, fuck!

'Ah, yes. I . . .'

'Are they your cannabis plants?' she asked, her pretty lips curling into a sexy smile.

'Cannabis? Er . . .'

'If they are, I was wondering if you'd sell one to me?'

'Sell one? Er . . . well . . .'

'If they're not for sale . . .'

'Yes, they are for sale but . . . What about your leader, your teacher or whoever she is?'

'She's all right. She wouldn't know a cannabis plant from a rubber plant!'

'Oh, I see. Well, in that case, let's go over to the greenhouse and you can choose one.'

Following the girl to the greenhouse, the priest gazed longingly at the backs of her knees, her thighs, her shapely bottom. God, she's a right little beauty! he mused as he looked around for the rest of the group. There was no sign of the others as he opened the greenhouse, eyeing the swell of her young breasts as she walked inside.

'How much were you thinking of?' he asked as she admired the plants.

'Oh, we girls never *pay* for anything!' she laughed.

'But I thought you wanted to buy one?' he queried.

'I do! I mean, we never pay with money.'

Is this really happening? 'Then what *do* you pay with?' he asked.

'With this!' she smiled, lifting her short skirt to reveal her knickerless pussy.

Gazing between the girl's legs, Father Will gasped. Her tight sex-groove was clearly visible through her sparse pubic hair, and he thanked God for the gift of young girls' tight cunts. Smiling at him, she lay on the ground, pulling her skirt up over her stomach as she opened her legs wide.

'Is it a deal?' she asked, opening her blouse and exposing her firm breasts, her erect nipples.

God, no bra! 'Er . . . yes, it's a deal,' he stammered, kneeling down between her legs.

'Don't take too long or they'll wonder where I am!' she giggled as he buried his face in her young bush and breathed in her pussy-scent.

Kissing her tight groove, he peeled her soft cushions of flesh back and licked the glistening pinken folds within. 'God, you taste good!' he breathed as he located her clitoris and sucked it into his mouth. Squirming, the young girl gasped as he flicked his tongue over the sensitive tip of her budling.

'Oh, yes, that's nice! But you must fuck me now!' she ordered as she arched her back.

'Come in my mouth, and then I'll fuck you,' he garbled through a mouthful of wet flesh.

Forcing her thighs open wider, the priest licked the entire length of her open slit, savouring her girl-cream as it flowed from her vaginal opening and trickled over her rubicund inner lips. Moving his attention back to her clitoris, he licked the surrounding flesh, teasing her until she begged to come. 'Please! I'm . . . I'm com—' Writhing, gasping, shuddering violently as he mouthed and sucked her clitoris, her orgasm exploded in a gush of pussy juice. Reaching up, he pinched her hard nipples, sustaining her pleasure as he continued to massage her clitoris with his tongue.

Shuddering her last shudder, she fell limp as he lifted his cassock and presented his cock to her wet pussy. 'And now for the payment proper!' he cried, thrusting his shaft deep into her tight pussy hole.

'Oh God!' she gasped as he impaled her young body on his huge organ.

'Big, isn't it?' he grinned as he began his pummelling.

'Christ! I've never known one so big! God, I'll tear open!'

'No, you won't. Put your legs over my shoulders and I'll give you a really good fucking!'

Following his instructions, she placed her slender legs over his shoulders, allowing him even deeper penetration. Her pouting pussy lips encompassing his massive shaft, her clitoris exposed, forced from its pinken hide, she lifted her head and gazed at her stretched girl-flesh. Thrusting his wet penis in and out of her tightening hole, his sperm rose quickly from his balls and jetted from his swollen knob, filling her young sheath, lubricating his pistoning shaft.

'I can feel it spurting inside me!' she cried as he rammed her young cervix even harder. 'Coming! I'm coming again!' she screamed as her young cunt tightened around his penis, gripping him like a soft vice as her body shook. 'Fuck me harder!' she pleaded. 'Ah, yes! That's it! Really give it to me!'

His balls drained, his shaft shrinking within her hot cunt, he lay over her young body and mouthed at her milk buds. 'That was good,' he whispered, sucking her nipple into his mouth. 'Shame you don't live nearby.'

'God, you're so big!' she giggled as he slipped his penis from her young vagina. 'I've had some big men in my time, but you're the biggest!'

'Thank you. And now you'd better be getting back to the others or they'll come looking for you.'

Adjusting her clothing as she stood up, she gazed at the row of potted plants. 'This one, I think,' she smiled, lifting a pot.

'Right, let's go,' said the priest, opening the door. 'You didn't tell me your name.'

'Jenny,' she replied. 'I'll go back alone – you'd better wait here for a while.'

'All right, Jenny. And, thank you.'

'Thank *you*!'

God, she's beautiful! he thought as he watched her disappear through the hedge with her cannabis plant. Wishing that she lived in the village, he grabbed the watering can and watered his plants. 'May I buy one?' a young girl asked as she appeared in the doorway. Her long dark hair framing her pretty face, her blouse open, revealing her cleavage, her skirt tight and short, the priest couldn't believe his luck.

'Er . . . did Jenny tell you how much they cost?' he asked, gazing into her big green eyes.

'Yes, she did – and I'd like to buy one,' she smiled, lifting her skirt.

His eyes wide with astonishment, he gazed at her youthful crack. Her pubic hair trimmed so short that it was barely visible, he smiled as she lay on the ground and opened her legs wide. 'Business is looking up!' he breathed, settling between her legs and kissing her puffy pussy lips. Reaching down, the girl peeled her pussy open, exposing her erect clitoris to the priest's hungry gaze.

'Be quick!' she said. 'We don't want to get caught!'

'I'd love to spend hours with you!' he gasped as he pushed his tongue into her snug pothole.

'I could always come and visit you,' she wavered. 'I only live thirty miles away.'

'Yes, do that!'

'Fuck me now, Father! Fuck me silly!'

Lifting his cassock, the priest displayed his huge penis. Wavering from side to side as he aligned the head with her open hole, he smiled. 'It's big!' he warned.

'God, I can see that!' she exclaimed, her eyes wide. 'You'll never get that inside me!'

'Don't you believe it! Now, open wide!'

Running his knob up and down her slit, he lubricated his weapon in readiness for the impaling. Pressing his purple head between her stretched pussy lips, he quickly drove his shaft into her tense body, causing her to gasp and grimace as he filled her tight young cunt, stretching it to capacity with his massive organ. Looking down, he grinned to see her taut outer lips gripping the base of his shaft, her abdomen rising and falling as he slipped his rod in and out of her tight sheath. Opening her blouse, she displayed her small breasts to his appreciative gaze. Her areolae darkening with her arousal, her nipples growing long and hard, she was a fine young specimen, and he wished he had his camera with him.

'Ever thought of being a model?' he asked as he thrust deep into her hot cunt again.

'God, I'll split open!' she cried. 'Yes, I have thought of . . . ah! Ah, yes!'

'I could take some nice pictures of you – you could earn a fortune, you know.'

'Yes . . . Oh, God – that's lovely! Fuck me harder, please!'

Leaning on his hands, he swung his hips back and forth, hammering her young cervix with his ballooning knob as she cried out in her sexual ecstasy. Two young girls in succession, he thought, watching his glistening shaft appear and disappear. 'I'm coming!' she cried as he took her young cunt with a vengeance, his heavy balls slapping her taut buttocks with every thrust. Tossing her head, rolling her eyes, she whimpered her release as her orgasm took her to her sexual heaven.

'And now to sperm inside you!' he gasped as his seed rose to the head of his throbbing penis and spurted deep into her tight pussy-hole.

Opening her legs to capacity, she closed her eyes, delighting in the sensations emanating from her clitoris, her stretched cuntal sheath, as he pumped out his offering. Her body rocking with each thrust, she begged him to stop, but he only continued with the beautiful fucking until he'd drained his balls and collapsed over her heaving body.

'Bloody hell!' she gasped as finally, he slid his rod from her steaming sheath. 'That was amazing!'

'It certainly was!' he agreed, climbing from her and sitting on his heels. 'You have a lovely cunt,' he observed as she massaged her clitoris with her slender fingers.

'And you have a lovely tool!' she reciprocated, lifting her head and gazing at his wet penis resting over his huge balls. 'I'd better go. I don't want to get caught.'

Helping the girl to her feet, Father Will asked whether any of her friends would like to buy a plant. They all wanted one, she said, but they had to leave. 'Will you be passing through Cumsdale again – on your way back, perhaps?' he enquired.

'Maybe. I don't really know what the plan is. But I'll ring you and let you know.'

'Good. The number's in the book under Cumsdale Church.'

'Right. My name's Lesbia, by the way.'

'Ah, Lesbia! Girl of Lesbos – how wonderful!'

'What's your name, Father?'

'Will.'

'Well, I hope to see you again – 'bye.'

'Bye, Lesbia – take care.'

The schoolgirl party gone, Father Will returned to the church to find Amber arranging flowers. Reaching up to place a vase on a high shelf, her delicate white blouse rose to display a band of naked flesh around her middle. The priest gazed at her, wondering why she'd not had a blackout – and praying that she would!

'Very nice!' he praised as she stood back to admire her work.

'Thank you, Father,' she replied bashfully, turning to face him. 'I've left the change on your office desk. By the way, those girls who were here . . . the woman with them was coming up from the basement when I got back. She looked quite stunned. She asked me if I'd worked here for long, and then ordered the girls to leave the church.'

276

'Oh, no! She didn't say anything else, did she?'

'She said that I'd be hearing from the authorities. I don't know what she meant by that, do you?'

'Er . . . no, I don't. Have you been down into the basement?'

'No, I've been busy, as you can see,' she smiled, waving her hand at several vases of flowers.

Leaving Amber to her work, Father Will sat at his desk and sighed. What the hell to do now? he wondered, lighting a cigarette. 'I thought I'd locked the basement door!'

'Sorry?' Josie smiled as she appeared in the doorway.

'Oh, Josie, it's you.'

'It is. Why are you talking to yourself? Are you going mad?'

'I've been mad all my life! I've got more problems, I'm afraid.'

'You and me both!' she sighed as she sat down.

'Why, what's *your* problem?' he asked, grabbing a can of lager from the desk drawer and offering it to her.

'Thanks,' she smiled, taking the can. 'You know about me, don't you?' she asked, her eyes gazing into his.

'Know what about you?'

'Who I am, what I've been up to.'

'Sorry, I'm not with you,' he replied, opening a can and taking a gulp.

'You mean . . . you really *don't* know what I've been doing all this time?'

Josie wanted to come clean, he knew, but the time wasn't right. If he let on that he knew her game, that he'd known from day one, it might ruin his chances of exposing the Reverend Mother and the bishop. On the other hand, she might be able to help him nail them.

'I don't know what you're talking about,' he bluffed. 'You'll have to tell me.'

'No, it's all right. It's nothing important. So, are you still being hounded by people trying to destroy you?'

'Yes, constantly! Anyway, what's your problem?'

'I've been sacked.'

I'm not surprised! 'Sacked? But, why?'

'Er . . . my sales figures weren't good enough.'

'Oh. So, what will you do now?'

'I don't know. I won't be able to keep my flat – not unless I find another job straight away.'

'There must be plenty of sales jobs around?'

'Well, yes, I suppose so, but . . . my work was rather special-ized. Anyway, when word gets round that I've failed miserably, no one will want to know me.'

'Failed miserably? You weren't *that* bad, surely?'

'Er . . . yes, I was, I'm afraid. I really thought that you knew about . . . Never mind.'

'I suppose you'll be going back to London now?'

'There's nothing for me there – or here, for that matter, so I don't know what to do.'

'You'll work it out, don't worry.'

'There's nothing *to* work out! No money, no job, and I'll have no flat soon. I haven't even got a boyfriend!'

'What about Brian?'

'No, no. Brian's been sacked, too. We both . . . anyway, my only hope is to find a man with some money and settle down. I don't suppose you'd like to take me on, would you?' she laughed.

Taking another swig from his can, Father Will gazed at Josie. This was the first time she'd been even half-honest with him, and the first time she'd hinted at a permanent relationship, although he recalled her asking him if he'd give his other women up if he had someone special. He pictured her on his bed, her pretty face, her pixie hair dishevelled in her arousal, her skirt raised, her shorn pussy grinning at him. Was she serious? Would she really consider having a permanent relationship with him?

Things were getting rough, too rough, he mused. Now that the bloody school teacher had joined in the battle to destroy him, he realized that his stint as Priest of Cumsdale Parish was coming to an end – possibly a sticky end, inside.

'I'd consider taking you on, yes,' he replied. 'As I told you the other day, I've had enough of the priesthood. It seems that I've made too many enemies to carry on now, anyway!'

'I don't think you have.'

'There's someone out there trying to destroy me, as you know, and there are others, too. I can't win, Josie. I might as well give up now, get out while I can!'

'Where would you live? I mean, you'd lose the presbytery, wouldn't you?'

'Yes, I would. I really don't know what I'd do, or where I'd go.'

'What about your parents? Wouldn't they put you up?'

'No, they've gone.'

'Oh. What was your mother like?'

'She was made in the image of God.'

'How do you mean?'

'I never saw her, never heard her, and I don't believe that she existed.'

'And your father?'

'I am my own father. I am a creation of myself.'

'What?'

'Forget it.'

'Well, my flat's big enough for two – provided I can afford to keep it on, that is. Anyway, I must be going.'

'Will you be around for a while or are you going straight back to London?'

'I'll stay on for a few days, I suppose.'

'Oh, good. Well, I'd better get on.'

'I'll see you again. 'Bye, Father.'

'Bye, Josie.'

The priest sat back in his chair, gazing at the ceiling, wondering what to do. He didn't want to appear too interested in Josie's offer, if it really was an offer. He didn't know what he wanted. Josie,

Sister Teresa, Chloë, Amber . . . they were all attractive, sensual, and bloody good in bed – and on the sofa, in the woods, in the church . . .

'I've finished the flowers, Father,' Amber announced brightly as she came into the office.

'Oh, good.'

'Who was that girl?'

'No one special. She's been . . . never mind. So, do you want to sort the Bibles out for me, or have you had enough for today?'

'Until my furniture arrives, I've nothing to do, so I might as well stay here.'

'Great. Look, they're on the shelves by the doors. The shelves need cleaning and the Bibles need stacking properly so . . .'

'Leave it to me, Father.'

Poor girl, he thought as she left the office – blackouts, no friends, lives on her own. Still, we've all got problems! Answering the phone, his face dropped as he heard PC Bridlington's dulcet tones.

'There's been yet another development, Father,' he said accusingly.

'And what's that, Constable?' Father Will asked, raising his eyes to the ceiling.

'I've had a woman come to see me. She claims that the church basement is full of alcohol and cigarettes. I told her that the idea was ridiculous, of course, but she insisted that there is also a fully equipped bar down there!'

Oh, fuck! 'Alcohol, cigarettes, a bar? The church doesn't even *have* a basement, Constable, let alone . . .'

'No basement?'

'No.'

'Oh, well . . . I'll call in and check this afternoon, about three o'clock, Father. It's not that I don't believe you, of course – it's just to set the record straight.'

'All right, Constable. Goodbye.'

'Goodbye, Father.'

What the hell am I going to do now? the priest thought as he banged the receiver down. Josie's offer was becoming more tempting by the minute, but he couldn't just up and run. 'I should never have sold the plants to those bloody schoolgirls! I'll be banged up for . . . oh, hallo, Amber – that was quick.'

'I haven't finished, I need a duster and some polish.'

'Oh, right. There's a cupboard in the corner, by the altar.'

'OK, thanks. Have you got problems?'

'You could say that, yes!'

'Can I help?'

'No, I don't think so. Thanks, anyway, Amber.'

Leaving the girl to her work, Father Will grabbed his camera from the presbytery on the off chance that he'd come across the archbishop screwing the Reverend Mother, and wandered down the lane, his head aching with worry. At least the bloody rain had let up for the time being. The photographs taken in the woods would put an end to the bishop's threats, he knew. But the Mother Superior was a constant problem. Josie no longer posed a threat, while Cheryl hadn't yet put her plan into action, whatever it was.

'No one's actually got any proof, as yet,' he breathed as he walked through the trees in the convent grounds. 'No pictures, no tapes – nothing.' PC Bridlington was a real pain in the arse, though, or he would be when he came sniffing round the church in search of the basement.

Wandering aimlessly across the damp lawn, he walked around the side of the convent to the Mother Superior's office window. Sitting under the window, he lit a cigarette, listening to the Mother scolding one of the girls for misbehaviour.

'You will be punished!' she threatened. 'You will pay for your obscenity! But before you take your punishment, you will recite aloud for the ears of your Maker the filth you chalked on the blackboard for all the world to see!'

'But, Mother . . .'

'I'm waiting, girl!'

Almost beside himself with anticipation, Father Will trained his ears to hear the girl's embarrassed mumblings.

> 'There once was a randy old priest,
> Whose dick was a bit of a beast.
> As he took Reverend Mother,
> He screamed "There's no other
> With a devil of ten feet, at least!"

'That's disgusting! Now, pull your knickers down, lift your skirt up and bend over my desk – you naughty little girl!' Rising to his feet, Father Will looked through the window to see the Mother Superior wielding a long, thin cane. The girl lay over the desk, her grey knickers round her knees, her skirt up over her back, her taut buttocks splayed.

'My God!' he gasped as the cane struck her buttocks. No point in taking any pictures, he thought. The Mother Fucker would only say that she was punishing a girl. There was nothing bent about that – well, nothing much!

Bulging beneath the dark crease of her buttocks, the girl's pouting labia were clearly visible. Her inner lips protruding from the dividing groove, glistening in the light, invited a kiss, a caressing tongue, and the priest prayed that the Reverend Mother would fall to her knees and suck between the girl's legs. Camera at the ready, he watched the thrashing, his penis threatening to tear its way out of his cassock, his eyes bulging.

Thin weals appeared across the girl's taut buttocks as the Reverend Mother delighted in the caning session, thrashing her victim harder and harder. The girl was obviously enjoying her punishment. Crying out for more, squirming, pushing her bottom out to receive the cane, she opened her legs wide, affording Father Will a perfect view of her bulging cunt lips, dripping with her teenage juices.

As he was about to lift his cassock to take his penis in hand, the Mother Superior stopped the thrashing abruptly and moved away from the girl. 'If you're going to make up limericks, you could at least do it properly!' she bellowed.

'Properly, Mother?'

'Something with substance!' she replied scathingly, her hands on her hips as she took a deep breath and brayed forth:

> 'There was a young nun called Theodora,
> The thick cream from whose pussy did appal her.
> She gasped: "God, what's that?
> I haven't a cat
> So who'll lick out this dreadful plethora?"

Her knickers still round her knees, the girl giggled as the senior nun lifted her habit and lay over the desk, her huge buttocks taut, her substantial cunt lips hanging between her thighs. 'Now for my defilement, *you* will punish *me*!' the excited nun cried.

Taking the cane, the girl began the beating, landing blow after blow across the Reverend Mother's wobbling orbs. His camera clicking and whirring, Father Will grinned triumphantly. 'At last!' he breathed. 'I've got the old hag!'

Suddenly dropping the cane, the girl followed the Mother's instructions and fell to her knees as the debauched woman lay further over the desk, spreading her legs wider to display her swollen pussy. The girl moved forward, licking the fleshy cushions, poking her tongue into the dividing crease to the accompaniment of the Reverend Mother's gasps. Pushing four fingers into the creamy flesh-cavern, the girl began her thrusting, bringing the nun closer to her climax. The camera shutter clicking again and again, the priest prayed that the light was strong enough to show the lewd scene in all its sordid glory.

Pulling her fingers from the Reverend Mother's dripping vagina, the girl took her place, lying on her back across the desk, her thighs wide, her youthful mound high, her swollen cunt lips gaping. Standing by her side, the woman of God massaged the girl's clitoris, dragging her lubricant from her hole up her slit to bathe her stiffening nodule. The girl gasped, tossed her head from side to side as her orgasm rose from her young womb and erupted between her legs. Moaning her ecstasy, she pulled her skirt up higher to reveal the creamy plateau of her stomach, her hairy mound.

Taking a huge vibrator from her desk drawer, the Reverend Mother presented the pink tip to the girl's vaginal entrance and slowly slipped the long cylindrical shaft deep into her trembling body. The girl reached down and peeled her pouting lips back, exposing her erect clitoris, her wet inner flesh encompassing the huge phallus. Taking several more shots, Father Will watched in amazement as the nun thrust the vibrator in and out of the girl's tight sex-duct, inducing a copious flow of girl-juice to flow from her stretched hole. Leaning over the girl, the Mother Superior licked the glistening flesh surrounding her clitoris, stiffening the budlette with her darting tongue.

Shuddering, the girl wailed, writhing as her young cunt gripped the phallus and her clitoris erupted in the nun's hot mouth. Slipping the vibrator from the girl's tight love-sheath, her mentor lapped up her slippery juices, cleansing her until the girl could take no more, rolling from the desk to hit the floor. Father Will couldn't hear her muttered words as she climbed to her feet and opened the desk drawer. But he soon realized what the Mother Superior had said. His eyes popping, he watched the girl strap a leather belt around her waist. Running another strap between her legs, she attached a huge rubber dildo to the crotch strap as the nun positioned herself over the desk again, her buttocks bared, her gaping pussy folds dripping with her cream.

Moving towards her goal, the girl gripped the dildo, aligning the rounded end with the Mother's gaping cunt. 'Put it in!' the nun cried. 'That's it!' she gasped as the girl thrust the phallus deep into the woman's vagina. Moving her hips back and forth, the girl rammed the Mother Superior's drenched cuntal cavern, taking her, using her as a man would. Harder and faster the girl fucked the older woman as the priest clicked his camera, knowing now that he'd got the Mother Fucker right where he wanted her.

Feasting his eyes on the incredible sight like a ghoul devouring flesh, he could barely believe the lewd scene. Still thrusting the dildo into the Mother's wet hole, the young girl hitched her skirt up. The leather strap disappearing between her burning buttocks, he prayed that she'd be caned again, thrashed for her sins.

'What *are* you doing?' a soft, lilting voice gasped. Turning, Father Will smiled to see Sister Teresa. 'Not spying on the old hag, are you?' she asked.

'Take a look,' he grinned. 'You've never seen anything like it in your life.'

Gazing through the window, Sister Teresa let out a rush of breath. 'I thought I'd seen everything,' she whispered. 'But never a schoolgirl and a Reverend Mother!'

'I've taken photographs, so now, at long last, we've really got the old bag nailed.'

'This is what we've been waiting for. My God, look, the old hag's coming!'

Taking more photographs as the Reverend Mother clung to the desk, shuddering in her depraved heaven, Father Will became aware of his solid penis. Taking Sister Teresa's hand, he placed it over his bulging cassock. 'God, you're stiff!' she breathed as she dropped to her knees and lifted his priestly garment. Taking the ballooning head into her hot mouth, she gently sucked, rolling her tongue over the silky-smooth glans.

Watching the girl slip the dildo from the Mother's drenched vaginal sheath, his eyes widened to see her stab the thing between the woman's buttocks and sink it deep into her bottom-hole. 'God!' he gasped as Sister Teresa mouthed and sucked on his throbbing knob. 'I'm going to come! A schoolgirl fucking the old bag's bum with a dildo, a young nun sucking my knob . . . God help me!'

His sperm jetting into the nun's hot mouth, he leaned against the wall to support his quivering body. Looking down at the nun, he watched her slip his glans from her mouth. His cream spurting over her pretty face, splashing her mouth, she licked the throbbing head of his penis, taking it between her full lips now before drinking from his fountainhead. Swallowing the last of his essence, she kissed his knob, licked his shaft, her eyes rolling as she savoured his fruits. Focusing the camera, the priest snapped the young nun, her mouth open wide, her tongue circling his purple glans.

'Now, *I*'ve got something on *you*!' he whispered as the Reverend Mother wailed in her coming.

'In that case, I'd better get something on you!' Sister Teresa giggled, grabbing the camera and lifting her habit. 'Go on, lick my cunt,' she ordered crudely. 'It's all hot and wet, so lick me out.'

Kneeling, Father Will peeled her swollen pussy lips apart and licked her wet inner flesh as she clicked the camera. Pushing three fingers into the heat of her tight love-sheath, he began his thrusting. 'My clit . . . lick my clit!' she breathed shakily as her body quivered and her legs sagged. 'Oh, God, that's good!'

Slipping a finger into her tight bottom-hole, he sucked her pulsating clitoris into his hot mouth and brought out her orgasm. Clinging to his head, she dropped the camera, her body crumpling as she tried to stifle her moans of pleasure. Her body bouncing up and down as he rammed her holes in unison, she fell back against the wall, her come oozing from her cuntal sheath, running down the priest's fingers before irrigating the ground.

Finally collapsing, she lay gasping for air, her cunt lips inflamed, open, dripping with juice. 'God, that was fantastic!' she grinned, pulling her habit down. 'Now I have a picture of you licking my cunt, and you have one of me sucking your cock.'

'A keepsake,' he smiled. 'Should we never see each other again, we'll always have the photographs.'

'What do you mean? You're not going away, are you?'

'I might have to, I'm afraid.'

'Why? You've got incriminating photographs of the old hag now, so she can't touch you.'

'Yes, I also have photos of the bishop in the woods screwing a young girl, so there's no problem there. But the police are on to me.'

'Police?'

'Yes, it's a long story but . . . Basically, I'm fucked!'

'Tell me what's going on.'

'Someone tipped the police off about the church basement, the drink, the fags, and the bar. The village bobby's coming to the church to see for himself. I told him that there is no basement, but he still wants to check it out.'

'What are you going to do?'

'God only knows!'

'When's he coming?'

'About three this afternoon, why?'

'If I'm there, perhaps I can distract him or something?'

'That's a thought. Look, I'll get back now. I've got enough on film to screw the Mother Fucker so you're safe enough, which is something, I suppose. Anyway, I'll see you at three.'

'OK. I'll fix him, don't worry!'

'Great! See you later.'

Back at the church, Father Will walked around the rear of the building and gazed at the basement doors. Looking round the graveyard, he noticed several plastic sacks full of grass cuttings left by the gardener. 'That's it,' he breathed, dumping the camera and grabbing a sack. Lugging it over to the doors, he emptied the cuttings over them. Grabbing another sack, he spread his camouflage. Finally, emptying the last sack, he stood back and smiled smugly. Just the inside door now, he mused, picking the camera up.

Although the heavy velvet curtain concealed the inside door to the basement, he was sure that PC Bridlington would discover it, even with Sister Teresa distracting him. But there was nothing he could do to hide the door. In his office, he sat down, praying for guidance as he took a can of lager from the desk drawer.

Che sarà sarà he mused, wondering where Amber had got to. Swigging his lager, he pulled his men's magazine from the drawer and opened it at the centrefold. 'What a beauty!' he breathed, gazing at a voluptuous young woman holding her pussy lips wide open to expose her inner girl-folds. If he was defrocked, he could always go into pornography, he thought with a smile, imagining the girl squatting over his face, his tongue licking inside her creamy vaginal sheath.

Placing his feet on his desk, he finished his lager and reclined in the swivel chair. 'Hard work, fucking all these young girls!' he sighed as he dozed off and dreamed of PC Bridlington screwing Sister Teresa's bottom-hole.

CHAPTER THIRTEEN

'Are you there, Father?' PC Bridlington called as he entered the church. Opening his eyes, Father Will glanced at his watch – three o'clock.

'Er . . . yes, I was just . . . oh, hallo, Constable,' he smiled, wondering why he'd slept for so long. 'What, er . . . can I do for you?'

'The basement, Father. I'll take a quick look around, just to set the record straight.'

'Oh, right.' *Where the fuck's Sister T got to?*

Watching the officer patrol the church, stamping his feet and banging the walls in an effort to find the basement entrance, Father Will knew he'd discover the concealed door and demand access. His hands trembling, he was sure now that the end had come.

'This way, girls!' Sister Teresa called as she bustled into the church. Walking over to the priest, tailed by forty or so school-girls, she smiled. 'Where would you like them?' she whispered, winking at him.

Squatting over my face! 'Group them over there, by that curtain,' he replied with a conspiratorial grin. Instructing her pupils to gather by the curtain, the young nun wandered over to PC Bridlington.

'Good afternoon, Constable,' she greeted him.

'Good afternoon, Sister,' he acknowledged, removing his helmet and bowing his head.

'We're here to learn more about the history of Cumsdale Church,' she enlightened him breezily. 'Father Entercock has been good enough to have allowed us to visit the church on several occasions, and we've discovered quite a lot. It's a school project, you see. Did you know that the church was built before the village came into being?'

'Er . . . no, Sister, I didn't,' he replied.

'And did you know that it's one of the few churches in this part of the country to . . . well, I won't waste your time, Constable. You're obviously a very busy man.'

'Yes, I am, Sister. By the way, from your research, do you know if this church has a basement?'

'Oh, no. It's built on a bed of granite. This was a deliberate move to stop smugglers using church basements to store their spoils, you see. It seems that some members of the clergy were . . . how shall I put it? They were easily bribed and corrupted in those days, and they allowed their basements to be used for storing smuggled goods. Not that anything like that would happen today, of course!'

'No, of course not, Sister. Well, if you'll excuse me, I have to be getting back to the station. Enjoy your visit,' he smiled, glancing over to the girls.

'We will, Constable – good day to you.'

'Good day, Sister.'

Whooping for joy, Father Will turned to his partner in crime. 'You're a little . . .'

'Er . . . not in front of the girls, Father!' Sister Teresa interrupted.

'Oh, right. That was brilliant, Sister T! What a story! You're a natural-born actress!'

'Yes, it was good, wasn't it? Well, I'd better take the girls back before you get any ideas!'

'*Me*? Oh, Sister! How could you? I *am* a priest!'

'I know what you are, and that's what worries me! Come on,

girls! Time to be getting back! I'll see you later, perhaps,' she said, turning back to Father Will.

'Right. And, thanks.'

'Any time. But you owe me one, all right?' she laughed.

'I owe you several damn good . . .'

'The girls, Father!'

'Yes, they're wonderful, are they not? Hot, young, fresh, tight, wet—'

'You and your evil thoughts!'

'Let us do evil, that good may come!'

'That *you* may come, you mean! Anyway, shut up or the girls will hear you.'

'Oh, right. I'll see you later. Thanks again.'

'Thank God for that!' breathed Father Will, opening a celebratory can of lager back in his office. But he knew that his troubles were far from over. PC Bridlington wouldn't give up on the mystery of Cumsdale woods, and if that bloody school teacher discovered that her girls had 'bought' some cannabis plants, she'd go straight back to the police!

Finishing his lager, he locked the church doors and wandered down the lane. The rain had stopped again and the sun was shining brightly after the downpour. But there were heavy black clouds rolling in from the horizon. The air was particularly still, close. An omen? he wondered. The rainstorm's over, so will we have calm seas? Or is this the calm before the real storm? Although things were looking better, he decided that he'd better get out while the going was relatively good. No sense in hanging around to make another buck, he mused. Might as well take the money and run!

He'd fared well from his illicit earnings, but he was still far from rich. Without the presbytery, he'd have to buy a house, which wouldn't leave him a great deal to live on – not in the manner to which he'd become accustomed, anyway! One last earner, he thought, remembering the soiled knickers. Five hundred pairs would bring in ten grand – a thousand pairs . . . But were there that many perverted punters out there? 'Damn right there are, Entercock!' he breathed, deciding to stay on to the bitter end.

'Hello, Father!' Samantha Lovejoy called as she ran up the lane.

Sexy little thing. 'Oh, Samantha, how are you, my child?' he smiled, eyeing her firm, rounded breasts ballooning her virgin-white school blouse.

'Fine, thanks. I'm sorry to hear that you're leaving.'

'Leaving? I'm not leaving. Whoever told you that?'

'Er . . . a friend of my father's . . . he's an MP. I met him at . . . he was at my parents' house and he told me that you're leaving the priesthood.'

'I know nothing about this! How come I cropped up during the conversation?'

'Well, we . . . we were talking about the convent and the church and he said that he'd been speaking to the archbishop about changes. He just said that you'd be leaving soon.'

Pillow talk? Grass talk! 'Well, it's news to me!'

'I thought it strange that you were leaving. I wonder why he said it if it's not true?'

'Yes, I wonder, too! Perhaps you got the wrong end of the stick.' *The candle!* 'Look, I must be going, Samantha. I'll see you around sometime.'

'OK, Father – 'bye.'

As the girl skipped down the lane, her short skirt lifting in the breeze to reveal her convent knickers, Father Will recalled her down by the pond with the Dishonourable Member for Piddlington South. As well as getting her pussy from her knickers, he'd obviously let the cat out of the bag during his orgasmic gaspings. Realizing the seriousness of his situation, that there were now people in high places involved, he knew he'd have to take some drastic measures.

'Go straight to the top!' he breathed, remembering the bishop telling Josie about the archbishop's trip to Brighton with a young blonde. Turning on his heel, he walked back to the presbytery, rehearsing his lines before dashing into the lounge and grabbing the phone. 'It's Father William Entercock, may I speak to the archbishop, please?' he asked the secretary.

'I'll see if he's available. Hold on, please,' she replied stiffly.

'Father Entercock?'

'Good afternoon, Archbishop. I'm sorry to trouble you personally but . . . well, I have a problem and . . . I thought I'd better tell you about it.'

'Problem? What sort of problem, Father? Can't you go to your bishop instead of bothering me?' he asked irritably.

'No, I can't. Allow me to explain why, Archbishop. It's a very long story, so I'll spare you the details. The point is that a newspaper reporter came to me with allegations of . . . I don't quite know how to put this. Apparently, a young blonde girl, a friend of yours, allegedly, has been trying to sell a story . . .'

'A young blonde girl? A story?'

'Yes, Archbishop.'

'I know nothing of young blonde girls, Father!'

'Allegedly, you were staying at a hotel in Brighton with her and . . .'

'Er . . . oh, yes . . . My . . . my secretary. She accompanies me on church business, you see.'

'Does she? That's odd, because this girl, allegedly, was registered at the hotel as Mrs Dixon, and that's not your secretary's name. The reporter has photographs and, apparently—'

'Photographs? I don't know what you're talking about, Father!'

'In that case, there must be some mistake, Your Remnants. I can't imagine you staying at a hotel with a young blonde girl – and as for registering as Mr and Mrs Dixon! But the photographs . . .'

'Mr and Mrs Dixon? Photographs? Where did these photographs come from?'

293

'I've no idea.'

'Have you seen them?'

'No, but she's going to bring them over to show me.'

'When?'

'She didn't say, Archbishop.'

'I'll . . . I'll get back to you, Father. We can't have these sort of allegations—'

'Oh, I almost forgot. The MP for Piddlington South—'

'Yes, I know him well. What about him?'

'He . . . this is ridiculous, I know, but apparently, he's making moves to have me defrocked. I really can't think why, can you?'

'Er . . . no, I can't. Look, Father, say nothing about this to anyone. As I said, I know the MP well. I'll have a word with him. There's obviously been a mix-up. I mean, we wouldn't want to lose you, would we?'

'No, that's what I thought. I really can't see why an MP is—'

'There were to be one or two changes within various parishes, yours included. I did speak to him about it and all I can think is that he's misunderstood me. I was talking to your bishop a short time ago, by the way, and we were saying how much we value you. You've done a fine job in Cumsdale Parish and . . . well, let's not talk about these silly allegations. I wouldn't want to see you defrocked, Father.'

Are you threatening me? 'Of course, Archbishop. Thank you for your time.'

'These photographs . . . When you get them—'

'I'll seal them in an envelope and send them directly to you, Archbishop.'

'Good, good! I think we understand each other very well, Father.'

'And so do I, Archbishop. Thank you again for your time.'

'Goodbye, Father.'

Replacing the receiver, Father Will rubbed his chin as he wandered around the lounge, deep in thought. Even though he was winning round after round, he knew that his luck would eventually run out. The archbishop wouldn't take kindly to being threatened by a mere priest. And the bishop wouldn't let the matter rest, with or without the incriminating photographs of him and Josie writhing naked in the woods.

Contemplating his plans, he realized that his intention to instate an all-girl choir would have to be shelved – not that anyone had come forward offering the oral services of their delectable young daughters! Opening the basement bar during the evenings would have to wait, too. Answering the telephone, he grinned to hear Cheryl's sensual tones.

'Want to meet me in the woods, Father?' she asked excitedly.

'Meet you in the woods?' he echoed.

'Yes, I feel like having some sexy fun, so . . .'

'The woods? Where, exactly?'

'Behind the village hall in that clearing we went to – it's a lovely spot.'

Everybody's favourite spot! 'I'm too busy, I'm afraid, Cheryl.'

'Oh, please, Father! You can spank me, if you want to.'

'I really can't spare the time . . .'

'You can't spare the time to enjoy my naked body?'

'All right, seeing as you put it like that. Give me twenty minutes.'

'I'll be there – ready and waiting!'

This was it – the trap! Sitting in his armchair, Father Will wondered whether the bishop would be there, hiding in the bushes with his camera. But no, Cheryl – Sister Felicity – didn't trust him so . . . Perhaps she was now working solely with the Mother Superior? What to do? he wondered, lighting a cigarette. Leaping from his chair in a flash of inspiration, he grabbed the phone and rang PC Bridlington.

'Hello, Constable, it's Father Entercock,' he said excitedly. 'I've just had word that something's going to happen in the woods behind the village hall. I know that you're interested in the activities that go on in the woods, so can you meet me there?'

'Yes, Father, of course. What exactly is going to happen? And when is it to take place?'

'I'm not sure, but word has it that there's some sort of most vile and perverted obscenity planned for an hour's time.'

'I'll be there, Father. But I think it best that you keep away. Being a man of God, you must hide your eyes from such—'

'All right, Constable. I hope you catch the culprits because we don't want things like this going on in Cumsdale village, do we?'

'Certainly not, Father! Thanks for the tip-off.'

'Any time, Constable. Good luck!'

Slipping into his jeans, the priest grabbed his Pentax and left the house by the back door. Jumping over the garden fence, he made for the woods, approaching from the rear so as not to be seen by anyone in the lane. His plan was muddled, but whatever happened, PC Bridlington would discover Cheryl, and her accomplice, and ask some very awkward questions.

Creeping through the undergrowth, Father Will slipped into a ditch not far from the clearing and waited. Within minutes, he heard a rustling sound and whispering voices nearing.

'Right,' Cheryl said, slipping her miniskirt off as she turned to the Reverend Mother. 'This is the spot. I'll get ready for him, and you find a good hiding place to take the photographs from.'

'I want some really good shots,' the Reverend Mother replied. 'Make sure that you get him in some compromising positions.'

'You leave the sex to me, Mother! I know what to do, don't worry!'

Reverend Mother Mary slipped behind a bush as Cheryl removed the rest of her clothes and lay on the grass under the hot sun. For what seemed like an eternity Father Will waited, gazing longingly at the young nun's breasts, her erect nipples, her beautiful mound of Venus. A fine young specimen, he mused as his penis stiffened. Shame to have to drop her in it, really. Still, she deserves what she has coming to her, as does the Reverend slag-bag!

Soon Cheryl became restless, asking the Reverend Mother in a loud whisper where she thought the priest had got to. Joining the young nun on the grass, Mother Mary checked her watch and sighed. 'He did say that he'd be here, didn't he?' she said agitatedly.

I am here!

'Yes, he said twenty minutes. He's obviously had a change of mind, or perhaps he had a visitor?'

'Are you sure this is the right place?'

'Yes, definitely.'

'Well, I don't think he'll turn up now. God, I'm baking in my habit!' the Reverend Mother complained, slipping out of the heavy black garment.

'And I'm too randy to wait any longer!' Cheryl returned, her hands now wandering between her parted thighs, her fingers exploring her glistening sex-groove. Removing her bra and stockings, the Mother Superior grinned at her naked novice.

'Here, allow me,' she breathed, parting the girl's legs and leaning over to kiss her soft mound.

Father Will gazed in amazement at the two women – God's women – wondering what PC Bridlington would say when he stumbled across them. Was it legal? he wondered. Two lesbians writhing naked in the woods – was it within the reach of the long arms of the law?

Moving on top of her, the Reverend Mother buried her face in the young nun's pussy, lapping at her gaping slit as she settled her own lioncat over the girl's face. Blessed with a perfect view, Father Will clicked his camera, taking shot after shot of the young nun's tongue licking between the Reverend Mother's bloated cunt lips. Pulling the woman's buttocks apart, Cheryl pressed her finger deep into the small hole lost within her vast orbs, continuing to lap up the creamy deluge flowing from her gaping vaginal crevice. Their bodies shuddering as they neared their illicit sexual heaven, both women began their gasping. 'Coming!' the young nun cried as the Reverend Mother sucked her throbbing clitoris into her hot mouth. 'Ah, God! I'm coming!'

'What the hell's going on here?' PC Bridlington cried as he emerged from the bushes into the clearing. Taking several shots of the PC standing over the naked women, Father Will thanked the Lord, beaming as he watched the horror on Reverend Mother Mary's flushed face. 'Mother Superior!' PC Bridlington gasped as Cheryl pulled her finger from the nun's bum-hole. 'I have never witnessed such . . . such lewd behaviour in all my days as a police officer!'

'Constable, I . . .' the Mother stammered as she climbed from Cheryl's glowing body. 'I . . . we were just . . .'

'I can see what you were doing! And you, Miss, what's your name?'

'Cheryl, sir,' the girl replied sheepishly as she climbed to her feet, her come pouring from her inflamed cunt, her elongated nipples hard and pointed before the police officer's astonished eyes.

'I must ask you both to dress and accompany me to the station. I must caution you both. You are under arrest for gross indecency in a public place, and anything you say will be taken down and may be used as evidence against you. Do you both understand the charge?'

Knickers!

'But, Constable . . .' the Reverend Mother began. 'Surely, we can come to an arrangement?'

'An arrangement?' he queried.

'Yes – I mean, you're a man. We could give you a little pleasure in exchange for you not mentioning this incident. Between us, we could pleasure you . . .'

'Are you trying to bribe me – a police officer?'

'No, no . . . I just thought that—'

'You will both accompany me to the station. I am also charging you with trying to pervert the course of justice by attempting to bribe a police officer!'

'Yes,' murmured the women as they dressed, their faces flushed with embarrassment.

Taking one last picture for posterity, Father Will kept his head low as the convent lesbians were led from the wood and taken to the police station. He could hardly believe his luck. They'd been arrested for gross indecency and would be the laughing stock of the village, once the local paper got to hear of it. What was more, any attempts they made to expose him would be dismissed as a futile effort to turn the spotlight away from themselves.

'Yes!' the priest cried triumphantly once they were well out of earshot. 'I've bloody well got the scheming little bitches now! Alleluia!'

'You get worse,' Josie giggled, approaching the priest from behind.

'Josie! What the hell . . .'

'What do you propose to do with the photographs?' she asked, gazing at the camera.

'I . . . Have you been here all the time?'

'Yes,' she smiled cheekily. 'I saw you sneaking across the field and wondered what evil you were up to, so I followed you.'

The time had come to be honest with the girl, he knew. There was no point in pussyfooting around any longer. But what did the future hold now? He couldn't stay on as Priest of Cumsdale Parish. Once word about the Reverend Mother and Sister Felicity got out, the village would be swarming with tabloid reporters who'd dig out all the filth – including his own.

'What are you two up to?' a woman's gruff voice called from across the clearing.

'Ah, Mrs Highmen!' Father Will greeted her. 'The mystery of the naked women has been solved! PC Bridlington has just arrested the Mother Superior of Hardmound Convent and one of her young nuns on a charge of gross indecency of a disgusting lesbian nature.'

'Good God! So the naked women I saw here on several occasions were . . .'

'Yes, Mrs Highmen – the Mother Superior and a nun.'

'I owe you an apology, Father. I have had bad thoughts about you – wicked thoughts! I thought that you . . . I had better come to confession.'

'You are forgiven, Mrs Highmen. Now, why don't you go home and have a nice cup of tea?'

'I think I will, Father. This is shocking news!'

'That it is. It's a reflection of the sad world we live in, I'm afraid.'

'If only there were more people like you in the world, Father – good men, strong men, men of moral fibre! You are an upstanding pillar of the community, Father! Churchill would have been proud of you! Onward Christian soldiers! Praise be to the Lord for delivering us unto Father Entercock! God save the Queen! God for Harry, England and Saint George! Land of hope and glory, Mother of the Free . . .'

'Yes, all right, Mrs Highmen. I think you'd better go and lie down for a while.' *Your brain's overheated!*

'Oh, yes, you're quite right, Father. I do feel a little queer.'

Watching the woman wander off, Father Will turned to Josie and smiled. 'Well, I think it's time we put our cards on the table, don't you?' he asked, gazing into her big brown eyes as he brushed her hair from her pretty face.

'Yes, I do,' she replied. 'Let's sit on the grass. We've a lot to talk about.'

Gazing at the girl's short, tight skirt, Father Will took a deep breath, wondering whether she'd enjoy a session of naked lust under the summer sun, the threatening storm clouds having now dispersed. After watching the lesbian scene, his penis was more than ready for the girl's hot, tight cunt! But first things first, he decided, wondering where to begin. This was it, the placing of cards on the table – the revelation!

'Josie, I . . . I do know who you . . .'

'Not yet,' she smiled, lifting her T-shirt over her head.

'But . . .'

'No buts. Right now, it doesn't matter who's who. All that matters is that we're together, the sun is shining down on us from the heavens, and . . . all this was meant to be, can't you see that?'

'Yes, I do believe that you're right,' he replied, gazing at her firm breasts, her elongated nipples as she slipped her bra off.

'Me coming to your church, losing my job, the whole thing was meant to be. It's all part of the plan, the great plan of life.'

'Don't worry about the great plan of life, Josie!' he gasped, gazing at her shaven pussy lips as she slipped her skirt and panties off. 'The only plan I'm interested in is the plan of your beautiful anatomy!'

'Well, we can't do much in the way of exploring each other's anatomies with your clothes on, can we?' she laughed, lying back on the grass and opening her legs.

'No, you're right!' he whooped, ripping his shirt and jeans off.

Settling between the girl's thighs, he peeled her shaven pussy lips apart and gently kissed her glistening inner sex-folds. Her juices already flowing in torrents from her young body, she gasped, reaching for her nipples and rolling them between her fingers and thumbs. Licking the entire length of her open groove, he savoured the taste of her slippery girl-come, breathed in her heady scent as she writhed in her sexual ecstasy.

'You're the best man I've ever had between my legs!' she gasped as he pushed three fingers into the heat of her gaping sex. Pressing his thumb into her tight bottom-hole, he mumbled through her rubicund flesh as he massaged her anal tube.

'And you've got the best pair of legs I've ever been between!'

Nearing her orgasm as the priest sucked her hard clitoris into his hot mouth, she tossed her head from side to side, gazing up at the green foliage towering high above her. The soft grass cushioning her naked buttocks as he rhythmically massaged and stretched her young cuntal sheath, she spread her limbs wide and gasped. 'That's it! Lick just like that! Don't stop, I'm . . . God, don't stop!'

Her cries of orgasm filling the wood, her body rigid, her cunt gripping the priest's fingers like a vice, she floated up to her sexual heaven, lost in her ecstasy. Father Will continued his mouthing, his sucking, his licking, working his fingers against her tightening muscles to sustain her shuddering sexual pleasure until she closed her legs, halting the incredible torture.

Before she'd come to her senses, he forced her legs apart and took his solid organ in his hand. Slipping his penis deep into her cunt, he began his thrusting, pushing the girl across the grass with every stab of his weapon. Josie shuddered, her mouth open, gasping as her tight cunt stretched to its limits. Lifting her buttocks off the ground, she met his every thrust, her body jolting as her cervix took the delicious pummelling. Almost delirious in her lust, she closed her eyes as her orgasm swirled within her womb and rose suddenly from her hot depths to erupt in her clitoris.

Grimacing, Father Will jetted his sperm deep into her spasming cunt as the girl cried out in her climax. Clinging to each other's hot glistening bodies under the summer sun, they shuddered uncontrollably, rolling over and over, his penis still solid within the grip of her fiery epicentre. Finally coming to rest with Josie on top, they lay still. Her legs splayed, her cunt lips encompassing the base of his massive organ, her firm breasts pressed against his chest, their mouths met, their tongues tasting, exploring, savouring each other's saliva. Finally rolling from his body, her sheath releasing his penis, she lay by his side, exhausted in her beautiful sexual fulfilment.

Lying under the hot sun, their bodies glistening with the sweat of lust, they relaxed, breathing slowly, their hands clasped. 'So, cards on the table,' Father Will whispered, rolling his head to one side and gazing into Josie's brown eyes. 'I've known all along that you're a newspaper reporter. The tape recorder in your bag, the radio bugging device—'

'Bastard!' she laughed. 'I thought that you might have guessed some of it, but not that much!'

'I listened to you and the Mother Superior talking in her office. The bug's still there, by the filing cabinet.'

'Bastard!' she cried again.

'*Praemonitus, praemunitus!*'

'What?'

'Forewarned, forearmed! I switched your tape recorder off when you first came to the presbytery to entice me to talk. Another time, I snapped the tape. I swiped the tape from your bag after I'd broken into the bishop's car and taken the video tape. By the way, you shouldn't rape bishops in the woods, you naughty girl!'

'Is there *anything* you don't know?' she asked, rolling on top of him.

'I don't think so. By the way, I had Brian's rolls of film snatched from The Woodman's Arms.'

'Oh, my God! You've been one jump ahead all the bloody way!'

'Yes, clever, aren't I? It's my MI5 training, you see.'

'You were never with MI5, were you?'

'Yes, but tell no one about it.'

'Liar! I ought to turn you over and thrash your bum!'

'I ought to thrash *your* bum, you mean! The bloody trouble you've caused me!'

'All's fair in love and war!'

'Yeah, but nothing's fair about investigative, bloody tabloid journalists! When are you going back to London?'

'I . . . I don't know,' she replied dolefully.

'Does your offer still stand? I mean, I'll miss you, and you'll miss me, so . . .'

'Yes, it does! But . . .'

'No buts. Let's do it today! Let's pack up and bugger off together today!'

Hugging him tightly, Josie kissed the priest passionately, pushing her tongue into his mouth as she pressed her pussy lips against his hard penis. 'Come on!' he said, pushing her away. 'We've things to do if we really are going to London today.'

'You're right!' she smiled, leaping to her feet. 'Come on, then, get dressed!'

Walking hand in hand with Josie through the woods, Father Will knew that he'd made the right decision. His life as Priest of Cumsdale Parish was over. 'I'll have my mail redirected,' he said, contemplating the convent knickers as he and the girl were about to emerge from the woods into the leafy lane.

'Christ, there's that newspaper reporter!' he gasped, dragging the girl back into the bushes, covering her mouth with his hand.

'Which paper is he from?' Josie asked, pulling his hand away as the man wandered by.

'I don't know, but he's posing as a water authority official. Right, he's gone! Let's go to the post office now and have my mail redirected.'

'There's so much to do,' sighed Josie.

'No, there's not. I've no real ties here. Apart from Bob, the Vicar of Hallworth Church, there's no one to say goodbye to, so . . .' Noticing a removal lorry pulling away from Amber's cottage, his words tailed off. 'Josie, will you sort the post office out? Only, I just want to . . .'

'To say goodbye to that girl?'

'Yes, do you mind?'

'No, of course not! Go on, and don't give her a goodbye fuck – you're mine now!'

Knocking on the front door, Father Will wondered how Amber would react to his news. Living alone, no friends, blackouts . . . Not a nice life, he mused as the door opened.

'Oh, Chloë!' he exclaimed. 'What are you . . .'

'Hello, Father!' Amber trilled as she appeared behind Chloë. 'Come in, please!'

'I see your furniture has arrived,' he said, wondering what Chloë was doing in the cottage.

'Yes, we've some sorting out to do, but we'll soon be settled in.'

'We?' he echoed.

Chloë dropped her head and Amber blushed as they went into the lounge. Sitting down, Father Will looked to Amber for an explanation, but decided to break his news first. 'I'm leaving the church, the village,' he said softly. The girls looked at him, beaming.

'That's good . . .' Amber began. 'What I mean is, we'll miss you. Chloë and I are . . . we've been seeing each other for a while and . . .'

'I understand,' Father Will smiled. 'And I hope you'll both be very happy. Amber, about your . . . your problem. Does Chloë know?'

'I have a confession to make, Father,' Amber said, lowering her head in shame. 'My blackouts are faked. You see . . .'

'I might have guessed!' the priest laughed. 'So, you knew all along about . . . you know exactly what I did to you during your blackouts?'

'Yes. I'm sorry, it's just that I've always had a thing about priests and cassocks, so I faked the blackouts, knowing that you'd take advantage of me. But I've got Chloë now, so all that's over.'

'But your identity bracelet?'

'That's all it is, an identity bracelet.'

'So you're happy, are you?' he asked, gazing at Chloë.

'Oh, yes. After my lesbian initiation with Cheryl, I . . . well, Amber and I have been friends for a while, but neither of us knew what the other was thinking so . . . after my initiation with Cheryl, I knew that I wanted a girl rather than a man. I soon realized that I was in love with Amber and I plucked up the courage to tell her, and that was it – bang! It's the best thing that's ever happened to me!'

'I'm happy for you both. Well, I've a lot to do so . . . I'll say goodbye.'

'Goodbye, Father,' the girls sang in unison as they followed him to the door.

'Will you visit us?' Chloë asked as he walked down the path.

'Yes, I will – I promise. Goodbye, and take care of each other.'

'Oh, Father . . .' Chloë said softly. 'Had you actually read my exercise book, you'd have discovered my feelings for Amber.'

'Really?'

'Yes, I wrote everything down. Anyway, keep the book – it'll remind you of your time here as priest.'

'Thank you, Chloë, I'll treasure it. Well, goodbye.'

Back in his office, Father Will rang John and asked if he'd like to buy the cannabis plants. 'Yes, nice one, Father!' John replied enthusiastically. 'I'll come over now. D'you want anything from France, only I'm going over soon?'

'No – thanks, anyway, John. I'm leaving today.'

'Leaving? What, for France?'

'No, no. I'm leaving the church, the village. It's all over, so you'd better get your van over here and take the plants.'

'Oh, right. So, I'm losing a valued customer, then?'

'Yes, sorry, but that's the way it is.'

'That's a shame. Anyway, I'll be with you shortly.'

'OK, John. I'll explain it all when I see you. Oh, by the way, talking of valued customers, I'll put my biggest outlet in touch with you.'

'Great! Thanks, Father. See you soon.'

A sad day in many ways, Father Will mused as he opened the desk drawer and grabbed a can of lager. But the money he'd accrued would pay off Josie's mortgage and he'd still carry on with the soiled knicker business – if Sister T could keep them

306

coming! Pressing the receiver to his ear, he rang Jack to tell him his news. Got to get rid of the stock, he mused as he waited for a reply.

'Jack, it's me, Father Will.'

'Hi, Will! What gives?'

'Got a couple of grand in cash?'

'Might have – why?'

'I want to sell off my stock, the whole lot. Two grand's a good price, I think you'll agree?'

'Bloody right it is, for that lot! Why are you selling it all?'

'I'm leaving.'

'Where you goin'?'

'London, a new life and all that.'

'When?'

'Today, hopefully. So, if you can arrange to pick the stuff up, I'll . . .'

'Where will I get my supplies from when you've buggered off?'

'You'll have enough to keep you going for a while. Anyway, I'll put you in touch with my supplier. You'll be better off – without me, the middle man, you'll be much better off.'

'OK, see you later, mate.'

Swigging his lager, the priest sighed. It was, indeed, a sad day, and he was beginning to wonder whether he was doing the right thing or not. But, he decided, he had no choice in the matter. With the Mother Superior and Sister Felicity in custody, there'd be a massive investigation by the church hierarchy, if not by the police. He'd be far better off in London, he desperately tried to convince himself.

Ringing Bob Cummings to put him in the picture, he sat back in his chair and smiled as the vicar recalled their communion with Cheryl at the altar. 'I still can't believe it!' Bob exclaimed. 'That girl was incredible!'

'Didn't I tell you? She was one of the fucking nuns from the convent! Anyway, I'll send you a copy of the video,' he laughed. 'You'll be able to watch it while you have a good old wank!'

'Christ, how many copies are there on the loose?'

'Only two, and I've got both of them, so relax.'

'Thank God for that! I'm going to miss you, Will. Are you sure you're doing the right thing?'

'Yes, I'm sure. I suppose I always knew in my heart that one day the end would come. Look, I'll call in and see you before I leave.'

'All right, mate. We'll have a last beer together.'

'Bloody good idea – see you later.'

'What's a bloody good idea?' Sister Teresa asked as she burst into the office lugging a plastic sack full of soiled convent knickers.

'Oh, hi! That was Bob Cummings . . . anyway, what are you doing here?'

'I've just heard some amazing news, so I thought I'd come and tell you – and I've managed to get you some more knickers. You'll never guess what's happened!'

'I already know.'

'What, about the Reverend slag-bag and Sister Felicity?'

'Yes. Good, isn't it?'

'It's brilliant! I'm not sure what'll happen up at the convent. I suppose they'll replace her soon enough. Anyway, I'm not going to hang around to find out. I'm off to London to work the strip clubs. That's the life I always wanted, and I'm going for it!'

'Great! This nun lark was never up your street, was it?'

'Bloody right it wasn't! At least you're safe enough now, what with the slag-bag banged up. I've arranged for another nun to bring you the girls' knickers: Sister Anne, she'll . . .'

'I'm leaving today.'

'What?'

'Yes, I'm off to London, too. Josie and I are . . . well, in love, I suppose.'

'Bloody hell! What will you live on?'

'I've made myself a tidy sum since I've been here. I'll still carry on selling the dirty knickers. I'll have to get Sister Anne to parcel them up and post them to me. I'll miss your little visits, Sister T. Shame we can't . . .'

'Any chance of a quick fuck before we part company? she grinned, lifting her habit and standing with her feet asunder to expose her tattooed thighs, her pouting pussy lips, to his lecherous gaze.

'I think that can be arranged!' he chuckled, taking her hand and leading her into the church.

'Where are we going?' she asked as he almost dragged her down the aisle.

'Ever been fucked over an altar?'

'No, I can't say that I have!'

'Well, you're about to be!' he laughed, lifting her from the floor and laying her over the altar. 'Come on, habit up, legs open wide!' he ordered, climbing up alongside her.

Pulling his jeans off, he displayed his solid shaft to the young nun's huge eyes. Kneeling between her open thighs, he pressed his purple knob between her splayed pussy lips and drove it deep into her tightening cunt. 'God, you get bigger by the day!' she gasped as he began his thrusting.

'And you get tighter and hotter and wetter by the day!' he replied as he kissed her full mouth.

'I thought you said that you were in love.'

'What's that got to do with your tight cunt?'

'I thought that monogamy came with love.'

'Well, you thought wrong!'

Placing her legs over his shoulders, Sister Teresa grabbed her ankles, opening her cunt lips wide, allowing the priest deeper penetration. Ramming her cervix as hard as he could with his ballooning glans, he quickly took the girl to her sexual heaven. 'I'm almost there!' she gasped as her body shuddered and her cunt muscles gripped his pistoning shaft. Grabbing a huge candle, she pushed the tip between her splayed buttocks. Easing the waxen shaft deep into her bottom-hole, she shuddered, crying out in her coming 'Ah, that's it! Come . . . coming!'

The priest's penis bulged within her tight cunt as he loosed his sperm, filling her spasming fleshy cavern to the brim, lubricating their inflamed genitals. On and on he rammed her young body, pushing her along the altar until her head hung over the side. Clinging on for dear life. she closed her eyes, ramming the candle in and out of her tight bottom-hole, taking the priest's gruelling battering until his swinging balls were drained.

'Christ, you're fucking good!' she breathed. 'God, I'm going to miss you!'

'We can meet in London,' he murmured as his body fell limp and he lay over her heaving breasts. 'We'll meet every day in London and fuck!'

'You bloody well won't!' Josie cried as she raced down the aisle.

'Oh, Josie! I . . . I was just . . .' Father Will stammered.

'I can see what you were just doing! Was it nice?'

'Well, yes, it was.'

'Good, then we'll *all* meet in London and fuck. You can come to the flat, Sister. We'll have some sexy fun, the three of us.'

'I can see that we're well suited, Josie!' Father Will smiled as he slipped his penis from the nun's sodden sheath and climbed from her trembling body. 'You . . . you won't want any other men to join in our . . .'

'You are a bastard, Will – you really are!' Josie laughed. 'But, to be honest, with you servicing me daily, I don't think I'll be in need of another superstud!'

Slipping the huge candle from her bottom-hole, Sister Teresa climbed from the altar and pulled her habit down. 'You're a lucky girl,' she said, turning to Josie. 'You've got a good man. He's got money, wit, charm – and a fucking great cock!'

'I am lucky, I know,' Josie smiled, taking the priest's hand.

'I'll leave you alone, then,' Sister T smiled. 'You'll not want me hanging around. Oh, you'd better give me your phone number.'

'Here, I'll write it down for you,' Josie smiled, opening her bag.

'No tape recorder in there, is there?' Father Will laughed.

'No, of course not!' Josie said, passing a slip of paper to the nun. 'There you are, ring us when you get to London.'

'I will. Well, 'bye for now.'

Installed in his office again, Father Will offered Josie a can of lager. 'I've been meaning to ask you,' he said as he sat at his desk. 'How did you, your paper, get on to me in the first place?'

'It was a stroke of luck. We'd been looking for a bloody good story concerning the clergy. I was sent out to church after church to see what I could unearth and I just happened to come across you, so to speak.'

'You weren't tipped off, then?'

'No, it was purely luck. If you hadn't gone on so much about sex when I first sat in here and talked to you, I'd have moved on to another church.'

'Ah, the great plan!'

'Yes, we were meant to meet, I know that. By the way, the woman in the post office wants your signature before she can redirect the mail.'

'Oh, right. Look, I've a couple of people coming to see me so . . . Why don't you go to the presbytery and make something to eat, a salad, perhaps? I'll be over when I've dealt with things here.'

'OK, I'll see you later. May I ask you something?'

'Anything.'

'What do you want out of life?'

'God only knows!'

'What do you want to do? I mean, what's your goal?'

To lose myself in girls' warm, moist panties! 'To be with you, Josie.'

'Oh, right. I'll see you later, then,' she smiled proprietorially, breezing out of the office.

Jack and John arrived at the church together. After filling them in on his news, Father Will helped to load the alcohol and cigarettes into Jack's van as John collected the cannabis plants. 'You'll be all right with John, he's a good bloke,' he said as they cleared the bar.

'Yeah, he seems on the level. I was worried about gettin' me stock when you told me you were buggering off!'

'Well, you've no worries now. I'll come and visit you from time to time – stay at the pub for a few nights, perhaps?'

'You're always welcome, Father – and you can stay as my guest. There's the dosh, two grand – and thanks for all you've done.'

Stuffing the money into his pocket, the priest waved Jack goodbye, thinking again that it was a sad day. One chapter closes and another opens, he mused as he said goodbye to John. Locking the church doors for the last time, he walked back to the presbytery.

Finding Annie in the kitchen with Josie, he was pleased that Josie'd told her the news. She turned to Father Will, frowning. 'The altar,' she said with a huge wink.

'There are the church keys,' he smiled. 'Drop them through the letter box when you've . . . when you've finished.'

'I'll miss you,' she said sadly.

'And I'll miss you, Annie. Sorry you've got to move your things out of the presbytery but . . .'

'That's OK. My old man's gone and run off with another woman, unfaithful bastard! Anyway, I can work from home again. Sod what the neighbours think! Mind you, when the news about the Reverend Mother is out, the neighbours won't be thinking of me!'

'That's true. Well, goodbye, Annie.'

'Goodbye, Father, thanks for everything. 'Bye, Josie. I hope you'll both be very happy.'

Munching on his salad, Father Will smiled at Josie. 'It's ironic!' he laughed. 'You came here to get your story, and I'm the one who's come up with the goods! Photographs of the Reverend Mother engaging in debauchery not only with Sister Felicity but also with a schoolgirl in her office, shots of you with the bishop, a video tape of me and Sister Felicity – alias Cheryl – screwing on the altar . . .'

'I'll tell you what!' Josie grinned.

'What?'

'I *can* run the story, after all! We'll sell it to a newspaper – the pictures, the tape, the lot!'

'Christ! Me screwing a nun over the altar with Bob? I'd be shooting myself where it hurts!'

'But you're leaving the priesthood, aren't you? So it doesn't matter. And we can edit the tape to keep the vicar out of trouble. We'll bring down the entire church – and earn ourselves a bloody fortune in the process! I'll write up the story and contact someone I know on one of the big Sunday tabloids. I reckon we're talking at least fifty grand, if not more!'

'And with the money I've already got, we'll be more than comfortable! I've also got something on the archbishop. I'll have to do some digging, but I reckon I can unearth enough to topple him, too.'

'The archbishop?' Josie frowned.

'Yes, as the bishop told you in the woods, the archbishop has been taking some young blonde down to Brighton and screwing her.'

'So the bishop wasn't lying! God, we might even hit the ton for this!'

Dashing to the lounge and answering the phone, Father Will

grinned to hear the archbishop's unsteady voice.

'I've . . . I've just heard the news,' he said softly. 'Look, Father, I don't know what your plans are but . . .'

'I have many plans, Archbishop.'

'The photographs of the blonde girl and . . . I don't want this to come out, you understand. Now that the Reverend Mother and that young nun are . . .'

What photographs? 'I'm leaving the priesthood, you'll be pleased to hear,' Father Will interrupted. 'But the bad news is that I'm selling the story to a newspaper, Archbishop.'

'I guessed you'd do something like that. Listen, keep me out of it, and I'll get the deeds to the presbytery signed over to you.'

'*What*? You'll give me the presbytery?'

'Yes, it'll take some doing, but I'll manage it. I'll fix the paperwork so that it appears that you've bought the place from the church. What do you say?'

'I say yes! You've got a deal, Archbishop!' *But it mightn't let you off the hook!*

'Good, I thought you'd see sense. I'll get on to it right away.'

'Fine, I'll look forward to hearing from you. Goodbye, Archbishop.'

Breaking the good news to Josie, Father Will couldn't stop grinning. 'You can rent out your flat, and we'll live here!' he cried triumphantly. 'We don't have to leave the village after all!'

'Thank God for that! I didn't relish the idea of living in London again, anyway.'

'We'll throw a party! Amber, Chloë, Sister T, Annie – they'll all come!'

'They can come to the party, but I don't want you making them all come!' Josie laughed.

'Talking of coming, I think it's time we christened the marital bed!'

'Marital?'

'Why not? If you want to stop me from roaming, from sneaking around the convent sniffing out the young girls' pussy cracks, then you'll have to marry me.'

'It's a deal!' Josie giggled, pulling her T-shirt over her head. 'Your friend Bob can marry us! I think you'd better carry me over the threshold!'

'Threshold?' he laughed, grabbing the reel of sticky tape.

'Carry me into the bedroom! What's the sticky tape for?'

'You'll see!'

Lifting her off her feet, Father Will carried the girl to the bedroom, kicking the door shut behind him. One door shuts, and another opens, he reflected, throwing Josie on to the bed.

'You *will* be faithful to me when we're married, won't you?' she asked as she slipped her skirt and panties off. Eyeing her swollen pussy lips, her creamy pink slit, he grinned.

'Of course, my angel!' he cried, picking at the end of the sticky tape with his fingernail.

Faithful to you, to Amber, to Chloë, to Annie, to Sister Teresa, to Rosa, to Samantha Lovejoy – to the entire convent school! Alleluia!

'Father Entercock!' an insistent voice interrupted through the letterbox. 'Father Entercock, I know you're in there! My name's Hydromann – I'm from the water authority! I am accompanied by a police officer! Please, open the door! I have to test your water supply for excessive quantities of algaecide!'

'Fuck off!'

Bloody journalists!